The Collected Supernatural and Weird Fiction of Barry Pain Volume 3

The Collected Supernatural and Weird Fiction of Barry Pain Volume 3

Eight Short Stories, Two Novellas & One Novel of the Strange and Unusual Including 'Rose Rose', 'The Grey Cat', 'The Girl and the Beetle', 'In a London Garden', 'The New Gulliver' and 'The One Before'

Barry Pain

LEONAUR

The Collected
Supernatural and Weird
Fiction of
Barry Pain
Volume 3
Eight Short Stories, Two Novellas & One Novel of the Strange and Unusual
Including 'Rose Rose', 'The Grey Cat', 'The Girl and the Beetle', 'In a London
Garden', 'The New Gulliver' and 'The One Before'
by Barry Pain

FIRST EDITION

Leonaur is an imprint of Oakpast Ltd

Copyright in this form © 2022 Oakpast Ltd

ISBN: 978-1-915234-74-2 (hardcover)
ISBN: 978-1-915234-75-9 (softcover)

http://www.leonaur.com

Contents

"Bill"   7

Entertainments of Kapnides   17

In A London Garden   29

Rose Rose   69

Smeath   75

The Girl and the Beetle   99

The Grey Cat   131

The New Gulliver   141

The Widower   185

Zero   191

The One Before   209

"Bill"

Bill came slowly up the steps from a basement flat in Pond Buildings, crossed the pavement, and sat down on the kerb-stone in the sunshine, with his feet in a delightful puddle. He was reflecting.

"All that fuss about a dead byeby!" he said to himself.

He was quite a little boy, with a dirty face, gipsy eyes, and a love for animals. He had slept the deep sleep of childhood the night before, and had heard nothing of what was happening. In the early morning, however, he had been enlightened by his father—a weak man, with a shuffling gait, who tried to do right and generally failed.

"Bill, cummere. Larst night there were a byeby come to be your sister if she'd grow'd. But she didn't live more'n hour. An' that's why your awnt's 'ere, an' mind yer do whort she tells yer, an' don't go inter the other room, an' don't do nothin' 'cep' whort yer told, or I'll break yer 'ead for yer, sure's death, I will!"

Then Bill's father had gone away to his work, being unable to afford the loss of a day; and Bill's vehement, red-haired aunt had come into the kitchen, and shaken him, and abused him, and given him some breakfast. Bill's aunt was one of those unfortunate people who cannot love one person without hating three others to make up for it. Just at present she was loving Bill's mother, her sister, very much, and retained her self-respect by being very strict with Bill's father, with Bill himself, and with the doctor. She instructed Bill that he was not to go to school that morning. He was to remain absolutely quiet in the kitchen, because he might be wanted to run errands and do odd jobs.

For some time, Bill had obeyed her, and then monotony tempted him to include the little yard at the back in his definition of the kitchen. All the basement flats in Pond Buildings have little yards at the back. Most of the inhabitants use them as drying-grounds. In some of them there is a dead shrub or the remains of a sanguine geranium

7

that failed; in all of them there are cinders and very old meat-tins. Now, when Bill went out into the yard, he found the black cat, which he called Simon Peter, asleep in the sun on the wall.

Simon Peter did not belong to anyone; she roamed about at the back of Pond Buildings, dodged anything that was thrown at her, and ate unspeakable things. She had formed a melancholy and unremunerative attachment to Bill; her name had been suggested to him by stray visits to a Sunday-School, forced on him during a short season when his father, to use his own phrase, had got religion. "Siming Peter," said Bill, as he scratched her gently under the ear, "Siming Peter, my cat, come in 'ere along o' me and 'ave some milk."

It is not at all probable that Simon Peter was deceived by this. She must have known that, with the best intentions in the world, Bill could not do so much as this for her. Yet she blinked at him with her lazy green eyes, and followed him from the yard into the kitchen. Bill filled a saucer with water, and put it down on the ground before her. "There yer are, Siming Peter," he said; "an' that's better for yer nor any milk." Simon Peter put up her back slowly, mewed contemptuously, and trotted out into the yard again. Bill, dashing after her, trod on the saucer and broke it, and overturned a chair. In another moment he was in the clutches of his fierce aunt.

"Do you want to kill your blessed mother, you devil? Didn't I tell yer to sit quoite? An' a good saucer broke, with the poor dead corpse of your byeby sister lyin' in the next room. Go hout! You're more nuisance nor you're wuth. See 'ere. Don't you show your ugly 'ead 'ere agin afore night. An' when yer comes back I'll tell your father of yer, an' 'e'll skin yer alive. Dinner? Not for such as you. Hout yer git."

So, Bill had been turned out, and now sat with his feet in a delightful puddle, reflecting for a minute or two on dead babies, injustice, puddles, and other things. It was a larger puddle, as far as Bill could see, than any other in the street, and it was this which made it so charming. But a puddle is of no use to anyone who has not got something to float on it. If you have something to float on it you can imagine boats, and races, and storms, and it becomes a magnificent playground for the imagination; otherwise, the biggest puddle is simply a puddle, and it is nothing more.

So, Bill started down the street to look for something which would float, a scrap of paper or a straw. He was stopped by a lanky unkempt girl with yellow hair, who was leaning on a broom that was almost bald, outside an open door. She was four or five years older than Bill, and she was very fond of him. The girls of the wretched neighbour-hood for the most part rather petted Bill; they did so, without know-ing their reason, because he was quaint, and pretty, and little. He was rather dirty it was true, but then so were they; and for the most part they were not so pretty,

"Bill," said the yellow-haired girl, "why awnt yer at school? You'll ketch it, Bill."

"No, I 'ont. They kep' me, 'cos we've got a byeby, an' the byeby's dead. Then they tunned me out for breakin' a saucer when I was goin' after Siming Peter what I were feedin', an' I ain't to 'ave no dinner, and I ain't to come back afore night, and when I do come back, I'm goin' to be walloped. I wish I was dead!"

"Oh, Bill, you *are* a bad boy; what are yer goin' to do?"

"Play ships at that puddle. I was lookin' for sutthin' what 'ud do for ships, an' can't find nothin'."

"An' what'll yer do about dinner?"

"I ain't goin' to 'ave no dinner," said Bill, solemnly, "I'm goin' to starve. They don't keer. Dead byebies is what *they* like."

The lanky girl leaned her broom against the wall, sat down on the doorstep, and commenced the research of a pocket; the pocket yielded her one penny.

"Look 'ere, Bill," she said, "you take this and git yourself sutthin' to eat."

Bill shook his head, and pressed his lips together. He was much moved.

"I 'ad it give me a week ago, and I sived it 'cos there warn't nothin' what I wanted. So, you take it. I don't want it. If yer like, yer can give us a kiss for it." She pressed it into his hand. "There ain't no other little boy I know what I'd give it to," she added rather inconsistently.

Bill nodded his head, and the lips grew a little tremulous. He had been treated cruelly all the morning, and this sudden change to sym-pathy and generosity was almost too much for him. He kissed the yel-low-haired girl once timidly and then suddenly with great affection.

"Why, Bill," she said, "I ain't done nothin' to 'urt yer, yer look om-must as if yer was goin' to cry."

"No, I ain't," replied Bill, finding words with difficulty, "but—but I 'ate ev'rybody in the world 'cep' you."

Then he walked away with great dignity, and every nerve in his excitable little body quivering. He felt on the whole rather more wretched than before. The contrast made him feel both sides of it

9

more deeply. He had forgotten now about the beautiful puddle and his intention to play ships. He wandered down the main street, and then down a side street which led behind a grim, frowning church. And here he found something which attracted his attention.

It was a dirty little shop which a small tobacconist and an almost microscopical grocer had used successively as a last step before bankruptcy. It had then remained for some time unoccupied. But now the whole of the window was occupied with one great bright picture, before which a small crowd had gathered. It represented a beautiful mermaid swimming in a beautiful sea, accompanied by a small octopus and some boiled shrimps. Her hair was very golden and very long; her eyes were very blue; she was very pink and very fat. Underneath was the announcement—

THE MERMAID OF THE WESTERN PACIFIC!
Positively to be Seen Within!!
For a Few Days Only.
Admission One Penny

An old man was standing in the doorway, with a tattered red curtain behind him, supplying further details of the history and personal appearance of the mermaid. He looked slightly military, distinctly intemperate, and very unfortunate, yet he was energetic.

"What it comes to is this—for a few days only I am offering two 'igh-class entertainments at the price of one. The performance commences with an exhibition by that most marvellous Spanish conjurer, Madumarsell Rimbini, and concludes with that unparalleled wonder of the world, the mermaid of the Western Pasuffolk. I have been asked frequent if it pays me to do this. No, it does *not* pay me. I am doing it entirely as an advertisement. Kindly take notice that this mermaid is not a shadder, faked up with lookin' glasses. She is real—solid—genuine discovered by a English officer while cruisin' in the Western Pasuffolk, and purchased direct from 'im by myself. The performance will commence in one minute. If any gentleman is not able to stay now, I may remark that the performances will be repeated agin this evenin' from seven to ten. What it comes to is this—for a few days only, etc."

Of course, Bill had seen shows of a kind before. He had seen a 'bus horse stumble, and almost pick itself up, and stumble again, and finally go down half on the kerbstone. That had been attractive, but there had been nothing to pay for it. Again, in his Sunday-school days, he had been present at an entertainment where the exhilaration of solid buns and dissolving views had been gently tempered by a short address. That too was attractive, but it had been free. And now it would not be possible to see this beautiful buoyant creature swimming in clear shrimp-haunted waters unless he paid a penny for it, the only penny that he possessed. Never before had he paid anything to go anywhere. The temptation was masterful. It gripped him, and drew him towards the tattered red curtain that hung over the entrance. In another minute he had paid his penny, and stood within.

At one end of the shop a low stage had been erected. On the stage was something which looked like a large packing-case with a piece of red baize thrown over it. There was a small table, on which were two packs of playingcards and a brightly coloured pill-box, and a tired fat woman in a low dress of peculiar frowziness. As the audience entered, she put a smile on her face, where it remained fixed as if it had been pinned. The performance commenced with three clumsy card-tricks. Then she requested someone in the audience to put a halfpenny in the painted pill-box and see it changed into a shilling.

The audience felt that they had been weak in paying a penny to see the show, and on this last point they were adamant. They would put no halfpennies in no pill-boxes. They were now firm. So also, was the Spanish conjurer, and this trick was omitted. She intimated that she would now proceed to the second part of the entertainment, the exhibition of the mermaid of the Western Pacific. She removed, dramatically, the red-baize cover, disclosing a glass case. The audience pressed forward to examine its contents. The case was filled for the most part with those romantic rocks and grasses which conventionality has appointed to be a suitable setting for stuffed canaries, or stuffed dogs, or anything that is stuffed.

There was a back ground of painted sky and sea; and in the front there was a small, most horrible figure, looking straight at Bill out of hideous, green, glassy eyes. It was not the lovely creature depicted in the window outside. It was a monstrous thing, a contemptible fraud to the practised intelligence, but to Bill's childish, excitable mind a thing of unspeakable horror and fascination. The lower half was a wilted, withered fish; then came a girdle of seaweed, and then something which was near to being human, yellow and waxy, with a ghastly face, a bald head, and those eyes that would keep looking at Bill. He shut his own eyes for a second; when he opened them again the monstrous thing was still looking at him.

There were two men standing near to Bill. One of them was a

11

very young and very satirical carpenter, with a footrule sticking out of his coat-pocket. "So that's a mermaid!" he remarked. "Yer call that a mermaid—oh!—indeed, a mermaid—oh, yes!"

"Seems to me," said the other man, middle-aged, cadaverous, and dressed in rusty black, "that it's a sight more like a dead byeby."

"Well, you ought to know," replied the satirical carpenter, grinning.

Bill heard this. So, in that basement flat in Pond Buildings, Bill's home, there was something lying quite still and waiting for him, to frighten him. He had never thought what a dead baby would be like. His mind began to work in flashes. The first flash reminded him of some horrible stories which his red-haired, vehement aunt had told him, to terrify him into being good. He had objected at the close of one story that dead people could not walk about.

"You don't know," his aunt had replied, "nobody knows, what dead people can do." In the second flash he imagined that he had gone home, had been lectured by his aunt, and beaten by his father, and had cried himself to sleep. He would wake up at night, when all was quiet—he felt sure of it—and the room would not be quite dark. He would see by the white moonlight a horrible, yellow, waxy thing crawling across the floor. It would not go to the right or to the left, but straight towards him. It would be his dead baby sister, and it would have a face like the face of the mermaid, and it would stare at him. He would be unable to call out. It would come nearer and nearer, and at last it would touch him. Then he would die of fright.

No, he would not go home, not until the dead baby had been taken away.

As the audience crowded out through the narrow doorway, Bill touched the man in shabby black:

"Please, sir, 'ow long is it afore they bury dead babies?"

The man stared at him searchingly. "What do yer want to know that for? Depends on the weather partly, and on the inclinations of the bereaved party. 'Soon as possible' 's allus my advice, but they let it go for days frequent."

Bill thanked him, and walked aimlessly away. He could not get the terror out of his mind. He walked through street after street, so absorbed in horrible thoughts that he hardly noticed what direction he was taking, and only just escaped being run over. He had been wandering for over an hour when he came across two boys, whom he knew, playing marbles. This was companionship and diversion for his thoughts. For some time, he watched the game with interest, and then one of the players pulled from his pocket two large marbles of greenish glass, and set them rolling.

Bill turned away at once, for he had been reminded of those green eyes. He imagined that they were still looking at him; but, in his imagination, they belonged not to the mermaid, but to the dead baby. He wished again and again that he had never been to that show. He was growing almost desperate with terror. Of course, his state of mind was to some extent due to the fact that he had eaten nothing for eight hours. But then, Bill did not know this. Suddenly he gave a great start, and a gasp for breath, for he had been touched on the shoulder. He looked up and saw his father. Now Bill's father had drunk two glasses of bad beer during his dinner hour, and in consequence he was feeling somewhat angry and somewhat self-righteous, for his head was exceedingly weak and poor. He addressed Bill very solemnly—

"Loit'rin' in the streets! loit'rin' and playin' in the streets! What's the good o' my bringing of yer up in the fear o' Gawd?"

Bill had no answer to make; so, his father aimed a blow at him, which Bill dodged.

"All right," his father continued, "I'm sent out on a jorb, and I ain't got the time to wallup yer now. But you mark my words—this very night, as sure as my name's what it is, I'll knock yer blawstid 'ead off."

At any other time, this would have frightened Bill. But now it came as a positive relief. There is no fear so painful, so maddening, as the fear of the supernatural. The promise that he should have his head knocked off had in itself but little charm or attraction. But in that case, he knew what to fear and from whence to fear it. It took his thoughts away for a few minutes from the horror of that dead baby, whose ghastly face he pictured to himself so clearly.

But it was only for a few minutes; the face came back again to his mind and haunted him. He could not escape from it. He was more than ever determined that he would not go home; he dared not spend a night in the next room to it. Already the afternoon was closing in, and Bill had no notion where he was to go for the night. For the present he decided to make his way to the green; he would probably meet other boys there that he knew.

The green to which he went is much frequented by the poor of the south-west. The railway skirts one side of it, and gives it an additional attraction to children. Bill was tired out with walking. He flung himself down on the grass to rest. His exhaustion at last overcame his fears, and he fell asleep. He slept for a long time, and in his sleep, he had a dream.

It was, so it seemed to him in his dream, late in the evening, and he was standing outside the door of the basement flat. He had knocked, and was waiting to be admitted. Suddenly he noticed that the door was just ajar. He pushed it open and entered. He called, but there was no answer. All was dark. The outer door swung to with a bang behind him. He thought that he would wait in the kitchen by the light of the fire until someone came. He felt his way to the kitchen and sat down in front of the fire.

It had burnt very low, and the furniture was only just distinguishable by the light of it. As he was waiting, he heard very faintly the sound of breathing. It did not frighten him; but he could not understand it, because as far as he could see there was no living thing in the room except himself. He thought that he would strike a light and discover what it was. The matches were in a cupboard on the right-hand side of the fireplace. He could only just reach the fastening, and it took him some little time to undo it. The moment the fastening was undone the door flew open, and something yellowish-white fell or rather leapt out upon him, fixing little quickly-moving fingers in his hair.

With a scream he fell to the floor. He had shut his eyes in horror, but he felt compelled to open them again to see what this thing was that clung to him, writhing and panting. A little spurt of flame had shot up, and showed him the face. Its eyes were blinking and rolling. Its mouth moved horribly and convulsively, and there was foam on the white lips. The face was close to his own; it drew nearer; it touched him. It was wet.

Bill suddenly woke and sprang to his feet, shivering and maddened with terror. The green was dark and deserted. A cold, strong wind had sprung up, and he heard it howling dismally. An impulse seized him to run—to run for his life. For a moment he hesitated; and then, under the shadow of the wall, slinking along in the darkness, he saw something white coming towards him, and with a quick gasp he turned and ran. He paid no heed to the direction in which he was going; he dared not look behind, for he felt sure that the nameless horror was behind him; he ran until he was breathless, and then walked a few paces, and ran again. As he crossed the road on the outer edge of the green, a policeman stopped and looked at him suspiciously. Bill did not even see the policeman. His one idea was escape.

It happened that he ran in the direction of the river. He had left the road now, and was following a muddy track that led through some grimy, desolate market-gardens. All around him there was horror. It screamed in the screaming wind with a voice that was half human; it took shape in the darkness, and lean, white arms, convulsively active, seemed to be snatching at him as he passed; the pattering of blown leaves was changed by it into the pattering of something ghastly, coming very quickly after him. For one second, he paused on the river's brink; and then, pressing both his hands tightly over his eyes, he flung himself into the water.

And the river went on unconcerned, and the laws of Nature did not deviate from their regular course. So, the boy was drowned. It was a pity; for he was in some ways a lovable boy, and there were possibilities in him.

★★★★★★★★★★★★

Bill's aunt was putting the untidy bedroom straight when his mother, opening her eyes and turning a little on the bed, said, in a low, tired voice

"I want Bill. Wheer's Bill?"

"I sent 'im out, dearie; 'e'll be back d'rectly. Don't you worry yourself about Bill. Why, that drattid lamp's a-shinin' strite onto your eyes. I'll turn it down."

There was a moment's pause, while the vehement woman—quiet enough now—arranged the lamp and took her place by the bedside. She smoothed the young mother's faded hair with one hand. "Go to sleep, dearie," she said.

Then she began to sing in a hushed, quavering voice. It was a favourite hymn, and for devotional purposes she rarely used more than one vowel-sound

"*Urbud wuth me! Fust fulls thur uvvun-tud.*"

Entertainments of Kapnides

No; it is not the story of the Spartan boy who lied about a fox, and subsequently died of the lies which were told about himself.

It is the story of an Athenian boy, who in the month of June sat quite alone in a thin tent by night. And the tent was pitched under the shadow of the long wall, and the night was hot and stifling.

He sat alone, for dead men are no company. His father and his eldest brother were in the tent with him; but he was alone. He had not been afraid to tend them in their sickness, for he had himself recovered from the pestilence; but it had taken away from him his beauty and his memory. He had been very beautiful, and his mind had been very full of fair memories. All were gone now. He kept only the few bare facts which his dying father had told him, that his mother had died long before; that they had lived in the country and had been ordered into the city; that Pericles had made a remarkably fine speech in the preceding year; and that his only surviving relation was his twin-brother, who had gone away into Euboea with the sheep. On these few poor facts, and on the two dead manly bodies before him, he pondered as he sat. And the night grew late, and yet he could hear outside the tent people passing busily, and quarrels, and long horrible cries.

And suddenly the poor Greek boy, with the ghost of an old beauty haunting his dull eyes and scarred cheeks, looked up, because he was conscious of the presence of a deity; and there before him sat an old gentleman in a silk hat, a frock-coat worn shiny under the fore arm, pepper-and-salt trousers, with a pen stuck at the back of his ear.

"I perceive a divine fragrance," the boy said. The fragrance was gin-and-water, but he knew it not. "And about thy neck there is a circle of brightness." In this he was correct, because the old gentleman was wearing an india-rubber dickey covered with luminous paint, which saves washing and makes it possible to put in a stud in the dark. "And

17

thy dress is not like unto mine. It cannot be but that thou art some god. And at the right time art thou come; for my heart is heavy, and none but a god can comfort me. And due worship have I ever rendered to the gods, but they love me not, and they have taken all things from me; and only my twin-brother is left, and he keeps the sheep in Euboea. And what name dost thou most willingly hear?"

"Allow me," said the old gentleman, and produced a card from his pocket, handing it to the boy. On it was printed: —

THE PROLEPTICAL CASHIER.
(Agent for Zeus & Co. , Specialists in Punishments?)

"The tongue is barbarian," said the boy, "and thy spoken words are barbarian, and yet I understand them; and now I know that the gods are kinder to me, because already I have greater wisdom than my fathers, and, perhaps, somewhat greater remains. Give to me, O cashier, the power to stay this pestilence."

"For a young 'un," said the cashier, "that's pretty calm, seeing that I *made* that pestilence. I just want to go into your little account. Your great-grandpapa, my boy, incurred a little debt, and Zeus & Co. want the thing settled before they dissolve partnership. They've just taken those two lives." He touched the body of the boy's father lightly with his foot. "They've taken your beauty and your memory. How sweet the girls used to be on you, my lad! but you can't recollect it, and you won't experience it again. You *are* a bad sight. Now we shall just kill your brother, and give the sheep the rot, and then the thing will be square. Now then, it's a hot night, and you'd better burn these two. I'll show you how to do it on the cheap, without paying for it. As long as Zeus & Co. are paid I don't care about the rest."

The boy sat dazed, and did not speak.

"There's a rich man built a first-class pyre twenty yards from your tent. They've gone to fetch his dead daughter to burn on it. We'll collar it before they get back. I'll take the old man, because he's the lightest. You carry your brother. He was a hoplite, wasn't he, one of them gentlemen that do parasangs? Oh, I know all about it."

Still the boy did not speak. They took up the two bodies, passed out of the tent, and laid their burden on the pyre.

"You look as if something had hurt you," said the old gentleman. "I like these shavings miles better than newspaper." He pulled a box of matches from his pocket, and set light to the pyre. It flared up brightly.

Then the boy touched him on the shoulder, and pointed first in

18

the direction of Euboea, and then at himself. A word came into him from a future civilisation.

"Swop?" he said gently.

"All right," grumbled the cashier. "I don't mind. It gives a lot of trouble altering the books. But I don't mind, I'm sure. It's a thirsty night."

For a moment the boy stood motionless; then, with a little cry, leapt into the flames. And his life went to join his beauty and his memory in a land of which we know too little.

THE STORY OF A CHILD SIREN

Ligeia never cared about the child from the first. It interfered with business. It absolutely refused to play her accompaniments, and said it could not bear to see the sailors tempted to their death. On this particular day it had interrupted Ligeia just as she reached the most tender, pathetic, touching part of her song. The sob of the child broke into the sloppy waltz refrain, and spoiled the spell. And the helmsman had turned the ship's prow out again from the coast, and there was another crew gone.

"You sinful little beast," said Ligeia. "Get out of my sight."

The child was not sorry to go. She climbed up the cliff, and then wandered on away from the sea, where the long grass came up to her waist. And as she wandered, the sun shone brightly, and the cool wind blew into her hair, and the birds sang above her, and only a little distance away sounded the drowsy murmurs of the waves.

And then for the first time in her life the passion for song came into her. She felt that she *must* sing. Always before she had shuddered at the thought of song, for the song of Ligeia and others had ever brought death with it. But now she felt that she *must* sing, and she knew not why; for a study of hereditary tendencies was not included in the Board School education of that period. She had reached an open space now. The ground was sandy, with here and there a stunted clump of grass, and in one place a beautiful golden poppy.

"No one will hear me," she thought, "and if I do not sing my heart will break." So, she sang, standing there white and naked, with the sunlight upon her, holding a lyre in her little hands.

And the music came out of her soul, but she knew not whence the words came.

She sang that it was not sweet for the golden poppy to bloom there alone, though the sun made it warm, and the wind was fragrant about

19

it. It was sweeter that she should pluck it in her little hands, which were warm with a better life than the life of the sun, and more fragrant than the west wind with its burden of the breath of the flowers. She paused, and her fingers rested lightly on the lyre. Her eyes were strained in looking up to the east, and she did not see that the poppy had bowed its golden head and withered away.

"And it is not sweet," she sang again, "for you, white bird, to fly on and on, and never to rest. It is better to lie here, and let me touch you, and fondle you, and love you."

And out from the eastern sky flew the white bird, and it nestled for one moment at the child's breast, and then fell dead on the sand.

And the child saw what she had done, and she flung herself down beside the dead bird and the withered flower, and sobbed in the foolishest way.

So, the afternoon wore on, and the sea still murmured, and she still lay there. And when it was evening a new wind sprang up from the south, and it whispered to her:—

"A girl's voice for a bird's life."

She stood up, erect, with eyes that flashed brightly, though the tears still stood in them. She held the white bird in her little hands. "I'll give you my voice," she said, as she kissed it. And the bird flew far away from her, and the girl was dumb.

For a little while she stood there, and the old passion of song came back to her, and tore at her heart; but she could not sing, for she was dumb.

"And I have nothing else left," she thought, "with which I may give back the life to the golden poppy."

"Crimson for golden," the south wind called softly in her ear.

So, she lay down once more, and put her pretty mouth to the dead bloom of the poppy, and she could not speak, but she thought the words "Drink my blood! Drink my life, and live!"

And the dead flower drained out her life, and she grew white and whiter, and when the moonlight fell upon her, not a tint of colour was in her cheeks.

Out of the forest the south wind crept, and he seemed a little excited as he saw the dead girl lying there.

"I'll never do it again," he swore; "if they want such things done, they must do them themselves. Curse them!" Then he howled, for his masters had overheard him and chastised him.

He went back to the forest, and brooded all day over what had happened. And that night he went mad, and came forth to do one or two things on his own account. There was the tall poppy growing by the head of the dead girl, and it had become crimson.

The south wind gave one puff, and blew it out of the ground into the sea.

And over the child's body it blew the finest white sand that it could find, until a heavy drift lay over it.

And it went away to a lonely place where a solitary tree was standing, and in the tree sat the white bird in her nest. And he blew down the tree, and broke the nest, and chased the bird for days and days over the water, till at last the bird sank.

And still the wind was not satisfied. He had a faint idea that he had not been doing much good. He ought, by rights, to have killed his masters. He knew that, but his masters could not be killed. How they smiled as they sat up in cloudland, and watched their angry servant snarling over a child, a bird, and a flower!

"He's not satisfied," said the first.

"Very few people are," grunted a second.

"You're right there," snorted a third.

Their conversation rarely rose above the intellectual level of a market ordinary; but they had the power, and could afford to be a little dull at times.

THE STORY OF THE CLOUD

It was a most beautiful cloud. Two highly respectable Athenians looked at it for a long time, and they understood beauty in Athens.

"Now, if anyone were to paint that," said the first, "everyone would say that it was not natural." He felt there was depth in the remark.

"I am not so sure of that," said the second, intending to be thought judicious but not disagreeable.

If the cloud had been painted, its chiefest beauty would have been omitted. For in the centre of the cloud sat the unborn soul of a girl-child. To all mortals it had no visible appearance. But the stars, as they crept slowly up for a night's work, saw with smiling eyes a graceful figure seated in the vapour, leaning a little backward, white against the crimson pillows of mist, with slender hands clasped behind a shapely head, and long dark hair and closed eyes. For it lived, but did not think, after the manner of unborn souls, which have ways distinctly of their own.

And as the sun poised over the cool, lighted sea that sang to welcome it, a noise of little tinkling silver bells was heard all down the sky; and there was some hurry and confusion amid Powers which were usually calm with the unjust, irritating, excessive calmness of a natural law.

When it was all over, no one exactly knew whose fault it was. But the Manager was summoned before the great Zeus, and reprimanded severely. "It's carelessness," said Zeus, "and that's what I can't stand. You ought to have been ready, and there are no two ways about it. You sit there in the office, wondering how long it will be before you can sneak out to your beastly lunch, and you forget that you're paid to be managing my business for me all that time."

Whether it was the Manager's fault or not, the fact remained. Down in the world, in the beautiful country just outside Athens, a boy-child had been born, and he had been born with the soul of a girl-child inside him.

"Such a piece of bungling!" grumbled Zeus, and went off to play at making orphans.

To play this game you have to be a god, and possess thunderbolts; every time you kill a father or mother you score one; if you miss, it counts nothing; if you kill anything else by mistake, you lose one.

Before the boy was grown Zeus had forgotten all about it. Perhaps this was as well for the boy, for Zeus had intended only to give him five years' life; and perhaps it was not as well.

At the age of twelve he was tall and straight. But his face was too delicate, and his eyes were the eyes that had slumbered a dreamless slumber under the closed lids of the unborn soul of a girl. And about his ways there was some sweet shyness and tenderness, or softness names do not matter although in courage and spirit and endurance he had no equal among his comrades. And with all his comrades he was gentle, and they loved him; but he, having no care for them nor for the parents who bore him, and angry with himself because he could feel no such care, went long, wandering walks alone, and heard strange stories told him by flowers and birds and winds.

And the years passed, and there was no change until the boy was sixteen, and then no one knew why he was so unhappy and quiet; he himself hardly knew. But now his wanderings would take him away for days at a time. A spirit of longing possessed him, for which he had no name, and the fulfilment of it was as a dim, dancing light before him, baffling and dazzling him, and leaving him no peace. And of this neither winds, nor birds, nor flowers told him anything. And the longing drove him to climb where no others had dared to climb, or to swim far out into the cool waters of the bay, that he might come back tired and sleep through the warm fragrant night in the long grass. And ever in sleep there came one dream and told him all; and ever when he awoke, the dream was gone from his memory. So he never knew, but always knew that he had known.

Comely maidens, with an intimate knowledge of their own best points, met him sometimes in his wanderings. And for them he cared nothing at all, and wondered why one or two of their number looked shyly at him as he passed them. They said nothing, for maidens are secretive animals; but one with shapely arms took to herself a new bracelet; and one with pretty pearly teeth got up a new sigh which just parted the lips without being ungraceful, and sounded extremely interesting. However, they might have painted themselves blue, and have had no effect whatever on the sorrowful youth. But they were not thus minded; and, seeing that this sad youth neither loved nor hated them, they looked out for those who understood love and hatred, and were married.

The boy's father thought it necessary to consult a physician about this strange melancholy. Besides, the youth was growing paler every day, and was listless, and cared for nothing but to lie asleep, or almost asleep, with the feathery grass rustling in a gentle whisper over him.

So, the physician came, and asked several impertinent questions. Then he delivered himself upon this wise:

"It is well known that much exercise and weariness consume the spirits and substance, refrigerate the body; and such humours which nature would have otherwise concocted and expelled, it stirs up and makes them rage; which, being so enraged, diversely affect and trouble the body and mind."

"Those are comforting words," said the boy's father, who couldn't understand them.

"Keep it vague," murmured the boy softly.

"It is to the immoderate use of gymnastics," said the physician, "that I ascribe your son's melancholy. Wherefore, let him drink of a syrup of black hellebore, confected with the boiled seeds of *anise, endive, mallow, fermitory, diacatholicon, hierologodium*—"

"Half-time—change ends," said the boy under his breath.

"Cassia and sweet almonds," continued the physician. "And in the meantime, he may drink of a broth of an exenterated chicken."

He had heard the youth's last remark. "And," he added severely, "let him beware of intempestive laughter."

So, the physician went away.

"What did he say?" asked the mother of the youth.

"Well," said the father, "he said that the boy had been growing too fast, at least he implied that, and he prescribed *hierolo*—French for chicken broth, you know."

But while the doctor's prescription was being prepared, the boy went off to the cliffs; and he stretched himself at full length on the thyme, and went to sleep, and dreamed the old sweet dream, and the sun drew near to its setting, and in his pleasant sleep the boy died.

Never had there been a happier and more desirable death.

And under the burning sun a cloud was stretched like a cloth of gold.

And the two highly respectable Athenians came out to look at it. "If I were to paint that exactly as it is," said the first, "everyone would say that my picture was intensely unnatural."

"Great Zeus!" ejaculated the second, for the first had made the remark nearly every night for rather more than sixteen years, and still thought there was a certain insight about it.

In the golden heart of the cloud were together the soul of a youth and the soul of a young girl, two souls that had done their work and were resting. He sat in careless happiness looking down at her: for she was stretched at his feet, making a daisy-chain with the souls of the daisies that were to bloom next year. And ever she would look up from her work into his eyes; and the eyes of the two were strangely alike, and soft and bright.

Into the cloud came the Manager. He was in a terrible hurry; for there had been great doings in Sicily, and an army had been cut to pieces, and consequently there was a press of business.

"I've called to take your numbers," he said.

They both gave the same number.

He seemed a little startled, then recovered himself, and jotted it down in his note-book. "I remember now," he said, half apologetically. "It was not entirely my fault. I had slipped out to get a glass of beer, and I told the boy to send for me if anything happened. But he thought he could manage it himself, and he blundered, and I was blamed. So, you both were born in the same body. I hope you were not crowded. Zeus had intended you to be born in different bodies, and fall in love with one another down below. But you can do it up here, you know. It's not the same thing, but some people think it's better: it's much more spiritual. You will have this cloud all to yourselves for as long as you like. At any rate it was not so hard on you as it was on the girl's body, which had to be born without any soul at all but I am told that she made money out of it. Well, I must be off; good evening."

So, the Manager departed, and they were alone, and they floated away into the night when the night came. And the sea sang beneath them, and the wind was warm and perfumed with flowers.

"I love you for ever and ever," he said.

The same remark had just occurred to her not strikingly original, perhaps, but both were satisfied with it.

THE STORY OF ZEUS & CO.

A general feeling of content prevailed in the house of Zeus & Co. "We shall declare," said Zeus, "such a dividend as never was."

"We shall," said Co.

Zeus & Co. occupied the two thrones at the back of the large hall. During the last spring-cleaning, Zeus had ordered his own throne to be regilded. Nothing had been done to the other throne, which was occupied by Co. But Co. was quite humble. As a general rule he merely echoed the sentiments of Zeus. If he felt the difference between the two thrones, he had never mentioned it. Perhaps it might be as well to notice that all the shares were in the hands of Zeus & Co. They were the directors, and also the shareholders. By this arrangement much unpleasantness was avoided.

But at this moment an old gentleman in a very shiny coat rose from the desk at the farther end of the hall, and stepped towards the thrones. He looked at Zeus, coughed a little nervously, and began:

"Mr. Zeus, and also Mr. Co., you will excuse me, but I've a little matter to bring before you, in my position as Chief Agent in the Punishment Department."

"By all means," said Zeus kindly. "There's nothing wrong, I hope. It's a good department."

"A very good and profitable department," echoed Co.

"Well, Mr. Zeus, you will probably remember that you assigned to me a young subordinate, a mere boy, called Eros."

"I remember," said Zeus. "He was not to draw any regular salary."

"Precisely so," replied the Agent. "He just took his small commission on every broken heart. Well, up to the present I've had no complaint to make of him. He did his work well and cheerfully. The

Suicide Section used to send me in most favourable reports of him. I had even intended to recommend him for promotion."

"But without increase of salary, I hope," said Zeus. "The shareholders would never stand that, you know."

"They simply wouldn't tolerate it for a minute," echoed Co. It was not supposed to be generally known that Zeus & Co. were the only shareholders.

"No, sir," answered the Agent. "I should have left the question of salary to you. I hope I know my place, sir. But, if you will believe it, that boy actually wants to resign the post he holds already. He got mixed up in that Psyche business a good deal, you know. I never knew the rights of the case exactly; but I do know that he's not been the same boy since, and takes no pleasure in his work at all."

"Well, show him in," said Zeus irritably, "and I'll have a word or two to say to him."

"I wonder," suggested Co., "if the Agent can have been fool enough to let the boy know that he was a punishment and not a blessing?"

At this moment the Agent, who had retired, reappeared with Eros. He was a handsome boy, but it was evident that he was very angry. His eyes flashed, and tears stood in them. He made no obeisance to Zeus, but with a rapid movement unslung his bow and quiver from his shoulders, and snapt bow and arrows, one after another, across his knee, flinging them down on the floor of the hall.

"I've had enough of that," he said shortly, setting his lips tight.

"Are you aware," said Co. solemnly, "that what you have just broken is the property of the shareholders? "

"And are you aware," thundered Zeus, "what the dickens you're talking about? Explain yourself."

The boy burst into tears. "I *won't* do it anymore," he sobbed. "I *won't*. I'm not a blessing; I'm a curse. And I'm not going to be your servant, because you hate everybody."

"No," said Co. quietly; "we love them."

"Then what does your first rule mean?" asked the boy fiercely.

"The first rule," replied Co., " is that twenty years shall not be enough to make a life, and ten minutes shall be more than enough to spoil it. We made that rule to stop people spoiling their lives."

Zeus rubbed his hands softly together, and smiled, and said nothing.

"I did not mind once," the boy went on, "when I made women weep and men rave. I do now. It's always the same thing. They long, and long, and cannot obtain; and then the weaker sort kill themselves, and the stronger sort grow cruel. Or, if they obtain, misery in one form or another follows. I resign my post."

"Just pass me that thunderbolt," said Zeus, in an unpleasant voice.

"Oh, you can kill me," the boy exclaimed, contemptuously, "I care nothing for that. I wish I had never lived."

"But you mistake," said Co., suavely, "you mistake; Mr. Zeus had no intention of killing you. You have a right to resign your post if you like. He was going to kill a young girl named Psyche."

"What for?" gasped Eros.

"Oh, for sport."

There was a moment's silence. Then Eros spoke in a hard, unnatural voice. "I will go back to my work, Zeus, and do it better than ever, if you will not kill Psyche."

"Very well," said Zeus kindly. "I don't want to be disagreeable; as long as I kill somebody, it doesn't matter. Now, trot along to your work, my boy, and I won't kill Psyche."

So, the boy went back to his work, and did it better than ever.

"That was a good idea of yours, Co.," said Zeus, after a moment's pause.

"Very much may be done by kindness," replied Co. "Don't you think this throne of mine looks a little shabby beside yours?"

"I'll give the order to have it regilded," said Zeus affably.

But, if things go on like this, it will be "Co. & Zeus" soon.

In A London Garden

My London garden is not really mine. I have it for a period of years
on conditions arranged between two legal gentlemen, the tenant paying the landlord's cost. Obviously, the person who owns the property
can better afford to pay those costs than the man who has to hire it.
And similarly, the man who is lending money on a mortgage can better afford to pay costs than the man who has to borrow it. But the
tenant pays, and the borrower pays. It is a principle of the law that the
poor man pays. But this reflection, into which bitterness of spirit has
led me, has nothing whatever to do with my garden.

I wasted more than a year. The thing looked quite hopeless. I left
my garden to the cats, the jobbing gardeners, the caterpillars, and the
other pests.

Of these the worst and most dangerous is perhaps the jobbing gardener. As the law stands at present you may kill a caterpillar, but not a
jobbing gardener.

Coming on the wrong day—and he never comes on the right
day if he can avoid it—he brings with him a mixed scent of beer and
lubricating oil. If the weather is wet, he sits in the potting-shed and
smokes. If it is fine, he may possibly mow the lawn. He prefers to mow
part of it and then to get on with something else, leaving it like a man
with one side of his face shaved. He takes no sort of interest in the
garden, and candidly there is no reason why he should take any interest. He only sees the place for a few hours every week, and he would
not see it then if he were not paid for it. He has untruthful testimonials, very dirty and decomposed, in his coat pocket, and he is aggrieved
when you sack him. This is quite reasonable.

A jobbing gardener who attends to the gardens of A, B, and C
naturally steals something from A's garden to sell to B, something from

B's garden to sell to C, and something from C's garden to sell to A, and thereout sucks he no small advantage. When he gets the sack there is nothing left for him but to steal your secateurs. He never forgets to do that. I will not say that even in my regenerate condition I never employ a jobbing gardener. There are days when it seems a fine, manly, and primitive thing to do a piece of digging or to mow the lawn. There are more days when such operations seem rather in the light of a nuisance. One would always sooner direct than perform. But the jobbing gardeners who come to me now are under supervision, and are compelled to do things that they hate most in the world—such as putting away their tools when they have finished with them.

I am not particularly fond of the expert and regular gardener either. Generally, he has the luck to be a Scotchman and is a man of few words and great knowledge. But his knowledge is always better than his taste, and he debases an art into a science. His ideals would not fit a London garden, and his feeling for colour is often wrong and poisonous.

The horticulturist-and-florist debases a science into a commerce. I have found him useful and shall continue to do so. He saves me trouble. I will deal with him, but I absolutely refuse to admire him.

The amateur gardener would be pleasant if you could cut out his conceit, but it is ineradicable. He comes into my garden and points out my principal mistakes and tells me of the much better things which he has in his garden.

I myself am not a gardener at all. I admit it. I should imagine that there is no man in Great Britain and her Dependencies who knows as little about gardening as I do. But that is not the sole reason why I write about my London garden. We can distinguish between the dog lover and the dog fancier. In the same way we may distinguish between the garden lover and the gardener. It is an important distinction.

The garden in London makes you love it, and it also breaks your heart. It has therefore all the charm of woman. I am not going to believe that any garden in the heart of the country, where everything is green and easy, can give the same pleasure as my half-acre reclaimed among the chimney-pots. It has its limitations, of course, but so have I. So have all human beings.

One does not ask a beautiful woman to be clever. One does not expect a clever woman to be beautiful. One does not even hope that an aggressively good woman will be either. Similarly, one does not ask the London garden for fruit and vegetables. All that one may really require is shade and flowers. Even that is something, when you remember how very few flowers will grow in shade.

Some blackguard who was allowed to use this garden before it fell to my lot planted rhubarb in a part of it. Most of the rhubarb has now gone, and the rest is going (as the politicians used to say), contrary, I believe, to the terms of my lease. But my landlord is more sympathetic than her solicitors. (The word "landlady" is not to be used. It gives totally wrong associations.) I have also a currant bush, and this shall remain. Its green does not displease me. It produces few currants and I never get or try to get any of them; but birds that are kept as busy with the slugs and caterpillars as the birds in my garden are, deserve an occasional change of diet.

I have a few old apple trees and pear trees, but I think I regard them chiefly for their blossom, though these last two years they have taken heart from the enrichment of the soil and have been covered with fruit. You will find parsley and mint in a secluded border, but these represent rather the ornament of nutrition than nutrition itself.

As a rule, parsley in London is terribly overworked. In the re-freshment-room at a London terminus late at night I have seen a barmaid collect the sprigs of wilted parsley from the tired sandwiches and sad hard eggs, and put it all in a teacup with a little water. It was heart-breaking to think that that parsley would have to go to work again the next day. But also, it presented the barmaid in a new light. It was so foreign to her abnormal stateliness and her unnatural gaiety. It tempted one to believe that after all she was human.

Sitting here in the shade on a hot summer day, with an Austrian brier in full bloom within a few yards of me, I wonder why on earth I ever neglected this garden.

In the first place it had been neglected before. I think for some two years previously a jobbing gardener had called one day every week on purpose to neglect it. Therefore, it seemed hopeless to do anything. In the second place it was too rectilineal. It was an exact rectangle, surrounded by straight paths and bisected by one straight path. In the third place I bought a book about gardening for amateurs and it frightened me. It began just about the point where I shall leave off if I live to be a hundred years old.

And then, neglected though it was, the garden made its appeal to me. All round it are tall trees—elm, and chestnut, and wild cherry, and plane, and sycamore. It offered me grateful shade on a hot afternoon, and I had done nothing to deserve it. In the springtime there were mauve blossoms on the lilac, and golden trails on the laburnum, that I had never earned. Later, tall hollyhocks, lavish sunflowers, crowded Michaelmas daisies, added their reproach. I became uneasy.

I went out and bought things, such as bast, and fertiliser, and green stakes. I began to wander about the garden, thinking what could be done with it. By the next summer the garden had got a fair hold of me. A man who can learn something fresh is not old, wherefore I am not old, but it surprises me that one of my youth should have learned so amazingly little about a garden in the time.

I began to see encouraging factors. I had not to think about fruit and vegetables. I had not to think about a greenhouse, because the garden has no greenhouse. It has not even got a frame. I shall buy one next year, or possibly the year after. London is simply crawling with florists, and for a few shillings you can buy things all ready to put in. The shilling that goes to the taxicab driver is gone for ever—sacrificed to a fit of laziness. The shilling that buys six sweet-williams provides pleasure for many weeks. The sweet-william is, I believe, a two-year thing, or as the sacred jargon of the gardener puts it, a biennial. You start it one year and it flowers the next.

It may be a mean and cowardly thing to do to let the florist do the first year's work on it, and buy it when it is ready to flower that season, but I do it, and I shall continue to do it. I shall continue to do everything that I can think of that will save me trouble in my garden without injuring the garden. But the Iceland poppies are from seed that I myself sowed. I have sown blood-red wallflowers and Canterbury bells to flower next year. One can be lazy without being wholly bad.

Things which looked hopeless at first sight proved better on further consideration. There was the lawn, for instance. The jobbing gardener turned up his nose at the lawn. It slopes. It slopes in several different directions simultaneously.

"There's only one thing to be done with that," said the jobber, "and the sooner you make up your mind to it the better. That all wants to be taken up, levelled, and relaid. It'll cost a bit of money, but it'll never be satisfactory till it's done."

He produced figures and they frightened me. The lawn still slopes deviously, and every day that I see it I am thankful for it. Nobody can possibly play lawn-tennis on it. I hate white rectilineal lines on grass almost more than I hate underdone mutton or "The Lost Chord". Therefore, it is a perpetual joy to me that my lawn slopes.

I asked the jobbing gardener what the roses were, planted in odd corners of the lawn.

"Roses!" he said scornfully. "They ain't roses. It's just some common sort of brier. What anybody put it there for, I don't know. It has never flowered for the last three years, and never will flower, and if it did, you wouldn't like it."

Those despised briers are all covered with flower at the present moment, and I like them very much. They are not gardeners' roses, but they are nicer to look at than the Putney bus.

Are there any plantains in my lawn? There are. There is also more grass than there used to be. You can do a lot of things with plantains. If you turn guinea-pigs loose on your lawn, so one newspaper informs me, they will eat the plantains and leave the grass. But I have not got any guinea-pigs, and I am not going to provide a manly but barbarous sport for the cats of the neighbourhood by buying guinea-pigs. Another method is to cut off the head of the plantain and apply lawn-sand. I shall very likely do that one day when there is nothing in the garden which wants doing more, and if I happen to feel like it. A part of a summer day you must work in a London garden, but it is equally true that for another part of the summer day you must just sit and enjoy it. Otherwise, you sacrifice the end to the means.

"As for that old box tree," said my jobbing Jeremiah, "it never ought to have been put there at all, right on the edge of a bed. If you take my advice, you will have it out. Of course, if it had been properly trimmed and looked after, that might have been made into a peacock, but it would take you years to get it into shape now. You can't grow anything under it, and it's no good trying."

I am glad the old box tree is not a peacock. It has grown the way it wanted to grow, and it suits it. It is perfectly true that nothing will grow under it, and therefore I have not tried to grow anything under it. I found me a handy man and sent him out to buy me a hundred bricks, what time I marked out under the box tree a place where one might sit—a place dry to the feet after the rain. I sent him for red bricks, and he came back with white, because the red bricks were (a) too expensive, and (b) too soft. But the white bricks have done very well with some old bricks mixed in with them, and soon lost their aggressiveness. So underneath my box tree is an L-shaped pavement of bricks, with room for a seat and a table.

People look at it and sniff. It is too unusual. Then they go away and buy bricks. It is astonishing, by the way, how very few bricks there are in a hundred. What I mean, of course, is what a very small pavement they make.

I made another seat under the big scarlet thorn, but this is more ambitious. I got me broken pavement stones—not very easy to get nowadays—and paved a semicircle. On that I put a semi-circular seat with a back to it. Irreverent people have compared it (*a*) to a pew, and (*b*) to a loose-box; but it is a pleasant place to sit in in the evening, and just catches the last of the sunlight. After that I dealt firmly with myself, and said that I could not be always making seats.

I began to see ways by which I might make the garden a little less rectilineal. I need hardly say that I wanted a pergola, because of course everybody wants a pergola. The best house-agents say that a riverside cottage lets better if it has a pergola and no dining-room than if it has a dining-room and no pergola. My pergola is built of rustic wood creosoted, which costs very little. It forms a big semicircle with a short tail projecting from the middle of the curve. On it I grow ramblers and glory-roses. I told an expert with some pride what I had done.

"Yes," said the expert sadly and thoughtfully, "almost any rose does well in London, except the Gloire-de-Dijon."

My glory-roses look all right at present, but he is probably correct. When you do a work and do not know how to do it, you are handicapped. Almost the first thing I did in the way of gardening was to put in some gaillardias, which I had bought in a box. Three of them died. It takes a good deal to kill a gaillardia. Things that I plant now do not die. I am certainly getting on. I shall soon be able to say Gloire-de-Dijon when I mean glory-rose.

Perfection is not for me. But there are some pleasant halting-places this side of it. I consult that book for amateur gardeners at intervals, principally because it is such a delight to be able to skip the long chapter about sea-kale. I still struggle, and tell myself frequently that I shall continue to struggle. But, as I have said, there are pleasant halting-places this side of perfection, and I have a great tendency to get out at the next station.

When that tendency comes over me, I try to remember the smallness of my garden. In a small garden you may cut the caterpillar nests off the scarlet thorn, and burn them to ashes so that no spark of life remains. You feel sure that not one caterpillar is left in the garden. You may then get to work and pick caterpillars off the rose trees. You may hunt the ubiquitous green fly. You may weed properly with a small fork, instead of perfunctorily with a hoe, after the manner of the jobbing gardener. In time of drought, you can water everything. In a small garden much is possible.

It is not exactly a garden yet, of course. The author of that book for amateurs would drop dead from shock if he saw it. But it is more like a garden than the cankered cat-walk it once was.

By the way, speaking of a garden in London, you may possibly have heard the story of—

The Pool in the Desert

There was once a desert. Now I come to think of it, there still is.

Across the desert, mounted on three camels, came the millionaire, the artist, and the analyst. During the day their diet had consisted principally of biscuits and sand. With this they had drunk as much dry sherry as happened to be left in the millionaire's gold flask with the diamond monogram on it. Therefore, at first sight they were glad when they saw the pool, and dismounted hurriedly from their camels. But self-respect, which is a splendid quality, came to their rescue. It was the millionaire who spoke first.

"I don't call that a pool at all. I have a lake in the park at my country-place at least four times the size of that. It is a wretched skimpy little business not worth our attention. Now if we had come to the cataract of Niagara, that really would have been of some interest."

Even as he spoke, the analyst had produced from his saddle-bags test tubes, and litmus paper, and a spirit-lamp, and all manner of mixed chemicals, and was busily engaged on a sample of the water which he had taken.

It was the artist who spoke next.

"Water demands green surroundings. To put a pool in a desert is to put it in a wrong setting altogether. Here we have one stunted and miserable palm tree, and no other vegetation. There is really nothing at all here that I should care to paint."

The analyst was now ready with his results.

"This is precisely what I feared. There can be no doubt whatever that this pool suffers from organic pollution. I do not say that it exists to such an extent as to be dangerous to life, but there is a very distinct trace. I will show you the figures in my analysis."

He did so. I have forgotten the figures. But that does not matter, because if I told you them, you also would forget them.

And then for a while these three good men sat and looked at one another.

"I believe I am dying of thirst," said the millionaire.

"So am I," said the artist.

35

"There is no known form of liquid that I would not at this moment gladly drink," said the analyst.

So, after all they turned their attention to the pool.

But in the meantime, the three camels—poor dumb beasts who knew no better—had drunk up the whole of that pool, and had gone on their way rejoicing.

OMISSIONS: AND THE STORY OF "THE GIRL WHO WENT BACK"

There are smuts in London.

There is also a tradition about the smuts in London, and it may be as well to differentiate the facts and the tradition. According to tradition, everywhere within a six-mile radius from Charing Cross smuts fall heavily and continuously. Nothing will grow. No green things can exist. A sheet of paper exposed to the open air becomes black in three seconds, and a thick layer of carbon covers everything. There are many people who believe this. I was told so only the other night by a beautiful lady to whom I had inadvertently jabbered about my garden. By the way, she was wearing a white dress. Why?

The fact is that there are as many smuts as one can reasonably want—and perhaps a few more—in the city and in Mayfair. There are not so many as there used to be, because there is less smoke. Electricity does not smoke. Up in St John's Wood and Hampstead the smuts are very much diminished. Probably if I climbed one of my trees, I should find my hands black. But I am not a boy nor a gorilla, that I should do this thing. I read or write in the garden, and I find that no smut settles on the white page. I dine under the tall trees, and the white cloth remains unpolluted. I may possibly get an elm-seed in my soup, but that is another matter. (Can anyone tell me, by the way, why the elm produces such an amazing lot of seeds and sows them broadcast, with a preference for places where they can never by any possibility germinate?) This is all quite contrary to tradition, but it happens to be the truth.

There is a good time coming—the time when smoke will be eliminated. The London garden will doubtless be an easier and cleaner matter then. But meanwhile the London garden is not impossible. The evergreens are distinctly shop-soiled after the winter; but with the summer comes the fresh green, and in the summer, London provides us with less smoke from fewer fires. Beautiful white dresses must be washed or cleaned, and after all the garden has its hose and its rain-showers.

The tradition is inept as it stands, but it has a basis of truth. There is very much that must be omitted in the London garden. There are flowers that never come to town. Speaking generally, bulbs will do less work here than they will in the country. After the first year the tulips get tired. But as a compensation for the many things which one must omit, come the many other things which one may omit.

The liberty of the subject is too much circumscribed, but I believe that there is no law in this country which compels a man to grow the Jacoby geranium. This does not seem to be generally understood. Look at the window-boxes of London, and look at the gardens. Mayfair as a rule is ambitious and kills quite pretty things in its window-boxes; but elsewhere all too frequently one finds the Jacoby geranium and the edging of blue lobelia. I think that people get these things and grow them just exactly as they pay their dog licence—not because they want to do it but because they feel they must. There is probably an organised conspiracy between florists and jobbing gardeners to promote Jacobys.

"You will be wanting some geraniums," says the florist decisively, and you are hypnotised into believing it. "What could we have in that bed?" you ask the jobbing gardener. "A few Jacobys," he says, with the air of a man who has had a bright idea. If he does not edge them with blue lobelia, he edges them with some yellow stuff which I think he calls pyrethrum. One has only to smell it once never to try it again. At the same time there are some super-cultured people who carry the hatred of the geranium to an unreasonable extent. There is a white one which does not make me ill, and a pink one which is not too hideous. But as it happens, the only geranium in my garden is the one which is grown solely for the scent of its leaves.

One year where geraniums might have been I had blue-violet verbenas, sweet-scented and just as easy to grow. I was told to hairpin them to the ground, but out of obstinacy I grew them upright. They did not seem to mind. I have no rage against the blue lobelia, if it is put in a safe place where its colour can do no harm. I do not know why the white lobelia has so much less popularity. One is not bound to grow it as an edging. Now I come to think of it, I believe I hate all edgings.

I am not very fond of those flowers which are distinctively villa flowers. I do not think there is any man alive who could sell me a yellow *calceolaria* or persuade me to find room for it in my garden. The fuschia too is rather a self-conscious and ostentatious thing, though I admit the tree-fuschia. To these I prefer musk, and mignonette, and heliotrope. They flourish in a wet summer, and I wish I did. Lilies and carnations of course one must have, and London permits it. London pride is common enough, but I like it and grow it. It is a generous thing that asks little and gives much. If only its graceful flower were expensive, it would be greatly admired. The white and yellow marguerites are of no dazzling rarity, but I welcome them. Hosts of the old-fashioned perennials are desirable and possible, though there are some of them that need to be watched. The sunflower, for instance, is distinctly greedy and would take the whole garden if it could get it.

If a general principle of omission and selection for a London garden could be formulated, it would probably run as follows—choose cottage-garden things and avoid villa-garden things. In this way you will get all that is simple and sweet-scented and easy of cultivation, and nothing which is formal and perky. There are men who at present do earn large salaries by making gardens perky. The pity of it!

I have myself seen a long bed covered with things of different coloured foliage in geometrical patterns. "You may see as good Sights, many times, in Tarts." Thank you, my Lord Verulam, for those words. Looking at such a bed one did not see the flowers only. The eye of imagination lingered on all that must have conduced to its preparation—all the pegs, and string, and perspiration, and misplaced cleverness. A garden may easily be over-educated, and that which is good in itself may suffer from improvement.

And that reminds me. You do not, perhaps, know the story of—

The Girl Who Went Back

There was once a girl whose name was Rose, and she was rather pretty and rather clever. She was not very pretty or very clever, but everybody said she was very sweet. She had great advantages. Her papa was a wise man. Her mamma—well, her mamma had the best intentions and was troubled with ambition. But they both loved Rose.

The ambitious mamma said to the wise papa: "Rose is now seventeen years old. She has faults which must be eradicated. She has good qualities which must be enhanced. The last year of her education must be peculiarly strenuous."

"As how?" said the wise papa.

"Well, I do not quite like the way she speaks. Her voice is pleasant in quality, and you can generally understand her; but she slurs her words and she is just a little weak on the letter 'r'. She must be made to pay far more attention to her personal appearance. Her waist is not as small as it might be; and her complexion—but these are not things which you will require to understand. She must learn German thoroughly. A smattering is no use. She must not be allowed to have her own way about the violin. Arithmetic is a very weak point with her. Are you attending?"

The wise papa opened his eyes, and said that he had heard every word, and that she was quite certain to be right, and that he would leave it to her.

Rose had no ambition and no wisdom. She liked play. She liked real music. She liked dancing. But as she was quite good, she did what she was told. Many tutors came about her, and she worked early and late. Her mother confided to her those secrets which should add to her beauty.

The elocution master was quite pleased with her. She learned to ar-tic-u-late her words and to speak dis-tinct-ly. She pronounced every "r" as if it had been a coffee-mill. It was a treat to listen to her.

Her proficiency in foreign languages was really remarkable.

Her music teacher said that she had improved enormously in technique and in taste. Her playing on the violin was a mixture of gymnastics and conjuring tricks. She learned to speak slightingly of melody. She understood advanced orchestration, and pronounced Tschaikowsky correctly. She occasionally annoyed people by giving Chopin the Russian pronunciation.

Her waist became smaller. You might have thought that her long hours of study would have made her pale, but there was always a delicate blush on either cheek-bone, except when she had just washed her face. Her hair became a work of art. It was marvellously arranged.

The college of domestic-training found Rose its most apt pupil. She could cook. She could housekeep. Her arithmetic was unfailing. She could detect at once the mistake in the tradesman's account, and she could get the right note of asperity into her voice in speaking to him about it. "Is it not rather an extraordinary coincidence that these frequent errors are always in your own favour?" This was obviously the kind of woman that a sensible man would be glad to marry. She was a highly developed helpmeet.

The ambitious mamma saw that Rose had improved out of all knowledge. She became proud of her. She now waited for Rose to make an exceptionally brilliant match. She continued to wait, for something had changed in Rose. People said she was very accomplished and very beautiful, but nobody said she was rather sweet. The boys who had played with her and danced with her did not seem to require her anymore; they shivered with fear in her splendid presence.

We should all improve ourselves, and try to do our best—this is the accepted view and there is no need to dispute it—but concentration on one's own self, even with the highest possible motive, is poison. And Rose had drunk of that poison.

And then the ambitious mamma died; and there were some people who thought that she was better dead. But Rose was overcome with grief. It was not until six weeks later that, standing before the cheval-glass, she noticed how very well she looked in black. She worked harder than ever at the task of self-improvement, until her health broke down. Then two things happened simultaneously. She was ordered into the country, and her papa went to take up an important post in Paris.

Rose lived now in a cottage up on a hill with a refined and elderly lady-companion. Beyond the garden of the cottage was common-land. Here the bracken grew waist-high, and you might see as many foxgloves in ten minutes as you would find in London in ten years. Sheep roamed among the bracken. The difference between the face of the lady-companion and the face of one of those sheep was hardly noticeable; they also had similarities in disposition.

When the lady-companion slept—and she was a perfectly grand sleeper—Rose wandered all the afternoon about the common. She was not improving herself any longer, because that was held to be bad for her health. She worried because she felt that she had lost the love of people. The longer she lived in the country, the more she wanted to be loved. She even put tentative questions to the lady-companion, to find out how it was that she was not loved. But these tentative questions were of no use, because the lady-companion maintained that Rose was loved very much indeed, being under the impression that this was the kind of thing that she was paid to say. She was a conscientious woman.

And then one night Rose had a dream. In her dream she heard a loud knocking at the cottage door, and she herself went to see who was there.

There stood a very ugly old pedlar with a leer on his face, and a pack on his back. He swung his pack round and took off the piece of American cloth from the top of it.

"And what can I sell you today, my pretty lady?" he asked.

"Nothing, thank you," said Rose.

"Don't say that," said the pedlar. "You have dealt with me before, you know."

"Never," said Rose. "You are mistaken."

"Yes, you did," said the ugly old man stoutly. "You bought a packet of Amoricide, and those that deal with me once must deal with me again."

"What is Amoricide?" asked Rose, who began to have a feeling that after all she did recognise the pedlar's face.

"Well, well," said the pedlar, "that's telling. I don't mind owning that there is a lot of the Air of Superiority in it, and there are other things. You have no complaint to make about it, have you? It does its work all right. I guarantee that it will exterminate love absolutely. It is death to love. Have you not found it so?"

"I have found," said Rose, "that it has destroyed the love of others for me, but not the love of me for others."

The old man chuckled. "That's it. That's right. That's why the people who deal with me once must deal with me again. You must have one more little packet."

"This time I want to know what is in it."

The pedlar began to look uneasy. "Don't ask too many questions. We call it *Taedium Vitae*. It is a splendid thing."

Rose was highly educated, and she told him that *Taedium Vitae* meant life-weariness, and that she would like to know how it acted.

"You go down the hill," said the old man absent-mindedly, as if he were speaking to himself, "and then, of course, you come to the pine wood."

Rose nodded. "Yes, I know it. Through the wood is the short cut if you are going to the station. The stile is rather awkward to climb over."

"You can manage it all right. You have done it before. And you know the dark pool under the trees?"

Rose nodded. This time she did not speak.

"That's another short cut," said the old man with a chuckle. "It's soon over. The sensation of drowning is said to be quite pleasant. Then there is no more trouble—no more worrying because you have lost love, and because life has lost its savour."

Rose was rather frightened. "When do I pay you?" she asked in a husky whisper.

"That's all right," said the old man ingratiatingly. "You don't pay me till afterwards. We give credit."

41

"Afterwards?"

"After the pool. Come, you will take this packet."

"I will not," said Rose with sudden determination, and shut the door in the old man's ugly face. He kept on knocking.

Then she knew that it was only the knocking of the maid who brought her one cup of China tea, one piece of thin bread-and-butter, one large can of hot water, and the news that it was a fine morning.

After that there was a change in Rose. Some of the change was very subtle. Some of it was quite obvious. Even a lady-companion with the mind of a sheep can detect a change in personal appearance. She did detect it, and she spoke about it with discretion.

Rose answered: "Yes, two inches bigger. I don't wear them at all now. Suppose I shall have to when I go back to town. And I find I simply cannot stand the other stuff. If I've got brown, that is because God's sun meant me to be brown."

"The merest touch would——"

Rose was good-humoured, but obstinate.

And in time she went back to town. She had lost the habit of thinking about herself or of asking why people did not love her. She gave them the music that they wanted, and not the music that she knew they ought to have wanted. She became very simple and friend-ly. The tone of her voice softened, and the "r" sound no longer buzzed properly. She had gone back. And when she was not thinking about it at all, people began to love her.

One man particularly. And this was fortunate for Rose.

Papa, who was a director of Kekshose & Cie—they make such big motor-cars that nobody ever dares to let them do as much as they will, and hardly anybody can afford to buy them—came back for the wedding.

I was just going to say, when that foolish story interrupted me, that Cardinal Newman wrote a book called *Apologia pro vita sua*. I mention it not as a discovery but as a reminder. I believe that almost every imaginative author writes an *Apologia pro vita sua*, though under a different title and in a different guise. I could name one author (and so, of course, could you) who has written several such *apologiæ*. If I have never done it myself, it is because I am not of the heroic type which undertakes lost causes. But I am not quite sure that I am not writing an *Apologia pro horto meo*. There is a serpent in every Eden, and its name is Pride.

If my half-acre of cat-walk can claim to be a remote descendant of Eden, the serpent exists there too. I point out the good things in the garden. I cover up the defects, or—which is even worse—I make elaborate explanations to prove that they are not defects at all. I cannot expect anybody to like my garden as much as I do, but I want them to respect it. Jokes about it always seem to me to be in bad taste. A very good amateur gardener once came into my garden and mentioned just a few of the things that he noticed. He did it in the kindliest way. He taught me quite a good deal, and I hope he will never know how near I came to beating him on the head with the business end of a large rake.

I think that what I have said about omission is true. Everybody who loves art loves omission. I should like, for instance, if I could, to write in the fewest words that lucidity requires. It has given me pleasure to omit certain things from my garden.

But all the same—and I may as well confess it—fewer things would be omitted from my garden if it were larger and in the heart of the country, and if I had somebody to help me, and if by chance I happened to know something about it.

Roses: And the Story of "The Blessed Artist"

The terminology of the botanist is a standard joke, but as a matter of fact, the botanist blunders into a good thing sometimes. It was rather a fine idea to have in plants an order of those that bear the cross—*cruciferæ*. The turnip and sea-kale are among those whose petals make the sign, but it need not shock us. Is there not loveliness in the flower of the potato, and poetry in the foliage of the asparagus? On the whole, I think the botanist makes me less angry than the horticulturist.

Why, for instance, are so many roses named after abominable horticulturists or their wearisome female relatives? How can you call a rose Frau Karl Druschki? I always call that great white rose Mabel, because it reminds me of a large, lymphatic, handsome girl, who was entirely without charm. Scent in a flower is charm in a woman. Frau Karl Druschki has no scent. Hugh Dickson has nothing wrong with it but its name. Fancy calling a beautiful apricot-tinted rose William Allen Richardson! Its godfathers and godmothers in its baptism showed a small sense of humour.

Besides, its name is quite obviously Doris. It is permissible to call a pink rambler Dorothy, but why add the unspeakable surname Perkins? Why should a red rose be named after a duke? It is insufferable, snobbish, and inept. No rose should be named after any man, and should never bear more than the first name of a woman. Niphetos is a possible name; it is the most sentimental of the white roses. But almost all roses have their counterparts in women. There is, for instance, in my garden a pink, useful, knobbly dumpling of a rose. I have not the faintest idea what the horticulturist would call it, but no one can see it without knowing that its real name is Kate.

I think the roses that I love best are those of the deepest and darkest crimson. They have velvety skins and the most perfect fragrance. It is part of the perversity of the thing that they should be so difficult to manage. You feed them and tend them, and they give you scanty and imperfect bloom, or they die, and the intelligent inquest results in an open verdict. When that happens, the only consolation is to find somebody else who has had the same trouble with the same rose. I have not ventured to ask one of them to put up with a London garden as yet, but I fancy one is coming to stay with me next year. Perversity haunts the garden, and the dock always grows as near as possible to some plant that you value.

"Now then," says the dock, "if you dig me up, you'll have to pay for it." But especially does perversity attach itself to roses. What have I done for the perennial lupins? Nothing. And they have given me numberless spikes of incomparable loveliness. What have I done for the Canterbury bells? Nothing. And they also seem to like it. But I did a good deal for that particular rose which I call Mabel, and then there was a late spring frost. It was no fault of mine. I was not even there when it was done. I was in bed at the time. But it annoyed Mabel. She seemed unable to forget it. Why must those loathsome and parthenogenetic green flies devour the tender roses? There is still a certain amount of rhubarb in the garden, and they are welcome to it. I would very much rather they ate it than that I should eat it myself. But the green flies will not look at it. They cling to the rose and suck its life out. Then, out of sheer devilry, they grow wings and migrate to some other rose tree.

The queen demands homage, and the rose has received it to the extent of countless volumes written by wise gardeners who have studied her specially. Their learning appals. They almost deter the poor blunderer in London from ever trying to grow a rose or to talk about one. A little knowledge may be a dangerous thing, but the expert runs his risks also. I was taken through a most beautiful rose-garden once, and I dared to admire one particular bed. "Yes," said the owner of the garden almost apologetically, "it's quite one of the old sorts." And then I was taken to other beds in which was the very last word in roses—kinds that had only been produced within the last year or so—and here the owner showed more enthusiasm. Has it come to this then—that fashion is to stray from the milliner's shop and find a place in the garden?

From motives of humanity, I refrain from bringing out once more certain over-worked quotations from Herrick and Omar; but in truth the poets, like the scientific gardeners, have not spared writing materials where roses were in question. They are ecstatic about the colour and fragrance, and generally sentimental about the thorns, and never by any chance allude to the culture. There is something feminine about poets. They like the result, but they ignore the process, just as a woman eats a lamb cutlet, but does not want you to talk about the slaughter-house.

Perhaps it is not to be expected that poets should mention the food of the roses, and yet I hate a shirker of facts. I am not sure that there is not something of poetry in the plain truth that in nature's impartial chemistry there is only one step from muck to glory.

And now, if you are tired of uninformative talk about roses, I will tell you the story of—

The Blessed Artist

There was once an artist who lived in a great town. He was painting a picture, and he took a great deal of trouble to make it as difficult for himself as possible. He tried for effects of lighting that needed miracles. In his work he sought and worshipped difficulties. In the garden beyond the studio, he found plenty of difficulty without seeking for it. But this was difficulty of a kind that maddened him. He wanted a garden, but he did not want to make a garden. So, he employed a man one day a week, and was profoundly dissatisfied.

One afternoon he had a dream. He dreamed that an angel came into his room—a beautiful angel of the accepted Doré Gallery type. The angel had a pleasant voice and said pleasant things to him.

"You have lived well," said the angel, "and you have worked well. You have earned for yourself the blessedness that belonged to the Garden of Eden. That blessedness shall fall upon your garden. Go and look at it."

So, the artist went out on to his lawn and was quite surprised. It was of one beautiful tint of fresh green all over, with never a brown spot. There had been many daisies on that lawn, but they had all gone now. It had suffered from moss, but the moss had vanished. It had been superficially irregular, but it was now level. The perfect grass was just three-quarters of an inch in height, and no tall bents stuck up anywhere. He went to look at his roses. He remembered them as they had formerly been—spindly bushes which he had forgotten to prune, and that bore leaves only at the extreme end of their branches.

They had changed to compact bushes that were green all over and flowered like an illustration in a seedsman's catalogue. Caterpillars had played havoc with them aforetime, but now he could find no caterpillar and no trace of the caterpillar's work. He went on to his two apple trees. They had borne no blossom that year that he could remember, and the white tufts of American blight had bedecked their trunks. The American blight was all gone now. The blossom had set, and the fruit was swelling, and each tree would bear exactly the right number of apples, neither more nor less.

The carnations were very large, numerous, and fragrant. The madonna lilies promised well. There was no weed to be seen anywhere, and the paths had been newly gravelled with the red gravel which he had always wanted, and never been able to get. The very quality of the soil had changed, and was now dark and rich. It was worthwhile to work in such a garden as this; he took his coat off and went into the potting-shed to get his tools.

And then he realised his blessedness. There was absolutely nothing for him to do in the garden. It was all quite good. The drought had not brought down the leaves nor cracked the surface. The strong winds had not dishevelled and laid low the sunflowers. He noticed, moreover, that things were tied up now with green bast to green sticks. He had always wanted green bast and green sticks, but had used the other kind because it was the only kind that the man round the corner sold.

He put on his coat and stretched himself on a deck-chair on the lawn in the evening sunlight in a great state of contentment. When it grew dusk, from the shrubbery at the end of the garden came beyond mistake the voice of the nightingale. He had always wanted nightingales, but so far, he had put up with imitative blackbirds. Blessedness had come to him indeed.

He lit a cigarette and reflected how he would show his garden to Smith, and how much Smith would be annoyed about it. Smith had a garden of his own, and was a toilsome amateur with a certain amount of knowledge. Smith would undoubtedly be green with jealousy. He would ask Smith to luncheon, and afterwards they would have coffee in the garden. He would carefully abstain from calling Smith's attention to anything; but he would watch him, as he slowly drank it all in and meditated suicide.

On the day that Smith was to come to luncheon, the blessed artist rose early in order that he might mow the lawn before breakfast. But when he went out, he found that it did not require to be mown. The grass grew to just the right height and then stopped. At luncheon Smith was inflated with pride, and talked freely about begonias. He mentioned other things which he had in his garden—things that that artist ought to come and see. The artist sat quite meekly, and was very polite until luncheon was over. Then he said: "I think we might have coffee in the garden, Smith, if you call that backyard of mine a garden."

"Ah," said Smith, "you should give a little more time and attention to it."

Then they passed out into the garden, and Smith was struck dumb. At last, he said: "How do you manage to get those fine dark wallflowers in full bloom at the end of June?"

"Takes a bit of management," said the blessed artist complacently.

Smith began to walk round the garden. He admired exceedingly. The confession that he had got nothing like that escaped him frequently; and when he had seen it all, he pulled from one pocket an old envelope and from another a short stub of a pencil.

"Look here," he said, "you might just give me the name of the chap who does your garden for you."

"The angels do my garden for me," said the blessed artist.

"Oh, all right," said Smith, "if you don't want to tell me, you needn't."

And he put back the old envelope and the pencil in their respective pockets, and he went away in a very bad temper. But this incident reminded the blessed artist to countermand the jobbing gardener—a man of intemperate habits and quite unfit to collaborate with angels.

The next day the artist went into his garden and enjoyed it extremely.

The day after he enjoyed it less.

The day after that he began to be dissatisfied. Dissatisfaction began to settle like a cloud upon him. He wondered why. It came to him slowly that he felt like a man who had stolen the Victoria Cross and was wearing it ostentatiously. He was exhibiting a perfection for which he had never worked; and there was no savour in it.

"Better," he cried, "imperfection towards which one has contributed something. Better even the sickly wilderness that this garden once was."

The sound of his own voice woke him.

He found that he was sitting in a deck-chair on the lawn. It was a decayed chair, having been left out in many rains. The lawn was just as bad as ever it had been. He could almost hear the caterpillars crunching up the surrounding vegetation. One glance showed him that his rose trees were still a shame and a reproach. And down the steps from the house came his old friend Smith, smiling and rubicund.

"Been asleep in this rotten old garden of yours?" he said. "It looks to me as if you would have done better if you had been working in it."

"I am inclined to think so," said the artist.

As a rule, it is easier to do much work than little. The man who is underworked rarely does the little that he has to do thoroughly and punctually. The more leisure one has, the more one desires.

I feel confident that if I had a thousand rose trees, I should be up bright and early in the morning to do for them all that they required. I should study the literature on the subject and become expert. Possibly I should not go so far as some experts, who provide a kind of conical tin hat for each rose bloom to shelter it from the rain. But it would not be slackness which would stay my hand; it would be because I cannot think that the conical tin hat adds greatly to the beauty of the garden.

But I have not got a thousand rose trees. It is none the less essential that I should cut off all the dead blooms. This labour, carried out with no unseemly haste, might possibly occupy me for five minutes.

And how many times have I shirked those five minutes of labour? I am shirking them now. Let me see, where are the scissors?

The Fountain: And the Story of "The Little Death"

I will admit that I very nearly erected a sun-dial in my garden. There was a kind of snobbery about it. So many artistic people have erected sun-dials in their gardens, that I supposed that I should be artistic if I erected a sun-dial in mine. But all the time, somewhere at the back of my head, was the conviction that the thing was rotten. I knew it was rotten some time before I knew the reason why.

Sun-dials are not used nowadays for the purpose of telling the time. It is therefore insincere and affected to put a sun-dial in a modern garden. It is not conscientious. It is like the artificial creation of worm-holes in the spurious-antique furniture. Where the sun-dial already exists in an old garden one may be glad of it, but one may not deliberately put a sun-dial into a new garden.

So, I put in a fountain.

The simplest and most satisfactory way to get a fountain in one's garden is to buy one from the fountain shop, make arrangements with the Water Company, and get a real plumber to fix it. This did not appeal to me. There was no adventure about it, it would cost too much, and I knew that I should hate shop-fountains. I therefore designed and made my own fountain, and will now instruct others how they may make one which will be nearly as bad and delightful.

The first step is to find among your acquaintances a family where the baby is grown up. Talk about babies. Ask if the baby had a tin bath with a lid to it, the kind that its things are packed in when it goes to the seaside in the summer. Ask further if that bath is still in existence. If it is, then make the family give you the bath. It is to serve as the reservoir for your fountain and is essential.

You proceed to the second step. In deciding where you would put your fountain, you will remember of course that fountains always look best among big trees with a green background. You now fix the disused bath firmly in the tree twenty feet or so from the ground, in such a position that it is secluded by foliage from the gaze of the curious and impertinent. The chestnut tree seems to have been specially designed by nature for this purpose.

Your third step would be to dig out the basin of the fountain. I chose a spot under the trees mid ferns and laurels. I bought from a stone-yard a cartload of material, half of it broken flat paving-stone and half of it chunks, and I may add incidentally that I paid too much for it. I paved the bottom of the basin with flat stone and concrete, leaving a space for the jet of the fountain to come up in the middle. I used the flat stone also for the border round the margin of the basin. At the back of the fountain, I built up the chunks to the height of six feet or so, putting in plenty of earth with them. I have golden and silver ivies climbing over the stones, and I have planted there anything which I thought would grow.

The reservoir being in its place and the basin constructed, the next step is to connect them. This is done by a compo pipe with a surreptitious tap in it.

And after that you fill the bath with the garden hose and turn the tap. As a rule, nothing happens the first time, because there is air in the pipe; but you can put the garden syringe to the fine nozzle in which the compo pipe terminates, and draw out the air. My own fountain will play for six hours continuously; and then when no one is looking one must fill up the bath reservoir again.

It is really extraordinary how gardening turns decent, God-fearing men into braggarts. I have said that I did this myself. I did design it. I did direct the work, and to some extent assist in it; but can I fix compo pipes on to holes in baths, or fine nozzles on to compo pipes? Can I fit taps? Can I manipulate stone and concrete? Certainly not.

It is very useful to know a man who can do everything, especially when one gets ambitious in a London garden. The same man who did the plumbing work of the fountain also did the stone work. He built the palace—it were an affectation of modesty to call it a kennel—in which the Pekinese puppy lives when it is not eating the Iceland poppies. He painted the garden seats. He is an expert in the removal of the American blight. He has diagnosed that my wild cherry is barkbound, and wishes me to let him cut a slit in it, but I dare not. He is wonderful and he is inexpensive.

The public fountain is always placed in an open space. There is a tendency even among quite decent private people to use the fountain as a lawn decoration. I like it better among trees myself; it is more classical. It recalls more lines of Horace. The fountain must never be allowed to play on a dull or cold day. And if you yourself are doing something strenuous in the garden, it is irksome to have the fountain playing while you are working. The fountain belongs to sunlight and repose, and the garden that is not a place of rest is no garden. The purr of the lawn-mower and the tinkle of falling water are the two most soporific sounds in existence. They should be used by the medical profession in the cure of insomnia. I do not know why, but people generally seem to be a little proud of insomnia. They like to tell you how many times in the night they heard the clock strike. One will do almost anything to be interesting, undeterred by failure in it. This, I suppose, it is which drives some to story-writing.

You may have chanced to hear the story of—

The Little Death

There was once (but it must have happened a long time ago and in some very distant island) a race of people who never slept. Occasionally they became tired and lay down, but they never closed their eyes and never lost consciousness. They had never heard of sleep. They had never learned it. And in consequence they did a great deal of work, but they died very young. They were quite happy about it of course, because one never misses what one has never had. There may be something quite as sweet as sleep which we ourselves do not miss, only because we do not know about it.

One day a shipwrecked man was cast up on the shore. These were hospitable people, and they took him up to the king's palace and entertained him. And when night came, after he had feasted and drunk, the king said: "And now what pleasure can we offer you? Would you like to hear music, or to see the dancing-girls, or to ride out in the moonlight?"

The man laughed. "None of these things, sir," he said. "The day has been long, and a feeling of weariness overcomes me. I should now like to sleep."

"That is some new game?" asked the king, intelligently.

"Sleep?" said the Princess Melissa. "We do not know that. What is this sleep?"

The man explained it as best he could, and his account was received with the greatest interest. Many questions were put to him.

"I perceive," said the king at last, "that this sleep is really a little death. For the time being you are dead. Take my advice, therefore, O stranger, and give it up. It is an awful risk, thus voluntarily to enter into the place of death. Suppose that one day you find something there that keeps you, and you cannot come back again."

The stranger explained that, so far was this from being the case, that every time when he went to sleep, he was more afraid that something would wake him, than that he would never wake at all.

"I fear," said the king, "that this shows that you have not thought about the matter profoundly."

"Possibly not," said the stranger. "But I am as I am constructed. I sleep because I must sleep. Had I but a couch to lie upon, I could be asleep now in five minutes."

"How exciting," said the Princess Melissa.

"May we all see it? May we watch you when you are dead of the little death?"

"Most certainly," said the stranger politely. "I am so tired that I am likely to sleep very soundly, but all the same noise or bright light would wake me again, and that would make me very angry. I must beg, therefore, that when you come to look upon me in my sleep, the light may be subdued and no sound may be made."

And to this condition they agreed.

A room was prepared for the stranger in the palace. It was thickly carpeted, so that no footfall could sound. It had a curtained entrance, that the stranger might not be disturbed by the sound of the door opening and shutting when people entered to see the show. The room was dimly lit by the flame of a small lamp. In five minutes, the stranger was asleep.

One by one they entered the room—the king, the princess, and all the people of the court—to see this new and awful phenomenon of a man who was dead of his own volition and would yet come to life again. Three ladies of the court fainted on leaving the apartment. The king became terribly anxious. "This is a dangerous game," he said, "and must be stopped at once. We do not wish to have the death of this stranger on our conscience. Bring, therefore, bright lights and make a loud noise——"

But here the Princess Melissa intervened. "No," she said; "he is not really dead, for he still breathes. I watched him most carefully and am sure of it. It is an experiment which he has often made. He tells me that he has had this sleep every night of his life."

"Doubtless," said the king, "he wished to make an impression; we are not bound to believe that."

But the king was bound to admit, though he did so grudgingly, that a man who breathed was not a dead man.

All the night through they watched outside the sleeping-chamber, and about the middle of the night they heard a terrific sound.

"That," said the king, "is the cry of his death agony. I know it. I am sure of it. We have done wrong."

As a matter of fact, the sound was the first snore which had ever been heard in that island. It made even the Princess Melissa nervous. But she investigated the phenomenon and reported that no interference seemed to be required. The man was not only breathing, he was breathing more strenuously than he did when he was awake.

Nevertheless, a great weight was taken from the king's mind when his guest came back to life again in the morning. It was noted that the man was none the worse for his strange experience. He seemed even better for it. He was more active and alert. His eye was brighter. He was instantly ready to undertake the fatigue of swimming for a long distance in the sea.

That morning, as he conversed with the Princess Melissa, he tried to explain to her something even more strange than sleep—the dreams that come to one in sleep. The two walked alone through the forest together.

"Tell me," said the princess, "do you think that I also could sleep and have a dream? I know it is bizarre and morbid, but I long passionately and above all things to have this strange experience."

"So far as I can judge," said her companion, "you are constructed precisely as the women of the rest of the world, where sleep is a nightly event. I may be wrong, but I should imagine that if the initial impulse could be given to you, you also would sleep."

The princess clasped her hands in ecstasy. "How perfectly splendid!" she said. "But then how am I to get the initial impulse?"

"What," asked the man, "is that glow of red amid the yellow in the field yonder?"

"That is where poppies grow among ripening corn. But what have they to do with the initial impulse?"

"They are it," said the stranger; "by means of those poppies I could prepare for you the secret of sleep. But there would be a risk."

"You told me just now that in a dream it seemed to you that you were sitting in a boat with an elephant, drinking tea, and the elephant had on a small white coat with a rose in its buttonhole. That seemed as real to you in the dream as it seems now that you are walking with me on the edge of the forest?"

"Quite as real, absolutely real."

"Then for such a miraculous experience as that, who would not run any risk? Come, we will go and gather poppies."

For the next few days, the stranger was shut up in his apartments in the palace, making the sleep-producing drug of which he knew. He had to test it many times, that he might be assured that the princess ran no risk. And during these days the Princess Melissa gathered dry bracken and carried it to the ruined temple that stood in the heart of the forest. For it was there that she meant to yield to her great adventure.

The man continued to sleep at nights, always before a good audience. For the wonderful story had been bruited abroad, and all the people in the land were eager to see. One night he slept for a charity in which the king was interested. Money was turned away at the doors, and the thing was a great financial success. But one newspaper of the island complained of the morbid character of the exhibition. "We cannot," wrote the editor, "approve that this poor sufferer should be made to earn money by what is doubtless his disease."

The time came at last on a hot afternoon in July. The princess drank the potion that was given her and lay down on the bed of bracken. The stranger watched by her side.

53

"It is going to fail. I am not asleep," said the princess; "I do not see elephants or boats or anything but what is really here."

"Close your eyes," said the stranger; "relax your muscles, breathe regularly, and count every breath you take up to ten. Then begin to count again."

"It is no use," said the princess wearily.

But in a few minutes, she was fast asleep.

The princess was young. Two years before she had fallen in love with a man whom she could not marry, and the man had fallen in love with her. There had been no scandal, such was the discretion that they used, but there had been material for a scandal. The matter was all over now, for the man in his wisdom had gone away.

When the princess awoke, she sighed deeply.

"You have slept?" said the man.

"I have."

"You have dreamed?"

"I have."

"Tell me your dream."

"I cannot tell you my dream, but I have been to Paradise."

"*Les yeux gris vont au Paradis*," quoted the man.

"Now give me more of the poppy juice," said the princess.

"No," said the man, "I have given you as much as you may take safely in one day."

So, the princess pretended to be meek and obedient, and said it was very well and she would think no more about it, and perhaps now sleep would come to her at nights even if she did not drink the poppy juice. That had broken down the barrier of the garden of sleep, and now she would be able to enter the garden freely when she would.

"Perhaps," said the man.

But when for many nights she tried and could not sleep, she grew rebellious, and going secretly to his apartments she procured the poppy juice he had prepared. With this treasure in her hand, she went back to the temple and stretched herself again on the bed of bracken. She drank the whole of the poppy juice.

"For," she said aloud, "if the little death be so sweet, then—then——"

And here she fell asleep.

For ten successive days I had forgotten to buy the weed-killer; therefore, on the tenth day, which was a Wednesday, I went out to weed the gravel paths with my own hands. It is not a pleasant operation. It is, I believe, the thing in gardening that I loathe most.

The faint burble of water led me towards my fountain. It was playing joyously, and some careless person had left beside it a garden-chair and the current issue of *Punch*.

Any man with a sense of duty and a reasonable amount of willpower would have turned off the fountain and got to work.

The sun was shining brightly. The day was warm. I had not seen that number of *Punch*. And I did not turn off the fountain, I turned off the work.

But the next day I remembered to buy weed-killer. The commonest saying of the Spaniard is not duly appreciated in this country, and is especially useful in the summer-time.

THE STRUGGLE: AND THE STORY OF "ALFRED SIMPSON"

The garden is peaceful, and this is the more extraordinary because it is really the perpetual scene of the bloodiest warfare, and this warfare is the more acute in a London garden because in London there are more enemies. One has the fight of the gardener against natural conditions, his fight against the enemies of his plants, and the fight of the plants among themselves.

One season there was a prolonged drought and the leaves of the trees fell prematurely. "That's due to the drought," said the experts. The following year the season was very wet, and once more my trees shed their leaves before the time. "What else can you expect after all the rain we've had?" said the experts. And in both seasons the dairymen, who seem to have a touch of the expert about them, raised the price of milk. Perhaps one year I shall find the kind of season which exactly suits my London garden.

To fight the drought, I got me a great length of hose, and made the usual arrangements with the Water Board. But once the question of a garden is raised, the Water Board also seems to be infected with the military spirit. I had a printed document from them, which was severe to the point of truculence. They reserve themselves rights. They do not guarantee. They are not responsible. They strictly forbid. With these and similar phrases they teach the man who dares to use a hose what a poor worm he is. They tell me that the hose must not be left unattended. What am I to do with it then? Am I to sit up all night with it and hold its nozzle?

A wet season brings home to me the awful injustice of Water Boards. Nobody who can get rain for his garden will use the hard, less satisfactory, but highly valuable products of the Water Board. But in the wet season, as in the dry, the consumer must pay. In strict justice, the amount one pays for the water supply for the hose should in any season be in inverse proportion to the rainfall during that season.

When the drought was here, I watered my lawn profusely (and the Water Board need not rage and swell, for I never left the hose unattended for one moment). A little later I walked over the lawn to collect its gratitude, as it were, and I saw hosts of strange and horrid things. They were white, and yellow, and yellowish brown. They had come out of the crevices, and they had crawled. When I thought that for weeks past, this, my garden, had been providing them with sustenance, I was moved to fury. But I did not lose my head. There is a right way and a wrong way of doing everything. There is even a right way of killing slugs.

I have read in books that the gardener takes the slug and crushes it under his heel on the gravel path; a jobbing gardener might possibly do that—jobbing gardeners will do anything. Any man who does that is not fit to have a garden. He is only fit to collect house refuse in an open cart during hot weather.

My own method is simple and refined. I have a large jar filled with a strong solution of salt and water. I have, moreover, a large pair of surgical forceps serrated on the inner edge, price one shilling at the shop in the Strand. With the forceps I lift up the slug and I place him in the salt water; he dies incontinently and very neatly. My best time so far is a hundred and one in a quarter of an hour.

I have found out the thing which the green fly absolutely cannot stand, and I give the green fly plenty of that thing with the syringe. I destroy earwigs. I destroy caterpillars. I have not yet reached the fine Tennysonian sensibility of the gentleman "whose eyes were tender over drowning flies." I kill some things that other things may live. They cannot all have it their own way in my garden, and I must settle which side is to prevail. All the same, I do sometimes try to look at it from the slug's point of view. What does the slug think about it? Let us hope and believe that the slug does not think about it.

With what brutality, too, does the gardener fight against the prolific impulses of nature. The dead flowers must be picked off from the sweet peas; otherwise, they give up work early. If you cut down the lupine spikes as soon as the beans have formed, you will get more spikes. (I am told that this will not weaken the plant if it is well fed, but I never do it myself.) And what does it all mean, when one comes to think of it? These poor beautiful things live and struggle only for the perpetuation of their kind. When that is done, their warfare is accomplished. We make lovely gardens by thwarting and baffling this natural instinct.

Even among the plants that I tend there is civil war. My garden is surrounded by tall trees, so that at any hour of the day I can get shade. I would not have it otherwise. I would not lose one of the trees. But they are all unprincipled robbers. Their roots spread far underneath the ground. The fight goes on, and they steal the sustenance that one has given to the roses.

I knew a man who admired in his neighbour's garden the golden stars of the stone-crop. He put a little piece in an envelope and planted it in his own garden. A few years later he turned out of his garden three cartloads of stone-crop; that, I admit, was in the country. Australian bamboo is determined and rapacious. It is easy to get it into the garden. It is next to impossible to get it out. The smallest fragment of root seems to be enough, and up it comes again.

The perennial sunflower is terrifically aggressive. It has a disregard of limits and wants the world. If its masses of yellow flowers were not so exhilarating, I would turn it out of my garden altogether. One would like to be able to argue with these things. I should like to say to those sunflowers: "Try to take example by the bergamot. It has the same perennial advantages as yourself, and it is quite beautiful. In addition, the scent of its leaves pressed in the fingers reminds one of Egypt. You do not find the bergamot shoving itself forward wherever it has a chance. Contemplate it and learn modesty." But argument does not avail with the perennial sunflower. The knife and the spade are the things that it understands.

I fight the weeds of course, but I have vague ideas as to what a weed is. I am quite merciless towards the bindweed, it is a murderer and a garrotter; but with the materials at my disposal I could not make anything quite so beautiful as its flowers. I found two low-growing things in a flower-bed, which seemed to be of the clover kind. One had small crimson-brown leaves with a flush of green on them; the other had a much larger green leaf with a delicate design in grey on it. The jobbing gardener said they were weeds; he would have turned them out. I saved their lives, and the one with the reddish-brown leaf rewarded me with any number of little yellow flowers. Were I a sentimentalist, I should say that this showed its gratitude. Next year some more of the same clovery thing came up in the middle of a gravel path, where it was not wanted; was that gratitude?

When one comes into my garden at the close of a fine summer day, one does really seem to come into a peaceful place apart, where the fight for life no longer exists. But the fight for life exists everywhere, and one can never get away.

Don't go, let me tell you the story of—

Alfred Simpson

Alfred Simpson was a nice-looking young man who had independent means and other attractions. People liked him, but when they spoke of him it was with a smile. "He is so easily influenced," said some. "He is so frightfully obstinate," said others. "He has such funny ideas," said both.

Simpson could be easily influenced by anything he saw in print. From views which he had formed in this way he could not be driven by spoken words of mature and skilled experience. He had the very unusual habit of acting upon his convictions, and the unusual is frequently funny. So possibly in what they said about Alfred Simpson people had reason.

"I have definitely made up my mind," said Alfred Simpson one day. "I will take no part whatever in the struggle. To struggle is vulgar. It happens that I have just enough to live upon; but if I had not, I should decline to earn anything. One cannot earn without beginning the struggle. Just as I set no value on property, so do I set none on my own rights. I would never resist anything."

Nobody minded. In spite of previous experience, nobody expected that Alfred Simpson would be as good as his word.

Hector Brown was quite a different type of man. His friends said that Hector was a rough diamond. His enemies said more briefly that he was a rough. Hector Brown went to a dance, danced with Mary, took her into the conservatory, and then and there kissed her—*contra pacem* and to the scandal of the government.

Mary was very angry. She had promised to marry Alfred Simpson, and it was to him that she complained.

"Now, what you've got to do," said Alfred's friends, "is to punch Hector Brown's head."

"Why?" said Simpson.

"What will you ask next? For infringing your copyright, of course."

"That," said Simpson coldly, "would be quite contrary to the views which I have already expressed to you."

So, he did not punch Hector Brown's head, and Mary told Alfred

Simpson that he could go away and play by himself. Mary's decision was warmly applauded by her parents, who had heard without enthusiasm of the noble resolve on the part of their prospective son-in-law never to earn anything. Three months later Mary married Hector Brown.

Now Alfred Simpson was not a coward. He was not quite so big and heavy as Hector Brown, but he was quicker, harder, and in better training. He had been boxing while Hector had been boozing. The instructor was of opinion that Alfred could punch Hector when he liked, where he liked, and as often as he liked. Of this Alfred's friends were well aware, and it made them the more angry with him. They despaired. What could they say to a man who banged the door on the primeval instincts and declared that struggle, resistance, and retaliation were repugnant to him?

Alfred's subsequent refusal to secure a highly valuable post by the medium of a competitive examination alienated his family, as he had already alienated his friends. It is probable that his friends would have refused to have anything whatever to do with him, but for one fact—it was possible to borrow money from Alfred Simpson. They all did it, except one man, but differed in the amount and the frequency of their borrowings, according as their self-respect hindered or their necessities encouraged them. The one man who would not do it was the most confirmed borrower of them all. To the professional money-lender he was well known. "But," he said, "I cannot borrow from Alfred Simpson; it is altogether too easy—it is inartistic and gives me no satisfaction."

Without working Alfred Simpson could very well have lived on his income. But his income depended on capital, and his capital rapidly dwindled to nothing under the inroads made upon it. When his last hundred had been lent to a young gentleman who wished to test practically his solution of certain mathematical problems in the neighbourhood of Nice, Alfred Simpson went with empty pockets to those to whom he had lent money, and inquired if the repayment of the whole or part would be convenient. He returned from this inquiry with one pound six shillings, and the happy consciousness that he had not been vulgar. He had never insisted, he had never urged.

His next step was to sell the furniture of his well-appointed flat in order to pay the rent for it. After that he lived on a fairly extensive wardrobe and a few small articles of jewellery that he possessed. He retained only the gold watch and chain which had been presented to him by his mother on his twenty-first birthday.

There came a day when he had lunched lightly on his last six dollars—or, to speak with pedantic accuracy, on the meal which had been provided with the money which had been acquired by the sale of those six dollars. In spite of this banquet, by eight o'clock in the evening he felt hungry again, and our sentiments yield to our necessities. He therefore went out to dispose of his watch and chain. He went through Regent's Park and was stopped by a man whose appearance was against him. He looked in so many directions at once that anybody else would have mistrusted him.

"Could you tell us the time, Gov'nor?" said the man.

Alfred produced his watch. The man snatched it and the chain therewith, and ran. He did not run remarkably well. It would have been perfectly easy for Alfred Simpson to have overtaken him and to have given him into custody. But such an act would have been inconsistent with the rest of his career. So, he gave up the idea of dinner and sat on the embankment.

On the following day he remained in the parks until closing time and then sat on the embankment again.

And the next night he dreamed that he died on the embankment.

And after death Alfred Simpson opened his eyes and saw that he was in a large and very plainly furnished room. He sat on a hard bench, not unlike that which had been his bed on the embankment, and many others, mostly of villainous appearance, sat there also.

"I say," said Alfred Simpson to the grey-haired reprobate next to him. "This isn't Heaven, is it?"

The reprobate chuckled. "Not exactly," he said.

"Then what is it?"

"It's the waiting-room for lost souls before they take their trial."

"But I'm not a lost soul," said Alfred Simpson indignantly. "I ought not to be here. I must have taken the wrong turning. I have never done anything very wrong in my life, and I have done heaps of good. I gave up the only girl I ever loved."

"I know," said the old man; "and in consequence she married a man she did not love out of pique. He's a brute, he ill-treats her, and she will die. You murdered her."

"This is terrible," said Alfred Simpson. "I had no idea of it. But I have done lots of other good things. I refused to go in for a competitive examination and take up a valuable post, in order that some other man might enjoy it."

"I know," said the old man again. "The other man got it; he had not your mental equipment and he was not equal to it. He bungled badly and disgraced himself. That's him over there, the man with the bullet-hole in his temples. It was his hand that held the revolver, but it was you who shot him, Alfred Simpson."

"This is most distressing," said Alfred. "If I could have foreseen this kind of thing, I should certainly have revised my ideas. I should have drawn out another scheme for my life altogether. But as it is, I must have done some good. I lent large sums of money without interest."

"I know," said the old man once more. "And by so doing you have turned various people who might have had self-respect and industry into worthless wastrels. The souls of some of them are waiting now to give evidence against you."

"It is very sad," said Alfred, "that things do not turn out as one intends. One of my last acts on earth was to allow a man to steal my watch and chain. I suppose it is useless to plead that this was a good action."

"Quite. How can you suppose it to be a good action to put such a premium on dishonesty?"

Then the door of the waiting-room opened and there stood there a most gigantic policeman.

"Alfred Simpson," he called, in a fruity and resonant voice.

"Here I am," said Alfred meekly. "Could you tell me what I am charged with?"

"You know perfectly well," said the policeman. "You are charged with starting the millennium before it was ready."

The shock awoke him. He rose and walked to his father's house. His dire necessities and abject condition broke down the alienation which had existed between him and his family, and he was welcomed as the returned prodigal. On the following morning, decently attired, with a bundle of IOUs in his pocket, he started across Regent's Park to call upon his solicitor. On his way he met a shabby man who looked in all directions at once. The shabby man saw him and ran. Alfred ran also. He caught the shabby man in an unfrequented part of the park, took from him fourpence in bronze, which was all that he possessed, and administered to him an extremely thorough hiding.

He handed the bundle of IOUs to his solicitor. Those who could pay in full were to pay in full. Those who could pay in part were to pay in part. Those who could not pay were to be left alone. Nobody was to be ruined, but Alfred Simpson was to have some of his money back.

And later, some two years later, he married the widow of Hector Brown. He is on his way to take up an important post in India, and she accompanies him. They say that she looks quite young and pretty again. She is certainly quite happy with her husband, though there are some who think him a little too selfish and dictatorial.

Night in the Garden: And the Story of "The Ghostly Music"

There are many things that may bring a man, normally sociable, into that state of mind when it is not desirable that he shall dine out. Too many wrong numbers on the telephone, too many visitors, too much talk—anything in fact that jangles the nerves may be the cause. In my case the cause was unimportant and uninteresting, but I was undoubtedly in that state of mind. I had to dine out, and I had not the feeling of gratitude which would have better become me. The idea of dining out filled me with rage and despair—disproportionate, ludicrous, but quite real. I recalled the words of a woman who had been through many seasons. "I want," she said to me earnestly, "to be asked to everything and to go to nothing."

And then the blessed sentence of reprieve came over the telephone. Never before had I known what a lovely word chicken-pox is. Postponed is another beautiful word; the long "o" sounds are like the coo of a dove. My more important nerves that had been revolving rapidly like large hot corkscrews began to shrink, to slow, and to cool.

Later, when it was dark, I went out into the garden. Lighted windows patterned themselves on the lawn, and half-way across it a warm wave of perfume met me from the white stars of the tobacco plants. The scents of flowers please me. Lavender and rosemary, lemon verbena and musk, rose and carnation—I have them all. But for scents in bottles or sachets, the chemist's products, I have only hatred and contempt. The bottled perfume is like mechanical music; the freshness and life have departed from it.

Even in the daytime but little sound of traffic reaches my garden, and at night there are such long stretches of precious silence that one seems to be far from London. As one grows older one values silence more—maybe a gentle providence, that in the end the great silence may not be unwelcome. The years change in so many things our sense of value. Property loses much of its attraction when one begins to think for how short a time one may hold it. This is consolatory if one be poor. I cannot own this scrap of London garden, but what matter? I may use it as if it were my own in return for—well, for so many stories a year. The transaction seems more estimable when the medium of exchange is not mentioned.

I sat and smoked, and drank the silence "like some sharp, strengthening wine". The great trees before me, motionless in the still air, were a flat dark grey against a sky a little paler. Below, where in the sunlight would be a riot of colour, were masses of velvety black out of which only the white flowers spoke. The tall white hollyhock would be a patient sentinel all night while its dark sister slept invisible. There is peace in the gardens of the country—gardens far richer and more beautiful than mine—but here the peace seemed deeper because of the near contrast.

Not far away the useful deadly motor-bus would be busy for hours yet. Theatres would be full, and Fleet Street would be strenuous, and (in houses which the chicken-pox had not yet reached) people would be dining out. Perhaps, without being too artistic and diseased, one who has sometimes liked crowds may sometimes like to escape them. Dusk and sweet scents, silence and solitude—the London garden has pleasant gifts for folks who are temporarily tired of things.

Across the lighted squares or mirrored windows on the lawn, slow yet alert, crept a cat with a heart full of sinful purposes. It flickered over the wall, poised clear against the sky for one moment, on its way to blood and passion in some valerian-scented hell. The nocturnal cat is supposed to be comic, but (in spite of many opportunities) I have never managed to see the joke. There is something terrific in those lower animals—there are several of them—that in certain moments produces the sound of the human voice. Strange too is that electric repugnance that a cat may set up.

Unseen and unheard, her presence is yet felt and loathed. She is a creature of the night, mysterious and satanic. Watch her as she starts for the black sabbath—a voluptuous sprawl with claws extended, steps of tense and measured stealth, and then a mad scurry. Presently, you shall hear her cry like a woman, even as the wounded hare sobs out her sisterhood. Tonight it was as though for a few moments a taint of monstrousness had passed through the peace of the garden.

Through an open window not far away came the sound of music— somebody was playing the piano. Music heard from another house is supposed to be a torture, and so (like the cat) has its place among the accepted jokes. But, because tonight I was to have the luck—who invented chicken-pox?—it was not distressing and funny. It was fine music played by an artist on a good instrument. It had the quality of the night, wistful and desiderious. Long ago and in a far country there was a king who suffered from a restless melancholy, or a bad temper, or something of that kind, and somebody made music for him. "So, Saul was refreshed, and was well, and the evil spirit departed from him." Surely, that nocturne was meant to be heard as I heard it—in a garden at night. Alas, these concerts, with their awful too-muchness, and professional smirks, and roars of ugly applause! I do not like to have music thus administered. But for the music that visited my garden that night I had the most grateful welcome.

When the chance things are charming, they far surpass the calculated, and love itself may be no more than a delightful accident. It was just by chance that somebody in a lighted room, without a thought of audience, went to the piano and remembered that music. Chance makes things grow on old stone walls; and in the rich man's rock-garden, wealth, skill, and calculation try to imitate the charm. The music ceased, and my gratitude must remain unspoken—unless, by a chance that were wellnigh miraculous, this page may carry it. But artists—be they makers of music or pictures, poems or stories—must not think too much of gratitude; for they will not always get it, and they will not always deserve it. That king of old once flung a javelin at the musician who played before him. Some lazy souls can never do their uttermost unless they are thrashed up to it. A moderate amount of javelin—avoiding vital parts—is not always bad for the artist.

My garden, they tell me, was once the garden of an old priory. Under one corner of the lawn is the well that provided the religious with water. It has been covered in with stone, and just over the stone the grass refuses to grow. It is like a tonsure. But though I have been in my garden I think at every hour of the night and of the early morning, I have met no shadowy figures counting their beads or reading their little illuminated books. These good people sleep long and quietly.

Let me tell you the story of—

The Ghostly Music

There was once a master of music, who, from the charity of his heart and from his love of excellence, took as his pupil without reward a young boy that was greatly gifted. And in time it came to pass that the pupil reached his zenith and the powers of the master had begun to decline, so that it was said by some that the pupil now surpassed the master. And the hints of this that came to the master's ears were to him bitter as wormwood.

Now it happened one day that, as the pupil walked in a wood, music came to him; and he hastened back to his house in order that he might sit down at the piano and play it. For although, being a musician, he knew quite well how the music would sound, he yet wished to hear it. And as he was on his way, though it was a calm day, the great limb of a treacherous elm fell upon him and crushed him so that he died. And in his music-room his piano waited in vain.

Upon his death all bitterness passed away from the heart of his master. Rivalry died with the rival. There came back to him old recollections of the boy and of the esteem and affection in which he had then held him. There was now no one who spoke of the dead musician with more generous praise than his master. In his own music-room the master placed the piano on which his pupil had been used to play. It had been specially bequeathed to him. It was the dead man's gift.

But now the old man became himself conscious that he was not as he had been. The fountains were dried up. Melody had ceased to come. He was arid and unproductive. His fear that his power was leaving him tended the more to diminish it. There were many long days and nights when he could do nothing; and at such seasons he would not enter his music-room upstairs, but sat in the room below it, trying sometimes to divert his mind by reading, and at other times cursing the wretchedness into which the course of nature had brought him.

After a long while it happened that one night when he sat late alone, his wretchedness seemed to him more than he could bear. In a few weeks he was to play before the king and there would be many great musicians in the audience. On such occasions it had always been his custom to produce some new work. Now he had nothing to give them. He would have to fall back on the compositions of his younger days. He could picture in his mind the meaning looks which the musicians would interchange. He could hear their polite applause, and it was like a torture. The king, himself no mean musician, might ask some question. He could not go into that company and thus fail. It was not possible. It could not be asked of him thus to debase himself. And there seemed to him but one alternative—a little more than usual of that laudanum in which he had lately sought inspiration.

But as he raised the glass to his lips, he heard something so unexpected that the glass crashed to the floor. In the music-room overhead someone was playing the piano. Who could it be? No servant of his had that skill, and besides, hours before his servants had gone to sleep.

It was divine music, entrancing, uplifting.

For a moment he hesitated, and then the desire to know overcame his fears. He went up the stairs, and in the passage outside the music-room he noted that a light showed under the door. Someone had switched the light on then. Was it the carelessness of a servant? "Quite possibly," he said to himself. "Quite possibly."

He opened the door and entered, and his eyes flew to the piano. No one was seated there, but the notes moved and the touch was human. He shrank back from the piano and stood in the farthest corner of the room, listening intently. When at last the music ceased, he had a great desire to say something, and yet could choose no words. And, as he hesitated, there was a sudden click and the lights were switched off. He fled from the darkness down the stairs to the brightly lit room below. For a while he was too overcome to be able to do anything; and then, for he had a musician's memory, he took paper and wrote down the music that he had heard.

A few days later it chanced that a great lady asked him what new music he would play before the king.

"I have decided," said the master, "to play a composition of mine that—if one must give these things names—I shall call 'The Sylvan Sonata'."

"Sylvan? How delightful. It represents scenes in the wood then."

The master shook his head. "Music represents nothing," he said. "Music is music. It is not an imitation of a sylvan scene, or church bells heard in the distance, or any other rubbish. I call this music 'The Sylvan Sonata' merely because it has in it different phases of woodland feeling. You understand me? It is the kind of music that might occur to the mind of a musician when he was walking through a wood."

"But how that reminds one," said the great lady. "It was in the wood that your favourite pupil died."

"I prefer," said the master sternly, "not to speak of that."

He preferred also not to think of it. The piano which had been bequeathed to him was kept closed and locked now, and it was on another instrument in another room that he prepared himself for the great occasion. He was a fine executant, as not every composer is. He tried to cheat himself. He said again and again to himself that what he had seen and heard in the music-room that night was illusion. The notes had not really moved. His brain had been over-wrought with worry and anxiety. The music was really his own. But the attempt to cheat himself was idle, for he knew too much of the characteristics of a promising young composer who was now dead. No one else but him could have written that.

The evening came and the occasion found him equal to it. His playing of "The Sylvan Sonata" was as near perfection as a man may attain. When he had finished there were a few seconds of silence before the audience could get back to the world again and begin their applause. And when that had died away, many came up to congratulate him, and a critic of music spoke.

"I am ashamed of myself," said the critic. "I confess that I had thought, in company with many others, that you declined in power, *maestro*. You have given us tonight something more superb than we have ever heard from you before. You are at your very highest at this minute."

The master did not seem to hear, did not seem to see the hands which were stretched out to him. He sat looking intently before him, as at some presence not visible to the others. And when he was summoned to speak to the king, he rose stiffly and moved mechanically, looking now and again over his shoulder, as at someone who followed him.

And when the king had finished his compliments, he drew a deep breath, as of one who makes an effort. He swung round and pointed with a wave of his hand.

"Alas, sir," he said, "I am not he who made 'The Sylvan Sonata'. But the composer is here. See him. He stands behind me. The face was somewhat crushed by the fall of the tree, but it is made well again. It is as it always was. It is his music, not mine, that I have played to you."

He stepped backward from the royal presence. The shiver of sensation went through the great assembly. This was clearly aberration. Someone should see to the old man. The trial had been too great for him, and his reason had been overcome. A doctor should be summoned.

But before anything could be done, the old man had slipped out of the assembly and left the palace and gone back to his own house. Once more he poured the laudanum, and this time his hand did not fail him. When he had drunk, he went up to the music-room again and unlocked the piano that had once been his pupil's. He opened it and began to play.

It was there they found him in the morning.

It was late at night and I had gone out to see the September moon. It was one of those nights which people like to say are as light as day.

It was not in the least as light as day. It was light grey and silver. It was even black in places. I heard a faint crackle and could smell the acrid smoke which mounted thin and straight in the still air from the fire which had been made in the morning. There burned things which had done their work and had been beautiful, but were now over.

The fire had been lit that morning and the lawn had been swept that morning; but there was a rustle of fallen leaves about my feet. The air was shrewd and chill. Next morning, I should still see flowers in my garden, but none the less the sentence had been pronounced. Summer was dead.

I suppose it is a question of temperament. Youth can enjoy the moment. Age must look forward. There is plenty of work to do in this garden in the autumn, and not a little in the winter. And all the time one is looking forward to the spring—to the coming of the new leaves and the fresh green.

But then, throughout the summer, one is haunted with fear and hatred of the coming winter. Even as one plants or sows, one seems to see the September weed fire.

It is better not to be wearisome, sentimental, and self-pitying on the subject, for one might get into that state of mind when, through-out the winter, one would no longer dare to look forward to the summer, because one would know the summer would be haunted with the hatred of the next winter. From which refinement and desolation may I be delivered.

Rose Rose

Sefton stepped back from his picture. "Rest now, please," he said.

Miss Rose Rose, his model, threw the striped blanket around her, stepped down from the throne, and crossed the studio. She seated herself on the floor near the big stove. For a few moments Sefton stood motionless, looking critically at his work. Then he laid down his palette and brushes and began to roll a cigarette. He was a man of forty, thick-set, round-faced, with a reddish moustache turned fiercely upwards. He flung himself down in an easy-chair, and smoked in silence till silence seemed ungracious.

"Well," he said, "I've got the place hot enough for you today, Miss Rose."

"You 'ave indeed," said Miss Rose.

"I bet it's nearer eighty than seventy."

The cigarette-smoke made a blue haze in the hot, heavy air. He watched it undulating, curving, melting.

As he watched it Miss Rose continued her observations. The trouble with these studios was the draughts. With a strong east wind, same as yesterday, you might have the stove red-hot, and yet never get the place, so to speak, warm. It is possible to talk commonly without talking like a coster, and Miss Rose achieved it. She did not always neglect the aspirate. She never quite substituted the third vowel for the first. She rather enjoyed long words.

She was beautiful from the crown of her head to the sole of her foot; and few models have good feet. Every pose she took was graceful. She was the daughter of a model, and had been herself a model from childhood. In consequence, she knew her work well and did it well. On one occasion, when sitting for the great Merion, she had kept the same pose, without a rest, for three consecutive hours.

She was proud of that. Naturally she stood in the first rank among models, was most in demand, and made the most money. Her fault was that she was slightly capricious; you could not absolutely depend upon her. On a wintry morning, when every hour of daylight was precious, she might keep her appointment, she might be an hour or two late, or she might stay away altogether. Merion himself had suffered from her, had sworn never to employ her again, and had gone back to her.

Sefton, as he watched the blue smoke, found that her common accent jarred on him. It even seemed to make it more difficult for him to get the right presentation of the "Aphrodite" that she was helping him to paint. One seemed to demand a poetical and cultured soul in so beautiful a body. Rose Rose was not poetical nor cultured; she was not even businesslike and educated.

Half an hour of silent and strenuous work followed. Then Sefton growled that he could not see any longer.

"We'll stop for today," he said. Miss Rose Rose retired behind the screen. Sefton opened a window and both ventilators, and rolled another cigarette. The studio became rapidly cooler.

"Tomorrow, at nine?" he called out.

"I've got some way to come," came the voice of Miss Rose from behind the screen. "I could be here by a quarter past."

"Right," said Sefton, as he slipped on his coat.

When Rose Rose emerged from the screen, she was dressed in a blue serge costume, with a picture-hat. As it was her business in life to be beautiful, she never wore corsets, high heels, nor pointed toes. Such abnegation is rare among models.

"I say, Mr. Sefton," said Rose, "you were to settle at the end of the sittings, but——"

"Oh, you don't want any money, Miss Rose. You're known to be rich."

"Well, what I've got is in the Post Office, and I don't want to touch it. And I've got some shopping I must do before I go home."

Sefton pulled out his sovereign-case hesitatingly.

"This is all very well, you know," he said.

"I know what you are thinking, Mr. Sefton. You think I don't mean to come tomorrow. That's all Mr. Merion, now, isn't it? He's always saying things about me. I'm not going to stick it. I'm going to 'ave it out with 'im."

"He recommended you to me. And I'll tell you what he said, if you won't repeat it. He said that I should be lucky if I got you, and that I'd better chain you to the studio."

"And all because I was once late—with a good reason for it, too.

Besides, what's once? I suppose he didn't 'appen to tell you how often he's kept me waiting."

"Well, here you are, Miss Rose. But you'll really be here in time tomorrow, won't you? Otherwise, the thing will have got too tacky to work into."

"You needn't worry about that," said Miss Rose, eagerly. "I'll be here, whatever happens, by a quarter past nine. I'll be here if I die first! There, is that good enough for you? Good afternoon, and thank you, Mr. Sefton."

"Good afternoon, Miss Rose. Let me manage that door for you—the key goes a bit stiffly."

Sefton came back to his picture. In spite of Miss Rose's vehement assurances, he felt by no means sure of her, but it was difficult for him to refuse any woman anything, and impossible for him to refuse to pay her what he really owed. He scrawled in charcoal some directions to the charwoman who would come in the morning. She was, from his point of view, a prize charwoman—one who could, and did, wash brushes properly, one who understood the stove, and would, when required, refrain from sweeping.

He picked up his hat and went out. He walked the short distance from his studio to his bachelor flat, looked over an evening paper as he drank his tea, and then changed his clothes and took a cab to the club for dinner. He played one game of billiards after dinner, and then went home. His picture was very much in his mind. He wanted to be up fairly early in the morning, and he went to bed early. He was at his studio by half-past eight. The stove was lighted, and he piled more coke on it.

His "Aphrodite" seemed to have a somewhat mocking expression. It was a little, technical thing, to be corrected easily. He set his palette and selected his brushes. An attempt to roll a cigarette revealed the fact that his pouch was empty. It still wanted a few minutes to nine. He would have time to go up to the tobacconist at the corner. In case Rose Rose arrived while he was away, he left the studio door open. The tobacconist was also a news-agent, and he bought a morning paper. Rose would probably be twenty minutes late at the least, and this would be something to occupy him.

But on his return, he found his model already stepping onto the throne.

"Good-morning, Miss Rose. You're a lady of your word." He hardly heeded the murmur which came to him as a reply. He threw

71

his cigarette into the stove, picked up his palette, and got on excellently. The work was absorbing. For some time, he thought of nothing else. There was no relaxing on the part of the model—no sign of fatigue. He had been working for over an hour, when his conscience smote him. "We'll have a rest now, Miss Rose," he said cheerily. At the same moment he felt human fingers drawn lightly across the back of his neck, just above the collar. He turned round with a sudden start. There was nobody there. He turned back again to the throne. Rose Rose had vanished.

With the utmost care and deliberation, he put down his palette and brushes. He said in a loud voice, "Where are you, Miss Rose?" For a moment or two silence hung in the hot air of the studio. He repeated his question and got no answer. Then he stepped behind the screen, and suddenly the most terrible thing in his life happened to him. He knew that his model had never been there at all.

There was only one door out to the back street in which his studio was placed, and that door was now locked. He unlocked it, put on his hat, and went out. For a minute or two he paced the street, but he had got to go back to the studio.

He went back, sat down in the easy-chair, lit a cigarette, and tried for a plausible explanation. Undoubtedly, he had been working very hard lately. When he had come back from the tobacconist's to the studio he had been in the state of expectant attention, and he was enough of a psychologist to know that in that state you are especially likely to see what you expect to see. He was not conscious of anything abnormal in himself. He did not feel ill, or even nervous. Nothing of the kind had ever happened to him before. The more he considered the matter, the more definite became his state. He was thoroughly frightened. With a great effort he pulled himself together and picked up the newspaper.

It was certain that he could do no more work for that day, anyhow. An ordinary, commonplace newspaper would restore him. Yes, that was it. He had been too much wrapped up in the picture. He had simply supposed the model to be there.

He was quite unconvinced, of course, and merely trying to convince himself. As an artist, he knew that for the last hour or more he had been getting the most delicate modelling right from the living form before him. But he did his best, and read the newspaper assiduously. He read of tariff, protection, and of a new music-hall star. Then his eye fell on a paragraph headed "Motor Fatalities."

He read that Miss Rose, an artist's model, had been knocked down by a car in the Fulham Road about seven o'clock on the previous evening; that the owner of the car had stopped and taken her to the hospital, and that she had expired within a few minutes of admission.

He rose from his place and opened a large pocketknife. There was a strong impulse upon him, and he felt it to be a mad impulse, to slash the canvas to rags. He stopped before the picture. The face smiled at him with a sweetness that was scarcely earthly.

He went back to his chair again. "I'm not used to this kind of thing," he said aloud. A board creaked at the far end of the studio. He jumped up with a start of horror. A few minutes later he had left the studio, and locked the door behind him. His common-sense was still with him. He ought to go to a specialist. But the picture—

★★★★★★★★★★★★

"What's the matter with Sefton?" said Devigne one night at the club after dinner.

"Don't know that anything's the matter with him," said Merion. "He hasn't been here lately."

"I saw him the last time he was here, and he seemed pretty queer. Wanted to let me his studio."

"It's not a bad studio," said Merion, dispassionately.

"He's got rid of it now, anyhow. He's got a studio out at Richmond, and the deuce of a lot of time he must waste getting there and back. Besides, what does he do about models?"

"That's a point I've been wondering about myself," said Merion. "He'd got Rose Rose for his 'Aphrodite,' and it looked as if it might be a pretty good thing when I saw it. But, as you know, she died. She was troublesome in some ways, but, taking her all round, I don't know where to find anybody as good today. What's Sefton doing about it?"

"He hasn't got a model at all at present. I know that for a fact, because I asked him."

"Well," said Merion, "he may have got the thing on further than I thought he would in the time. Some chaps can work from memory all right, though I can't do it myself. He's not chucked the picture, I suppose?"

"No; he's not done that. In fact, the picture's his excuse now, if you want him to go anywhere and do anything. But that's not it: But that's not it: the chap's altogether changed. He used to be a genial sort of bounder—bit tyrannical in his manner, perhaps—thought he knew everything. Still, you could talk to him. He was sociable. As a matter of fact, he did know a good deal. Now it's quite different. If you ever do see him—and that's not often—he's got nothing to say to you. He's just going back to his work. That sort of thing."

"You're too imaginative," said Merion. "I never knew a man who varied less than Sefton. Give me his address, will you? I mean his studio. I'll go and look him up one morning. I should like to see how that 'Aphrodite's' getting on. I tell you it was promising; no nonsense about it."

★★★★★★★★★★★★

One sunny morning Merion knocked at the door of the studio at Richmond. He heard the sound of footsteps crossing the studio, then Sefton's voice rang out.

"Who's there?"

"Merion. I've travelled miles to see the thing you call a picture."

"I've got a model."

"And what does that matter?" asked Merion.

"Well, I'd be awfully glad if you'd come back in **an hour.** We'd have lunch together somewhere."

"Right," said Merion, sardonically. "I'll come back in about seven million hours. Wait for me."

He went back to London and his own studio in a state of fury. Sefton had never been a man to pose. He had never put on side about his work. He was always willing to show it to old and intimate friends whose judgment he could trust; and now, when the oldest of his friends had travelled down to Richmond to see him, he was told to come back in an hour, and that they might then lunch together!

"This lets me out," said Merion, savagely.

★★★★★★★★★★★★

But he always speaks well of Sefton nowadays. He maintains that Sefton's "Aphrodite" would have been a success anyhow. The suicide made a good deal of talk at the time, and a special attendant was necessary to regulate the crowds round it, when, as directed by his will, the picture was exhibited at the Royal Academy. He was found in his studio many hours after his death; and he had scrawled on a blank canvas, much as he left his directions to his charwoman: "I have finished it, but I can't stand anymore."

Smeath

1

Percy Bellowes was not actually idle, had a good deal of ability, and wished to make money. But at the age of thirty-five he had not made it. He had been articled to a solicitor, and, in his own phrase, had turned it down. He had neglected the regular channels of education which were open to him. He could give a conjuring entertainment for an hour, and though his tricks were stock tricks, they were done in the neat professional manner.

He could play the cornet and the violin, neither of them very well. He could dance a breakdown. He had made himself useful in a touring theatrical company. But he could not spell correctly, and his grammar was not always beyond reproach. He disliked regularity. He could not go to the same office at the same time every morning. He was thriftless, and he had been, but was no longer, intemperate. He was a big man, with smooth black hair, and a heavy moustache, and he had the manners of a bully.

At the age of thirty-five he considered his position. He was at that time travelling the country as a hypnotic entertainer, under the name of Dr. Sanders-Bell. At each of his entertainments he issued a Ten Thousand Pound Challenge, not having at the time ten thousand pence in the world.

He employed confederates, and he had to pay them. It was not a good business at all. His gains in one town were always being swallowed up by his losses in another. His confederates gave him constant trouble.

But though he turned things over for long in his mind, he could see nothing else to take up. There is no money nowadays for a conjurer without originality, an indifferent musician, or passable actor. His hypnotic entertainment would have been no good in London, but it did earn just enough to keep him going in the provinces.

Also, Percy Bellowes had an ordinary human weakness; he liked to be regarded with awe as a man of mystery. Even off the stage he acted his part. He had talked delirious science to agitated landladies in cheap lodgings in many towns.

Teston was a small place, and Percy Bellowes thought that he had done very well, after a one-night show, to cover his expenses and put four pounds in his pocket. He remained in the town on the following day, because he wished to see a man who had answered his advertisement for a confederate. "Assistant to a Hypnotic Entertainer" was the phrase Mr. Bellowes had used for it.

He was stopping at the Victoria Hotel. It was the only hotel in the place, and it was quite bad. But Percy Bellowes was used to that. A long course of touring had habituated him to doubtful eggs and indistinguishable coffee. This morning he faced a singularly repulsive breakfast without quailing. He was even cheerful and conversational with a slatternly maid who waited on him.

"So, you saw the show last night," he said.

"Yes, sir, I did. And very wonderful it was. There has never been anything like it in Teston, not in my memory."

"Ah, my dear. Well, you watch this."

He picked up the two boiled eggs which had been placed before him. He hurled one into the air, where it vanished. He swallowed the other one whole. He then produced them both from a vase on the mantelpiece.

"Well, I never!" said the maid. "I wonder if there's anything you can't do, sir?"

"Just one or two things," said Mr. Bellowes, sardonically. "By the way, my dear, if a man comes here this morning and asks for me, I want to see him." He consulted a soiled letter which he had taken from his pocket. "The name's Smeath."

Mr. Smeath arrived, in fact, before Bellowes had finished his breakfast, and was told he could come in. He was a man of extraordinary appearance.

He was a dwarf, with a slightly hunched back. His hands were a size too large for him, and were always restless. His expression was one of snarling subservience. At first Bellowes was inclined to reject him, for a confederate should not be a man of unusual appearance, and easily recognisable. Then it struck him that, after all, this would be a very weird and impressive figure on the stage.

"Ever do anything of this kind before?" he asked.

"No, sir," said Smeath. "But I've seen it done and can pick it up. I

76

think I could give you satisfaction. You see, it's not very easy for a man like me to find work."

All the time that he was speaking, his hands were busy.

"When you've finished tearing up my newspaper," said Bellowes.

"Sorry, sir," said the man. He pushed the newspaper away from him, but caught up a corner of the tablecloth. It was frayed, and he began to pull threads out of it, quickly and eagerly.

"Ever been hypnotised?" Bellowes asked.

"No, sir," said Smeath, with a cunning smile. "But that doesn't matter, does it? I can act the part all right."

"It matters a devilish lot, as it happens. And you can't act the part all right, either. My assistants are always genuinely hypnotised. I employ them to save time on the stage. After I have hypnotised you a few times, I shall be able to put you into the hypnotic state in a minute or less, and to do it with certainty. I can't depend on chance people from the audience. Many of them cannot be hypnotised at all, and with most of the others it takes far too long. There are exceptional cases—I had one at my show only last night—but I don't often come across them. Come on up with me to my room."

"You want to see if you can hypnotise me?"

"No, I don't. I know I can. I simply want to do it."

Upstairs in the dingy bedroom Bellowes made Smeath sit down. He held the bright lid of a cigarette-tin between Smeath's eyes and slightly above the level of them.

"Look at that," he said. "Keep on looking at it. Keep on!"

In a few minutes Bellowes put the tin down, put his fingers on Smeath's eyes, and closed them. The eyes remained closed. The little hunchback sat tense and rigid.

An hour later, in the coffee-room downstairs, Bellowes made his definite agreement with Smeath.

"You understand?" said Bellowes. "You'll be at the town-hall at Warlow tomorrow night at seven. When I invite people to come up on the platform, you will come up. That's all you've got to do. Got any money?"

"Enough for the present." Smeath began to pull matches from a box on the table. He broke each match into four pieces. "But suppose that tomorrow night you can't do it?"

"There'll never be a day or night I can't do it with you now. That's definite. Now, then, leave those matches alone. I might be wanting one of them directly."

After Smeath's departure, Percy Bellowes sat for a few minutes deep in thought. In that dingy room upstairs, he had seen something which he had never seen in his life before, something of which he thought that various uses might be made. He picked up the newspaper, and was pleased to find that Smeath's busy fingers had spared the racing intelligence. Then he sought out the landlord.

"I say," he said, "I've got a fancy to put a few shillings on a horse. Do you know anybody here it would be safe to do it with?"

"Well," said the landlord, "as a matter of fact you can do it with me, if you like. I do a little in that way on the quiet."

"The police don't bother you?"

"No; they're not a very bright lot, the police here. Besides, they're pretty busy just now. We had a murder in Teston the day before you came."

"Who was that?"

"A Miss Samuel, daughter of some very well-to-do people here. They think it was a tramp. See that plantation up on the hill there? That was where they found her—her head all beaten to pulp and her money gone."

"Nice set of blackguards you've got in Teston, I don't think. Well now, about this race today."

When Percy Bellowes left the Victoria Hotel on the following morning, he was not required to pay a bill. On the contrary, he had a small balance to receive from the landlord.

"Bless you, I don't mind," said the landlord, as he paid him. "Pretty well all my crowd were on the favourite. Queer thing that horse should have fallen."

2.

At Warlow the entertainment went very well. When it was over, Bellowes asked Smeath to come round to the hotel. They had the little smoking-room to themselves.

"You remember when I hypnotised you yesterday?"

"Yes, sir. Yes, Mr. Bellowes."

"Do you remember what you did, or said?"

Smeath shook his head.

"I went to sleep, the same as I did tonight. That was all."

"Know anything about horse racing?"

"Nothing. Never touched it."

"You mean to say you've never seen a horse race?"

78

"Never."

"What did you do before you came to me?"

"I had not been in any employment for some time. I was once in business as a bird-fancier. I had bad luck and made no money in it. You ask me a great many questions, sir."

"I do. That's because I've been turning things over in my mind. I want you to put your name to an agreement with me for three years. A pound a week. That's a good offer. A man who's been in business, and failed, ought to appreciate an absolute certainty like that."

"It would be the same kind of work?" Smeath asked.

"Pretty much the same. When I've finished this tour, I am thinking of settling down in London. I should employ you there."

"No, thank you, Mr. Bellowes," said Smeath. "I would rather not."

"Oh, all right," said Bellowes. "Make an idiot of yourself, if you like. It doesn't make a pin's-head of difference to me. I can easily find plenty of other men who would grab at it. I thought I was doing you a kindness. As you said yourself, chaps of your build don't find it any too easy to get work."

"I will work for you for six months—possibly a month or two longer than that. But, afterwards, well, I wish to return to the bird-fancying again."

"No, you don't," said Bellowes, savagely. "If you can't take my terms, you're not going to make your own. If you won't sign for three years, out you get! You're talking like a fool, too. How can you go back to this rotten business in six months? D'you think you're going to save the capital for it out of a pound a week?"

"I have friends who might help me."

"Who are they?"

"They are—well, they're friends of mine. You will perhaps give me till tomorrow morning to think it over."

"Very well. If you're not here by ten tomorrow morning to go round to the solicitor's office with me, I've finished with you. Now then, I'm going to hypnotise you again."

"What for?"

"Practice. Now then, look at me."

In a few moments Smeath sat with his eyes open, but fixed.

"Tell me what you see?" asked Bellowes.

"Nothing," said Smeath. "I see nothing."

"Yes, you do," said Bellowes. "There are horses with jockeys on them. They are racing. See? They get near the winning-post."

"Yes," said Smeath, dully. "I see them, but it is through a mist and a long way off. Now they're gone."

"Yesterday when I hypnotised you, you saw clearly. You actually described a race which afterwards took place. You gave me the colours. You gave me the names that the crowd shouted. You described how the favourite crossed his legs and fell. Can you do nothing of the kind today?"

"No, not today. Today I see other things."

"What?"

"I see a street in London. There is a long row of sandwich-men. My name is on their boards. There are many fashionable people in the street. Expensive shops. Jewellers' shops, picture-galleries. I can see you, too. You have just come into the street."

"Where have I come from?"

"How can I tell? It may be your own house or offices. Your name is on a very small brass plate by the side of the door. You have got a fur coat on, and you are wearing a diamond pin. You get into a car. It is your own car, and you tell the man who opens the door for you to drive to the bank. You look very pleased and prosperous. Now the car starts. That is all. I can see no more."

Bellowes leaned forward and blew lightly on Smeath's eyes. The tenseness of his muscles relaxed. He rubbed his eyes and stood up.

"Do you know what you've been saying?" Bellowes asked.

"I've been saying nothing," said Smeath. "I have been asleep, as you know. You made me go to sleep."

Bellowes looked round the room. His eye fell on an empty cigarette-box, lying in the fender.

"Pick that up, and hold it in your hands," he said.

Smeath looked surprised, but he did as he was told. There was a loose label on the box, and his fingers began to tear it off in small pieces.

"Now then," said Bellowes, "can you tell me anything about the man who had that box, and threw it down there?"

"Of course, I can't. How should I be able to do that? It's not possible."

"Very well," said Bellowes. "I'm going to put you to sleep once more."

"I don't like this," whined Smeath. "There's too much of it. It's bad for one's health." "Nonsense! Look here, Smeath. I want you for three years, don't I? Then I'm not likely to do anything that will injure your

80

health. You'll be all right."

When Bellowes had hypnotised Smeath, he again put the cigarette-box in his hands.

"And now what do you see?" he asked.

"This is quite clear. It is a short, thick-set man who takes the last cigarette out of the box and throws it down. As he smokes it, he walks up and down the room, frowning. He is puzzled about something. He takes out his pocket-book, and as he opens it a card drops to the floor."

"Can you see what's on the card?" "Yes. It lies face upwards. The name is 'Mr. Vincent.' And in the left-hand corner are the words 'Criminal Investigation Department, Scotland Yard.' Now he closes his note-book."

"What was written in it?"

"I only saw one word—the name 'Samuel ... Now a waiter comes into the room, and the man asks for a time-table."

Once more Bellowes restored Smeath to his normal state.

"That'll do," he said. "That's all for tonight. You can be off now, and think over that offer of mine."

At ten on the following morning Smeath kept his appointment. He said he would sign an agreement for two years only, and that he would want thirty shillings a week.

"What makes you suddenly think you're worth thirty shillings a week?"

"I have no idea at all, but I know you need me very much. I have that feeling."

"It was three years I said, not two. If I pay you thirty shillings a week, you can sign for three years."

"I cannot. I want to get back to my birds. I will sign for thirty shillings a week for two years, or I will go away."

"Oh, very well," growled Bellowes. "You're an obstinate little devil. Have it your own way. I hope to goodness I'm not going to lose money over you. I've never paid more than a pound to an assistant before. By the way, Smeath, were you ever in London?"

"Yes; several times." "Do you know Piccadilly, or Bond Street, or Regent Street?"

Smeath shook his head.

"I have only passed through in going from one place to another. I know the names of those streets, but I've never been in them."

"Very well," said Bellowes. "Come along with me, and we'll fix up the agreement."

About a month later Mr. Bellowes, who had come up to London for the purpose, called at the office of Mr. Tangent's agency in Sussex Street.

"Appointment," said Bellowes, as he handed in his card, and was taken immediately into the inner office. Mr. Tangent, a florid and slightly overdressed man of fifty, rose from his American desk to shake hands with him.

"Well, my dear old boy," said Tangent, "and how are you?"

"Fit," said Bellowes. "Remarkably fit."

"And what can I do for you? I had an enquiry the other day that brought you to my mind. It's not much. A week, with a chance of an engagement if you catch on."

"Thanks, old man, but I don't want it, on to something a bit better. What I want from you is a hundred and fifty pounds."

Tangent laughed genially.

"Long time since I've seen so much money as that. Well, well! What's it for? Tell us the story."

"I've had a bit of luck, Tangent. I've got a man booked up to me for the next two years who is simply the most marvellous clairvoyant the world has ever seen."

"Clairvoyants aren't going well," said Tangent. "Most of them don't make enough to pay for their rent and their ads. in the Sunday papers. The fact is there are too many of them. I don't care what the line is—palmistry, crystal-gazing, psychometry, or what you like. There's no money in it."

"Let's talk sense. You say there's no money in it? Do you remember when Merion fell, and a ten-to-one chance romped home?"

"Remember it? I've good reason to. I'd backed Merion both ways, and didn't see how I was going to lose."

"Well, I backed the winner. Not being a Croesus like yourself, I only had five bob on. I backed him, because my clairvoyant saw the whole thing, and described it to me before the race was run."

"Can he do it again?"

"He has not been able to do it again yet. He has seen what happened in the past many times, and he has never been wrong. He is exceptional. He is only clairvoyant when he is hypnotised. In the normal state he sees nothing. He's an ugly little devil, a dwarf, and if I bring him to London, he'll make a sensation. What's more, he'll make money. Pots of money. I know the crowd you've been talking about.

They're a hit-or-miss lot. They're no good. This is something quite different. We shall have all the Society women paying any fee I like to consult him. There's a fortune in it."

Tangent lit a cigarette, and pushed the box across to Bellowes. "What is it you propose to do?" he asked.

"Rooms in Bond Street. Good furniture. Uniformed servant. Sandwich-men at first, Once the thing gets started, it will go by itself. Any woman who has consulted him once is absolutely bound to tell all her friends. The man's a miracle. I'll tell you another thing I'm going to do. When the next sensational murder turns up, and Scotland Yard can't put their hands on the man who did it, I'm going to turn my chap on to the job. I'll bet all I've got to sixpence that we find the man."

"There was the case of that girl—Esther Samuel."

"Yes, I remember that. But by this time most of the public have forgotten it. A better chance is bound to turn up soon."

"I don't see how you're going to start on a hundred and fifty."

"I'm not, my boy. I've got money of my own that I'm putting into it as well."

"Let's see," said Tangent, picking up a pencil. "What did you say was this man's name and address?"

Bellowes laughed. "Oh, no, you don't," he said. "At present that's my business. Make it your own business as well and you shall be told everything."

"I don't know why you should call it business at all. You ask me to lend you a hundred and fifty. You offer no security. All I've got is your story that you've found a clairvoyant who's really good."

"Very well. If you satisfied yourself that the man was really good, would you lend the money then?"

"On terms, yes. But they'd have to be satisfactory terms."

"They would be. Well, you shall see for yourself. The man's waiting in a cab downstairs."

"You might have said that before."

"Why? Anyhow, I'll go and bring him up now."

It was a chilly morning, and Smeath shivered in a thick overcoat, which he refused to remove. No time was wasted on preliminaries. Bellowes hypnotised him at once.

"Now then, my boy," said Bellowes. "You shall see for yourself. Give me any article which you or someone else has worn, or has frequently handled."

Tangent opened a drawer in his desk, and produced a lady's glove. "That," he said, "was left in my office a week ago. Let's see what he makes out of it."

Bellowes put the glove in Smeath's hands. Smeath began to pull the buttons off it. He dragged and tore at the glove like a wild animal at its prey. Then suddenly he began to speak.

"I see a handsome woman with bright golden hair. I think the hair has been dyed. It has that appearance. She is talking with Mr. What's-his-name in this room. Each is angry with the other. She is accusing him of something. Suddenly—yes—she picks up an ink-bottle and throws it at him. Ink all over the place. He bangs on a little bell, and a man comes in who looks like a clerk. That is all. I cannot more see any more."

"Wake him up and send him down to the cab again," said Tangent. "Then we can talk."

"Now," said Bellowes, when they were alone together. "Had he got that right?"

"Absolutely. The woman was Cora Vendall. She wanted a particular berth, and thought I ought to have got it for her. She's fifty-six if she's a day, and not in any way suitable for it. If I had proposed it, the people would simply have laughed at me. She did get into a blind fury with me, and she did throw the ink at me. She's been made to pay for that, and she's been told not to show her powdered nose inside my office again. Your man is remarkable, Bellowes. There can be no two opinions about it. There is certainly money in him."

"You will find the hundred and fifty, then?"

"Yes, I'll do that. Mind, I must have a word to say in the management. The right sort of people will have to be got to see that man. Once that has been done, I do believe you're right, and the thing will go by itself."

"What interest do you want?"

"I don't want interest. What I do is to buy for a hundred and fifty pounds a share in your profits from your agreement with the clairvoyant."

"You shall have it. It's a jolly good thing I'm putting into your way, Tangent. I had never meant to part with a share, and I'd sooner pay you fifteen *per cent.* on your money. However, if you insist, you can take a sixteenth."

"Rats!" said Mr. Tangent, impolitely. "This is not everybody's business. Step across to the Bank of England, and see how much they'll advance you on it. There are three of us in it. Him and you and me. I'm going to take a third. Do just as you like about it. If I go into it, I can make it a certainty. I can get the right people to see the man."

"A third's too much. You must be reasonable, Tangent. I discovered him."

"A man once discovered a gold-mine. He had no means of getting the gold out. He was a thousand miles from anywhere, and he was all alone. He died on the top of his blessed gold-mine. However, I'm not arguing. I'm simply telling you. Give me a third, and my cheque and the agreement will be ready this time tomorrow morning. Otherwise, no business."

Mr. Bellowes hesitated, and then gave in.

4

At six o'clock on a summer evening, in a well-furnished room that overlooked the traffic of Bond Street, Smeath and his employer sat and quarrelled together. Both of them wore new clothes, but Bellowes had the air of prosperity, and Smeath had not.

"It's no good to talk to me," whined Smeath. "I know what I'm saying. Where an essential consideration has been intentionally concealed, an agreement cannot stand. You never told me I was a clairvoyant."

"No," said Bellowes, "I did not. And I don't tell a man what the colour of his hair is, either. Why? Because he knows it already. You knew that you were a clairvoyant."

"I did not. I swear I did not!" said Smeath, raising his voice.

"Now, don't get excited. Don't squeal."

"I'm not squealing. Do you think that if I'd known, I would ever have come to you for a wage like that? We've had fourteen people here today. What did they pay?"

"Mind your own business!"

"But it is my own business. And as you wouldn't tell me, I've taken my own steps to find out. Not one of them paid less than a guinea. You had as much as five guineas from some. And here am I with thirty shillings a week. I can get that agreement set aside. I can prove what I'm saying. I had never been hypnotised until I met you."

"Look here," said Bellowes. "Let us get this fixed up once for all. I don't know who's been cramming you up with these fairy-tales about my fees, but I don't get what you think, or anything like it. I get so little, that I don't want to waste any of it on lawyers. Besides, it would do the business no good, and it would do you no good. I should leave you, and then where would you be? Remember that you are not clairvoyant until I make you clairvoyant."

"You think, perhaps, I have not read what the newspapers say about me? I can find a hundred hypnotists very easily. But there is no other man who's clairvoyant as I am."

"And there is no other man who can run a show as I can. Who brought the newspaper men here? Who paid for the advertisements? Who did pretty well everything? However, I'm not going to argue. If you want more money, you can have it. Name your figure. If it is in any way reasonable, you shall have it, on the understanding that this is the last advance you get. If it is unreasonable, you'll get nothing. You can take the thing into the Courts, and I'll fight it. And, mark my words, Smeath. If I do, you may get a surprise. You know nothing at all about hypnotism. You may find yourself in the witness-box saying things that you did not intend to say. Now, then, name your figure."

The little man took time to think it over. He rubbed his chin with his fingers reflectively. He seemed on the point of speaking, and then stopped. Suddenly he snapped out:

"I want four pounds week!"

"It's simply bare-faced robbery," said Bellowes. "But you shall have it. Mind you, you will have to sign another paper tomorrow, and this time there shall be no doubt about it."

"If you pay me that, I'll sign anything. With four pounds a week I can keep some very good birds again. But you are right that it is bare-faced robbery, and I am the man who is being robbed."

There had been many disputes between the two men during the six weeks that they had been associated. It was by Tangent's directions that Bellowes acted in the present quarrel.

"It would be better to pay the little devil twenty pounds a week, and keep him, than to refuse and lose him," said Tangent. "I believe he's right, and that your precious agreement isn't worth the paper it's written on. Anyhow, I'll get a new agreement ready. Pay him what he wants, and he'll sign it."

"Well," said Bellowes, doubtfully, "if you say so you're probably right. But in that case, we ought to get an extension of time out of him."

"No," said Tangent, "the chap's suspicious of you. He hates you. If you try any sort of monkeying, he'll be off. Besides, with the fees you're charging, two years will about see it through. There are not such a vast number of people who can afford the game."

"As things go at present, it looks as though it might last for ever. You should see the engagement-book. We've got appointments booked for two months ahead. It isn't only a game you see. It's not just a pastime for fashionable women. We get men from the Stock Exchange, business men of all sorts, racing-men. Yesterday morning we had the Prime Minister's private secretary. He didn't give his right name, but Smeath was on to it, and then he admitted it."

"Hot stuff, Smeath. Do you get much out of him in the way of prophecy? Foretelling the future?" "Not very often. He has done some wonderful things that way, but more usually he deals with something that is past."

"Why don't you get him to foretell your own future, Percy?"

Bellowes shook his head.

"Not taking any," he said. "He shall have a shot with you if you like."

But Tangent also refused.

Their business had certainly progressed very rapidly. Tangent arranged a report in a newspaper. He communicated with one or two doctors whom he knew to be interested in the subject. He sent a couple of popular actresses to Smeath. He arranged a special *séance* for a cabinet minister, whose principal interest was psychology. After the first week they no longer employed sandwich-men and advertisements. The ball had begun to roll. Everybody who came to Smeath sent somebody else. Everybody in Society was talking about the hideous little dwarf and his marvellous powers. Bellowes was regarded as a showman and a charlatan, but Smeath was clearly the genuine thing.

Despite their mutual dislike, Bellowes and Smeath both lived in the same house—the Bloomsbury lodging-house. It was Bellowes who had insisted on this. He had never felt quite safe about Smeath, and even after the new agreement had been signed, he had his suspicions. He was afraid that Smeath would run away. Bellowes occupied fairly good rooms on the first floor. Smeath had one room at the top of the house, but this happened to suit him. Through his windows he could get out on to a flat, leaded roof. There he made friends with the pigeons and sparrows. The maid-servant at the house, who one day saw him out on the roof with the birds all round him, said that it was witchcraft.

"They were 'opping about all over 'im. Sometimes he put one down and called another up. I never saw anything like it in my life before."

She had the hatred of the unusual which is prevalent amongst domestic servants, and gave notice at once. But before the month was up, she had grown quite accustomed to seeing Smeath playing with the birds, and the notice was revoked.

5

Bellowes still used for business purposes the name of Sanders-Bell, but he no longer called himself a doctor. He was meeting too many real doctors, and Tangent had advised against it. The room in Bond Street was divided in two by a curtain. The outer part served as a waiting-room, and here, too, Bellowes had his bureau. In the inner part of the room the actual interview between the client and the clairvoyant took place. Their usual hours were only from eleven to one and from two to four, but Bellowes would sometimes arrange for a special interview at an unusual hour and an increased price.

On these occasions he always took care to pacify Smeath. Sometimes he gave him money, and sometimes other presents; on one occasion he gave him a big book about birds, with coloured illustrations, and Smeath remained docile and in a good temper for days afterwards.

"Yes," said Bellowes. "You have complained once that I was robbing you. You can't say that now. You have fixed your own salary. If there is the least little bit of extra work to be done, you always get something for it. You are not as grateful as you ought to be, Smeath. Where would you have been without me? What were you doing before you came to me?"

"Nothing. For some weeks I had been very hungry. I make no complaint against you, but when my time's up I shall stay no longer. I go back to the birds again."

"It would be more sensible of you," said Bellowes, "if you banked your money. What did you want to buy that great owl for? He makes the devil of a row at night. We shall have people complaining about it."

"She is a very good friend to me, that owl," said Smeath. "I am teaching her much. She will be valuable."

At this moment there was the sound of a footstep on the stairs, and Smeath stepped behind his curtain.

The man who entered was not at all the type of client that Bellowes generally received. He was a thick-set man of common appearance, and he was unfashionably dressed. He did not look in the least as if he could afford the fee. Bellowes saluted him somewhat curtly.

"It is ten minutes to eleven, sir, and our hour for beginning is eleven. However, as you have called, if you like to pay the fee now—two guineas—I will make an appointment for you, but I'm afraid it will have to be in nine weeks' time."

The visitor looked reflective, turning his seedy bowler hat round in his hands.

"Don't think that would do," he said. "Nine weeks —that's a very long time. Couldn't Mr. Smeath see me today? Couldn't he make an exception?"

"Only by giving you a special appointment. And for that a very much higher fee is charged."

"How much?" asked the man. "He could give you ten minutes at one o'clock today. But the charge for that would be six guineas. You see, Mr. Smeath is only clairvoyant while in the hypnotic state, and that cannot be repeated indefinitely."

The visitor took an old-fashioned purse from his hip-pocket. He pulled out a five-pound note, a sovereign, and six shillings.

"There you are," he said. "Please book me ten minutes with Mr. Smeath at one o'clock today."

"Very good," said Bellowes, opening the engagement-book. He looked up, with his pen in his hand. "What name shall I put down?"

"I am Mr. Vincent."

"You'll be careful to be punctual, of course. Mr. Smeath will be ready exactly at one o'clock."

"I shall be here," said the man.

He had no sooner gone than Smeath emerged from behind the curtain again. "What on earth did you do that for?" he asked excitedly.

"Keep your hair on, Smeath. It's all right. I'm going to buy you a big cage for that owl of yours."

"I do not want any cage. My birds are not kept in cages. It is not the extra work that I mind. It is that I cannot do anything for that man. I tell you he is dangerous."

"In what way dangerous?"

"I don't know. He is dangerous to me."

"He looked to me an honest man enough. He had the appearance of a chap up from the country. Probably wants to know what his best girl is doing. I shouldn't worry about it if I were you. Don't stand in the way of business, Smeath. You don't know what the expenses are here. I've got to pay the rent next week, and if I told you what that was, you wouldn't believe it. If you don't want the bird-cage, you shall have something else."

But it was necessary to show Smeath a sovereign, and to present him with it before he would consent. Even then, he did so with great reluctance.

Clients with appointments came in, and the ordinary business of the morning began. Smeath no longer spoke when in the clairvoyant state, for he was often consulted upon matters requiring secrecy, and what he said might have been heard by other clients in waiting. He had a writing-block, and scribbled down on it in pencil what he saw.

At one o'clock precisely Mr. Vincent returned, and was at once brought behind the curtain. Smeath sat there motionless. His eyes were open, but he did not look up at Mr. Vincent.

"Now then, sir," said Bellowes. "What is it you want?"

Mr. Vincent drew from his pocket a comb wrapped in paper. It was of the kind that women wear in their hair, and it had been broken.

"I want him to tell me about the girl who wore this at the time when it was broken."

Bellowes placed the comb in Smeath's hands. Smeath held it for a moment, and then the fingers relaxed, and it dropped to the floor.

Bellowes again placed it in his hand, and this time Smeath flung it from him. But immediately he began to write, Mr. Vincent watching him narrowly as he did so. He wrote with an extraordinary rapidity. Presently Bellowes, who had been standing behind him, and reading what he wrote, asked Mr. Vincent to wait in the outer part of the room. As soon as he was alone with Smeath, he took the writing-block out of his hands, tore the sheet from it, folded it, and put it in his pocket. Then he rejoined Vincent.

"I am extremely sorry, sir," said Bellowes, "that the experiment has failed completely. There is perhaps some kind of antipathy between Mr. Smeath and yourself. These things do occasionally happen. I find that he can tell you nothing at all, and under the circumstances, I should perhaps return your fee."

Vincent did not seem particularly surprised.

"Very well," he said. "I had hardly expected to get what I wanted, but I thought I might as well try. I paid you six guineas, I think. You seem to be treating me fairly, and I have given you a certain amount of trouble. Supposing you return me five of them."

The money was handed over, and Vincent departed. Bellowes went back to Smeath and brought him out of the trance.

Smeath shivered. "Is he here still?"

"No. Gone."

"Was it all right?"

"It was quite all right."

"I'm glad he's gone," said Smeath. "I was horribly afraid of something. Now I can go out and get my lunch, and I have to buy food for the birds too."

"I shouldn't spend too much money on it if I were you," said Bellowes.

Smeath laughed.

"It is not very expensive," he said. "And I have made one extra sovereign. Why not?" "Because, in future, Smeath, you are going to work for me for much less money—for a pound a week, to be precise."

"I shall not," said Smeath, loudly. "I told you once before not to squeal. I don't like it. You will do exactly as I say, and for a very good reason. If you don't you will be taken to prison, and you will be tried before a judge, and you will be hanged, Smeath. Hanged for the murder of Esther Samuel in the woods at Teston.".

6

"What makes you say that? How do you know it?" asked Smeath. The fingers of his big hands locked and separated and locked again. His eyes were fixed intently on Bellowes. He looked excited, but not frightened.

"How do I know it?" echoed Bellowes. "I have it here in your own handwriting." He tapped his breast-pocket. "You do not remember what happened when you were hypnotised. I put a broken comb into your hands. It was a comb which the murdered woman had worn. You began to write at once. You've put the rope round your neck, Smeath."

"And that man—the man that I knew to be dangerous?"

"Mr. Vincent? I told him that the experiment had failed, and returned his fee. He knows nothing. So long as you do exactly what I tell you, you are quite safe."

"Who was he, this Vincent?"

Bellowes shrugged his shoulders.

"How should I know? Possibly one of the Samuel family. Possibly a 'tec. If I had given him what he had paid for, we should have had the police in here by I have saved your skin for you, Smeath. Don't now, forget it."

"Will you read it out to me, the thing that I wrote down?"

"No. It tells one everything, except the motive."

"The motive was obvious enough. I was hungry and had no money. I had tramped to Teston and reached there two days too soon. I had nowhere to go, and I lived and slept in the woods. I begged from the girl at first, and if she had given me a few pence she might have been alive now. She was not the least bit afraid of me. Why should she have been? I was small, misshapen, and looked weak. She was tall and strong. As she turned away from me, she said the tramps in the neighbourhood were becoming a nuisance, and she would send the police after me.

"Even then I only meant to hit her once, but that is a queer thing—you cannot hit a human being once. You see the body lying at your feet, and you have to go on striking and striking. When I knew she must be dead, I flung the stick down. I took nothing but the money, nothing which could be traced. Even the money made me so nervous that I hid most of it—buried it in a place where I could find it again. If the police had found me, there would only have been a few coppers in my possession, and I did not look like a man who could have done it. But they never did find me."

"I see. That was why, when I offered to advance your railway fare, you told me you had money. You had a pair of new boots on when you turned up at Warlow. I remember what an infernal squeaking row they made on the platform. Well, you've done for yourself, Smeath. You've got to work for me on very different terms now."

"No," said Smeath. "That is not so."

"Very good. I'll write my note to Mr. Vincent now. He'll do the rest."

"No, you won't, and I'll tell you why. You can destroy me very likely, but if you do, you'll destroy your own livelihood. And you always take very good care for yourself, Mr. Bellowes."

"Destroy my livelihood?" said Bellowes, thumping on the table with his fist. "That's where you make your mistake, you little devil! Because you're useful, you think you're indispensable. You're not. There's a reward of two hundred pounds out for anyone who finds the murderer of Esther Samuel. I'm a born showman. With two hundred pounds capital I can chuck this and start something else that will pay me just as well."

"It looks as if I shall have to give in. Well, there's no help for it. I must get a much cheaper room, of course."

"No, you won't. You'll stop in the same house as me. D'you think I haven't worked it all out? After you've paid your rent, you've a shilling a day for food, and better men have lived on less. I'm not going to give you a chance to bolt. And mark my words, Smeath, if you do bolt, the very moment I find you've gone I give you up. Don't imagine you can get away. There are not many men of your build. The police would have you for a certainty within twenty-four hours."

"Then I become a slave; I can do nothing. There were other birds that I meant to buy. And in time I could have started a business again. That must all go."

"Quite so. That must all go. In fact, before a fortnight is out, I expect you'll sell that big white owl of yours. You'll grudge him his keep."

"It is a she-owl, and I shall not let her go. She can do things that would surprise you."

"Can she?" said Bellowes. "It might be rather effective if you brought her down here. She would impress clients."

"I shall not. I keep her for myself!"

"Don't talk like a fool! You are forgetting that I hold you between my thumb and finger. If I tell you to wring that bird's neck you will have to do it."

Smeath rose to his feet in fury.

"Where's my hat?" he said. Give me my hat!"

Bellowes stood in front of the door.

"What's the matter with you? Where are you off to?"

"Checkmate for you, Mr. Bellowes. I am going now to give myself up. Where is your two hundred pounds reward, eh? Where is the money that you make out of the clairvoyant?"

"Sit down, and don't talk in that silly way. I never told you to kill the bird. I was only speaking in your interests when I said I doubted if you could afford to keep it. As a matter of fact, I don't care a pin's head about it either way. If you set so much store by it, keep it by all means."

"In that case," said Smeath, "I will go on working for you, and on the terms that you have said."

"That's all right; and now you can go out to lunch. Remember that you have to be back at two o'clock. If you are not here by ten minutes past two, I shall send the police to look for you."

"I shall be here, Mr. Bellowes."

★★★★★★★★★★★★

Every Saturday morning at half-past nine Tangent called on Bellowes in Bond Street, to look over the books and to collect his share of the profits. Tangent had no great faith in Mr. Bellowes. Smeath was never allowed to be present on these occasions.

On the Saturday after Mr. Vincent's visit, Tangent was well pleased with the results.

"Mind you," he said, "the little dwarf isn't doing so badly out of it either. He gets his regular four pounds a week. This week I see he's had one pound ten in cash for extra work, and you're charging twelve-and-six for a present to him. What was the present?"

"Oh, a bird of sorts. The little beggar's simply mad about birds. That did more good than if I'd given him the actual cash."

"Oh, I'm not grumbling, Bellowes," said Tangent, surveying with complacency the diamond ring on his finger. "If, by giving him a trifle extra now and then, you can keep his goodwill, it's quite worth our while to do it. No man will work for nothing, and I suppose he finds this clairvoyance game rather exhausting. Not over and above good for the health, eh?"

"He says it's exhausting. He seems to me well enough."

When Tangent had gone Bellowes smiled. To swindle Tangent was a real pleasure to him, even apart from the profit he made for himself. He remembered the terms which Tangent had forced him to accept for the provision of capital for the enterprise.

The introduction of a large white owl into the Bloomsbury lodging-house could have but one effect. The maidservant gave notice at once on general principles. It was Smeath this time who persuaded her to remain.

"You must not be afraid of the white owl," he said. "Owls are wise birds. She knows who my friends are, and who my enemies are. You are my friend, and she will never hurt you. She will let you feed her and stroke her feathers. They are very, very soft, the feathers of an owl."

In a week's time Jane was neglecting her work to play with the white owl out on the leads.

7

For several weeks no change took place. Smeath did his work with patience and docility. He addressed Mr. Bellowes with respect. He made very little objection to private engagements. As a munificent reward, on two occasions Bellowes took him out to luncheon, and once presented him with some Sunday tickets for the Zoo, which he himself did not want. Every Saturday Tangent inspected, with satisfaction, some purely fantastic accounts. Bellowes was specially careful that Smeath and Tangent should never meet, lest the discrepancy between the statements in the books and the actual facts should be discovered.

And then business began to fall off. There was no excessive drop, but the previous standard was not quite maintained. That astute show-man, Mr. Bellowes, decided that something would have to be done. Some new feature would have to be introduced, to set people talking again.

"Smeath," he said one day, "didn't you tell me something once about a white owl?"

"Yes," said Smeath, "I have one."

"It does tricks, don't it?"

"It does a few things," said Smeath, grudgingly. "You do not want it. You said that you would leave me my owl."

"You needn't get into a stew about it, and do for goodness sake keep those great hands of yours still. They get on my nerves. Nobody wants to take your blessed owl away from you. The only thing that I was wondering about was whether it might not be worthwhile to keep the bird here, instead of at your lodgings."

"No, sir! No, Mr. Bellowes! It is in my leisure time that I want my owl."

"Well, I was talking to Mr. Tangent about it, and he thought it was a good idea; in fact, he said I ought to have done it before. We must think about it. I have been pretty easy with you, Smeath."

"Also, I've worked very hard for you."

"You've done what you were told, and of late you've given me no trouble. You might let Tangent and myself have a look at the bird, any-how. It would be effective, you know—the dwarf clairvoyant and the great white owl on the back of his chair. Tangent spoke of a poster. I'll tell him to give us a call in Bloomsbury on Sunday morning."

"I do not want my owl to be taken away. It lives there on the leads outside my window. Here it would be unhappy. How could I leave it here all night alone?"

"Don't be unreasonable, Smeath. You will see more of the bird then than you do now."

"No," said Smeath. "The greater part of the time when I'm here I'm like a dead man, and know nothing."

Bellowes had quite realised that this was the point on which Smeath would have to be handled carefully.

"Look here," he said, "I wouldn't do anything to hurt the bird. At any rate, let Mr. Tangent and myself see it. Let us see if it can really do the things that that girl Jane jabbers so much about. If Tangent and I think it would be an asset to the show, I am prepared to go quite beyond our agreement. I'll give you two or three shillings for yourself, Smeath. You can give yourself a treat. You've not been having many treats lately; in fact, you look just about half starved."

It was true. The little dwarf had grown very thin. His eyes seemed to have got bigger and brighter. There was a look in them know which would have made Bellowes suspicious if he had noticed it.

"Jane," said Smeath, as he met her on the stairs that night, "they are coming on Sunday morning to see my owl."

"Then they'll see miracles," said Jane, with confidence.

"And they're going to take it away."

"If that bird goes, I goes!"

Smeath burst into a peal of mirthless laughter.

Mr. Tangent arrived in a taxi-cab at the Bloomsbury lodgings at eleven on the following Sunday morning. He was in a bad temper, and swore and grumbled profusely.

"So, I've got to turn out on Sunday morning and work seven days a week, just because you're such a damn bad showman, Bellowes? You've let the thing down. The books on Saturday were perfectly awful."

"I'm not a bad showman, and it's not my fault. The weather's been against us, for one thing. And, besides, no novelty lasts for ever. We must put something else into it to buck it up, and we must get that poster out."

"That means more expense. I don't see why we should keep on paying Smeath four pounds a week if business is falling off. And as for that rotten old owl of his, I'm no great believer in it. It will look all right on the poster, but it will do no good in your Bond Street rooms. I know those tricks. The bird picks out cards from a pack, or shams dead, or some other nursery foolery. Stale, my boy, hopelessly stale."

"According to what I hear, the bird does none of those things. It's a new line."

"Is it? I'll bet a dollar it ain't. However, tell Smeath to bring it down, and let's get it over."

"Smeath won't bring it down. We shall have to go up to it. He makes a great favour of showing it to us at all. And, if you will take my tip, you'll say nothing to Smeath beyond a good morning. I can tell you he wants devilish careful handling about this bird of his. If you interfere, you'll spoil it. All you've got to do, if you think it at all remarkable, is to say to me that it might possibly do. I shall understand. Now then, come along up!"

96

"All those stairs!" groaned Tangent. He was a heavy and plethoric man. When they reached Smeath's room he stood for a minute, panting.

The room was ordinarily dingy enough. It was a fine morning, and the sun streamed in through the window. On the leads outside they could see the great white owl perched on the bough of a tree which had been fixed there. Smeath, with his hat off, stood beside it, and seemed to be talking to it. Around his feet were a flock of pigeons and sparrows. He nodded to the two men, and then gave one wave of his hands. The pigeons and sparrows flew off and left him alone with the white owl.

"Funny sight!" grunted Tangent. "Devilish funny sight!"

Smeath opened the window, and called into the room: "Good morning, gentlemen! Will you come out?"

"Don't much like it," said Tangent. "I've no head for this kind of thing."

"Oh, you're all right!" said Bellowes. "You needn't go anywhere near the edge."

He placed a chair for him, and Tangent climbed out onto the roof, followed by Bellowes.

"I will leave you to look at the bird by yourselves, gentlemen," said Smeath, and stepped down into the room.

"Then who's going to make the bird do its tricks?" asked Tangent. "It's a fine-looking beggar, anyhow. Seems about half asleep. Tame enough." He passed his jewelled hand over the snowy plumage on the bird's breast. "There's a feather-bed for you," he said, laughing.

The bird opened its eyes, and leaped straight into the face of Bellowes. Its plumage half stifled him, its sharp claws tore his eyes. He screamed for help.

Tangent, in horror, had flung himself down flat on the leads, covering his face. Within the room Smeath stood with folded arms, watching the scene with the utmost calmness.

Bellowes tore at the bird with his hands, but step by step it forced him back. There came one final scream from him, and then two seconds of silence, and then the thud as his body struck the stones below. Up above, the white owl flew swiftly away.

The dwarf rubbed his hands and laughed. And then, changing his expression to one of extreme dismay, went to the help of the prostrate Tangent.

The Girl and the Beetle

A Story of Here and Hereafter.

On the brushwood and groups of trees that here and there broke the monotony of the flat and sandy common were the marks of autumn. The wind was soft and mild, and the leaves fell gently, and the white clouds sailed away into the distance steadily and unquestioningly. Far off the glint of sunlight fell on the narrow, sluggish river. Winds and leaves, clouds and river—all were going home, with a calm meekness that aggravated the dying beetle. It was a good day to die on, and the beetle knew it; but yet he was dissatisfied.

Above him there hovered two unkempt birds, tormented by a sense of what in all the circumstances was the correct thing to do. Each bird had sighted the beetle, and neither would come and take it; for each thought that the other would suppose him to be greedy. Of these two birds the one was magnanimous and the other was nervous, and both were hungry.

"There's a large beetle down there," the first remarked, "but I don't know that I care about it particularly. Won't you take it?"

There was nothing that his companion would have liked better, but his unfortunate nervousness prevented him from availing himself of the generous offer. "No, thanks" he stammered, "I couldn't deprive you."

"But I really don't want it," said Magnanimity.

"Nor do I," replied Nervousness. "Let's go for a little fly."

So, they flew slowly away, feeling empty and mistaken, with a sense that the world must be out of joint where there were nearly always two birds to one beetle, and both the birds understood etiquette. And the beetle went on dying.

He had not during his previous life been a good beetle. He was strongly built, and his constitution, which had now given way, had always been considered robust. Female beetles had thought him

99

uncommonly handsome; yet with all these gifts he had not been a good beetle; on the contrary he had been extremely immoral. He lay stretched on the sand by the edge of the pathway, enjoying the warmth of the afternoon sunlight.

"Mary," he called, a little querulously, "come out."

It is difficult to understand how the beetle could call without making any noise. It should be remembered, however, that sound is to beetles very much what silence is to us. A certain kind of silence, on the other hand, answers to what we call conversation, and can be varied so as to express all that we can do by changing the tone of the voice. The small female of depressed appearance, who hurried from the shelter of a stone in answer to this summons, quite understood that she had been called querulously. The two unkempt birds should undoubtedly have waited.

"Thomas," said the beetle who had been addressed as Mary, "I think you called me?"

"Have you stopped crying?"

"Yes, dear; I won't cry any more, if you don't like it."

"You know I don't like it. Have you got any new ideas?"

"Well, Thomas, nothing that could be absolutely called new, perhaps; but I remember a little story that my poor dear mother used to—"

"Stop!" said Thomas, "you're a stale, heavy-minded female, and you can get back under the stone. I was going to let you see me die. I shan't now!"

"Do let me stop!" pleaded Mary.

"No, I won't!—stay, what's that pestilential insect creeping towards us?"

"It's the Dear Friend. He looks small and meagre, but we must not judge from looks, Thomas. Beauty fades."

Thomas surveyed Mary slowly. "It does," he said.

The Dear Friend was so named from his habit of calling indiscriminately on other beetles, and excusing himself on the ground that he wanted to be their dear friend. He lived a very good life, and he wanted other beetles to be good. The want was noble, but he had not sufficient tact to conceal it. Some beetles thought him a bore, and did not care to hear him discuss their sins in his plain way. Others, seeing that he knew so little about this life, thought that he might have unusual knowledge of the next. Beetles, as a class, have a tendency towards mysticism. Mary had a firm belief in the goodness and spirituality of the Dear Friend, although she was dimly conscious that he was not clever. She was very anxious that he should have a few words with the dying Thomas.

"You will see him, dear, won't you?" she said. "You're drawing near to your end, you know, and it would do you good to experience a word in season. You have been such a bad beetle."

"I have," said Thomas, with a chuckle of intense self-satisfaction, "I've been a devilish bad beetle."

The thought of his own exceeding immorality seemed quite to have restored his good temper. "Heavy-minded female, you are become brilliant. Never before have I experienced a word in season. You may stop, and we'll interview the Dear Friend."

Mary, like some females of higher organisations, was rarely able to understand the precise value of a satirical silence. Everything was cloudy in her brain, and nothing precise. She had vague ideas that she ought to be good, and that served her for aspirations. She had at least three decided opinions—that her mother had been very good and very kind to her, that Thomas was horribly bad and very unkind to her, and that of the two she infinitely preferred Thomas. She was emotional and rather self-seeking. At present she was very pleased at being praised, and welcomed the little visitor kindly as he crept across towards them. They formed an extraordinary trio even for beetles. It is not generally known that the lower the physical organisation the more complicated is the character. A beetle is as a rule much more contrary and difficult than a man. The character of a *tubercular bacillus* is so complex as to absolutely defy analysis.

"Mr. Thomas," the Dear Friend began solemnly, "I am pleased to see you—in fact, I have come a long way with that intention. I had heard that you were very ill and like to die, and I had also heard—you will excuse me—of your past life."

"Quite right," said Thomas encouragingly, "I am guilty of having had a past life. Oh, sir, you can't think how many beetles of my age have had a past of some kind or other. It is true that it was my own life—I have not taken anyone else's, not yet—but still I've had it. I feel that deeply."

At this the Dear Friend warmed to his work, but made a fatal mistake—he grew slightly enthusiastic. Now Thomas could stand no manner of enthusiasm, because it always seemed to him to show an exaggerated conception of the value of things.

"Oh, Mr. Thomas, I am so very glad to hear you talk like that. This is indeed no time for idle compliments, and you recognise the fact. You have the sense of guilt. You see how disgusting, and loathsome, and abominable the whole of your life has—"

Here he was interrupted by a curious stridulating noise which Thomas made, thereby rendering it impossible to catch the remainder of the Dear Friend's silence. The poor little insect cooled down again at once. He saw that enthusiasm would not do; that he had been taking matters too fast, and that Thomas was a beetle who required to be treated with a good deal of tact. The Dear Friend himself was unable to stridulate, and had sometimes felt the want of it; but it is not a gift which belongs to every kind of beetle. Perhaps it would be as well to show some interest in the process, and then gradually to lead up to more serious subjects. He waited till the last whir had died away, and then he said:

"May I inquire how you make that noise? It is most interesting."

Thomas knew all about it.

"It is caused," he answered drily, "by the friction of a transversely striated elevation on the posterior border of the hinder coxa against the hinder margin of the *acctabulum*, into which it fits."

"Ah!" gasped the Dear Friend; but he speedily recovered himself. "That is indeed interesting—really, extremely interesting." He was trying to think in what way it would be possible to connect this with more important matters. "Talking about fits," he said, "I have just come away from such a sad case, quite a young—"

"I was not talking about fits, sir," interrupted Thomas, a little irritably. The Dear Friend hastened to agree with him.

"No, Mr. Thomas, you were not. I see what you mean, and it's very good of you to correct me. I was wrong. I was quite wrong. But you happened to use the word fits, and that suggests—"

"And talking about jests," retorted Thomas severely, "I don't think this is the time for them. When you're calmer, my friend, and have got over your inclination to make sport of serious subjects, you will see this. Please don't get excited; I'm not equal to it. You come to see me on my deathbed, and when I try to talk about my past life, you wax ribald, and begin to make puns that a schoolgirl would be ashamed of. I'm sorry for you, sir—very sorry. Mary, show that bug out. I want to think of my latter end, and he interrupts me."

"Oh, dear, dear!" said the poor, well-meaning little insect, almost whimpering, "I'm afraid I've made a very bad beginning. I didn't intend to offend you, and I do hope you'll make allowances. I know I'm not very clever, and I'm very young, and I've never had any education to speak of, because I've always been going about in my humble way trying to teach others. But I do want to be your really dear friend, and my heart does yearn—"

"Mary," said the exasperated Thomas, "I asked you to show that bug out. Will you kindly go away, sir, and drown yourself? I insist upon thinking of my latter end, and I simply cannot do it when you are here."

"I will go away, if you wish it, Mr. Thomas, but you will let me come back this evening?"

"You won't be able to come back, if you drown yourself."

"But I'm not going to drown myself."

"Well, you said you were, and you ought to, anyway."

"Oh, Mr. Thomas, I never, never—"

"Don't contradict. It's excessively rude, especially in a young bug like yourself. You promised to drown yourself, if I'd bequeath Mary to you in my will. You can take her now, if you like, and you may both go away and drown yourselves. I shall be dead before this evening; and if I am quite dead, you may come back. Now go."

The Dear Friend turned slowly and sadly away.

"Are you going to take Mary?" Thomas called after him. "You can if you like. She's nearly as fat-headed as yourself, and you'd get on splendidly together. Pray take her. I'm nearly dead, and I don't want her."

The Dear Friend made no reply. The wretched Mary was crying again. Thomas had worked himself up to the climax of fury, and was now lapsing from it into a series of chuckles. "Moist one," he said, turning to Mary, "you don't love me."

"Indeed, I do," sobbed Mary. "I love you ever so much too well but you're so cruel and you make fun of a good cause and you're going to die."

"Let us," said Thomas, drily, "be categorical. You, like most other females, say too much at once. Your remarks must be sifted and answered categorically. Firstly, you state that you love me. Yet you display a lot of wet, horrible emotion, in order to hasten my end. Don't speak; you know you did; and you asked the Dear Friend to come and bore me in my last moments; and you refused to sit on his head, or show him out, or stop him in any way. Consequently, I had to stop him myself. I had to be almost rude to him. Perhaps you'd better go after him if you're so fond of him. He's only half way across the path, and you'll

103

be able to catch him up."

"Oh, Thomas! I'm sure I never—"

"*Will* you keep quiet? Can't you see that I'm being categorical? Secondly, you say that I'm cruel. I am, and it's not my fault. If you and other people were not so abominably heavy-minded, I should not be cruel. You provoke me. You needn't tell me that you can't help being heavy-minded. I know that, and I never said that it was your fault; but it certainly isn't mine. Nothing that I know of ever is anybody's fault. Thirdly, you said that I made fun of a good cause. You muddler! I love most causes, and hate most of their promoters. Most causes are noble, and most promoters are presumptuous. So far from making fun of the good cause, I did it the greatest service by asking the Dear Friend to seek an early death. That reminds me—you said that I was going to die. So I am, if you don't mind waiting ten minutes. Why this unseemly haste?"

At this point Mary became all tears and disclaimers. "If you do that," said Thomas, "you really will have to go. I am about to die, and I intend to die my own way, without any weeping females or dear friends. It's much the same with you that it is with man and the other lower organisms. The good heart generally goes with a bad head; and if you have a good head, you probably—there, I thought so. Do you see? The Dear Friend on the further side of the path has just been trodden on by a passing labourer. If he'd had a little more head, he would have kept out of the way, and then he would not have died. Intellect is practical: spirituality is not. Now that is very curious, for although I have always been a most practical beetle, I have frequently had strong spiritual desires. For instance, I often after supper yearn to leave this gross and uncomely world, and bask in an impossible hereafter."

"Ah!" cried Mary. (She liked the ring of his last sentence.) "Those are beautiful words. If only you would always talk like that, instead of insulting those who only come to do you good. I know the Dear Friend made you angry; but then it's not so much what he said as what he wanted to say that we must think of."

"Ah, yes, my dear Mary, most moist and muddle-headed, and it is not so much what I am as what I want to be that the deceased bug should have considered. You were born with a wrong head, and so you form wrong judgments. It's not your fault; nothing's anybody's fault. The Dear Friend was good, but it doesn't matter. I am bad, and that doesn't matter either. Nothing matters, and I can't understand

104

anything, and I want to die."

Thomas threw himself on his back and kicked petulantly. Mary entreated him not to give way to temper; however, he declared that he was doing no such thing: that he was trying to think very fast, and that the action of kicking made it possible to think faster. Suddenly he stopped, and recovered his normal position. "Mary," he said, "it is clear to me, and I will make it clear to you, that nothing matters. Suppose something had an optical delusion, and the optical delusion died, and had a ghost—"

"But it couldn't, Thomas."

"I know that. I am only asking you to suppose it and the ghost went to sleep, and dreamed that he was dreaming, that he was dreaming—"

"Oh, don't go on! you'll only make your poor headache!"

"Do you think the something would care very much what happened in fts optical delusion's ghost's dream's dream's dream? Yet the innermost of the three dreams would seem to be perfectly real, and the apparent reality would be due to part of the previous experience of the something, which would be filtered—or, rather, reflected—through the whole series."

"That will do. Please don't go on. I don't understand a word of it, and it's no use. Oh, do let us talk good."

"You are going to understand it, fat-headed one. You think that you exist; that everything is real. How do you know that it is so? When you dream, you imagine that the dream is quite real; but you wake up and find that you are wrong. Now suppose the something one day had a thought, that went through a million optical delusions, a billion ghosts, and a trillion dreams—"

"It's not a bit of good," interpolated Mary. "I can't imagine numbers like that."

"That thought might ultimately take the form of this world, of which I, Thomas, the beetle, am a considerable part. There is nothing impossible about that. It may be so, and I am inclined to think that it is so, because something inside me seems to be struggling to get back to its origin. But if it is so it must be perfectly clear to you that nothing matters, because nothing is real, and nothing will be real till it gets back again to the—the something!"

"I don't understand it," said Mary; "are you quite sure that it doesn't confuse you at all to think that way?"

"Absolutely sure," said Thomas, which was untrue.

"And how do you get back again to the something?"

"That," said Thomas drily, "I will show you in a few minutes if, as I said before, you do not mind waiting."

For a short time neither of them spoke. The sun, like the spoiled child who promises to be so good if you will only let him stop, was growing more beautiful than ever as the time drew near for his departure. He had nothing but vapour and light with which to work, and yet he produced some very pretty effects. The gravel path, near which Thomas and Mary were lying, led into the road which skirted the edge of the common; along this road was a line of detached villas. The sun did the best that he could with them, but felt that he could not do much. The last house in the line was much larger than the rest, and stood in much larger grounds.

The advertisement had described them as being park-like, and they certainly contained quite enough trees almost to hide the house from the views of those who passed on the road. The sun had found out one of the windows through the foliage and was making it blaze. He liked doing that. He could see a good deal of the house and grounds in point of height he had the advantage of passers-by. He could see two tennis-courts, the players, groups who had gathered to look on, others who strayed aimlessly about and tried to prove they were not suburban. It was all cup and conversation, and it rather bored the sun, who has a masculine mind. None of the people in that garden were aware that rather less than half a mile from the house a remarkably fine beetle was dying in his sins; if they had known it, they might possibly not have cared.

When Thomas began to talk again, he appeared to be continuing a line of thought of which he had not considered it worthwhile to give the beginning.

"So, the truth of the matter is that a beetle did once get there—right up beyond the stars, but he never Carried a man there. Aristophanes said he did, but that was an aetiological myth. He made up the story to account for a prevalent belief that man could rise to higher things."

"That was what the Dear Friend always said," murmured Mary reflectively. "Cows, and pigs, and men, and fowls can never get up there—only beetles. It's all kept for them."

"And it's not what I say," retorted Thomas sharply. "I've got better things to do in my last moments than to waste them in agreeing with anybody. The mistake the man made was not in supposing that he could rise. All beasts can rise, as much as we can. His mistake was in rejecting the supernatural, and thinking that he could be raised only by a beetle. We may have more spirituality than men. That is quite possible: they are a lower organism. We may perhaps find it easier to soar than they do. But I am sure that all are going there, just as we are, beyond the stars."

"That may be true," said Mary, plucking up a little spirit; "but it certainly was not the opinion of the Dear Friend. Only beetles can rise."

"Do you prefer the opinions of the Dear Friend to absolute truth?"

"I do," said Mary proudly.

"Oh, blind and fat of temperament!" (This does not read quite right, but it is a fairly literal translation. There are no polite English words that exactly express the silence which Thomas used on this occasion.) "A few days ago, I was down in the grass by the river. It looks sweet and green from here. It grows long, and it makes a pleasant shade above one; but at the roots it's all mud and muck. That is the way of the world; instead of grumbling at the mud we might just as well be thankful for the grass; however, that's not my point. The cows came down to drink while I was there. They are nasty, lumpy animals; you can see their slobbering mouths and great yellow teeth as they bend over one to crop the grass. Some beetles get nervous, but I don't fancy there's any danger.

"As one of those brutes stooped down, I looked up and saw right into its eyes. It was like looking into immeasurable distance. They were sad, humble, trustful eyes; but there was something in them which signified the consciousness of a purpose in being. That is my point. A poor devil of a cow! it couldn't have told anyone why it existed, it could not even have put the reason clearly in its own mind; but it knew. I am much like the beast. I know, but I cannot say, not even to myself, the reason for my existence. Sometimes I think that if all sounds were in my power, I could get the whole thing out in music.

"It is a thing which defies ordinary processes and all logical connexion. I see the fading sunlight writing something on the under edge of a cloud; the intellectual part of me cannot read that language, but something else in me reads it, and understands it, and answers it almost piteously. 'Oh that I might fly away and be at rest!' And suddenly the conviction is strong in me that I know why I am here, and what I shall be hereafter. In the awful silence of the night that conviction comes dropping down my dark mind like a falling star. In moments of acute *dyspepsia* I always feel it."

He grinned pleasantly. He had spoiled his own poetry, and that pleased him. In his former life he had always been trying to make pretty things, and had always broken them up again. The grin passed from him, and he continued:

"Cows, therefore, have souls. You needn't contradict me, and thrust that omniscient Dear Friend down my throat, because I won't stand it. I tell you that I saw into their eyes, and I know. If you want to get at the bottom of things, you must leave all ordinary processes, all logical processes. You can't crawl down that way: you must jump. The people who dare not jump see that you have got to the bottom of things, and comfort themselves with saying that you must have hurt your poor head terribly. Have I hurt my head, Mary? For my intellect is all gone, and the light is fading very quickly.

"You hate men, I think. Never despise them anymore; for they have souls. They cut down the grass, and it dies. They pull the flowers, and they die. They tread on the beetles, and they die. They kill the animals, cut down the trees, and poison the rivers. Where a man comes, death always follows. They are murderers; they are hideously ugly; they make unpleasant noises, and do not understand silences; they are the very lowest of all creatures, but they are on their way to a hereafter. Nothing's wasted: the very strictest economy is practised."

"I can't understand you, Thomas; and I am afraid that you are getting worse. It tries you to talk. Why did you say the light was fading? The sun is still shining all over us. Oh, Thomas, you'll be gone soon—may I cry now? I must."

Thomas did not seem to have heard her. "I have been wicked, and yet not I," he said. "It was something bad in me that will pass. And the world did provoke me terribly; it would be so emotional and stupid."

Mary was crying unreservedly, but Thomas did not notice it.

"Something," he said, "has come into my head which wants thinking out, but I will not bother myself. I have the easier way. Goodbye—for the sake of old times—Mary, darling. I am going to know everything."

Then he curled up his legs quietly, and died.

Mary stopped crying, and examined the body. Yes, he was quite dead. Then she started away on a journey.

Thomas had been a wicked beetle, and he had talked wrongly in his last moments, and she was afraid to be near his body. Besides, she had heard of a vacancy.

The sun had quite finished with the window of that villa now, and the park-like grounds were nearly empty. On one of the courts a few enthusiasts were still playing, and would continue to play until they went in to dress. Out through the gate a young man sauntered into the road. The look of an escaped animal was on his face. He had been talking to a number of people whom he neither knew nor wanted to know. He had seen nothing of Marjorie, his host's daughter, a child who always pleased and generally amused him. He felt that he had done much for his hostess; he had suffered privations. And now he was glad that the bulk of the visitors—all who were not staying in the house—had gone. He took the path across the common, pausing to light a pipe with a wax match and an air of relief. He walked in the direction of the spot where the dead body of Thomas was lying.

One of the two unkempt birds came slowly flying back again. It was he to whom the surname of Magnanimity has been given. He had got rid of his companion by some pretext of an appointment, and he had come back again to look for that beetle. He swooped down close beside the dead body of the insect, and turned it over with his beak.

"That's just my luck," he murmured softly. "I never could stand cold meat." But that was affectation.

At this moment a small stone struck the ground within a foot of where the unkempt bird was standing. He hopped away in an aggrieved fashion.

"I won't fly away yet," he said sulkily, "it would only make the man conceited. They're always chucking stones, these fools of men, and they hardly ever hit anything. They like to think that we're afraid of them, and I'm not the least bit afraid."

Another stone missed by a sixteenth of an inch the bird's tail-feathers, and Magnanimity with one scream of bad language flew upwards. When he got there, he found that his nervous and unkempt companion had come back again, and had been watching him all the time. Then the magnanimous fowl swore worse than ever. There was no doubt that the nervous one would have a pretty story to tell about that pretended appointment.

The young man, who had thrown the stones, sauntered slowly up and surveyed the dead beetle, taking it in his hand to examine it more closely. He knew something about beetles—he had collected them in his schooldays—and he saw that this was a large one of its kind, a fine specimen. He slipped it into one of his coat pockets, and strolled slowly back again to the house. He had originally meant to go further, but he had changed his intention. He was comparing in his own mind his favourite Marjorie, a child not quite fifteen, with the finished and ordinary girl as turned out in large numbers for the purposes of suburban tennis. He was also wondering casually why there were any beetles in the world, and why he had once been so interested in them.

When he got back to the house, he paused in the hall for a second, and then went slowly upstairs to a room at the top of the house, used as a schoolroom by Marjorie and her governess, Miss Dean.

Marjorie was seated at the table writing. She had a large French dictionary by her side. She was dressed in dark blue serge. Her long hair had become a little untidy in her struggle to be idiomatic. She had a pale, intelligent face. She looked up as the young man entered.

"I'm awfully glad you've come," she said, smiling. "It was getting rather dull, being all alone. Did you have some good setts?"

"No, not particularly—didn't play much. I talked, and made myself useful, and ate ices, and drank things most of the time. You can't see like that." He struck a match, and lit the gas, and then he seated himself at the piano. "Where's Miss Dean?"

"Oh, she went away as usual at half-past five, and left me this stuff to do for tomorrow. I'm doing it now, because I am going to be down in the drawing-room tonight. Only three more days to the holidays!"

"Have you got any tea?"

Marjorie nodded her head towards a table at the side of the room. "They brought it up about an hour ago," she said. "It's quite cold—will you ring for some more?"

"No, thanks," he answered, as he got up and helped himself. "This will do very well. I am not really thirsty, because, as I said, I have been drinking during the whole of the afternoon—more or less. But I never feel absolutely sociable unless I am either smoking or drinking. Have you got much more to do for the estimable one?"

"Oh, no, only a few words. It was a shorter bit than usual, and I expected to have got it finished ever so long ago. But when it came to doing it, there were a lot of words that I'd never seen before. I know the French for a plate, or a glass, or a horse, or a hat, or anything like that. But I always have to look up words like buttercup or gridiron. Now here's a word of that kind. What's the French for beetle?"

"*Escarbot*, I believe, but" I wouldn't swear to it."

"Look here, Maurice," Marjorie said very earnestly, leaning her pretty little chin on one hand, "I'll tell you what I've noticed. When a thing's different in one way, it's always different in another. If a piece for translation is extra short, there are always more words to look up. If I have an awfully bad morning, and Miss Dean is savage, and Aunt Julia patronises me, and Miss Matthieson makes me kiss her—bah!— I'm always glad at the end of it, because I know I am going to have a specially good afternoon or evening."

"Marjorie, I believe you're right. You'll have a bad morning to-morrow if that wretched piece about the gridirons and beetles isn't done for the inestimable Dean."

"Well, I'll finish in less than two minutes. Play something while I'm doing it."

He opened the piano and took down the first piece that came. It was a drawing-room piece, and had the entire absence of soul which always appealed to the corresponding vacuum in the chilly Miss Dean. It was moderately difficult, and sounded *very* difficult. Miss Dean well knew that when a girl like Marjorie, not yet fifteen, played that piece properly, it would be acknowledged to reflect great credit on her teacher. Maurice Grey opened the piece, looked at it suspiciously, skipped the introduction, played a few bars from the first page, glanced at the fifth page, then shut it up, and put it back again on the top of the piano with a sigh.

"I hate that too," said Marjorie. "Play the thing you played to them last night in the drawing-room."

"You weren't in the drawing-room last night."

"No, but my bedroom's just above, and I could hear it. It went like this." She hummed a few bars.

Maurice began to play once more. It was a mischievous, tender, eccentric little dance that went laughing about the piano as if it were mad. Marjorie had finished her work, and rose from the table and stood beside him, watching him with dark, attentive eyes as he played. She was thinking that she liked Maurice. He knew the right way to treat her. Aunt Julia treated her like a baby, and other visitors often appeared to be under the impression that children like inanity. Her father was rather an apathetic man, yet he had the sincerest affection for his wife, his only daughter, and young Maurice Grey. He had many acquaintances, but no other friends.

He had been "Meyner and Sons," who did great things in iron, but he disposed of his business to a company soon after his marriage. He was absorbed in the study of psychology, and made many curious experiments upon himself. In one or two of these young Maurice had been of some service to him. But in his family affections, his studies, or his experiments, he showed very little enthusiasm. He never expected to get great results.

"The evidence is so bad," he said to Maurice once, speaking of his favourite pursuit. "On my subject men lie often intentionally; and often deceive themselves and lie unintentionally, and rarely speak the truth. Also, I find out more and more that I cannot even trust my own senses. The human brain is a shockingly defective instrument."

He was a little sensitive, and to visitors in his house—with the exception of Maurice—he would talk of anything but psychology. Psychology, he found, was a thing they never understood at all, and at which they generally laughed. Marjorie's mother, Mrs. Meyner, was not so apathetic or so pessimistic, but then her horizon was not extended. The circle of her friends and relations gave her enough to think about and to make life worth living. She was a very gentle, unselfish woman, and had a provoking knack of sincerely liking nearly everybody. Her half-sister, Julia, had the opposite knack of hating nearly everybody. Julia was old and unmarried, and had a wonderful tongue; she dressed perfectly, had snowy hair, a kind face, a sweet smile, gentle ways, and a perfectly venomous disposition. Marjorie did not like her Aunt Julia. She did not like Miss Matthieson much better—a sentimental woman. Miss Dean was too chilly a person to like exactly; Marjorie respected her sometimes. But she did like Maurice, and she liked the music that he was playing now.

"That is awfully nice," she said, when the piece was finished. "What is it?"

Marjorie's Aunt Julia had asked the same question of him the night before in the drawing-room, and he had told her that the piece was by Grieg, which was untrue, and which he knew to be untrue. He was not aware that that cheerful, spiteful, and horribly intellectual old lady also knew that he was lying. He had felt it better to blaspheme the name of Grieg than to give her a chance by owning that he had composed the thing himself. He was a young man of dangerously diverse talents. He was just at the end of his first year at Cambridge, and was reading for the Classical Tripos. Now the Classical Tripos is a jealous mistress, and admits of no rivals. Nevertheless, he had become a very fair oar, was socially popular, and had devoted much time to psychology and more to music. The end of such a course is generally failure. He did not mind telling Marjorie about the little dance he had just been playing.

"Well," he said, "I have a general impression that it is mine; but there's a touch of Grieg about it. In fact, I risked telling your Aunt Julia last night that it was Grieg's. I daren't tell her it was mine."

"Yes," said Marjorie sadly, "she is awful. She pats me gently on the head, and tells me I'm a good little child, and that I may run away to the nursery and play. It's perfectly maddening. She knows as well as I do that, I'm nearly fifteen, and that it's absolute nonsense to talk like that. She does it on purpose to make me angry, and I hate being angry."

Maurice took a long sip at his cold tea.

"Yes," he said, "the people in this world want sorting. Have you finished your piece about the beetle and the gridirons?"

"Oh, yes! There's nothing in it really about gridirons, but a beetle comes into it—a dead beetle—"

"By Jove!" said Maurice suddenly, thrusting his hand into his pocket, "that reminds me!" He pulled out the dead body of Thomas, and laid it carefully on the table.

"There," he said, "what do you think of that?"

"It's perfectly horrible," said Marjorie. "Where did you get it? What did you do it for?"

"I strolled on to the common after tennis for a smoke, and I happened to find it. I used to collect these things when I was at school. I suppose I picked it up from force of habit, but I'm sure I don't know. You ought not to call it horrible, you know. It's really a fine specimen of its kind."

Marjorie looked at it more closely, turning it over with the end of a penholder.

"Do you remember saying just now," said Maurice, "that things which were different in one way were generally different in another? Beetles are different from us; they can't do the same things; we despise them; they haven't as good a time. Perhaps they can do things we don't know anything about; perhaps they despise us; perhaps they are going to have a better time in some other world. What are all the stars for?"

Marjorie wrinkled her brows, and kicked one tiny slipper half off.

"I almost think I see what you mean—"

"I am not at all sure I meant anything," said Maurice. "It was just a suggestion."

Marjorie had thrown down the penholder, and taken the body of Thomas in her hand.

"Beetles might have some secrets that we know nothing about. But Miss Dean says that all insects were sent into the world for the birds to eat."

Maurice was silent for a moment. He was remembering that Miss Dean had remarked to him the day before that she considered that the birds had been created to kill the insects. "I should like to talk the question over with a beetle. Now I must be off and dress."

When he had gone an old trick of Marjorie's younger days came back to her. She had often, in her babyhood, held conversations with voiceless or inarticulate things, such as dolls or cats, and on one occasion, after a stormy music lesson, she had made the piano promise to make the music come out right next time. She had always to do the speaking for them, so it was not quite convincing; but it was helpful and consolatory in its way. And now she began to talk to the beetle aloud, holding it on the palm of one little white hand—

"Beetle, tell me your secrets. Tell me all your secrets."

There was silence.

"I want to know if beetles are as good as men. Are they? Are they better than men? Are there better things than we ever think of doing, which we might do if it was only possible to think of them? *Do* tell me. I won't tell anybody, except Maurice and mamma, if she asks me, but she won't. You *might* tell me—it's quite safe."

There was only silence; but then it has been proved already that silence is a beetle's method of speech. Perhaps the spirit of Thomas was there and answered her; perhaps it was elsewhere; perhaps Thomas never had a spirit.

Marjorie put the beetle down again on the table, with a laugh at herself for her silliness.

In the drawing-room that night, she saw very little of Maurice. Aunt Julia looked as perfect and sweet and gentle an old lady as ever; and her conversation was just as poisonous as usual. Her temper must even have been a little worse than normal. She commenced to talk about psychology with Mr. Meyner, because she knew that he hated discussing it with the uninitiated. She insisted that he was joking—the poor man never joked; he was half earnestness and half apathy—and she told him untrue stories.

When he escaped, she fastened on to Miss Matthieson, who was a sentimental and ignorant woman, with a desire to love art. She invented an entirely fictitious picture of Turner, described it, and gave its precise position in the National Gallery; she finally made Miss Matthieson talk about it, become enraptured about it, and confess what her sensations were when she first saw it. She did not enlighten her;

that would have been too crude an enjoyment for Aunt Julia. Her smile became just a little sweeter, and she assured Miss Matthieson that she had learned much from her. Maurice Grey had, for reasons of his own, been playing Chopin's Funeral March. "And is that also by Grieg?" she asked him, looking interested.

"No, it is not," he said shortly. He knew very well that Aunt Julia knew very well what he had been playing; and he saw what she meant by her question.

"Oh, please don't be angry with me," she said. "I'm no musician, you know, Mr. Grey,"—her knowledge of music was, as Maurice was aware, considerably above the average—"and I make stupid mistakes. Last night you played a little dance which you told me was by Grieg. Now, I never should have known it; I thought it was pretty enough, but just a little weak and—well, almost amateurish, you know. You played it again in the schoolroom this afternoon, and you altered the last part of it. What *is* that thing you played just now?"

"Chopin's Funeral March."

"Are you going to make any—any improvements in it, as you did in the Grieg? And why did you play a funeral march? I suppose the sight of an old woman like myself, among so many young people, suggested the thought of death. Ah, yes—very natural."

This was absolutely intolerable, but Maurice was not allowed to protest or escape.

"It is a great mistake," said Aunt Julia, earnestly, "to give one's self up to trivialities. We must all die. It is always better to think about death, even in the drawing-room after dinner. I mean that it's better for the aged, like myself. To the young it might perhaps seem a little gloomy and morbid, but I like it—I enjoy it. I shall be going to bed directly. Won't you play a few hymn tunes, Mr. Grey, before I go? You might play the *Dies Irae*."

She did not go to bed until she had maddened about half the people in the room. Even Mrs. Meyner found it difficult at times to make excuses for Aunt Julia. Maurice Grey managed to be moderately polite to her as a rule; he generally shammed stupidity, and refused to see the point of any of her sarcasms. He found afterwards that this style of treatment had impressed Miss Julia Stone. When Marjorie came round to say goodnight to Maurice, she spoke to him about the beetle.

"Do you want that dead beetle?" she asked. "Shall I keep it for you?"

"Yes, keep it."

"Are you going on collecting again then?"

"No, I don't think so—but it is too good a specimen to throw away just anywhere. How would you like to be thrown away?"

"It's not quite the same thing, you know, Maurice. I'm more important. But we'll treat this beetle very well—you've just played a funeral march for it—and then, perhaps, its ghost will come and tell us all about beetles, and what beetles think about men, and if they know anything that we don't."

"Yes, treat it kindly," said Maurice, smiling. "Much can always be done by kindness."

Marjorie went out of the room laughing; but on the following morning, when she appeared at breakfast, she was very quiet and subdued. A note came from Miss Dean, regretting that—"owing to a slight indisposition"—she was unable to come to teach Marjorie that morning. Even the prospect of a day's holiday did not seem to cheer her up. Maurice found her alone in the garden about an hour afterwards.

"What's up, Marjorie?" he said. "Aren't you well?"

"Oh, yes, I'm always well—I've got something to tell you though. I saw it last night."

"Saw what?"

"The beetle."

Maurice was a little startled. He too had had a curious dream in which the beetle had figured. "Look here, Marjorie," he said; "I've nothing particular to do this morning, and I believe you'd be the better for a walk. We'll go over to Weyford, and then go up to St. Margaret's, if you don't mind climbing the hill."

"Oh, that would be lovely! That's just the thing. We shan't get back to lunch, you know."

"That's all right. We'll lunch in Weyford. I'll go in and talk to Mrs. Meyner about it, and you go and get ready."

The morning sunlight and the cool wind made walking pleasant. That unkempt bird, whom we have called Magnanimity, was taking out quite a young bird for a little exercise. They saw Maurice and Marjorie walking together.

"Those are men," said the young bird. "Bless your heart—I've seen lots of 'em."

"Just drop that," said Magnanimity, sternly. "There's nothing more sickening than to hear a mere chick like yourself setting up to be a complete bird of the world. Fancy taking any notice of contemptible,

116

ugly men!"

"That young she-man," said the mere chick, "isn't at all ugly. I often wish I were a man."

"You'd soon wish you were a bird again," retorted Magnanimity. "Are you aware that men can't fly, or lay eggs, or talk our language, or do anything really worth doing? Are you aware that we old birds lead them the very devil of a life?"

"How do you do it?" asked the mere chick, quite unable to keep the wonder and admiration out of the tone of its voice.

"Why, we mock at 'em—sneer at 'em till they can't bear themselves."

Marjorie and Maurice walked on, talking of indifferent things. They climbed the hill, resting occasionally in the shade of the plantations that grew on its sides. They reached the summit at last, a solitary place where the ruined chapel of St. Margaret stood in a little deserted grave-yard. The wind was fresh and cool. They could see far away into the distance; they could see the river winding along down the valley, until it was a mere thread of silver; they could see the smoke curling up from low, red-roofed cottages and farm-buildings, scattered here and there. Maurice stretched himself at full length on the grass, and endeavoured to light a cigarette. There was just enough wind to blow a match out. There always is.

"Now then, Marjorie, you had a dream last night."

"Yes!"

"And it frightened you."

"No—no—well, it didn't exactly frighten me—it made me think. It was all nonsense, you know, and yet it was the realest dream I ever had in my life."

"Stop a minute. You had some coffee in the drawing-room, and that kept you awake for a long time, you turned about from side to side, and thought about the beetle. Your bedroom seemed hot and stifling."

"Yes, that's all true—how did you know, Maurice?—but it has not got anything to do with it."

"Marjorie, if you'd never had that coffee, you'd have never had that dream. Now, then, let's hear it. I'll try to keep awake, but walking always makes me sleepy."

"After I had said goodnight to everybody, I went up into the schoolroom and got the beetle, because I was afraid the servants might throw it away in the morning, and you said you wanted it. I took it into my own room, and put it down on a table. All the while I was undressing, I kept thinking about it and wondering if beetles and other things could really understand, or if it were only men and women who knew about things, and if all the world were just made for us alone. Before I got into bed I picked the beetle up, and said to it, 'Beetle, you've got to come into my dream tonight, and tell me all about it. Don't forget.' Of course, that was just a fancy. I didn't really think it could understand what I said, or that it would come. I'm not a baby, though Aunt Julia treats me like one sometimes. Well, for a long time I couldn't get to sleep, but at last I did."

"And then the beetle came and suffocated you, or threw you over a precipice," remarked Maurice, drowsily.

"No, that's not a bit like it. I don't know how long I had been asleep, but I dreamed that I woke up suddenly, and that the moonlight was streaming in at the window. Right in the middle of the moonlight was the beetle, standing up on his hind legs. He had grown ever so much bigger, and was as tall as I am. 'Come on, now,' he said. 'How much longer are you going to keep me waiting? I'm late, as it is.'

"I didn't feel the least bit afraid of him. I just asked him where we were going. He opened the window, and pointed upwards. 'Well,' I said, you must wait till I'm dressed, else I shall catch cold.' However, he wouldn't wait, and so I got out of bed. We climbed up on to the table in front of the window. 'Now then,' he said, 'you must keep hold of my fore leg, or you'll fall.' We didn't fly or walk; we floated out of the window, and then upwards, going very quickly and steadily, as if a wind were blowing us. As we were floating up, the beetle's head changed till it became just like Aunt Julia's. 'Marjorie's an unnatural child,' it said in Aunt Julia's voice. 'She doesn't care for dolls doesn't care for anything except music and Maurice.'"

Maurice had an unworthy and needless impression that the girl was making some of this up. He looked at her curiously, as though he were going to say something; but he refrained, and she continued her dream—

"I didn't quite know what to say, but I told the beetle that he was entirely wrong—that I liked papa and mamma very much indeed, and rather liked almost everybody. Then I asked him how he managed to speak, being a beetle, and how he could hear me speak. He told me that neither of us had spoken a word: when I contradicted him, he said that if I had gone back to my own room, I should have found that my real body was still lying asleep in bed. 'Now,' he pointed out, 'you can't speak without your body—so that is proved.'Then he said that beetles never spoke, and that as a matter of fact we were not speaking, but just understanding each other's silence. Still, it seemed just like speaking.

"We must have moved very quickly, because by this time we had got quite beyond the moon. I could see it ever so far beneath my feet, and the stars all scattered about the darkness; yet I didn't remember passing them on our way up. I didn't feel at all cold. As the beetle went on talking—it was just like real talking, so it doesn't matter whether it was real—or not he stopped being like Aunt Julia. He got his own head back again, and his own voice—except that sometimes it began to be rather like yours. You haven't gone to sleep, have you?"

Maurice had not gone to sleep, and said so.

"The strangest thing was that although his body had not really changed—except that it was so much bigger—it didn't seem at all ugly now. In fact, I liked to look at it, and didn't at all mind keeping hold of its fore-leg. I think the beetle must have known what I was thinking about, for all of a sudden he said, as if he were sorry for me: 'Poor Marjorie! Poor little Marjorie! They've taught you all wrong, and they taught me all wrong. But I had a glimpse of the right thing: I always knew that human beings were not half as ugly as they seemed to be. I said as much, but it was of no use to talk to the Dear Friend. As for Mary—that fat-headed female had believed so many other things that she had no capacity left for believing any more. I, however, had got plenty of room left—oh, yes, plenty of room.' When he said that he chuckled in the most horrible way you ever heard. 'Now I come to think of it,' he went on, 'I believe I did *say* that the human breed were ugly. It was such a tame thing to believe anything that one said; it was a thing that Mary always did, and so I didn't. Marjorie, if the good people hadn't been good, I should have liked goodness.'"

"But who were Mary and the Dear Friend?" asked Maurice.

"I don't know any more than you do. I don't think he liked the Dear Friend very much; sometimes he seemed to hate Mary, and sometimes he seemed to love her and pity her. Now do you know what he told me? He said positively that all beetles believed that they had souls which never died, and that the sun, and stars, and everything were made for them alone. They believed that men, and other animals, had no souls at all. I told him how very absurd that was, and tried to explain to him what was really the case; but he only chuckled horribly again. But as we went up higher and higher, he got more grave, and he didn't laugh anymore; and once or twice he said to me quite sadly,

'Poor little Marjorie, you are very young to bother yourself about these things. You only know part—only part—and I cannot tell you the rest—I may not!'

"I began to get quite sorry for him, because it seemed to trouble him; I think he really wanted to tell me some more things. Just then I saw up above us a River of Light. It was flowing very swiftly and smoothly, and looked like melted gold. I don't know why, but I wanted to plunge into the river. It seemed to be the only thing worth doing, or that ever had been worth doing. I never wanted anything so much before in my life, but the beetle would not let me go. Last of all I began to cry; I really did, and you know, Maurice, that I hardly ever cry. But it was of no use; he still kept tight hold of my hand. The darkness was all grey darkness, except one black piece which stuck up like a mountain. We stopped on the top of it, and looked down at the river. I kept on crying—I do not know why, but I think it was because it all seemed strange and awful. I may have been frightened a little, but it was not quite like being frightened. There was a long pause, and then the beetle said, 'Ah, if you only knew now, Marjorie! And if I had only known then!'

"Just then out of the grey darkness came a thread of light, like a little snake, moving very quickly and curling about as if it were glad; it hurried towards the great River of Light, and melted into it and was gone. I was eager about it, and asked the beetle what it was. 'I may tell you that,' he replied. 'It was a soul going home!' I stopped crying then; I felt something the way I feel at an evening service in a church in summer time, when they are singing one of the hymns, I like best. It was a sort of quiet happiness; I can't explain it properly, but I never felt so happy as I did then. 'Beetle,' I said, 'you must tell me the rest now.'

"'I will tell you one thing,'" he said.

"What was it?" asked Maurice quickly.

For a few seconds Marjorie did not answer. There was a queer dreamy look in her eyes. At last, she said,—

"Maurice, I'm afraid you'll think now that I have been making all this up, but I haven't. I can't tell you what the beetle said, because I *don't know*. It was about you, and it was very important. I don't even know whether it was good or bad. It has gone straight out of my memory, and I *can't* get it back again. I'd give anything to be able to remember it. I've been thinking about it all the morning.'

"I believe you entirely," said Maurice thoughtfully. "I have had much the same kind of thing happen to me in a dream."

120

He did not add that much the same thing had happened to him on the same night. "How did the dream end?" he went on.

"I awoke directly after the beetle told me that thing that I have forgotten. It was broad daylight. But when I got up, the beetle was not on the table where I had put it. I could not find it anywhere."

"You probably moved it in your sleep. Did you ever walk in your sleep?"

"Once, when I was quite little—almost a baby. I had got out into the garden, and my nurse found me there."

Maurice rose, and the two went down the hill together. "I wouldn't trouble about all that if I were you," said Maurice. "These things can generally be explained in the simplest way when one goes through them carefully. Coffee, the action of the heart, the position of the body in bed, the sounds that one hears while asleep, all help to explain a good deal, you know."

He did not tell her his own dream. He thought, perhaps rightly, that a young girl, unacquainted with the study of mathematics, might be unduly impressed by coincidences which were unusual but did not require a supernatural explanation. He did not want to frighten her, or let her grow superstitious. Yet during the day he thought a good deal about the two dreams.

He had dreamed that he was seated on the one side of the fireplace in his rooms at Cambridge, and that the beetle, with the same exaggerated dimensions with which Marjorie had seen him, was seated in a lounge chair on the other side. They were discussing Maurice's psychological studies, and Maurice was describing to him some of the curious experiments which he had made in conjunction with Mr. Meyner. Every difficulty that Maurice propounded the beetle made clear at once. He even suggested fresh problems which had not occurred to Maurice before, and was equally ready with their solution. His last words before Maurice awoke were: "There are many things besides which you ought to know, and of which you have not realised your own ignorance. You will know them all one day."

This was all that Maurice could remember of his dream. The difficulties propounded and the explanations given had passed completely out of his recollection. He was only conscious that during his dream he had felt an exhilarating sensation of having known for certain things which he had thought it impossible that anyone, at least in this life, could know at all.

Shortly afterwards he returned to Cambridge. By this time Marjorie seemed to have recovered her normal spirits. She made no further allusion to her dream. She was unaffectedly sorry at the departure of Maurice.

Maurice had not been long at Cambridge before he received news of the sudden death of Mr. Meyner. Apart from the friendship he had always felt for Mr. Meyner, the death seemed to him peculiarly distressing and pathetic. The man had worked hard at a study which fascinated him, not from any desire for gain, or fame to be derived from it, but with the most genuine devotion to the study itself; and he had died before his work was done, before he had arrived at any large and definite result. Yet Maurice felt assured that Meyner's patience, and judgment, and freedom from prejudice, would, if he had but lived longer, have brought him some reward, some light. He had always distrusted and undervalued himself; his humility was genuine, but almost irritating.

He had been at school, and subsequently at college, with Maurice's guardian, and had first met Maurice when he was a boy of fifteen; the friendship between the boy and the middle-aged man had formed, slowly, but surely, since then; yet, although he gave every sign of his liking for Maurice, he never seemed to expect Maurice to like him in return; he certainly never realised the admiration which Maurice had for his knowledge and attainments. So too he loved his wife and only child dearly, and he knew that they loved him; but he had never realised how much they loved him, and would very possibly have thought such love almost irrational.

To some extent, perhaps, his studies had spoiled him; he had been groping in the darkness after great things, and the one result that he seemed to have found there was a sense of his own insignificance. Yet, illogically enough, he had never thought others insignificant; he had never reached the cynical conclusion that nobody matters very much. If his friends and his sympathies were so few, it was not because the outside world did not matter to him, but because he could not believe that he mattered to the outside world. He had died without ever having learned his own value.

A parcel which was forwarded to Maurice from Mrs. Meyner shortly afterwards contained the many note-books which her husband had filled with the evidence he had collected, and the work he had done, until death interrupted him. With them was a simple and pathetic letter that he had written to Maurice on the day before he died.

"Look through them," the letter said, in reference to the note-books. "You will see and understand what I was aiming at. If you think it worthwhile, carry on the investigation which I began; I own that it is some pleasure to me to think that it is possible that you may do so; that one who was intimate with my views, and who shared some of my opinions, which are not generally held, may be able to give those views and opinions their justification. But I do not want you to pledge yourself in any way, nor do I ask you to give up your tripos or your career at college for the purpose."

Maurice paused as he read this last sentence. How often he had thought, as he turned English verse into indifferent Alcaics, that this classical work could only lead, was only educative, could never be considered as an end. But he came to no final decision until he had spent nearly a month in a rapid survey of those note-books. They startled him; the minute accuracy and patience shown in the collection of evidence were only what he expected from such a man as Meyner, but the brilliant audacity of his theories, the almost savage independence of an original mind, looked far different when plainly stated in black and white, than when they had fallen humbly and almost hesitatingly from the man's own lips.

The romantic side in Maurice's character was touched most by what was worst in Meyner's books; the finished and unprejudiced scholar would have shaken his head over much that looked like vain imagining, that was extravagant, and, so far, unsupported. Maurice was younger; Meyner's fierce opposition of an accepted view attracted him, and awoke his pugnacity. He would linger over page after page of what seemed to him splendid conjecture, of what might have seemed to others very useless stuff, and say to himself: "If only one could prove that this *is* so, instead of longing that it *may* be so!" The air of conviction with which Meyner wrote down his own views on his own subject gained immeasurably in Maurice's eyes from the personal knowledge which Maurice had of Meyner's perpetual tendency to undervalue himself, and to distrust himself in all other matters.

Even with these views in his mind, he had expected no great results; he had been too honest to support them with any evidence that was not thoroughly tested. They seemed to Maurice to be the guess of genius; the air of conviction had for him the strange attraction of a religious, not wholly rational, faith. He decided to abandon his university career, and to devote his time to a further prosecution of Meyner's investigations.

His guardian, who was also his uncle, made very little opposition. Maurice had given so much evidence that he was stable. He had an unusually large allowance for a young man at Cambridge, and yet he had not run into debt. At Cambridge the wealthy are the most in debt, because they have most credit and most temptations. As a matter of fact, Maurice never had considered the financial side of anything; it had simply happened that he had never wanted more than he could well afford. But this weighed very much in Maurice's favour with his guardian. He felt that his nephew was a man who understood value, and could be trusted. The property to which Maurice would succeed, when he came of age, made it unnecessary for him to adopt any profession; nor did it bring with it any of those special responsibilities for which a special training is supposed to be necessary.

Maurice, therefore, spent the next two years abroad, for the most part in Paris. He had carried with him an introduction to a physician at one of the Paris hospitals, who sympathised with him in his work, and was able to be of great assistance to him. In this man he gained a friend; in other respects, these were years, it seemed to him, of disillusion. One by one the great, beautiful theories had to go; a tiny meagre fact would start up, a fact that meant but little to the ordinary observer, and it would be strong enough to overthrow years of work, and send the conjecture on which they were founded to some limbo for lost absurdities. He had long ago been aghast when he had tried to realise how vast is the amount of the things that no man knows. And now for "knows" he put "can know."

Mrs. Meyner and Marjorie had also been abroad, but he had seen them very seldom in those two years. Marjorie seemed to be slowly changing; he was no longer the recipient of childish confidences. She was grave and more beautiful, perhaps, than she had been; and she was also more quiet and reserved; she was friendly with him, up to a limit; she told him news, of a kind; she sympathised with his disappointments in his work, within decent bounds. At the end of the second year, when Mrs. Meyner and Marjorie were staying for a few days in Paris, and Maurice was at last awakening to the fact that he could not expect childish confidences from one who was no longer a child, Marjorie told him some news which surprised him.

"Aunt Julia has changed very much. I like her now."

"She must certainly have changed then," said Maurice smiling.

"I don't mean," Marjorie explained, "that she is different to other people—only to mamma and myself. Her servants are in terror of her, and her tenants hate her, and so on; but she has been really kind to me. I think she likes me. We were staying with her a few weeks ago. You'll be surprised to hear that she likes you too."

"Of course," said Maurice, "it is surprising that anyone likes me, as you say."

"I don't think I said that. She told me quite suddenly once that she liked Maurice Grey, because he was the cleverest man she knew in one respect. Mamma suggested that it was because you understood her. 'No, my dear,' said Aunt Julia, 'the village people do that, because I speak plainly, and they try to pay me back again for it. He always misunderstood me. I like him. He will not do much, because he can't concentrate himself on one thing; but I like Maurice Grey all the same.'"

Marjorie did not repeat any more of Aunt Julia's conversation; but the old lady had gone on to say that Maurice, however, would probably concentrate himself on one person. She added, in her point-blank way, that she intended him ultimately to marry Marjorie. She did not appear to think that Marjorie, or Maurice, or Mrs. Meyner, could have a voice in the matter; the marriage was one of the things that the perverse old woman had made up her mind to arrange.

"I'm glad that dear old lady likes me," said Maurice. "I always liked her—I really did. She was full of such striking and impressive contrasts the soft, purring voice and the ill-tempered words—her gentle, peaceful face and her fearful pugnacity. And I like her more because she has been good to you, you say."

"Did you ever," asked Marjorie, hurriedly going to another subject, "find out anything new about the intelligence of the brute creation?"

"I think I used to tell some lies about a favourite terrier of mine once, and made myself believe them. No, Marjorie, that has not been my line. It has been quite enough to find out that I and you, and all the rest of us, have got no intelligence worth mentioning, none that will do a thousandth part of what we want it to do. What made you ask that?"

"I was thinking about that beetle you found on the common when you were stopping with us once, and about the dream I had."

"Ah! I remember that."

"I never found the dead beetle, although I hunted everywhere for it, and I never remembered what it told me about you."

"I did not tell you at the time, Marjorie, but I had a dream about the beetle that same night. It came to me that night and told me everything I wanted to know—the things I have been working at for the last two years. Of course, they were all gone when I awoke, but I can remember it saying that I should know them all one day. I am afraid that dead beetle lied."

"Maurice," said Marjorie suddenly, "sometimes a thought flashes across my mind that in a minute I may be dead. I don't know even what life and death mean; yet I have to live and die. There are stars above me, but I do not know why they are there. There are beasts, and birds, and insects everywhere, and I do not know how important they are. I feel lost and horrible. No, I feel like a prisoner beating against an iron wall. For a few moments it is torture to be like that; I should kill myself or go mad if it went on. But it always passes away, and three minutes afterwards I am wondering if I will do my hair a different way—"

"Don't!" murmured Maurice, softly.

"Or I can be really angry because my maid knocks something over, or does something clumsy; when one speaks of it, it seems absurd enough. Speaking spoils everything. Lovers—in books, I mean—talk the worst nonsense, and yet that nonsense is the expression of a very fine thing. I do not think that silence is enough appreciated. I want, for instance, to let you know what I am thinking. Well, when I put the thought into words, I lose some of it, or add something to it, or I alter it by an accident with the tone of my voice. Now if I could just look at you and you at me, and we could understand one another exactly through silence, it would be splendid."

Maurice agreed with her. After two years of disappointment silence seemed to him almost the only thing left. There was, however, one thing even more consolatory. About a year after this conversation with Marjorie the two met once more, and Maurice put his failures behind him and told Marjorie that he loved her. So, they both spoke the nonsense which they deprecated. We all believe that in affairs of the heart we are not as the others, and we are all mistaken. With him there was an iteration of "I love you," with a deep tremble in the voice; and with her there was a sighing echo of the same words, coming up between blushes.

The expression of the feeling was almost ludicrous; the feeling itself was so sacred that the lightest touch of thought seemed to soil it, and a writer, after turning over his vocabulary in disgust, can find nothing explanatory which at all matches it. But when it took place, it seemed to Maurice the only important thing that ever had happened to him; the psychological studies, which had brought him so much disappointment, appeared in a new light as a plaything that had seemed to amuse him until love came.

This did not happen at Paris. Maurice had returned to England, and all of them—Mrs. Meyner, Marjorie, and Maurice—were staying in Aunt Julia's house. It was a lonely old house, much too big for that one wicked old lady; it stood outside a North Yorkshire village, just where a grand, dignified old hill drew back its skirts, with a sharp sweep, from contamination with human dwelling-places. Aunt Julia owned quarries at the foot of the hill, and got therefrom more money than was good for her. The time was December, and the moors looked bleak and cold. But it was a comfortable house. Aunt Julia had devoted her many years to the study of comfort—her own comfort.

"There is nothing to shoot," she explained to Maurice, "except my tenants down in the village. You can shoot them, if you like. There's the library, though, which is good, and you can smoke anywhere you like—"

"But you used to hate smoking?" said Maurice.

"My dear Maurice, there are two of me, and you used to know the wrong one. Down in the village they mostly know the wrong one, and they call her, I am told, the hellcat, which is rude of them. Yes, you can smoke anywhere. If you and Marjorie want to go out of the house—which is a thing, I never do in December—I believe there are some horses round at the back. If there is anything wrong about the horses, or Pilkin, or anything that is his, just tell me, and I will say a word or two. I believe the man presumes on my ignorance. You can go and see my quarries, or my cottages; but you had better not go to the cottages, because they have no drains. I should like to give them some drains, but the tenants won't let me. They are poor people, and a strong smell makes a difference to their colourless existence."

So, Maurice did a certain amount of reading, riding, and smoking. But, of course, Marjorie made for him the chief charm of the house. Mrs. Meyner had willingly consented to the engagement; even if she had desired to oppose it, her more strenuous half-sister would have reasoned her out of it; or, to use her own gentle euphemism, would have said a word or two. The days passed quietly enough. To Maurice they were a pleasant rest after his three years of wasted laboriousness.

"Marjorie," he said to her one afternoon, when they had wandered over the dignified hill, and as they came back saw the bare boughs of the trees in the plantation black against a red blot of sunset,

"Marjorie, I have done with all questions. I am here, and you are here, and that is enough for me. I am going to live and love, and enjoy. Blessed be my fate that has saved me from the sordid worry of life. (Just wait a second, will you? can't get a match to light in this wind.) We will make a beautiful house, with beautiful things in it, with good books on shelves, and good wine in the cellar, and a good cook in the kitchen. And no one shall enter into that house who is not either very beautiful, or very clever, or too good for this world."

"But I shall be so lonely there without you," said Marjorie, gently, with her sparkling eyes looking groundwards.

Maurice laughed. "Ah, Marjorie, you and I will be one, and you are more beautiful, and clever, and better than anyone in the world. That is how I shall have a right to come into my own beautiful house. We will trouble ourselves with no theories about anything. We will not get excited about anything; an excited man always has been, or will be, dull. We will make life one long, gentle enjoyment."

He spoke half in jest and half in earnest, telling his soul of beautiful things laid up in that house for many years; bidding himself to eat, and drink, and enjoy judiciously.

Perhaps it was because Marjorie at that moment looked towards the sunset. It seemed so far away from her, and yet so desirable. She had the fancy, common among children and poets, that the dying light looked the gate of some wonderful place to be seen hereafter.

"Maurice, Maurice!" she cried. "Look at that. I have the lost, prisoned feeling again when I look at it. It is too far away."

That night ended all. There were beautiful things to come, so it seemed to both of them, such poetry and love as never had been before; and all was stopped by an accident, one commonplace accident, almost too poor to be put into a story.

Marjorie had been subdued, almost depressed; she had talked but little at dinner or afterwards. Mrs. Meyner and Marjorie both went to bed rather early. Maurice, restless from his love-passion, had gone to walk and smoke for an hour on the fell-side. Aunt Julia sat before the fire in the drawing-room, waiting for Maurice to return, reading a favourite chapter of Gibbon.

For some time, one would have said that Marjorie was sleeping quietly and peacefully. Then suddenly she sat up in bed, her eyes still closed. She began talking in her sleep. "Tell me! Come back again and tell me. I *will* know. I am on the verge, and—and—." She stopped talking; quickly she moved from the bed to the dressing-table, and her fingers fumbled impatiently with the opening of her dressing-case. She had drawn up the blind, and the moonlight shone straight upon her. Her lips were still moving, but no sound came. She opened the dressing-case and took from it a glass jar which was filled with old dead rose leaves. She had filled it herself long before, when she was a child. She unscrewed the silver top, and began to take out the rose leaves very carefully. At the bottom of the jar, she found the thing for which she had been looking, and laid it on the palm of her little white hand. It was the withered body of a large dead beetle.

For a moment she stood thus. And then she drew a long breath, and opened her eyes wide. She was awake, and she had remembered the horrible thing which she had heard in a dream and had forgotten. Quivering and almost breathless she hurried from the room, just as she was.

Aunt Julia had good nerves, but she was a little startled when the door of the drawing-room was flung open, and she saw, standing in the doorway, the figure of Marjorie, white-robed, bare-footed, with both hands stretched out, and struggling in vain, as it seemed, to speak.

"Marjorie! What is it?" cried Aunt Julia in a shaking voice.

She found words at last.

"Maurice is dead—dead! He fell—I saw him fall—over there, against the plantation, down into the quarry. He is dead!"

There followed a burst of hysterical laughter, more bitter than any tears, and then she fainted away.

★★★★★★★★★★★★★

Aunt Julia stood in the porch, looking out. She was white to the lips. By the moonlight she could see the procession coming nearer—two men carrying lanterns, four men carrying a hurdle with a burden upon it, covered up altogether because it was broken and ghastly.

The Grey Cat

I heard this story from Archdeacon M———. I should imagine that it would not be very difficult, by trimming it a little and altering the facts here and there, to make it capable of some simple explanation; but I have preferred to tell it as it was told to me.

After all, there is some explanation possible, even if there is not one definite and simple explanation clearly indicated. It must rest with the reader whether he will prefer to believe that some of the so-called uncivilized races may possess occult powers transcending anything of which the so-called civilized are capable, or whether he will consider that a series of coincidences is sufficient to account for the extraordinary incidents which, in a plain brief way, I am about to relate. It does not seem to me essential to state which view I hold myself, or if I hold neither, and have reasons for not stating a third possible explanation.

I must add a word or two with regard to Archdeacon M———. At the time of this story, he was in his fiftieth year. He was a fine scholar, a man of considerable learning. His religious views were remarkably broad; his enemies said remarkably thin. In his younger days he had been something of an athlete, but owing to age, sedentary habits, and some amount of self-indulgence, he had grown stout, and no longer took exercise in any form. He had no nervous trouble of any kind. His death, from heart disease, took place about three years ago. He told me the story twice, at my request; there was an interval of about six weeks between the two narrations; some of the details were elicited by questions of my own. With this preliminary note, we may proceed to the story.

★★★★★★★★★★★★

In January, 1881, Archdeacon M———, who was a great admirer of Tennyson's poetry, came up to London for a few days, chiefly in order to witness the performance of *The Cup*, at the Lyceum. He was not present on the first night (Monday, January 3), but on a later night in the same week. At that time, of course, the poet had not received his peerage, nor the actor his knighthood.

On leaving the theatre, less satisfied with the play than with the magnificence of the setting, the archdeacon found some slight difficulty in getting a cab. He walked a little way down the Strand to find one, when he encountered unexpectedly his old friend, Guy Breddon.

Breddon (that was not his real name) was a man of considerable fortune, a member of the learned societies, and devoted to Central African exploration. He was two or three years younger than the archdeacon, and a man of tremendous physique.

Breddon was surprised to find the archdeacon in London, and the archdeacon was equally surprised to find Breddon in England at all. Breddon carried off the archdeacon with him to his rooms, and sent a servant in a cab to the Langham to pay the archdeacon's bill and fetch his luggage. The archdeacon protested, but faintly, and Breddon would not hear of his hospitality being refused.

Breddon's rooms were an expensive suite immediately over a ruinous upholsterer's in a street off Berkeley Square. There was a private street-door, and from it a private staircase to the first and second floors.

The suite of rooms on the first floor, occupied by Breddon, was entirely shut off from the staircase by a door. The second-floor suite, tenanted by an Irish M. P., was similarly shut off, and at that time was unoccupied.

Breddon and the archdeacon passed through the street-door and up the stairs to the first landing, from whence, by the staircase-door, they entered the flat. Breddon had only recently taken the flat, and the archdeacon had never been there before. It consisted of a broad L-shaped passage with rooms opening into it. There were many trophies on the walls. Horned heads glared at them; stealthy but stuffed beasts watched them furtively from under tables. There was a perfect arsenal of murderous weapons gleaming brightly under the shaded gaslights.

Breddon's servant prepared supper for them before leaving for the Langham, and soon the two men were discussing Mr. Tennyson, Mr. Irving, and a parody of the *Queen of the May* which had recently appeared in *Punch*, and doing justice to some oysters, a cold pheasant with an excellent salad, and a bottle of '74 Pommery. It was characteristic of the archdeacon that he remembered exactly the items of the supper, and that Breddon rather neglected the wine.

After supper they passed into the library, where a bright fire was burning. The archdeacon walked towards the fire, rubbing his plump hands together. As he did so, a portion of the great rug of grey fur on which he was standing seemed to rise up. It was a grey cat of enormous size, larger than any that the archdeacon had ever seen before, and of the same colour as the rug on which it had been sleeping. It rubbed itself affectionately against the archdeacon's leg, and purred as he bent down to stroke it.

'What an extraordinary animal!' said the archdeacon. 'I had no idea cats could grow to this size. Its head's queer, too—so much too small for the body.'

'Yes,' said Breddon, 'and his feet are just as much too big.'

The grey cat stretched himself voluptuously under the archdeacon's caressing hand, and the feet could be seen plainly. They were very broad, and the claws, which shot out, seemed unusually powerful and well developed. The beast's coat was short, thick, and wiry.

'Most extraordinary!' the archdeacon repeated.

He lowered himself into a comfortable chair by the fire. He was still bending over the cat and playing with it when a slight chink made him look up. Breddon was putting something down on the table behind the liquor decanters.

'Any particular breed?' the archdeacon asked.

'Not that I know of. Freakish, I should say. We found him on board the boat when I left for home—may have come there after mice. He'd have been thrown overboard but for me. I got rather interested in him. Smoke?'

'Oh, thank you.'

Outside a cold north wind screamed in quick gusts. Within came the sharp scratch of the match on the ribbed glass as the archdeacon lit his cigar, the bubble of the rose-water in Breddon's *hookah*, the soft step of Breddon's man carrying the archdeacon's luggage into the bedroom at the end of the L-shaped passage, and the constant purring of the big grey cat.

'And what's the cat's name?' the archdeacon asked.

Breddon laughed.

'Well, if you must have the plain truth, he's called Grey Devil—or, more frequently. Devil *tout court.*'

'Really, now, really, you can't expect an archdeacon to use such abominable language. I shall call him Grey—or perhaps Mr. Grey would be more respectful, seeing the shortness of our acquaintance. Do you object to the smell of smoke, Mr. Grey? The intelligent beast does not object. Probably you've accustomed him to it.'

133

'Well, seeing what his name is he could hardly object to smoke, could he?'

Breddon's servant entered. As the door opened and shut, one heard for a moment the crackle of the newly-lit fire in the room that awaited the archdeacon. The servant swept up the hearth, and, under archidiaconal direction, mixed a lengthy brandy-and-soda. He retired with the information that he would not be wanted again that night.

'Did you notice,' asked the archdeacon, 'the way Mr. Grey followed your man about? I never saw a more affectionate cat.'

'Think so?' said Breddon. 'Watch this time.'

For the first time he approached the grey cat, and stretched out his hand as if to pet him. In an instant the cat seemed to have gone mad. Its claws shot out, its back hooped, its coat bristled, its tail stood erect; it cursed and spat, and its small green eyes glared. But a close observer would have noticed that all the time it watched not only Breddon, but also that object which had chinked as Breddon had put it down behind the decanters.

The archdeacon lay back in his chair and laughed heartily.

'What funny creatures they are, and never so funny as when they lose their tempers! Really, Mr. Grey, out of respect to my cloth, you might have refrained from swearing like that. Poor Mr. Grey! Poor puss!'

Breddon resumed his seat with a grim smile. The grey cat slowly subsided, and then thrust its head, as though demanding sympathy, into the fat palm of the archdeacon's dependent hand.

Suddenly the archdeacon's eye lighted on the object which the cat had been watching, visible now that the servant had displaced the decanters.

'Goodness me!' he exclaimed, 'you've got a revolver there.'

'That is so,' said Breddon.

'Not loaded, I trust?'

'Oh yes, fully loaded.'

'But isn't that very dangerous?'

'Well, no; I'm used to these things, and I'm not careless with them. I should have thought it more dangerous to have introduced Gray Devil to you without it. He's much more powerful than an ordinary cat, and I fancy there's something beside cat in his pedigree. When I bring a stranger to see him, I keep the cat covered with the revolver until I see how the land lies. To do the brute justice, he has always been most friendly with everybody except myself. I'm his only antipathy.

He'd have gone for me just now but that he's smart enough to be afraid of this.'

He tapped the revolver.

'I see,' said the archdeacon seriously, 'and can guess how it happened. You scared him one day by firing the revolver for joke; the report frightened him, and he's never forgiven you or forgotten the revolver. Wonderful memory some of these animals have!'

'Yes,' said Breddon, 'but that guess won't do. I have never, intentionally or by chance, given the "Devil" any reason for his enmity. So far as I know he has never heard a firearm, and certainly he has never heard one since I made his acquaintance. Somebody may have scared him before, and I'm inclined to think that somebody did, for there can be no doubt that the brute knows all that a cat need know about a revolver, and that he's scared of it.

'The first time we met was almost in darkness. I'd got some cases that I was particular about, and the captain had said I could go down to look after them. Well, this beast suddenly came out of a lump of black and flew at me. I didn't even recognise that it was a cat, because he's so mighty big. I fetched him a clip on the side of the head that knocked him off, and whipped out my iron. He was away in a streak. He knew. And I've had plenty of proof since that he knows. He'd bite me now if he had the chance, but he understands that he hasn't got the chance. I'm often half inclined to take him on plain—shooting barred—and to feel my own hands breaking his damned neck!'

'Really, old man, really!' said the archdeacon in perfunctory protest, as he rose and mixed himself another drink.

'Sorry to use strong language,' but I don't love that cat, you know.'

The archdeacon expressed his surprise that in that case Breddon did not get rid of the brute.

'You come across him on board ship and he flies at you. You save his life, give him board and lodging, and he still hates you so much that he won't let you touch him, and you are no fonder of him than he is of you. Why don't you part company?'

'As for his board, I've known him to eat anything except his own kill. He goes out hunting every night. I keep him simply and solely because I'm afraid of him. As long as I can keep him, I know my nerves are all right. If I let my funk of him make any difference—well, I shouldn't be much good in a Central African forest. At first, I had some idea of taming him—and, besides, there was a queer coincidence.'

He rose and opened the window, and Grey Devil slowly slunk up to it. He paused a few moments on the window-sill and then suddenly sprang and vanished.

'What was the coincidence?'

'What do you think of that?'

Breddon handed the archdeacon a figure of a cat which he had taken from the mantelpiece. It was a little thing about three inches high. In colour, in the small head, enormous feet, and curiously human eyes, it seemed an exact reproduction of Grey Devil.

'A perfect likeness. How did you get it made?'

'I got the likeness before I got the original. A little Jew dealer sold it me the night before I left for England. He thought it was Egyptian, and described it as an idol. Anyhow, it was a niceish piece of jade.'

'I always thought jade was bright green.'

'It may be—or white—or brown. It varies. I don't think there can be any doubt that this little figure is old, though I doubt if it's Egyptian.'

Breddon put it back in its place.

'By the way, that same night the little Jew came to try and buy it back again. He offered me twice what I had given for it. I said he must have found somebody who was pretty keen on it. I asked if it was a collector. The Jew thought not; said it was a coloured gentleman. Well, that finished it. I wasn't going to do anything to oblige a foreigner. The Jew pleaded that he was a particularly fine gentleman, with mountains of money, who'd been tracking the thing for years, and hinted at all manner of mumbo-jumbo business—to scare me, I suppose. However, I wouldn't listen, and kicked him out. Then came the coincidence. Having bought the likeness, next day I found the living original. Rum, wasn't it?'

At this moment the clock struck, and the archdeacon recognised with horror that it was very, very much past the time when respectable archdeacons should be in bed and asleep. He rose and said goodnight, observing that he'd like to hear more about it on the morrow.

This was extremely unfortunate, for it will be seen it is just at this part of the story that one wants full details, and on the morrow, it became impossible to elicit them.

Before leaving the library Breddon closed the window, and the archdeacon asked how 'Mr. Grey,' as he called him, would get back.

'Very likely he's back already. He's got a special window in the kitchen, made on purpose, just big enough to let him get in and out as he likes.'

'But don't other cats get in, too?'

'No,' said Breddon. 'Other cats avoid Grey Devil.'

The archdeacon found himself unaccountably nervous when he got to his room. He owned to me that he had to satisfy himself that there was no one concealed under the bed or in the wardrobe. However, he got into bed, and after a little while fell into a deep sleep; his fire was burning brightly, and the room was quite light.

Shortly after four he was awakened by a loud scream. Still sleepy, he did not for the moment locate the sound, thinking that it must have come from the street outside. But almost immediately afterwards he heard the report of a revolver fired twice in quick succession, and then, after a short pause, a third time.

The archdeacon was terribly frightened. He did not know what had happened, and thought of armed burglars. For a time—he did not think it could have been more than a minute—fear held him motionless. Then with an effort he rose, lit the gas, and hurried on his clothes. As he was dressing, he heard a step down the passage and a knock at his door.

He opened it, and found Breddon's servant. The man had put on a blue overcoat over his night-things, and wore slippers. He was shivering with cold and terror.

'Oh, my God, sir!' he exclaimed, 'Mr. Breddon's shot himself. Would you come, sir?'

The archdeacon followed the man to Breddon's bedroom. The smoke still hung thickly in the room. A mirror had been smashed, and lay in fragments on the floor. On the bed, with his back to the archdeacon, lay Breddon, dead. His right hand still grasped the revolver, and there was a blackened wound behind the right ear.

When the archdeacon came round to look at the face, he turned faint, and the servant took him out into the library and gave him brandy, the glasses and decanters still standing there. Breddon's face certainly had looked very ghastly; it had been scratched, torn and bitten; one eye was gone, and the whole face was covered with blood.

'Do you think it was that brute did it?'

'Sure of it, sir; sprang on his face while he was asleep. I knew it would happen one of these nights. He knew it too; always slept with the revolver by his side. He fired twice at the brute, but couldn't see for the blood. Then he killed himself

It seemed likely enough, with his eyesight gone, horribly mauled, in an agony of pain, possibly believing that he was saving himself from a death still more horrible, Breddon might very well have turned the weapon on himself.

'What do we do now?' the man asked.

'We must get a doctor and fetch the police at once. Come on.'

As they turned the corner of the passage, they saw that the door communicating with the staircase was open.

'Did you open that door?' asked the archdeacon.

'No,' said the man, aghast.

'Then who did?'

'Don't know, sir. Looks as if we weren't at the end of this yet.'

They passed down the stairs together, and found the street-door also ajar. On the pavement outside lay a policeman slowly recovering consciousness. Breddon's man took the policeman's whistle and blew it. A passing hansom, going back to the mews, slowed up; the cab was sent to fetch a doctor, and communication with the police-station rapidly followed.

The injured policeman told a curious story. He was passing the house when he heard shots fired. Almost immediately afterwards he heard the bolts of the front-door being drawn, and stepped back into the neighbouring doorway. The front-door opened, and a man emerged clad in a grey tweed suit with a grey overcoat. The policeman jumped out, and without a second's hesitation the man felled him. 'It was all done before you could think,' was the policeman's phrase.

'What kind of man?' asked the archdeacon.

'A big man—stood over six foot. He never waited to be challenged; the moment he knew that he was seen he hit out.'

The policeman was not a very intelligent fellow, and there was little more to be got out of him. He had heard the shots, seen the street-door open and the man in grey appear, and had been felled by a lightning blow before he had time to do anything.

The doctor, a plain, matter-of-fact little man, had no hesitation in saying that Breddon was dead, and must have died almost immediately. After the injuries received, respiration and heart-action must have ceased at once. He was explaining something which oozed from the dead man's ear, when the archdeacon could stand it no longer, and staggered out into the library. There he found Breddon's servant, still in the blue overcoat, explaining to a policeman with a notebook that as far as he knew nothing was missing except a jade image or idol of a cat which formerly stood on the mantelpiece.

The cat known as 'Grey Devil' was also missing, and, although a description of it was circulated in the public press, nothing was ever heard of it again. But grey fur was found in the clenched left hand of the dead man.

The inquest resulted in the customary verdict, and brought to light no new facts. But it may be as well to give what the police theory of the case was. According to the police the suicide took place much as Breddon's servant had supposed. Mad with pain and unable to bear the thought of his awful mutilation, Breddon had shot himself.

The story of the jade image, as far as it was known, was told at the inquest. The police held that this image was an idol, that some uncivilized tribe was much perturbed by the theft of it, and was ready to pay an enormously high price for its recovery. The foreigner was assumed to be aware of this, and to have determined to obtain possession of the idol by fair means or foul. Fair means failing, it was suggested that he followed Breddon to England, tracked him out, and on the night in question found some means to conceal himself in Breddon's flat.

There it was assumed that he fell asleep, was awakened by the screams and the sound of the firing, and, being scared, caught up the jade image and made off. Realising that the shots would have been heard outside, and that his departure at that moment would be considered extremely suspicious, he was ready as he opened the street-door to fell the first man that he saw. The temporary unconsciousness of the policeman gave him time to get away.

The theory sounds at first sight like the only possible theory. When the archdeacon first told me the story, I tried to find out indirectly whether he accepted it. Finding him rather disposed to fence with my hints and suggestions, I put the question to him plainly and bluntly:

'Do you believe in the police theory?'

He hesitated, and then answered with complete frankness:

'No, most emphatically not.'

'Why?' I asked; and he went over the evidence with me.

'In the first place, I do not believe that Breddon, in the ordinary sense, committed suicide. No amount of physical pain would have made him even think of it. He had unending pluck. He would have taken the facial disfigurement and loss of sight as the chances of war, and would have done the best that could be done by a man with such awful disabilities. One must admit that he fired the fatal shot—the medical evidence on that point is too strong to be gainsaid—but he fired it under circumstances of supernatural horror of which we, thank God! know nothing.'

'I'm naturally slow to admit supernatural explanation.'

'Well, let's go on. What's this mysterious tribe the police talk about? I want to know where it lives and what its name is. It's wealthy enough to offer a huge reward; it must be of some importance. The man managed to get in and secrete himself. How? Where? I know the flat, and that theory won't do. We don't even know that it was him who took that little image, though I believe it was. Anyhow, how did he get away at that hour of the morning absolutely unobserved? Foreigner are not so common in London that they can walk about without being noticed; yet not one trace of him was ever found, and equally mysterious is the disappearance of the Grey Cat. It was such an extraordinary brute, and the description of it was so widely circulated that it would have seemed almost certain we should hear of it again. Well, we've not heard.'

We discussed the police theory for some little time, and something which he happened to say led me to exclaim:

'Really! Do you mean to say that the Grey Cat actually was the foreigner?'

'No,' he replied, 'not exactly that, but something near it. Cats are strange animals, anyhow, needn't remind you of their connection with certain old religions or with that witchcraft in which even in England today some still believe, and not so long ago almost all believed. I have never, by the way, seen a good explanation of the fact that there are people who cannot bear to be in a room with a cat, and are aware of its presence as if by some mysterious extra sense. Let me remind you of the belief which undoubtedly exists both in China and Japan, that evil spirits may enter into certain of the lower animals, the fox and badger especially. Every student of demonology knows about these things.

'But that idea of evil spirits taking possession of cats or foxes is surely a heathen superstition which you cannot hold.'

'Well, I have read of the evil spirits that entered into the swine. Think it over, and keep an open mind.'

The New Gulliver

1

(The first few pages of the account of his travels by Mr Lemuel Gulliver, junior, have unfortunately been damaged by fire
and are for the most part illegible. They contain reference to
a sea-fog and to a shipwreck. He appears to have escaped by
swimming, and his record of the number of days he spent in
the water and the distance covered verges upon the incredible.
His statement that he lived principally upon the raw flesh of
those sharks which made the mistake of attacking him will also
be accepted with reserve by those who remember the latitude
in which the Island of Thule is traditionally placed. The leg-
ible and consecutive manuscript begins with his arrival at the
island.)

I now wrung the water from my clothes as well as I might, and
spread them on the rocks in the sun. After an hour, perhaps, I was so
far recovered from my exertions that I thought I might now see what
manner of island this was to which my ill-chance had brought me.
Donning my clothes again I climbed up the low cliff.

The land that now lay before me appeared to be for the most
part flat and bleak in character. There were long stretches of sand and
coarse grass, and here and there a group of stunted shrubs. Presently, in
the far distance, by the aid of my perspective-glass, I made out several
cultivated plots, but nowhere could I detect any building which might
serve as a human habitation. At one point, which I guessed to be about
two miles away, a column of smoke arose, as if from the interior of the
earth. This I imagined to be of volcanic origin, but it puzzled me not
a little that the land should be under cultivation and that yet I could
find not so much as a single house or cottage.

So intent was I upon my survey of the distance that I did not note

141

the approach of a human being until I heard the footsteps close beside me. I speak of it as a human being, but in many respects the creature differed from humanity as previously known to me. Particularly noticeable was its manner of progression. It walked very slowly and laboriously on all fours, the arms being longer and the legs shorter than in the normal man.

Its body was clothed in two garments of a thick grey woollen material, and loose boots with tops of a similar material, but with leather soles, were worn both on the hands and feet. The size of the head was disproportionately large and seemed too heavy for the slender neck. It was bald save for a fringe of scanty grey hair. Large spectacles of high magnifying power distorted the eyes, and the toothless mouth was absurdly small. The grotesque object was more likely to inspire laughter than fear, for the body was small and its movements slow and feeble, but indeed it showed not the slightest sign of hostility.

"I see," said the creature, "that you are from the old world. Who are you?" He spoke in a gentle voice and with an accent not unlike that which we call American.

"My name is Lemuel Gulliver, a shipwrecked mariner, at your service. Will you tell me what island this is on which I find myself, and to whom I am speaking."

"The island is Thule—Ultima Thule—the one spot of earth that has emerged from barbarism. Chance has done great things for you in bringing you here."

He slipped one hand out of its boot, removed his big spectacles, and blinked his weak eyes. I watched him narrowly. His face was hairless. It might have been the face of an old woman or of an old man. A look of cunning now crept over it.

"I think," he said, "that I grasp your difficulty. You may speak of me as a man; but for beings of the first class, to which I belong, sex is abolished. It was perhaps the worst of nature's evils that our triumphant civilisation in the process of centuries overcame."

"But in that case," I said, "your race, or that class of it to which you belong, must be rapidly dying out."

"It is undoubtedly dying out," said the strange creature with a complacent smile, "but less rapidly than a barbarian would suppose. Increased knowledge has brought with it increased longevity. I am myself one hundred and ninety-two years of age. The end must come, of course, but after all, why not?"

As I looked at him I did not from the aesthetic point of view see why not. The creature had replaced the spectacles now, and lay at full length on the sand, as if wearied by the standing position. He went on speaking:

"Death in the individual is, of course, to some extent a confession of failure. It means inability, mostly due to ignorance, to adapt oneself to one's environment. Death of a race may be quite a different matter—an exhaustion of utility. However, that may be, it is clear that the last of us to survive will represent the highest possible development of human potentiality. I speculate sometimes on the question of who the ultimate survivor will be. It may possibly be Professor YM6403 of the Outer Office. Some think so. I believe he thinks so himself. On the other hand, I may be the last survivor. However, there are still some thousands of us in existence, and for the present these disquisitions may appear to you idle."

My clothes were damp and I was chilly, hungry, and tired. His jabber about professors and survivors had no interest for me. I ventured to point out to him that I was at present in urgent need of rest and refreshment.

He rose on all fours again, and did so with extreme awkwardness. "True," he said. "I will attend to it. We are hospitable people, though it is seldom that a stranger visits us. I will proceed at once to conduct you to my house."

"Your house? I fear that must be at some great distance, for there is no house in sight."

For a moment he looked puzzled, and then light dawned again in his short-sighted eyes.

"I see your mistake," he said. "You come from the old world, where the old type of house is still in existence. The history of the old world is the special study of my friend, the Professor. But of course, there is general knowledge that every educated being may be supposed to possess, and I know the type of house you mean. I have seen pictures of it in the museum. Now in Thule, when many centuries ago aviation became the cheapest and most popular form of transit, it also became obviously impossible that we should have houses above ground. Aviation is a source of danger to such houses, and the houses themselves were dangerous to the aviator. Our buildings are all subterranean. We avoid danger of every kind. We dislike risk. You cannot see my house to which I am taking you, but as a matter of fact it is less than a quarter of a mile away."

He went so slowly that I had to abate my usual pace, lest I should outstrip my guide. As he moved, he looked a little like a very small tired elephant.

"Aviation," I said. "I suppose that with you that has been carried to a great point of perfection."

"On the contrary," he said, "it is superseded. It is a back number. We no longer use it. But we have seen no reason to change our style of domicile, which possesses many advantages."

"And what is it?" I asked, "that has superseded aviation?"

"It is the power to dissipate and subsequently reconstruct identically at some different point the atoms of any organism or group of organisms."

"I don't think I understand," I said.

"It is natural that you should not. However, here we are at my house."

It looked to me rather as if we had come to an ordinary well, the interior of which was occupied by a spiral descending incline.

"You will observe," he said, "that when I am weary of exertion and return to my house, I descend. In the old type of house, it was customary to ascend."

I should calculate that we descended some thirty-five or forty feet below the surface. At this point we were confronted by a perfectly ordinary door with a brass knocker on it and an electric light above it. On the door were painted the letters and figures MZ04. He opened the door with a small latchkey, which he produced from one of his boots. The keyhole and the handle were placed at such a height that it was easy for him to reach them without assuming the erect position. We went through into a small hall, brightly lit and containing no furniture but a door-mat, on which my guide wiped his four boots carefully. He then requested me to come with him into the dining-room, as indeed I was by no means reluctant to do.

On entering this room, however, I was disappointed, for it bore no resemblance whatever to a dining-room, and there was no look of good cheer about it. Its walls were lined with shelves, and the shelves were filled with numbered bottles containing what looked like small pills. In the middle of the room, immediately under the light, was a low table, on which were a row of small aluminium cups and a leather-bound book. There was no other furniture of any description.

"You are looking for a chair perhaps," said my host presently. "We have none. To stand erect on the feet is a precarious position, and to sit is hardly less precarious. We avoid all risk. On all fours or in a recumbent position one is safe. However, if you would like to sit on the floor, pray do so, while I make up the prescription which you require."

I sat down on the floor, which was very hard and discouraging. I did not greatly like that use of the word "prescription," and my inner man cried rather for butcher's meat than for chemist's stuff. However, a man must take his adventures as he finds them.

My guide slipped his hands out of his boots and consulted the volume on the table. "From long use," he said meditatively, "I know most of the numbers by heart; but I cannot recall what is taken for a chill caused by prolonged submersion in sea-water. I have never had occasion to use it. Ah, here we are! Number one hundred and one."

He took down the bottle which bore that number, and dropped one pill from it into an aluminium cup. I noticed that the shelves were all placed low on the wall. But indeed, the whole of the appointments and furniture of the house was adapted for beings who used the quadrupedal position. I noticed, moreover, both now and afterwards, what very little furniture there was in these houses. The hatred of superfluity was a marked characteristic of the people of Thule.

My host took down one bottle after another from the shelves, talking as he did so. Each bottle had an ingenious stopper, which allowed one pill, and only one, to fall out each time that the bottle was reversed.

"I have never eaten shark, cooked or uncooked," said my host, "but I should imagine that a diet confined to this meat would give an excess of nitrogen. We correct that with one of number eighteen. To this I add our ordinary repast—numbers one, two, and three—a corrective for exhaustion from number sixty-four, and a pill of a narcotic character from sixty-eight."

He handed me the little aluminium cup with the pills in it. "I think," he said, "that is all you require."

"I am extremely thirsty," I said.

"No civilised man eats and drinks at the same time." He whisked down another bottle and dropped one more pill into my cup. "You will find," he said, "that little addition will remove all sensation of thirst. You shall drink when the right time comes."

I took my pills obediently and was now conducted by him into a much smaller room on the same level. I afterwards saw other subterranean houses in the island. They were all alike in plan, and the rooms were all small and so low that when I stood erect, I could easily touch the ceiling with my hand. The total absence of decoration, and the simplicity and scarcity of the furniture, were not specially characteristic of my host. Aesthetic pleasure was very slightly appreciated by any of the first-class beings in Thule.

A pneumatic mattress lay at one end of the room which we had now entered, and there were two dials on the wall, each provided with a moving hand. There was no other furniture of any kind.

"There is your bed," said my host. "Now sleep."

"I should hardly have called it a bed," I said dubiously.

"It is not the barbarian idea of a bed. We abandoned bed-clothes of every description long ago. They are not hygienic. All that is necessary is to raise the temperature of the room in which the sleeper lies. This you can easily do by altering the hand on the first of these dials, which controls the heat. It stands at present at fifteen. When I sleep I generally put it up to twenty. We will try it at twenty, and you can advance it farther if you find yourself chilly. The other dial controls the lighting and gives you five degrees of light down to absolute darkness."

"I wonder," I said, "if I might have my clothes dried. They are still damp, I fear."

He looked at my garments with marked distaste.

"If you will put them outside the door," he said, "I will see that they are thrown into the refuse-destructor, and will order proper clothes to be provided for you in their place. You will sleep for one hour, and shortly after that I shall return. By the way, how comes it that you speak our language?"

"I speak English," I said.

"English," he said meditatively. "English. I have heard that word somewhere. No, don't explain. I can easily obtain the information."

He now left me. I put the hand on the heat dial at twenty-five. Although I had no clothes of any description, I felt pleasantly warm, and in spite of the excitement caused by the novelty of my experience, I soon fell asleep. This may be ascribed either to the fatigues I had undergone or to the potency of the drugs administered to me.

2

When I awoke, it seemed to me that I must have slept for some six or eight hours, yet it had been but one hour only. I felt perfectly refreshed and well. I had shut off nearly all the light before falling asleep, and I now groped my way to the light dial and moved the hand round until the room was brightly illuminated. The silence of the place was remarkable; it was almost as if I had been in an uninhabited house. I opened the door of my room a little way, and was pleased to find a bundle of clothes awaiting me outside. I brought the bundle in and investigated it.

At first sight it looked as if some mad and malicious tailor had made two pairs of trousers out of a material suitable for an overcoat. The reason of course was that the suit had been made with a view to the conformation and habits of the natives of this curious island. They wear two garments only, and therefore require them to be of considerable thickness, and their arms are of about the same length as their legs. (The difference in our own case is much less than most people imagine.) I soon put the two garments on, and found that they fitted me well enough if I rolled back the sleeves to leave my hands free. I was also provided with a pair of boots similar to those my host wore. They were too large for me, but could be kept on by a buckle and strap fastening at the ankle.

I now made some examination of the room itself. The walls and ceiling were covered with a hard shiny substance, which I at first thought to be paint, but afterwards decided to be of the nature of our water-glass. The usual right-angles between floor and walls and ceiling were in every case softened into a curve, which I recognised to be an advantage from the point of view of cleanliness. The floor itself was covered with the same material as the walls and ceiling, but in this case had a minute corrugation all over it, to prevent slipping. In the middle of the floor was a small grating, about one foot square. As I inspected this, a fan below it began to whirl rapidly, but without the slightest sound. As I was looking at it my host knocked and entered. I was pleased to see that he brought with him a sealed bottle and two aluminium cups that would have held about half a pint apiece.

"We now drink," he said briefly.

"An excellent idea," I began, but he immediately bade me to be quiet, saying that it was not customary to talk while drinking was in progress.

He divided the contents of the bottle (not quite fairly) between the two cups. He gave himself the advantage of the choice and finished his drink at a draught. I followed his example and found that I was drinking distilled water. At this I was somewhat disappointed, but the more disposed to forgive him for the injustice of the division.

"And now, my friend," he said, "we can talk."

"Then," I replied, "you will perhaps tell me what is the reason for the custom which prevents you from taking your drink in a sociable

147

manner. In the country from which I come we like to sit and chat over our glass."

"So, it was here also in the dark ages," said my host. "At that time our drink was for the most part of an alcoholic character, and it was found that the more one talked, the more one drank; and the more one drank, the more one talked. It was a vicious circle of foolishness and ill-health, and the practice was made illegal. Alcoholic drink is quite unknown now among the first-class beings of Thule. But the custom of not speaking when one drinks, although we now only drink water, still remains. It is one of the many instances in which the ritual has survived the religion."

I pointed now to the grating in the floor. "A ventilator, I suppose."

"Exactly. It is actuated once every hour for two minutes. It draws out carbon dioxide, which being heavier than air is in the lower part of the room, and at the same time draws in fresh air through the corresponding grating in the ceiling, which communicates with a shaft to the open. The great point about it is that it is absolutely noiseless. Our study of longevity has shown us that irritation is one of its deadliest enemies. The noise of an electric fan is irritating, especially in a bedroom. I dare say the crude appliances you have in the old world still whir or clatter."

"I notice that all your electric lights are fixed in the ceiling itself. Is there any reason for this?"

"Naturally. Anything which hangs may subsequently fall. We do not court dangers. It is curious that you should mention it, because I was speaking of this point only last week to my friend, the Professor. He showed me a picture of an old-world chandelier. He also told me it was the custom in England and other uncivilised parts of the world to daub oil-paints on a piece of canvas. This was surrounded by a heavy frame and was suspended on walls. It was called a framed picture. You will find nothing so reckless here. By the way, I have found out about England. I cross-spoke to the Outer Office, and they told me it was a piece of land at the back of Scotland."

I found later that "to cross-speak" meant in Thule to send a wireless message.

"The mention of the Professor," my host continued, "reminds me that today is his birthday and mine. On this day I generally make him a ceremonial visit, and I shall be pleased to take you with me. As a specimen you will interest him."

"Might I ask what you mean by the Outer Office?"

148

"The Central Office deals with utilitarian knowledge and is separated into Controls. I, for instance, am at the head of the Heat and Light Control. The Outer Office deals with academical knowledge, and our friend is the Professor of Old-World History. The Inner Office decides questions of justice. But there is no time just now to explain our simple constitution to you. We should be starting for the Professor's house."

"One more point," I said. "May I ask your name? I should have done so before."

"We do not have names. Beings of the first class have a distinguishing formula, and only use names for plants and the lower animals. The second-class beings, the workers, may possibly use names among themselves, but of that I have no knowledge. My own distinguishing formula is MZ04, and as no two people have the same formula, much confusion is prevented. By the way, your hair is untidy."

"Naturally," I said. "I was going to speak of it."

"And your hands are not clean. That is as it should be. You are now ready to pay a ceremonial call. You perhaps don't understand. All our houses are on the same pattern, and each is provided with a fitted room for the purposes of the bath and the toilet. But when we pay a ceremonial call, it is our invariable custom to do so in a soiled and dishevelled condition. On arriving we make ourselves clean and tidy in our host's toilet-room. This is done by way of compliment. It implies that he possesses conveniences which we do not."

"It seems to me singularly foolish, if I may say so."

"From one point of view all compliments are foolish, but from the point of view of longevity all compliments are wise. They have a slightly emollient effect. We recognise this so much that we even employ at times professional optimists."

"Won't you tell me about them?"

"It is a very simple matter. If a being of the first class gets worried and depressed, he knows that this is lowering his vitality and lessening the period of his life. This knowledge only tends to increase the worry. He therefore sends at once to the Central Office for a professional optimist. The optimist comes and talks. He slightly emphasises all that is most favourable in the being's circumstances. He dwells on the strong points in his character. He listens to his stories. He shows himself impressed by his abilities. We have but a few of these professional optimists, and they are extremely well paid—that is to say, their power of ordering from the Central Office is very considerable."

"Some of this seems to me rather childish," I said. "And some of it I do not understand."

"You, a barbarian, can hardly be expected to grasp at once the refinements of a higher civilisation. You will do so gradually. Now, please, I have only just time to see the Professor before I keep my appointment at the Heat and Light Control. Come along, please."

We passed up the spiral slope, my host going very slowly and breathing heavily. The Professor's house was scarcely a hundred yards away, and I think we took nearly five minutes to get to it. The outward appearance was precisely similar to that of the house we had just quitted.

When we reached the outer door, my guide knocked once. The door immediately opened, as if of itself, and we passed into an empty hall. From this a door led us into a large room devoted to the purposes of the bath and the toilet. I subsequently found that in all these subterranean houses this room was the largest. I remarked to my guide that no servant had admitted us, and there seemed to be no one to introduce us into the presence of the Professor.

"There are no servants," said my companion. "We have the second class, the workers, but we should not admit them to live in our houses. We have so far simplified life that one being can very well look after one house, his own. As a matter of fact, two second-class beings are sent from the Hygienic Control of the Central Office every morning to clean each house, but it is a question whether this should continue. We are discussing it. It looks just a little like luxury, and luxury is dangerous to longevity. Why should we have a servant to announce us? If the Professor knows the visitor, it is not necessary. If he does not know him, the visitor can supply the information just as well as the servant. If the Professor had not wished to receive, the outer door would not have opened."

We did not find the Professor in the first room we entered, but in the dining-room, where he was taking pills out of one of those small aluminium cups. He went on taking his pills and we watched in solemn silence until he had finished. In appearance the Professor closely resembled my guide, but his fringe of hair was darker and more abundant, and something in his face seemed to betoken a love of study rather than high practical ability. I now witnessed another curious piece of etiquette.

"I hope you are ill," said my guide genially.

"Wrong absolutely," said the Professor, "but I trust that you yourself are suffering from some malignant disease."

"Nothing of the kind," said MZ04.

Subsequent inquiries showed me the reason for this. The principle was that the guest should take the earliest opportunity to make his host feel in a superior position. Therefore, etiquette required the guest to arrive unkempt, as if he did not possess the conveniences which his host had at his disposal. It also required him to make an obviously false statement as to his host's health, in order that his host might have the power of correcting him. A well-bred host, such as the Professor, immediately replied by giving his guest a similar opportunity to correct and in consequence to feel in the superior position.

They now exchanged rather ponderous compliments on their respective birthdays. But in spite of their politeness, I somehow got the impression that these two beings were in strong antagonism to one another, and that however much the emotions might be discouraged in Thule, feelings of jealously still existed.

"On this auspicious occasion," said the Professor, "it is generally my custom to make you some slight offering. I have placed a power to read a manuscript to your order at the Central Office."

"I thank you sincerely," said MZ04. "I had intended to do the same thing, but I think I have found something even more to your taste." He pointed at me with his booted hand. "Here," he said, "is rather a curious thing that I have found. You make a study of the old world and might be interested in it. I have no use for such curios myself and am happy to present it to you. In many respects—notably in its foolish use of the erect position—it resembles our second-class beings, but I believe it to be a genuine old-world relic."

"I am of the same opinion," said the Professor, "and I am obliged to you for your generosity. Can it talk?"

"Fluently," said MZ04, "but with a bad accent."

I now said very decisively that I was a free man, that I did not belong to either of them, and that I absolutely declined to be handed as a slave or a chattel from one to the other. I repeated this in varying terms more than once. They took not the slightest notice of it, but waited patiently till I had finished.

"I am busy today at the Heat and Light Control," said MZ04. "I fear that I must now leave you."

"Going to walk?" asked the Professor.

"No. I have taken my exercise for today. I shall disintegrate."

Even as I looked at him, his substance became a smoky shadow, shimmering and vibrating. It grew rapidly fainter and fainter until it had vanished altogether.

3

"And now," said the Professor, "before we go any further there is one point on which I wish to be assured. You came from the house of MZ04 just now?"

"I did."

"Did you observe in him as he came up to slope from his front-door any tendency to puff and blow?"

"He certainly did seem slightly short of breath."

"Poor fellow! Poor fellow! It breaks my heart to hear it. I don't give him another hundred years to live. Sad that so intelligent a being should be snuffed out like a candle."

The Professor did not look in the least as if it had broken his heart. So far as I was able to judge he seemed rather pleased than not.

"That being settled," he continued, "I may now devote myself to you. You made some protests just now, based, as most protests are, on ignorance. You are not going to be a slave. You may regard me as your host. I shall treat you as a guest and I shall look upon you as a curiosity. Tell me at once what I can do for you."

"I want to know where I am. I want to know the history of this place—the meaning of first-class and second-class beings—how sex came to be abolished—what is implied by a power of order from the Central Office. I have been here but a few hours and I find everything puzzling and incomprehensible."

"This," said the Professor, "is Thule. I cannot give you its exact geographical relation to the world, for it has no geographical relation. How do you imagine that you came here?"

I gave him some account of the shipwreck and of my fight with the sharks, showing him in proof my large clasp-knife, which, together with my perspective-glass and some other trifles, I had found means to secrete in the clothing provided for me by my former host.

"I have no doubt," said the Professor, "that you speak with sincerity. But you are wrong. That is not how you came here. Nor shall I put you in possession of the actual facts, or you would be able to use them to ensure your return. You are not a prisoner, but at present I wish to detain you. And now, if you will, I will give you roughly and in as few words as possible a sketch of our history and constitution. This being in the nature of a lecture, I shall lie down. It is the custom

152

in this country for every lecture or public speech to be delivered in a recumbent position, the greatest physical ease being consistent with the greatest mental concentration. Come to the sleeping-room."

He led the way to a room provided with a pneumatic mattress. It was in all respects the counterpart of the room I had seen at my former host's house. He stretched himself on this mattress, and as there was plenty of room, I saw no reason why I should not do the same. He noticed it and approved.

"You are wise," he said. "Your carcass will now cease to attract your attention and you will be able to attend to me."

He lay on his back with his eyes fixed on the ceiling, and his two long arms crossed over his protuberant stomach. Presently he began to speak in a solemn and magisterial voice, as if he were addressing a large class. I did from time to time interrupt him with question or remark, but have not thought it worthwhile to place such interruptions on record.

"To understand the conditions of Thule at the present day we must go back to the great social upheaval of centuries ago. At that time the equality of all men was claimed and the community of property. Successful agitation backed by armed force carried the matter. Community of property does to some extent remain to this day, although a more civilised view of the value of property is now held by us. But within a very few years of the social upheaval the fallacy of universal equality declared itself.

"It is a rare thing for two men to be facially alike, and no two men are ever equal in all respects. Such inequalities soon declared themselves. We had on the one side a minority who contributed more to the State in actual benefit than they received from it, and on the other side a majority who received more from the State than they contributed to it. The minority naturally became a discontented class, and healthy discontent produces activity. The majority, getting more than they gave, were quite satisfied with the state of affairs. They babbled of the blessings of an assured democracy. They took no trouble with themselves. They thought they were at the end of the social revolution when they were only at the beginning of it.

"The formation of a secret society, including most of the minority, was the natural result. You must not make the mistake of confusing this minority with the old aristocracy. The old aristocracy was based on lineage and wealth. The minority of which I speak was based on mind. They were the people who could acquire knowledge and could

153

use knowledge. They included in their number some members of the old upper classes, but many also of the old lower classes. The aim of the secret society which they formed was not only the acquisition of knowledge, principally of a practical character, but also the seclusion of it.

"The members were sworn not to impart the secrets of the society to any of the great but inactive majority. In this secret society we have the origin of what are now called first-class beings. In the glutted and lazy democracy who formed the majority we have the origin of what we call second-class beings—beings who today are permitted to acquire no other knowledge whatever than that which is necessary for the work which they do under compulsion from us. At this moment by far the greater number of them are unable to read or to write or to perform the simplest operations of arithmetic.

"It is of course a commonplace of the text-books that no social evolution follows exactly on lines laid down and planned. The secret society, which was known as the Crypt, was formed originally for the purposes of self-defence. The only means by which a few superior beings could protect themselves against the aggression of the many inferior was by the possession of secret knowledge. To take a case in point: improvements of the first importance in the accumulation and transmission of electricity were made by a member of the Crypt whose formula was H401.

"H401 was called upon to specify and to explain what he had done. He produced a written statement which was from the first word to the last abject nonsense veiled in pompous scientific phraseology. It was accepted as perfectly satisfactory and deposited in the archives. Every electrician—every man of sufficient education to detect the fraud—was already a member of the Crypt. With this came the first inkling of the tremendous power which was now in the hands of comparatively few men. By the simplest dislocation of machinery, they could deprive the great majority of light and heat, and could, if they would, choose a severe mid-winter for the operation. Many other secrets of knowledge came into the hands of the Crypt. I will not weary you with a catalogue of them, but I will mention one of which our friend MZ04 gave you just now a practical demonstration.

"I refer to the power to dissipate and subsequently to reconstruct identically at some different point the atoms of any organism or group of organisms. You saw just now how MZ04 dissipated himself as it were into smoke in order to reconstruct himself instantaneously at the Heat and Light Control, over which he presides. It is a secret of this kind which makes one being the master of many armies. This was realised by the Crypt and a course of offensive action was at last decided upon.

"At this juncture the voice of the Crypt was practically the voice of that extraordinary and commanding personality Q666—a formula that will be for ever remembered in our history. He was not a being of high scientific attainments. His life was irregular. He had neither scruples nor mercy; but he saw clearly the thing to be attained and the means towards it. At his instigation the General National Assembly was declared to be dissolved, and the whole of the second-class beings were enjoined under penalty of death to yield the strictest obedience to the orders of the Crypt as issued.

"The proclamation was received with ridicule by the second class. Democracy had always triumphed and would triumph again. It relied much upon the fact that the army was entirely democratic. That is to say, no officer or man was a member of the Crypt. The army was not deficient in courage. Its officers included even some few men who took their profession seriously. It was confidently anticipated that after a few days of civil war the Crypt would be compelled to submit.

"I have said that Q666 was a being without scruple. His declaration was made in mid-winter and the whole land was ice-bound. And on the night that followed the declaration heat and light were cut off from the dwellings and camps of his opponents. Some thousands died that night and many more in the course of the next few days. The water which they drank was mysteriously tainted and produced death. Their army found no objective for attack, so rapidly, by virtue of that power which I have described, did the members of the Crypt come and go.

"On the day when the democracy submitted and received the new constitution by which they ranked as second-class beings, they had actually become inferior in numbers to the beings of the first class. The rule which Q666 established remains to this day. Sentimentalists had in the old days clamoured for the abolition of capital punishment. Q666 abolished every other kind of punishment except this. The punishment for idleness after three warnings was death. The punishment for any intentional disobedience was death without any warning at all.

"I have given you quite roughly and simply with little or no detail the story of the struggle between the Crypt and the democracy, ending in the establishment of first-class and second-class beings.

"I have shown how from an attempt to establish universal equality and to abolish all class distinction there came into being two classes between which there was a distinct cleavage—a class of masters and a class of servants. The end of the struggle was only what could have been expected. While all the harnessed forces of wind and tide provided radiance and warmth for the members of the Crypt, their opponents froze in the darkness. The same water that poisoned the democracy that drank it refreshed the masters without injuring them. The old-fashioned disciplined stupid army was powerless against opponents whose mobilisation, swift as lightning, rendered them practically invisible. There is still much to relate to you, but I grow weary of talking. I propose to take you to see my plants."

"Got a nice garden?"

"We have no gardens. I keep my plants as pets here in my house. Without awakening any emotion which might be prejudicial to longevity, they provide a mild interest and a salutary change from more serious occupation. Follow me and I will show you them."

He rose from the mattress and I noticed that he did so with more ease and agility than had characterised the movements of my poor friend MZ04. I followed him to a room so small that it might almost have been called a cupboard. It was intensely lit by a tinted electric light. In it were two tall plants in tubs.

The leaves of the plants were large and of a tropical character. Each had a stem about three feet in height, surmounted by a ball which looked as if it were made of fine silk. The colour of the ball or flower in one case was a peacock-blue and in the other dead black. I noticed a slight movement of the leaves as we entered the room and assigned it to the opening of the door.

"The plant with the blue head is Edward," said my host. "He is rather an affectionate little thing. Observe."

He called Edward twice in a caressing voice, and immediately the stem of the plant bent downwards and the silky blue ball rubbed itself caressingly against my host's cheek. Almost immediately the other plant began to agitate its leaves violently and to waggle its black ball backwards and forwards.

"You observe?" said my guide. "Frederick is jealous."

He gave each of them a little water and we then went back to the sleeping-room again.

"I never saw anything like that in my life before," I said. "Plants with us cannot move of their own volition. They——"

"Surely you mistake," said the Professor. "I am no botanist, but I have made a special study of what went on in the old world, and I think I am correct in saying that there were creeping plants there which moved to find their supports, and plants whose leaves shrivelled up at a touch, and others that actually devoured the insects which formed their sustenance. Almost anything can be done with plants and knowledge. The old world produced many new varieties—some of them of real utility, as for instance the thornless cactus. We have merely gone a little further. We live in solitude and a companion of some kind is a necessity. I think you will find that every first-class being here keeps one or two pet plants."

"You don't keep dogs or cats?"

"We keep nothing which can be both offensive and provocative of strong affection. Cats and dogs, common though they were in the old world, stand condemned under both categories."

4

"This," said the Professor, "is the hour at which on fine and warm days we go out and bask in the sun. Sunlight is the enemy of disease and the friend of longevity. You would perhaps like to come with me. We shall find many more engaged in the same occupation."

We passed out of the house and up the spiral incline. The scene before me reminded me somewhat of certain stretches of grass in our public parks on a hot day. Here and there on the coarse grass or sand were stretched the grey-clad bodies of beings of the first class. I did not see any engaged in conversation or in reading or even in sleep. They simply lay still in the sun. Some of them had brought rugs with them. One who appeared to be very infirm was carried in a kind of litter by four finely built men who walked erect.

"That," said the Professor, "is the grandson of the great Q666."

"And who are the fine-looking men who are carrying him?"

"Merely second-class beings detailed for the work. Take no notice of them. They will not, of course, venture to remain in our presence."

The four men deposited their master gently on a bed of tufted grass and marched away again without a word. So far as I could compute, there were now some two hundred first-class beings stretched out motionless under the pleasant and vivifying warmth of the sun.

"May we not," I asked as we reposed ourselves, "take this opportunity for some continuation of your lecture? There is still much about which I am curious."

"On what point would you wish me to speak first?"

"I am told that among beings of the first class at any rate sex is abolished."

"Can sex be of interest to any thinking being? It is of no interest at all to me."

"It happens," I said boldly, "to be of the very first interest to myself."

"Very well," said the Professor. "We must withdraw to some distance, so that our voices do not disturb the meditations of others."

I followed him to the spot that he selected. We lay on our backs on the sand and he continued his discourse.

"The practical abolition of sex has with us been a very gradual process extending over centuries. It began with that great social upheaval of which I have already told you. To declare the complete equality of men was to declare the complete equality of the sexes. It ended about one hundred and fifty years ago when the words "men" and "women" ceased to be used by first-class beings, and no distinction of sex was admitted. That I think is all you want to know."

"Pardon me," I said. "You give me no explanation whatever."

"The thing explains itself. Take first the case of a male. You will find in him so many factors mental and physical which belong to the race and so many which belong to the individual. In the case of a male the factors which belong to the individual are very much in excess of those which belong to the race. In the female we find the reverse of this. The factors which belong to the race are in her largely in excess of those which belong to the individual. She is the martyr and trustee of humanity. That was the state of affairs before the great social upheaval of which I have spoken. When women began to mix in every business, profession, and sport, a new type of woman very soon declared itself—unusually tall, flat-chested, small in the hips, destitute of femininity.

"Briefly, the male type and the female type began to assimilate. Now sex assimilation is the death of sex attraction. All that women spent on their individual development they stole from the race. Marriages became rare and where they existed they were frequently sterile. Gradually, all that made man man and all that made woman woman became rudimentary and atrophied until, as I have told you, one hundred and fifty years ago the distinction between man and woman was abolished. Since that time, and indeed for some ten years previous to it, there has been no instance of birth or marriage or love-making

158

among beings of the first class. The last word of civilisation has been reached. It is a splendid consummation."

"Splendid?" I said doubtfully.

"How can you doubt it? Now that the burden of racial responsibility has been cut off from our backs, our longevity is trebled and more than trebled. This may be assigned in part to our increased knowledge and to the fact that we do no laborious or dangerous work. Laborious and dangerous work is confined to the second class. With them, of course, sex still exists. They are a lower order. They breed up children. When the number of workers is deficient, we keep those children. When the number tends to be excessive, they are destroyed. Have you never thought into what a quandary racial responsibility led men and women in the dark ages? No married man lived as an unmarried man, no married woman as an unmarried woman. Life became a string of compromises and concessions. There were complicated households with nurseries in them.

"It must be clear to you that the man who works for six people must work just six times as hard as the man who works for himself alone. Work is dangerous. And if work is dangerous, worry is deadly. Worry is enormously increased where there is any emotional attachment. Look how we have simplified things. To one being one house. The emotions never paid for their keep, and it is civilised to get rid of them. Tears are as little known among the first-class beings of Thule as is the gross and unhygienic kiss. The tortures of modesty do not affect us, for where there is no sex distinction there is no modesty. We are emancipated. We are free. Love implies death. The loveless live long. I may tell you that it is whispered already that we are on the edge of discoveries which may make it possible for us to live for ever."

"Well," I said, "I am not constituted as you are. You would hardly expect me to like what you like."

"I do not expect any man from the old world to be civilised. It would not be reasonable. But what objection can you possibly offer to the state of things among the first-class beings here?"

"Well, to take the first point that occurs to me, it seems to me that you must all be most horribly bored."

"Never," said my host emphatically. "Boredom is the result of living too fast. Those who work too hard or those who enjoy too much must in the intervals of their work or enjoyment be bored. Here we have found by experience the exact pace at which one should live. Every one of the first-class beings has an occupation of some kind for which he was originally fitted by training and is now specially fitted by long experience. Take the Central Office alone. It is divided into many Controls and in each Control, there are many sections.

"The being who made me a present of you, our friend MZ04, is at the head of the Heat and Light Control. In that alone there are forty-two sections and each section finds work for two first-class beings. Love never stimulates us to an excess of work. Love never takes our minds from the thing on which we are engaged. We do what we can do well and we do it under the best possible conditions, and we have no entertainments of any kind. How then can we be bored? I have said enough. Let me meditate."

"There is just one thing more I should like to ask."

"What is your name or formula?"

"My name is Lemuel Gulliver."

"Well, Gulliver, we are kindly and hospitable people. For some weeks I shall be keeping you here and obtaining from you first-hand information on various details of life in the old world. You will be catechised for one hour or so a day. You may take your revenge in advance. I will answer one more question."

"You told me that community of property still practically existed among you."

"It does. Money is not used. In proportion to the work, he does a first-class being has the power of ordering what he requires from the Central Office. It is an extremely rare thing for any first-class being to order all to which he is entitled. The wisest are those who reduce property to the barest necessities. At a man's death all that he has reverts to the State. Here we have no appalling families. Here no man has to make provision for prodigal sons and worthless daughters. We are free from the insanity of love and we find it more easy to believe in friendship when friendship must always remain unremunerated."

"And still I do not envy you," I said. "You are not free from all emotions yet. I have already found two in existence among you, and they are two which I do not greatly love."

"What are they?" the Professor asked.

"Fear and jealousy."

"Lie still. You disturb my meditations."

For half an hour he remained silent with his eyes closed, but not, I think, asleep. Then rising suddenly on all fours, he said that we would return to his dwelling, take our pills and compose ourselves for the night.

"I would make a request to you," I said. "These pills which you take are wonderful and I have already experienced their good effects. But I do not think I could live upon them. Evolution has brought your digestive apparatus to a pitch of perfection that I cannot hope to possess. What can you do for me?"

"Our workers, the beings of the second class, are accustomed to kill an ox, cut off a piece of it, subject it to the action of heat, and then devour it. They make also a drink which has great attractions for them. It has even led them to disobey, and to disobey is of course to die. I am sorry to mention such filthy diet, but I can think of nothing else. After all it might suit an old-world barbarian."

"I think it might suit me admirably."

"Then I will have second-class rations sent you every day from the Central Office. I will cross-speak the Central Office now in order that they may send you a piece of dead animal before you sleep. The one condition I make is that I shall not see you engaged in tearing it to pieces with your teeth. You will take it in your own room."

"And which will that be?"

"Oh," he said carelessly, "I shall keep you in the cupboard with my two other pets, the plants. You shall have a mattress to lie on."

A few minutes later one of the working class brought a covered tray, deposited it just inside the Professor's door, and departed.

"Your food," said the Professor. "Take it to the cupboard."

I did so with pleasure. I found on the tray a plate of excellent cold roast beef and a knife and fork of rough workmanship and some flat hard biscuits. There was also a bottle containing about a quart of strong old ale. With this I was very well satisfied, and stretching myself on my mattress, for which there was barely room in the cupboard, I composed myself to slumber.

5

I passed a wretched night. I cannot assign this to the small size of my sleeping-room, for I was able to stretch myself at full length and the admirable system of ventilation kept the air always fresh. Such sleep as I had was haunted by dreams in which these four-legged human beings figured largely. Early in the morning I rose and switched on the light, hoping that by pacing my cell or the passage without for a few minutes I might again induce sleep. I saw a strange sight. The silky heads of the two plants swayed gently to and fro continuously. Their leaves rose and fell. Somehow, they seemed to suggest to me a caged lion.

"You poor devils," I said aloud.

When I had put out the light and stretched myself on the mattress again, I felt the silky head of one of these plants rubbing against my cheek. It startled me at first. I touched it with my hand. It was about the size of a man's fist. I felt its thousand fibres vibrating under my touch.

In the morning another covered tray was brought me, precisely the same as on the previous evening. A bad night gives one little appetite for strong ale in the morning and I begged a drink of distilled water from the Professor. I took that opportunity to explain to him the kind of food that I should require in the future, and to beg for some facilities by which I might cook myself a hot dish. This last he refused, but agreed that my evening ration should be brought to me hot in the future.

I remained with the Professor for fifteen days. Every day for about an hour he catechised me closely on the manner of life in my own country—the old world, as he called it. His knowledge and his ignorance alike amused me. For example, he made a drawing of a hansom-cab which was really fairly accurate; but he was under the impression that hansom-cabs were used in Rome at the time of Julius Caesar. All his ideas about dates were wrong and confused, and perpetually I had to correct him. He made notes of all that I told him with an ink pencil.

"You are writing a book on this subject?" I asked him one day.

"I am. That is my duty."

"And when will it be printed and published?"

"Upon the defeat of the democracy and the establishment of first-class and second-class beings, the extremely wise course was taken of breaking up all printing-machines and destroying all books, except those copies, mostly manuscript, which were especially selected for the library of the Central Office. We neither print nor publish."

"Why do you call this a wise course? It seems to me the wildest folly. It is to cheap printing and cheap books that the spread of education in my own country has been largely due."

"Undoubtedly. The question of course is whether the spread of education—or rather what you mean by education—is in any way desirable. It seemed to us that one might as well admit children and fools under no supervision to a menagerie of wild beasts and provide them with the keys of the cages. We respect letters. We consider it a dishonour to letters that books should be cheap or easily obtainable.

Here it costs a first-class being more to read one manuscript from the library of the Central Office than it would cost you in your own country for a year's subscription to King Mudie."

I informed him that Mudie was not a king and that I did not know how he had got the idea. He accepted the correction as he always accepted every correction, with considerable irritation.

"It seems to me," he continued, "that you use the word education in a very narrow sense. I myself should say that the whole of our second-class beings were educated. Each is trained to the work that he has to do. We have for instance a group of them who are familiar with the ordinary process of plant culture. They can dig, they can prune, they can plant. They have the education for which they are fitted. They are not versed in those extraordinary modifications which can be produced in plants by chemical changes caused artificially in the nature of the sap. That branch is naturally reserved for beings of the first class.

"They are taught how to weave and how to make the garments which we all wear. They are taught how to clean our houses in the quickest, most silent and most effective manner. Briefly, they do any work which their intelligence and judgment entitle them to do. Beyond that we do not go. We do not give them knowledge which would be dangerous to them and to us. When you return home, my friend, if ever you do return home, preach to your poor benighted people the inequality of man and the advisability of restricting all really important knowledge to the higher grade."

One day while we were chatting about indifferent subjects, he mentioned quite casually that he had been cross-speaking the Central Office and that he found that MZ04 had died that morning.

"I am sorry to hear it," I said. "For after all he received me kindly—fed me and clothed me. When is the funeral?"

"Funeral?" said the Professor. "We have no funerals. The body of MZ04 went into the refuse-destructor hours ago. Death is a confession of failure, a sure proof of a blunder somewhere, and therefore ordinary politeness tells us that we should take as little notice of it as possible."

"Who will take his place?" I asked.

"That has already been decided by the Inner Office."

"You had no ambitions in that direction?"

"None whatever. There is no reason why in addition to my present appointment I should not now be holding a post—and a highly placed post—in the Inner Office. It is merely a want of appreciation and, I am afraid I must add, a certain meanness in the minds of some first-class beings which keeps me a humble professor. However, merit will tell; I can trust to that."

The boasted civilisation of Thule had at any rate not extirpated human vanity. The vanity of the Professor was colossal. No compliment was too gross for him to accept with avidity. His nature was indeed very curious and difficult for a simple man like myself to comprehend. In spite of the casual way in which he spoke of death, I was convinced that he lived in hourly dread of it.

"In spite of the fact that he spoke of every known form of religion as an idle superstition, and professed the most absolute materialism, I think he was unable to disbelieve entirely in the future life. His nerves were not good. Sometimes in the middle of the night he would tap at the door of the cupboard where I slept and ask me to come out and speak to him. There was always some excuse, and I think the excuse was never the true one. The fact of the case is that the extreme solitude in which most of these first-class beings lived had its inevitable effect upon them. They had, as the Professor observed, no entertainments. They had really no social gatherings. Occasionally one friend would pay a brief and formal visit to another friend, but there was nothing beyond that. When they went abroad for exercise or to bask in the sun, they as a rule passed one another unnoticed.

I was myself the reason why for a time the number of visitors to the Professor's house increased considerably. People came to see me, and he produced me and lectured upon me in terms which were sufficiently humiliating.

"Observe," he would say, "the ludicrous smallness of the head and the short and attenuated forelegs. In this respect one might almost believe him to be a second-class being. He is probably, however, a still lower type. The skin is whiter from deficient pigmentation, and the size of the body is smaller than in a second-class male. In the land from which he comes I find that they learn nothing by experience. The child born into the world there naturally adopts the safe quadrupedal position and has the use of its toes. The creature that we have here can do absolutely nothing with his toes and is uncomfortable in the quadrupedal position. In fact, the deformity of his body prevents him from adopting it easily."

At this point in his lecture, he would change to a different language and continue. This second language was used by first-class beings among themselves when they wished to say anything without being understood by those whom they considered their inferiors. In the presence of a second-class being it was that language which the first class always adopted. Among themselves and in my presence, they spoke English, except on the occasions when they did not wish me to understand them.

I began to rebel against the kind of life which I was leading. I disliked to be made a curiosity and a show of. The monotony affected me. The horrible familiarities of those two plants in my sleeping-room got on my nerves. I began to hint to the Professor that I must have change and more freedom or that the source of his information would possibly be dried up.

"If you became useless to me," he said carelessly, "you would be killed, of course. You would have failed and your body would go into the refuse-destructor."

"Very likely," I said. "But you would not get the information which you want. And you do want it, you know."

That was my trump card. He really did want to acquire all possible information about what he called the old world. In return for this I was always able to obtain concessions, and I did not fail in this case. I told him that I wished to explore the island, to go right over to the other side of it and see the places where the second class lived and the work they did. At first, he tried to dissuade me. He pointed out that the distance to the other side of the island was not less than eight miles, and refused to believe that this would not be beyond my strength. He painted in lurid colours the dangers of the mountain which I should have to cross and of the forests which I should find on the other side.

"I, however, remained obstinate in my purposes and at last obtained his permission to go, on condition that I returned in ten days and that I never spoke with any second-class being whom I might encounter, lest I should inadvertently betray important knowledge to them. This promise I gave readily enough, but I must confess, with no intention of keeping it. He gave me some further instructions and a pass written with the ink pencil, which he said would entitle me to protection and help from any first-class being whom I might encounter.

Thus, then on a fine sunny morning I started out with no more equipment than I could easily carry on my back. The prospect of adventure lured me. For the first time for days, I felt in good temper and spirits.

The Professor had been well within the mark in stating that the breadth of the island was not less than eight miles. By sundown I must have covered thirty miles at least and encamped for the night by the side of a swift and narrow stream. I had still the low hill to cross which the Professor had spoken of as a mountain. In a flat country such as Thule, all hills are mountains.

The Professor's mistakes in regard to time and distance interested me a good deal. I could understand that they rendered him professionally unsuitable for the practical work of the Central Office and that they probably helped to debar him from the post which he desired in the Inner Office. It may be, perhaps, that one cannot have an over-development in one direction without a compensating defect in another. The Professor showed the same anxiety to conceal his want of time-sense that an engine-driver might show to conceal his colour-blindness. After all, instances of this want of time-appreciation are common enough among my own people in dealing with the past.

One knows the vagueness with which the ordinary man assigns a fact to the sixteenth or seventeenth century—a fact which in reality belongs to the eighteenth. The further back we go the more vague we become. It is difficult for us to realise that the difference between the tenth and eleventh centuries is a difference of a hundred of those very years which we are now living. So far as the present was concerned, the Professor's time-appreciation was clear and accurate enough. He never forgot the hour at which he should take his pills or his *siesta* in the sun. Watches were unknown in Thule, but there was a clock in every room, and all clocks were wound and synchronised electrically from the Central Office.

I had never been able to persuade the Professor to tell me where the Central, Outer, and Inner Offices were domiciled. I guessed at first it would be where I saw that shaft of smoke ascending when I landed at the island, but afterwards I saw several other similar smoke columns and assigned them to subterranean factories of some kind. But in the course of my day's ramble, I came upon many other features that interested me. I reached a long stretch of fields in which a veritable army of the second class was at work.

Each field was numbered and seemed to have its separate gang. Each gang was in the charge of one first-class being. As a rule, he lay in the sun with one hand removed from the boot and covered with a rubber glove. In this hand he held a thick rod some three feet in length which seemed to me to be made of aluminium. His quick and watchful eyes surveyed the whole of the field, and every now and then he called out an order to some individual labourer. The order was in every case instantly obeyed. In every one of these fields, I was challenged by the overseer with a loud "Who are you?" I replied as the Professor had directed me and showed my pass.

I was then allowed to go on unmolested. I may even say that I was treated with kindness. One of these beings had water fetched for me that I might drink. Another, astounded by the distance which I had covered on foot, offered to provide four labourers with a litter to carry me, and seemed surprised to find that I really preferred walking. In many of these fields there was grain ready for harvest—of the same kinds, I think, as we have in our country, but with the ears much larger and heavier and of a very dwarf-like habit. I found barley and oats full grown standing scarcely six inches above the ground.

Beyond these cultivated fields was a gently undulating plain, not unlike common land I have seen in England. The bracken was near waist-high, and often I had to force my way through a tangle of bramble and gorse. This part of the country seemed to be entirely deserted, and with no one to direct me I steered by the sun. After some miles of this I came upon a small clump of elm trees and stretched myself in the shade for food and rest.

As I lay asleep, I felt a gentle touch upon my shoulder, and opening my eyes I saw one of the first-class beings. I judged him to be one of the overseers, for from one of his big loose boots an aluminium rod projected.

"Who are you?" he said.

I showed him my credentials. He seemed satisfied.

"Go on your way at once," he said, "and bear well to the right, for here you are in danger."

I could not tell what the danger might be, but thought it best to take his advice. As he trotted away from me, I fastened up my pack again and slung it on my back, and almost instantly I saw what the danger was. Out from a dip of the land which had concealed them came a herd of about twenty wild cattle. Their size was enormous. The leader, a white bull, scented or sighted me and charged at once towards me. There was but one thing to do. I gripped a low bough and easily swung myself up into the tree, even in the moment of my activity speculating how long I should be kept there and what would happen to the overseer who had spoken to me and was now scarcely a hundred yards distant. The bull paced round and round the tree, pawing the earth and striking the trunk with his great horns. From my perch I could see that the overseer now stood still. He had slipped one hand out of the boot and now grasped that aluminium rod. At that moment the bull sighted him and charged him. The rest of the herd waited huddled and motionless.

When the bull was within about twenty yards of him the overseer raised his hand and pointed that rod towards the beast. There was a flash as of lightning, a loud crackling sound, and the bull rolled over stone dead. The rest of the herd turned tail and galloped off in panic. Without a word to me the overseer replaced the rod in his boot and went on his way.

I could understand now how one of these beings could easily control a gang of thirty or more of the second-class labourers, and could ensure punctual and complete obedience. Yet, grateful though I was to this overseer, I regarded the beings of his type more with wonder than with admiration. They were a selfish and sterile race. Their mode of walking suggested to me too vividly things that I had seen in the great ape-house in Regent's Park. Physically they were not, according to our notions, to be compared with the second class whom they controlled.

Those that I saw of the second class were all men of fine stature. Their skins were darker than the European and of a reddish brown. Their faces were handsome, gloomy, and sombre. They seemed more akin to me than did this four-legged thing with the monstrous head and the death-dealing rod in his boot. But as yet I had spoken to no being of the second class. As I passed through the cultivated fields, I was all the time under the eyes of the overseers, and deemed it inadvisable to break through the Professor's injunctions.

I saw nothing more of the wild cattle nor of any living being until I reached the stream beside which I camped for the night. I had been told that on the farther side of the hill I should find a forest and beyond the forest the dwellings of the second class and the sea.

As I lay stretched on my rug, I heard beneath me a curious rumbling sound and guessed correctly what it might be. It was commonplace enough—an underground train taking the workers back to their homes. Commonplace, at least, in London, but strange in the environment in which I found it. I slept well, as I ever do in the open on a warm night, and in the morning after a refreshing swim in the stream set out to climb the hill.

The air was clear and from the crest of the hill I obtained a fine view. Beneath me lay a forest that covered, I should imagine, some four or five miles. Beyond was the blue sea, and close to the shore what looked like a small town or village of much the same character as we are familiar with in England. These were the first buildings above ground that I had seen in Thule, and constituted the dwellings of beings of the second class.

The attitude of the first class towards the second was rather puzzling. The restriction of the numbers of the workers was quite ruthless. Children that were not wanted were destroyed as we destroy superfluous kittens, fewer girls than boys being allowed to live. The punishment of death was given for any act of disobedience, and even, after due warning, for carelessness and incompetence. But the workers whom I had seen so far—all men—were evidently well treated. They showed no signs of over-work, or under-feeding, or disease. They were tall, stout fellows, all of them, and evidently in fine condition. Not one of them adopted or attempted to adopt the quadrupedal position. They walked erect, and were obviously the physical superiors of their masters. Doubtless utilitarian views had prevailed with the first-class beings, and they gave such treatment to the second class as would ensure the maximum of effective work from them.

The clothing of the workers was of the same thick woollen material as that of their masters, but of a different colour—a reddish brown. The men threw off their upper garment when working in the fields. It will be remembered that on my arrival I was provided by the late MZ04 with grey garments similar to those worn by the first class. I was thus in the nature of an anomaly to everyone who met me. I walked erect and therefore did not belong to the first-class beings. I wore the grey garments, the sleeves of which had now been abbreviated to suit me, and therefore did not belong to the second class. To tell the truth my stature was inferior to theirs, and would by itself have distinguished me.

Standing on the crest of the hill I made my plans. It was in my mind to get away from this island as soon as might be. In a forest of that extent, I might easily lie hidden for weeks, and I doubted if, with all his knowledge and cunning, the Professor would be able to find me. Meanwhile I would establish friendly relations with some of the second class. Living as they did upon the sea-shore, I expected that they would have contrived boats for their own use, and thus I might make my escape. I had the whole day before me, and began now to explore the forest, intending to go on to the village on the shore when the workers had returned in the evening.

I followed the course of the stream that trickled down the hill-side. There was no wind, and except for the burble of the stream and the call of the birds all was still in the forest. Here and there the stream broadened out into wide shady pools, where it seemed to me there might be the chance of tickling a trout. Presently I heard below me a loud splashing. The trees and undergrowth were so thick that I could see but a very little way before me. I still followed the stream in the direction of the sound, but I went with extreme caution, taking care that my footsteps should not be heard. I did not know what danger might not be awaiting me below.

Presently I reached the pool from which the sound had come. Peering through the bushes I saw, seated in a dejected attitude by the edge of the pool, a very beautiful woman. In spite of the fact that she had been swimming, and her long dark hair hung dankly about her brown shoulders—wet hair is ever unbecoming to a woman—her beauty was amazing. The brown shoulders peeped from the heavy folds of the garment which she had thrown round her after her swim. It was of the colour prescribed for beings of the second class. The women of that class wear but one garment—a long piece of stuff like a plaid, that they drape about them. As I came into view she started up and gave a scream of terror.

"Do not be afraid," I called. "I mean you no harm. I will not hurt you."

As she looked at me further, she seemed reassured. "I thought," she said, "at first that one of the gods had come to take me."

"What gods?" I asked.

"The gods that walk on four legs and against whom no man can do anything. Your dress is of the same colour that they wear."

"I am no god, but an ordinary man enough—a shipwrecked mariner cast up on this island a few weeks ago, and now planning to escape from it again."

"There is no escape," she said mournfully. "The gods know everything."

"Let me come down and speak with you."

"Come," she said. "I am not afraid anymore."

"What do you do here?" I asked, as I sat beside her.

"I have fled from death. It was ordained by the gods that I should

170

die at sundown seven days ago. I escaped and hid myself here. But there is no escape really. Sooner or later, they will find me. They never fail. In their coming and going they are unseen. Suddenly before you stands one of the gods, and he points his rod at you and you are dead. It is not possible to hide from those whom one cannot see in their approach."

"Has no one ever escaped?"

"Years ago, a girl like myself fled to the forest, and for three months in the summer she lived there. It was I myself who found her lying dead. Her garment over her breast was scorched by the lightning of the gods, and her heart was burned within her. It was all one; for in the winter, she would have perished of cold and starvation. I love life. I want every day and hour that I can get. But I have no hopes."

"Tell me, what is your name?"

"To the gods I have no name. When I am at work a number is put upon me; it may be a different number every day. Among my own people I am called Dream."

"And why was it that seven days ago you incurred the anger of your masters and were to die?"

"Seven days ago, I had the care of a loom. By sundown so much work was to be finished. It is easy work. Our gods never give the women hard work. All the same, that which is appointed must be done. It was just at the beginning of the first spell of hot weather. The forest called me. It was stronger than I was. When I went to my mid-day meal I slipped into the forest and swam in the pool, and could not go back to the loom again. After that I dared not go back, for those who have disobeyed die instantly. Such is the will of the gods, and we cannot alter it."

"Listen to me," I said. "Those whom you call gods are not gods. They are descended from those who, many years ago, were men and women just as you are. They are not all-powerful. I myself mean to escape from them. Generations of slavery have crushed your spirit, but in the country from which I come there are no slaves. I shall escape and I shall take you with me."

"You are good. I will do as you say. But how can one escape?"

"In the town on the shore I hope to be able to find a boat."

She looked at me with her dark and lustrous eyes wide open in sheer wonderment.

"What is a boat?" she asked.

Her ignorance I found was not assumed. The making of a boat had been prohibited so long by the beings of the first class that now even the recollection of it had passed from the workers. They regarded the sea with terror. It was the grey liquid wall of their prison-house. To touch it was to die. They bathed in the forest pools, and never in the sea. The fish that they ate were fresh-water fish only. Their masters had told them numberless strange lies about the sea.

"Dream," I said, "there is one thing which I cannot understand. You live in daily terror of these people whom you miscall gods. You are fairly well treated, but you are not free. You live as slaves. Why do you tell me, then, that you want every hour and every minute of life?"

She dipped a bare foot in the water below her, passing it slowly to and fro.

"There is always love," she said pensively.

8

"What do you know of love?" I asked.

She shrugged her pretty shoulders. "Almost nothing, except of the lesser loves—the love of children, the squirrels in the forest."

"Of parents," I suggested.

"No," said Dream decisively. "You cannot love those whom you do not know."

"But how does it happen that you do not know your parents?"

"How should I? Sometimes for two years, sometimes for three—as the gods decide—the child remains with its parents. After that it is taken away from its parents and brought up by the gods. That is the law."

"But these women who have their children taken away from them—how do they bear it?"

"Sometimes they are so sad that they go away into the forest and eat the nightshade and die. More often they weep for a long time and then they forget. When a thing is the law and it cannot be altered, there are very few who become angry or grieved about it. What would be the use? The gods are very careful about the children, you know."

"In what way careful?"

"If a child is weak, sickly, or misshapen, it is killed instantly. If it is unable to learn how to do any work it is killed. The strong which remain are well treated. For some years they do little work, they are well fed, they are healthy and happy."

I thought of the gangs of magnificently built men that I had seen at work in the fields. I looked at the strong and beautiful girl beside me.

The drastic methods of the lords of Thule had at least brought about one thing—the highest possible physical condition of the race.

"Tell me," I said, "do your gods interfere also in the matter of marriage?"

She gazed at me with her sincere and wondering eyes. "What is marriage?" she said, in much the same tone as she had inquired what a boat was.

I told her something of the marriage ceremonies existing in my own country, and she was very much amused.

"But why?" she asked; "that is a very great to-do about very little. If a man loves a woman and the woman also loves the man, what more is there to say? Why write down things in books and call many people to a feast?"

"Dream," I said, "you are an immoral heathen."

"Those also are words that I do not know. You will tell me about them."

I did not tell her about them. I had already been rather struck by the curious simplicity of her own speech. Her phrases were at times biblical, though she knew nothing of any religion, and could not have read a bible if she had possessed one.

"And when, as you say, a man and woman love one another, is it customary with you for them to live together for the rest of their lives?"

Dream yawned. I was wearying her.

"It is so strange," she said, "to have to tell you the things that everybody knows. Also, what you ask is so funny. Of course, people who love live together. Is not that right?"

I hardly knew what to tell her. She had the innocence of the first garden. After all it may be that the notions of right and wrong which are very properly accepted in my own country are not to be imposed upon every people in every form of civilisation. I did not wish to judge her. I therefore changed the subject.

"This evening, Dream, I want you to take me to that town where you all live. I am going to save you and take you away from this island. To do that I must make a boat or a great raft. I must have men to help me."

"I will take you there if you wish, but if I do, I shall die immediately. Every day and every night the overseeing gods go up and down there. It is well known that I left my work at the loom, and that I am to die. The gods have said I am to die, and what they say always happens. Any one of them who saw me in the town would point at me with his death-rod and I should fall. Still, no one has ever escaped, and as I must die anyhow, I will take you to the town if this gives you pleasure."

I could not of course hear of this. My first step to secure her safety could not reasonably be a step which would ensure her death. I asked her, however, how these overseeing gods—the police of the town, as I figured it—would recognise her.

"By the pictures," she said. "They have pictures of every one of us. My picture is put up throughout the town on the walls of houses."

"I see," I said. "If I go to the town at all I will go alone. Shall I be in any danger from your people?"

"None. You wear the grey garments. True, you do not walk like a god, and you suffer from short arms, as I do. But would you be safe from the gods themselves?"

"Yes," I said. "I have something that was given to me to show them. It is a sign that they are not to injure me."

"Injure?" she echoed. "The gods injure nobody. They kill when it is necessary, but they do not injure. If one has a crooked spine, or if one falls sick, or if one has lived too long, or if one refuses obedience, as I have done, then of course they must die. It is the law. The gods themselves have told us that in the old days our forefathers were beaten or shut up in prisons or their goods were taken away from them. This was called punishment. We are free from all that. We have food and shelter, we have light and warmth, we have times of work and times of play. No one punishes us. That is why it is our duty to love the gods."

"Who taught you to say that?"

"They taught it me themselves. It is one of the first things that a child learns. But I grow weary of sitting here and telling you the things that everybody knows. Will you come with me through the forest and down to the shore where the caves are where I sleep?"

I assented. She rose up and draped her garment anew about her. As we walked side by side, I asked her if she was not afraid of sleeping in the caves. Surely there first of all the gods would go to look for her.

"No," she said. "Never. No god has ever been inside those caves since the creature came out of the sea and lived there."

"What creature?"

"How should I know? It was more than fifty years ago, and none of us live for fifty years. But I have heard the story as it is told by my

174

people. The creature that came out of the sea was something like a serpent, but larger than all serpents. Those who looked into its eyes died of horror. Two of the gods died. It went away into the caves, and no one has ever seen it again. I suppose it still lives there waiting for something. But it is far away in the very heart of the caves where I never go. If I heard it moving, I should awake at once, for I sleep but lightly, and so I should save myself. If I could remain always in the caves, I need have no fear of the gods, but one must have the sun, and water to swim in, and food to eat. Is that not so?"

I agreed with her. "But," I said, "in the forest you are in constant danger."

"Only on calm days. When the wind blows the gods will not go into the forest. That is well known, but I do not know what the reason is."

I knew perfectly well. I had already learned their fear of something falling on them. Over-civilisation had broken up their nerves and rendered them flaccid and spiritless. They had no reason to fear the wild cattle with the death-rod in their hands. They had no reason to fear the docile race that they had tamed in ignorance to serve them. But the limb of a tree might fall, or a cave might be haunted. I grew to hate these first-class beings, as they called themselves.

She began now to ask me questions about the land from which I had come, and all that I told her was subjected to her barbarian criticism. She was perfectly shocked at hearing of hospitals, and regarded the whole of the medical fraternity as impious. "If those who are weak and sickly are patched up and made to live a little longer, is there not a danger that they will have children who will also be weak and sickly, and so much more trouble be made? We see that this is so with the beasts that we rear, and the plants that we cultivate. Is it not so with men also?"

I had to admit that it was. But I pointed out to her that in my country we regarded many other things besides physical perfection.

"So, I have already observed," she said, with almost embarrassing frankness. "Are the women of your country beautiful?"

"Some of them are very beautiful. Some, I fear, are not beautiful at all."

"Then why do they live? It must be very unpleasant. Are any of them more beautiful than I am?"

"I have never seen anyone, Dream, as beautiful as you are."

"Say that again," she said, "it makes a pleasing sound."

175

I did not say it again. I felt my responsibilities towards this beautiful but wholly barbarous creature. It seemed to me my duty at the very first to purge her mind of her superstitions about that deformed, intelligent, and learned section of humanity in whose divine character she had been taught to believe.

"If your masters are indeed gods, as you say, why did they not destroy the creature from the sea?"

"Two of them went out to kill it, but they saw its eyes and horror overcame them so that they died. After that they saw that this was a very evil creature, and in their wisdom, they left it alone."

"They must be poor creatures to be so easily frightened to death. In my country we could not believe in gods that ever die. Yet the very first of your masters that I saw when I reached this island has since died and his body has been burned."

"His body—yes. But he himself still lives. I was taught these things by the gods when I was a child, and it is wrong of you to try and make me think otherwise."

I began to realise the tremendous strength of early impression. I could call to mind that I had seen evidence enough of it before ever I came to Thule. It seemed almost impossible for me—one man— to fight against this crafty and complex organisation of tyranny and slavery that was here blindly accepted. I turned to another of her terrors—her terror of the sea.

"Do you swim well?" I asked her.

She laughed. "One swims as one walks or runs. Why not? You ask such strange things."

"Very well then," I said, "you shall swim in the sea."

"No. The sea is the evil water. If one had only that water to drink, one would die. Is that not so?"

"It is, but——"

"Very well then. We are rightly taught not to touch the sea. You speak to me sometimes very much as if you were a god, and you boast of freedom, and you have come all the way from a far-off country; but you yourself would not dare to enter the sea."

It was my turn to laugh. "I am going to swim in it this evening," I said.

"I implore you not to do it," said Dream.

"I shall come to no harm."

"You will most certainly die."

"You will see that I shall not."

"It would be a pity, because I myself perhaps may escape death yet for a few days longer, and I might begin to love you."

We had now reached the entrance to the caves.

9

The side of the brown sandstone cliff was perforated like a gigantic rabbit warren. I judged the cliffs to be natural in character, but in the labyrinth of passages and rooms upon which one first entered, much artificial work had been done. In places columns of brick upheld the roof, and the walls had been trimmed and levelled by a tool. I guessed—for it was a point upon which Dream could tell me nothing—that the lords of Thule had at one time some intention of making use of these natural excavations, and that they had been frightened from their task by the absurd superstition which Dream had recounted to me. I could not believe in the marvellous amphibious monster that had come out of the sea, and for fifty years or more had lived in the heart of these cliffs.

I told Dream of my doubts, but she was not to be shaken. The track of the animal when it went in had been clearly visible, and no track had been found to show that it had gone out again.

"On what then does it live?" I asked.

"Things that it finds in the water."

"But you tell me that it has never gone back to the sea again."

"Never. But far within the caves—much farther than I have ever gone—there is a great lake. It lives there. I will take you to a place where you can hear the roar of the water falling into the lake. Follow me closely or you may lose yourself."

She took me through many winding passages until she reached a point where she knelt and put her ear to the ground. She made me do the same. I could certainly hear the sound of running water below me, but that did not prove the existence of the lake, much less of the monster that was supposed to inhabit the lake. I told her this, and she did not like it.

"When you found me in the forest," she said, "I was very sad because I had spoken to no one for many days, and I was to die and there was no escape. Then because of your companionship and because you seem to hope and to fear nothing, I became lifted up again. It is necessary for you to think as I think, or I shall grow sad again. Therefore, you must believe in the great serpent."

"We will not speak of him. Show me where you sleep."

177

She took me by a passage that rapidly grew narrower until I could hardly force my way into the chamber beyond. It was a simple sleeping-apartment containing a bed of dried bracken and nothing more.

"Yes," she said, "I chose this place because the passage was so narrow and the great serpent which was in the lake was so big. Here he could not get to me."

"And how do you manage about food?"

"I have plenty—far too much. Every night someone or other of my people brings food and puts it at the entrance of the cave. They do not go near to the cave because they believe in the serpent, not being so wise as you are. I would not go into the cave myself were it not that I have to die anyhow."

"But do your gods permit this?"

"I do not know. They do not care to come very near to the caves. I myself think that they do know that food is brought to me and do not wish to prevent it. They have only one punishment. They would not starve me slowly. They would point the death-rod at me and burn my heart out in an instant. But you remind me that I have become very hungry after my swim. You also must think as I do and be hungry too, and we will eat together."

She showed me another room nearer to the entrance where she kept her supplies. They were simple enough. There was a pile of thin sweet biscuit and another pile of dried fruit. This in colour and flavour was like a raisin, but four times the size.

"That grows in the forest," said Dream. "In the autumn when the fresh fruit is ripe it is very good indeed. I shall not live to pick any more of it, and for that I am very sorry."

She was still, I think, rather offended with me for my disbelief in the creature that came out of the sea, but on the whole we chatted amicably enough. I can see now that I did a clumsy thing in thus suddenly and crudely trying to upset a tradition in which she had grown up. It is not perhaps very desirable to shake the faith of anybody in anything, unless that faith be distinctly and immediately harmful. I am a simple seaman and unused to missionary work, and it is small wonder that I bungled it.

After we had feasted, Dream went off to her bed of bracken and I once more climbed the hill to watch the sea. All that afternoon I watched, using at times my perspective-glass, but never once could I make out a sail.

I may admit that my plans were now changed and that the change

178

was entirely due to the strong fascination which Dream had for me—far stronger than I cared to let her know at present. I no longer cared to explore the town or to find out more of the condition of the workers than Dream herself could tell me. I had decided to throw in my lot with her and, if it were possible, to save her from the cruel death with which she was threatened. How I was to do this I did not know. I could only wait and see what chance might offer itself.

I cut bracken for my bed, and laden with this I made my way back to the cave again. There Dream awaited me and all traces of her ill-humour had vanished. I did not insist on my swim in the sea that night, lest it should pain her further. We sat and talked together until the stars came out. It was the first time since I had been on the island that I had looked up at the stars. I could find nothing that I recognised. I wondered where in the world or out of the world I now found myself. The problem did not disturb me greatly. It was pleasant to sit and hear Dream's recital of her story of the squirrel that she captured and tamed. Her voice was curiously soft and caressing.

Soon she went back to her bed and I spread my bracken in the door of the cave and lay down. It was in the night that her people came to bring her food, and I wished, if possible, to see them and to speak with them.

But this experiment turned out ill. I had slept but an hour when I was awakened by a footfall, and looking out from the cave I saw striding towards me a man who bore a tray on his head. But when he was within a hundred yards of the cave, he set the tray down and turned back again. I called out that I was a friend and would speak with him, but I do not think he understood what I said, and the sound of a strange voice filled him with terror. He ran off at the top of his speed.

Early that morning I had my swim in the sea, but on my return, I said nothing to Dream about it. I told her, however, how the man had run away when he heard my voice the night before.

"You did not do this very well," said Dream. "You told me that you did not wish to go to the town anymore and that you would remain with me. But it seems that I am not enough and that you do wish to speak with others. Very well then. This night I will watch outside the cave and I will go to the man who brings the food and I will bring him in to you. He is, I think, a man who loves me very much indeed."

I told her that I had changed my mind and did not wish to see the man. A brisk wind was blowing and we spent most of the day in the forest together. Again, from time to time I scanned the horizon with

179

my perspective-glass, and again with no result whatever. I wondered in what deserted sea this island might be placed. Throughout the day Dream was silent and thoughtful, but she was in no immediate fear, knowing that on such a day her gods would not enter the forest. Next morning, I went for my swim in the sea again, and on my return, Dream told me that she knew what I had done. She had seen me swimming far out.

"Why did you not tell me you had done this?"

"I feared to disturb your mind."

"I am not a child and am not to be treated as a child. I can think as you think about the sea if I like. I dare do anything that you dare to do."

I told her that I had no doubt of it. Rain fell for the greater part of that day and we remained in the cave talking. She told me of the life she had led and of the laws by which her people were governed.

I have said that I had begun to hate the lords of Thule—the first-class beings as they designated themselves—the gods, as the poor ignorant workers supposed them to be. I hate them still. I despise their sexless emasculate nervousness. I despise their want of the warmer sins and their subjection to the colder. I despise their selfishness even while I admire their wisdom.

Yet, if I am to speak honestly, their despotism—not benevolent and wholly self-interested—produced a finer race of workers than is to be found in my own country today. They were better fed, better clothed, better housed. They were healthier—disease was almost unknown—and they were happier. I use the last word deliberately. The cruelty with which they were treated—and to our modern minds it was abominable cruelty—was after all not capricious cruelty. It proceeded on laws as immutable as the laws of nature. The mother of the weakling who saw her child destroyed at any rate knew why; and when the lightning strikes the best and most promising of us, we do not know why.

Every man was specially trained for special work, and his own inclination was always taken into account; for the greater the inclination, the greater—as a rule—the aptitude. The view taken of women was definitely animal, and only in exceptional cases were women allowed to live beyond the age of forty-five. On the other hand, no woman was worked hard; women who were about to be mothers or had recently become mothers, were treated with a delicate consideration far beyond anything to be found in our Factory Acts; and no woman was influenced in her choice of a mate by vulgar claims of a financial or social character.

The children were free from the thwarting and snubbing and the curse of competitive examination which we are pleased to call education. Each child was taught a few essentials very thoroughly. The training was in each case individual and based on a clever study of the child's nature. If reading or writing or arithmetic was unnecessary for the work which the child would ultimately be called upon to do, then none of these things was taught. It might almost be said that the children were spoiled. But they learned early the immutable and inexorable nature of the laws imposed on their race.

Towards the close of this day Dream became once more sad and depressed. Suddenly she rose and said that she was going back to her own people in the town.

"But," I said, "you know that this means death."

"There is one thing worse than death which may happen to a woman. It is useless for you to try to prevent me. If I cannot go to the town, then tomorrow I shall eat the poison berries in the forest."

I had intended, if ever I could find the way, to take Dream back with me to my own country and there to marry her. It seemed to me now that there was no hope of this. I make no defence of what I said or did. I do not know if under those circumstances any defence is needed. But I told Dream that she need not seek the death-rod of her gods or the poison berries of the forest, because the one thing which is worse than death had not happened to her.

10

There followed sixteen days of such great and idyllic happiness that for that alone it seems worthwhile to have lived my life. Dream lost her terror of the sea and every morning swam out with me. Sometimes we would catch trout in the forest pools, and these I would clean and cook in the manner I had learned in the South Seas, on hot stones and ashes, getting fire from the sun by means of the lens of my perspective-glass. But this we could only hazard on days when the wind blew strongly, lest the smoke of our fire should signal our whereabouts. I was not able to shake Dream's belief in the creature that came out of the sea, but she seemed no longer to have any fear of that or of anything.

"When death comes," she said, "it will come to both of us. Every day is a gain. Yet, when one cannot possibly be happier, it is not hard to die. One has drunk the wine of life."

I had it in my mind to attempt some further exploration of the caves. In this I had been so far prevented by the fact that we had no means of lighting ourselves. It was on the morning of the sixteenth day that I found in the forest wood of a very resinous character which I guessed would make good torches. I got me a store of this and carried it down to the cave, telling Dream what I meant to do.

"I shall go with you," she said. Nor could I dissuade her from it.

We kept a small fire burning at the entrance to the cave that day, and when the sun had gone down, we lit our torches from the fire and started off, taking no other equipment than my clasp-knife and a lump of chalk with which to mark our way in the labyrinth.

We soon reached a point where but two roads were left, each so wide and lofty that a coach and four might easily have been driven along it. One of these roads led upwards, and I made no doubt emerged on the farther side of the hill. The other one struck more abruptly downward, and this was the road which we took. Here, if it existed at all, I should find the subterranean lake. As we went on, the noise of falling water became more and more distinct. I was excited by the adventure and eager to see more.

Presently the road widened into a vast hall, so vast that our torches could not illumine the farthest recesses of it. And here it was as well that I looked carefully to each step, for I found myself suddenly on the edge of a precipice. Lying flat on my stomach and holding out my torch, I could see a vast stretch of black water below, into which at one end a cataract thundered. In the middle of this lake there projected something which looked like a smooth boulder of rock. I wondered what it might be.

"We have plenty of torches?" asked Dream.

"Plenty."

"Then we will see what it is."

She waved her torch round her head till it was all ablaze and then flung it down. It fell on that great mass in the middle of the lake. The mass turned slowly over, showing shaggy hair matted with slime. The smell of burning hair came up to us and with it a deep groan that seemed to shake the cave.

We fled in panic. I must indeed ascribe it to chance and to no courage of my own that I kept my grip of the torch. We did not even pause to look at the chalk marks we had made for our guidance, and in consequence found ourselves lost for a while in the labyrinth of

182

passages at the entrance to the cave. At last, we found the way out and made our way to the forest. There we spent the remainder of the night, wakeful and talking of the wonders we had seen. It was the last night that we spent together.

The sun had scarcely risen when I saw a few feet away from us a little smoke flickering over the powdered soil.

"What is that?" I asked.

"That is the end," said Dream. "We shall die together."

Rapidly the smoke, which did not rise and disperse, became more opaque, vibrating until it took solid shape. Before us leered the misshapen head and bright beady eyes of the Professor.

His right hand covered with a rubber glove slipped out of the boot and drew forth the death-rod.

"The stranger dies first," he said, and pointed the rod at me. Dream clung to me. I felt a sensation as of fire in my throat.

And now comes what seems to me—though it may not so seem to others—the strangest part of my story. Passing through a kind of swoon, I found myself gently rocked as on board a ship. Opening my eyes I saw two men bending over me. One of them held a glass containing brandy to my lips.

"You see?" said a voice triumphantly. "The beggar's alive and I win my bet."

I found afterwards that I was on board the steamship *Hermione* bound from Alexandria to Cardiff with a cargo of cotton seed. I had been found senseless at the bottom of an open boat. I was treated with plenty of rough kindness and brought back to my own country; but over the story which I told them the crew shook their heads gravely.

Since then, nothing of import happened to me until I was brought to this great barrack-like place where I now live in fair comfort. There are many doctors here and many guests. Some of the guests, I fear, have an aberration of the intellect, for they say strange things. I am well contented. I have lived my life. But since no one will listen to my marvellous experiences in the island of Thule—or if they listen at all make a jest of them—I have written them down here for the service of another and a wiser generation.

The Widower

The decision of Edward Morris to marry again was one of the few practical things of his record. He had married first at the age of eighteen without the knowledge of his parents. His wife died two years later. He had no children by her. At her death he was desolate.

He was as desolate, that is, as one can be at twenty. He was free from the annoying minor-poet habit of advertising his afflictions, but it was quite dear to himself that there was nothing more left. Yet it is idle for a man to say he will stop when Nature, his proprietor, says that he will go on. There is no comedy at ninety, and there is no tragedy at twenty.

After he had deposited the remains of his wife in Brompton cemetery—she had a strong aversion to cremation and inwardly believed that it destroyed the immortal soul—he went off into the country, selecting a village where he knew nobody. Here he learned by heart considerable portions of the poems of Heine, neglected to return the call of the rector, and bored himself profusely. It must not be understood that he resented the boredom. That was what life was to be in future, a continuous dreariness.

After a brief stay in the village, he went off to Paris to study art. At the time when he thought of giving himself to music all noticed his ability in painting. When he took to art, they remembered that he had musical talent. A year later, when he returned to England to live the life of a hermit, to teach in song what he had learned in sorrow, some said that he was a lost artist, and some that he was a lost musician, and others that he was a well-defined case of dilettantism. It is, however, difficult to be a hermit in London. London has many tentacles; it puts them out and draws you into the liveliest part of itself. A claim of relationship, an old friendship, a piece of medical advice, a chance meeting—anything may become a tentacle.

Almost before he knows it the misanthropical hermit is dragged from his shell and is writing that he has much pleasure in accepting her very kind invitation for the thirteenth, and wonders if that man in Sackville Street will be able to make him some evening clothes in time, his others being not so much clothes as a relic of those pre-hermit days when his wife, his only love, still lived and took him out to dinners, and would have the glass down in the hansoms. The thought that he resented this last action at the time saddens him, but the acceptance is posted. He is drawn into the vortex.

Once in, Edward Morris had to explain to himself how he got there. Nobody else wanted any explanation. Nobody else knew that the first time he took his hostess in to dinner he looked down the long table towards his host's right hand and remembered. His explanation to himself was that he did it to avoid comment. One could not wear one's heart on one's coat sleeve. One must go somewhere and must do something. One must unfortunately live, even when the savour of life has gone. So, he lived, and in living the savour of life came back again.

It was on a muggy December evening that he accompanied Lady Marchsea and her eminent husband to a first-night performance. When the eminent man was grumbling at the draught, and Lady Marchsea was, with justification, admiring herself, her dress, and everything that was hers, Edward Morris looked up. Out of the gloom of the box above him a brown-faced girl with dark eyes, her chin leaning on her white gloves, bent forward and looked down.

Yet it was not till the end of the first act that he asked who she was and was told that she was nobody, but was apparently with the Martins, who were very, very dear friends, and would Mr Morris take her round? That was the beginning of it, and the end of it was his engagement to Adela Constantia Graham, who was nobody. Everybody who knew Adela Constantia knew that it was an excellent thing for her—a much wealthier man than she had any reason to expect. Everyone who knew Edward Morris knew that it was the best thing for him. "Ballast," said Lady Marchsea, emphatically, "that is what marriage means to a man like Edward Morris. He needs ballast; something to make him concentrate himself and trust himself; something to encourage him and urge him on."

Her notions of the general uses of ballast were vague, but her conviction was sincere that Edward Morris, happily re-married, would achieve something in one, or possibly in all, of the arts. Her eminent husband said: "Nice sort of man, but no good really." But still he paid for the dinner-service with the sanctifying mark on the bottom of all the plates, which they forwarded to Edward Morris a short time before the wedding—the wedding which never took place.

About a week before the date fixed for that wedding it occurred to Edward Morris in a moment of leisure—he was naturally very busy at the time—that his first wife had been a jealous woman, and he wondered what she would have thought and said if she had been alive. He could laugh at the illogicality. If she had been alive there would have been nothing to think or to say. The haunting face with the chin pressed on the white gloves against the darkness at the back of the box would have been merely a face and nothing more, and would not have haunted. He collected his old love-letters and burned them.

Other little relics of his first wife he gathered together, had them placed in a box and deposited at his bankers. The old life was done; the new life was beginning. Yet one night as he stood in a darkened room with Adela Constantia in his arms the door opened with a little quick click some few inches. She stepped back from him, thinking it was a servant, and he turned white, thinking, in a moment of madness, that it was someone else; then he went to the door and opened it wider. No one was there.

The position of the widower who marries again is irritating to him if he be, as Edward Morris was, a man of nice feeling. He has to say, and to believe, that he loves as he never loved in his life before. Scraps of used romance must be whipped up out of his respectable past to set against the virginal fervour of the young woman who has just begun to love him. Yet he feels that all this is an insult to the dead—to the woman who loved him before. A man of the world has a happy habit of forgetting and of ignoring. He may marry for the second or third time quite easily. He takes nothing too seriously. He may order a new overcoat, but he does not feel that the coat will be worthless unless he swears and tries to believe that he never wore a coat like that before. Morris, however, was a sentimentalist, and so he became irritated with himself. The next step inevitably followed. He became irritated with his dead wife. She had got her cold arms round his neck and was dragging him down and holding him back from the joyful development of his life.

When in London it was his custom to visit her grave in Brompton cemetery at regular intervals, once every month. During his engagement to Adela Constantia, he made up his mind that this regular visit must be dropped. Some arrangement could be made to have the grave kept in decent order, but he could not go near it again. He remembered having been told a story of a widower who married again and went hand-in-hand with his second wife to stand by the grave of the first. It had been told him as something pathetic. He had never been able to see in it anything but a subject for a humorous paper; Guy de Maupassant would have done wonders with it.

He settled the day when the last visit should be made. He selected an appropriate wreath, in which everlastings and dead leaves were symbolically interwoven. But that afternoon more than ever before his hatred to his dead wife grew within him. He recollected her strange belief with regard to cremation. Fire destroyed everything, even the immortal soul, and it seemed as if fire destroyed love too. He remembered that he had burnt her letters. As he drove down Regent Street an old friend, a man whom he had not seen for some time, recognised him. He stopped the cab and his friend came up.

"Why do I never see you now?" said the friend. "But of course, I know. Very much engaged, aren't you? (That's not bad for an impromptu, by the way.) I suppose you are going there now?"

"No," said Morris, "as a matter of fact I am not."

"Well, you are evidently going somewhere, and you carry a big box with you with a florist's label on it, so all I can say is that if you are not going there, you ought to be."

Edward Morris laughed, and to laugh was the last touch of horror.

"Well," the friend said, "if you are really not going to see Miss Graham, I have no scruples in annexing you. Come round to the club for a game of billiards."

"Thanks," said Morris, "I am afraid I am very busy this afternoon."

However, he let himself be persuaded. The box containing the wreath was left in the charge of the hall-porter at the club. On the following day Morris despatched the wreath to Brompton cemetery by a messenger-boy, where the symbolical offering was deposited on the grave of Charles Ernest Jessop, who died at the age of two and a half, and of whose death or previous existence Morris was unaware.

Messenger-boys are so careless. Morris never even attempted to visit the cemetery again. It was not only anger, it was not only hatred; it was also fear that kept him away. He was assured in his own mind that the dead woman was awake again and was watching him jealously.

The moment when he had just awoken from sleep was always a horrible one for him. The fear of the dead woman was in his mind then and nothing else was very dear. He left the electric light on all night and, as a rule, slept fairly well and without any haunting or painful dreams. But the moment of waking was always a trial. He kept on expecting to see something that he never did see. He would not have wondered if, as he awoke, someone had touched his hand, or the electric light had been suddenly switched off.

Of course, everybody noticed that he looked wretchedly ill. Adela Constantia was in despair about his health. There were things about him which were very queer; that he did not like dark rooms. That when he was talking to her, he would suddenly look over his shoulder—at nothing. The comforting doctor told her that Morris has been very busy indeed with the preparation for his married life and, the doctor added, a lot of worry upsets the nerves. This is quite true.

On his wedding morning he certainly looked much fitter to be buried than to be married. His best man gave him champagne and told him to hold his head up more. The bride made an adorable and pathetic figure; a beautiful young girl is always a pathetic figure on her wedding-morning. Her sisters fluttered around her, ready to cry at the right moments. Her father looked a little nervous and elated. He had had quite a long talk with Lady Marchsea, whose husband was kept away by the toothache. The ceremony went with its customary brilliance until that point when the bridegroom was required to say: "I, Edward, take thee, Adela Constantia." He said this in a loud voice, but he did not say "Adela Constantia"; he gave another name. There was a moment's pause, and while everybody was looking at everybody he fainted and fell.

At the inquest it was found that the blow on the head from the sharp edge of the stone step satisfactorily accounted for the death. All the evening papers had readable paragraphs headed "Tragic End to a Fashionable Wedding Ceremony."

And Adela Constantia married somebody else.

And the dead woman went to sleep again.

Zero

1

James Smith was a trainer and exhibitor of performing dogs. His age was forty-five, but on the stage, he looked less, moving always with an alertness suggestive of youth. His face was dominant, but not cruel. He never petted a dog. On the other hand, he never thrashed a dog, unless he considered that the dog had deserved it. He had small eyes and a strong jaw. He was somewhat undersized, and his body was lean and hard. This afternoon, clad in a well-cut flannel suit, and wearing a straw hat, he sat on the steps of a bathing-machine on the beach at Helmstone. He was waiting for the man inside the machine to come out. Meanwhile he made himself a cigarette, rolling it on his leg with one hand, and securing the paper by a small miracle instead of by gum.

As he lit the cigarette the door of the bathing-machine opened, and a tall young man of athletic build came out. He was no better dressed than James Smith. At the same time, it was just as obvious that he was a gentleman as that Smith was not.

"Hallo!" said the young man. "You're all right again, I see. What was it—touch of cramp?"

"No, sir," said Smith. "I'm not a strong swimmer, and I've done no sea bathing before. I never meant to get out of my depth, but the current took me. What I want now is to do something to show my gratitude."

"Gratitude be blowed!" said the young man cheerfully. "It was no trouble to me, and I happened to be there."

"Well, sir," said Smith, "will you let me give you a dog? I've got some very good dogs. I should take it as a favour if you would."

He took from a Russia leather case a clean professional card, and presented it to the young man.

"That, of course, is not my real name. That's just the French name they've put on the programmes. I'm James Smith, and I have a two

191

weeks' engagement at the Hippodrome here. I've got my dogs in a stable not far from there."

The young man glanced at his watch.

"Well," he said, "I've got nothing to do this morning, I'll go and have a look at the dogs, at any rate. They're a pretty clever lot, I suppose."

"They can do what they've been taught," said Smith; "all except one of them, and he can do what no man can teach him."

There was a great noise when they entered the stables. Twenty dogs, most of them black poodles, all tried to talk at once. Smith said something decisively, but quietly, and the dogs became silent again. Smith made a sign to one of the poodles and held out his walking-stick. It looked quite impossible, but the dog went over it.

"My word, but that's a wonderful jump!" said the young man.

"It is," said Smith. "You won't find another dog of that breed in this country that can do the same. He's yours, if you like to take him."

"No; hang it all! I'm not going to do that. I'm not going to take a dog which you can use professionally. What about the beggar that you said you could not teach?"

Smith pointed to a huge brindled bulldog, who lay in one corner of the stable absolutely motionless, watching them intently.

"That's the one," he said. "He's never been on the stage at all. He couldn't even be taught to fetch and carry."

"And you just keep him because you're fond of him?"

"Fond of him? No, I'm not fond of dogs. They're my livelihood, and I don't do so badly out of it. But I'm not fond of 'em—know too much about 'em."

"Then what do you keep him for?"

"You may call it a sense of justice, or you may call it curiosity. He's a rum 'un, that dog is, and no mistake."

"In what way rum?"

"I'll tell you. He's a dog that sees dangers ahead. He knows when things are going to happen. I had him as a puppy, and when I found I could teach him nothing, I made up my mind to get quit of him. I was going off by train that day to a village fifteen miles away, and I knew a man there who I thought might take a fancy to Zero."

"Zero, you call him?"

"Yes; that was a bit of my fun. As a performing dog he was just absolutely last—number naught, see? Well, as I was saying, there was I on the platform with the dog at my heel and the ticket in my hand.

Just as I was going to get into the train, he made a jump for that ticket, caught it in his mouth and bolted with it, nipping in among a lot of milk-cans. I called him, and he wouldn't come out. Then I went in after him, and he bolted again. By the time I did get him I had missed my train, and I didn't give him half a jolly good hiding for it, I don't think! If I'd gone by that train, I shouldn't have been talking to you now. Collision three miles from the station. Well, you don't apologise to a dog. All I could do was to keep him. But that wasn't the only instance. The beggar knows things."

"Apparently he didn't know that you were going to drown yourself this morning."

"If he knew anything about it, he knew that I wasn't."

"Good-tempered dog?"

"Oh, all bulldogs are safe! You want to look after him with collies. He doesn't like 'em. If he gets hold of one, it's bad for the collie. Otherwise, a baby could handle him."

Zero had crossed over to them, and the young man stooped down and patted him. The dog expressed delight.

"I can send him round to your hotel," said Smith; "or, for that matter, he'd follow you. He's taken a fancy to you, he has."

"Look here," said the young man, "let me buy him. I'm not a millionaire, but I can afford to buy a dog. I'd like to have this one, and there's no reason on earth why you should give him to me."

"You'd like to have him, and I can afford to give him to you, and I want to give him to you. You must let a man indulge his sense of gratitude. It's only fair."

"Very well, if you say so. Many thanks. I'll step over to the Hippodrome and see your show tonight."

"Do. You'll be surprised."

The two men talked for a few moments longer, and then Zero's new owner said that he must be getting back to lunch.

"You really think the dog will follow me?" he said. "I don't want to take a lead?"

"I know he'll follow you. I tell you I know dogs. They take fancies sometimes. You can take that dog out, and if I call him back myself, he wouldn't come."

"I bet you a sovereign he would."

"I'll take that," said Smith. "You go on with him, and I'll wait here."

The young man walked a few yards away with the dog at his heels, and then Smith called the dog back, loudly and insistently. The dog did not give the slightest sign that he had heard anything at all. When his master stood still, he remained standing patiently at his heel, and never once looked back.

The young man laughed as he took out his sovereign-case.

"Queer chap, Zero. Well, you've won, Mr Smith. Catch!"

Mr Smith caught the sovereign adroitly, and went back into the stable.

"Yes," he said to the cleverest of the black poodles, "I don't know that I wouldn't sooner he'd taken you."

It was seldom that Smith addressed any of his dogs, except to give an order. The poodle did not know what to make of it. He whined faintly.

Richard Staines went back to his hotel, with Zero at his heels. He had his own sitting-room opening into his bedroom at the hotel, and he intended to keep the dog there at night. This was against the laws of the hotel; therefore, Staines had to pause a few moments in the hall to get the laws altered. One of the arguments he used was that he would only be there two days longer, and it would not matter for so short a time. The other argument was bribery and corruption. After which he and Zero went up in the lift together.

2

Staines was a partner in succession to his father in an old-established firm of stockbrokers with a good connection. He had a small flat in St James's Place, and thither he brought Zero. Zero accepted metropolitan life philosophically. There was a dingy cat in the basement of St James's Place, and he was quite willing to make friends with her. He looked mildly puzzled at her definite assurance that she would kill him if he came a step nearer. It never occurred to him to attempt to injure her. But for one slight lapse—he had killed a collie, and cost Staines compensation—his behaviour was admirable.

He was fortunate in having a master who was fond of outdoor life, and not at all fond of London. Every weekend, and occasionally on a fine afternoon, if business was slack, he got away into the country. He never quite seemed to understand the terror which his appearance inspired in some young or foolish people. When children rushed from him shrieking, he would look up at his master as much as to say, "Can you understand this?" And he was careful not to increase their terror by running after them.

One day in the park a muddy-faced little girl of six, who feared nothing at all, came up and patted him, examined his teeth with curious interest, and finally sat on him. These attentions Zero received with great joy. Weeks passed, and he had not given the slightest sign of the curious instinct with which his former master had credited him.

Staines liked him, principally because he so obviously liked Staines. Staines thought him a faithful and affectionate beast, with nothing to distinguish him from the normal. When he recalled Smith's story of the snatched railway ticket, he explained it all as a chance. These flukes did happen sometimes.

And then one afternoon he went to call upon the Murrays—a practice that was becoming rather common with him—and as Jane was particularly fond of Zero, Zero accompanied him. When they reached the square, Zero sat down on the pavement. Staines called him, and the dog wagged his tail, but did not move. Staines went on without him, but presently had to stop, for Zero had now changed his tactics, and was running round and round Staines' legs. The incident of the railway ticket flashed across his mind. He was a business man, and not superstitious; however, it did not matter to him in the least which two sides of the square he took, and he determined to turn back and take the other two sides, and see what would happen. As soon as he turned back, Zero followed at heel in his usual quiet and unobtrusive manner.

A loud crash caused him to look round. A heavy stone coping had fallen from a roof, and if the dog had not brought him back it would have fallen upon him. Here was a nice little story with a mildly sensational interest for Staines to tell over the teacups.

Mr Murray was matter-of-fact.

"Your story is true, of course," he said. "Your dog did make you take the other two sides of the square, and the fact that you turned back probably saved your life. But, all the same, the dog didn't know. By what means could the brain of a dog recognise the imminent dissolution of part of the roof of a house?"

"Zero did know," said Jane. She was Mr Murray's only daughter, and without being wildly beautiful, was an extremely pleasing and friendly young woman to look at. At present she was feeding Zero with thin bread-and-butter. Zero had been told, even by Jane herself, that this form of diet was bad for his figure, but he accepted it with resignation—rather an enthusiastic kind of resignation.

"What makes you say that Zero knew?" her father asked, with indulgent superiority.

"Because I know he knew," said Jane firmly and finally.

"And then," said Mr Murray, "women tell us they ought to have the vote."

"Miss Murray," said Richard firmly, "that dog is not to be fed any more, please."

"Last piece," said Jane. "And he's promised to do Swedish exercises."

Richard was inclined to agree with Mr Murray. The coincidence was again remarkable; it might even be called very extraordinary. And, given a choice of two things, Richard preferred to believe the easier. Why, fond though he was of Zero, he had to admit that the dog was not even clever.

He had tried to teach Zero to find a hidden biscuit, but though he had hidden the biscuit in all manner of places he had never yet selected a place that Zero had been able to discover. He was just a dear old fool of a bulldog, and it was absurd to suppose that he was a miracle.

But Jane Murray remained firm in her belief, and even condescended to be serious about it.

"Look here," she said, "if you put your horse at a jump, and you're feeling a bit shy of it yourself, do you mean to say the horse doesn't know?"

"Of course, he knows. But he only knows it by the way you ride him."

"Well, I've had it happen to me. All I can say is that I wasn't conscious of riding any differently. It was my first season in Ireland, and I wasn't used to the walls. I said to myself, 'It's got to be.' I did really mean to get over. But the horse knew the funk in my head and refused. However, I'll give you another point. How do you explain the homing instinct of animals?"

"I've never thought about it. I suppose when a pigeon gets up high it can see no end of a distance."

"That won't do. Dogs and cats have the same instinct—especially cats. For that matter, crabs have been taken from the sea and returned to it again at a point eighty miles away, and have found their way back. It's not done by sight, scent, or hearing. It must be done by some special sense which they have got and we have not."

"It sounds plausible."

"It's the only possible explanation. And when once we've admitted that animals have a special sense which we have not, I don't quite see how we are to say what the limitations of that sense are. It is not really a bit more wonderful that Zero should have the sense of impending danger than that a crab, eighty miles from home, should be able to find its way back."

"Well, you may be right. I wish now that I'd asked that chap Smith a bit more about the dog."

A few days later one of the partners in Richard's business announced his intention of getting married. He was a junior partner, two years younger than Richard.

"Well, Bill," said Richard, after he had offered his congratulations, "what shall I give you for a wedding-present?"

"Give us that dog of yours."

"Never. Try again."

"Oh, I was only rotting. But seriously, I'd as soon have a dog as anything. Not a bulldog—they're too ugly."

"It's a good, honest kind of ugliness. What breed then?"

"Gwen's keen on black poodles."

That settled it. Richard hunted up Smith's card. He had always meant to do some business with the man if he got an opportunity, and here was the opportunity. On the following day he journeyed to Wandsworth and found Smith. Smith looked less spruce and prosperous than before. He did not actually declare that the performing dog had had his day, but he admitted that business was not what it had been.

"Too many of us in it. And, I tell you, I'm afraid to bring out a new idea—it's pinched before you've had a week's use of it. Public's a bit off it, too. I'm doing practically nothing with the 'alls. I train for others, and I'm trying to build up a business as a dealer. Only first-class dogs, mind."

"That's what I want. I came here to buy a dog."

"Let's see. Bulldogs were your fancy. Well, I've got one of the Stone breed that's won the only time it was shown and will win again."

"This is not for myself. It's a present. Black poodle."

"I see. Well, you've come to the right market. How far were you prepared to go?"

"Show me a really valuable dog and I will pay the real value. I'm not buying for the show-bench; but I want the best breed, good health, good temper, cleverness and training—two years old for choice."

"Ask enough," said Smith, smiling. "Well, if you don't mind stepping into the yard, I can fit you. I'm asking twenty guineas, and he's worth every penny of it—he'd bring that money back, to anybody who cared to take it, before a year was out."

The dog was shown—an aristocrat with qualities of temper and intelligence not always to be found in the aristocrat. Richard Staines thought he would be paying quite enough, but decided to pay it. He returned to the house to write his cheque.

"There you are, Mr Smith. By the way, do you remember Zero, the dog you gave me? He's sitting in my taxi outside."

"I remember him. He'd never win prizes for anybody—not like that poodle you've just bought. You couldn't teach him anything either. But he could see ahead, that dog could."

Smith heard how Richard Staines had been saved from the falling roof, and evinced no surprise at it at all. "Yes," he said, "that dog always knew. Did I tell you about the milk?"

"No. What was that?"

"Me and Cowbit next door got our milk from the same man. I went out one morning to take the can in, when Zero came bullocking past me and knocked the can over. He never tried to drink the milk that was spilled, but just stood there, wagging his old tail. Mind you, sir, that was after he had saved me from the train smash. 'Well,' I said to him, 'I suppose you know'; and I went in to Cowbits' to tell them not to touch that milk. Cowbit laughed at the story, and took milk in his tea. But his missus wouldn't have any, and wouldn't let the baby have none either. Cowbit was ill for days and pretty near died. Mineral poison it was, from one of the milk-pans going wrong."

"How do you suppose the dog knew?"

"Me suppose? Why, I never asked myself the question. He did know—that was all about it. Still, if I had to explain it, I should say it was some kind of an instinct."

And Richard mercifully forbore to ask Mr Smith how he would explain that particular kind of instinct.

3

Richard was best-man at his partner's wedding. He afterwards attended a crowded reception. It was too crowded; and there were far too many people there who wanted to talk to Jane Murray. She was popular, and there was a group round her all the time. Not for five minutes could Richard get her to himself. It was this selfishness on the part of others which depressed him, not the reception champagne, which was no worse than is usual on such occasions.

The crowds bored him and when he got back to his flat the solitude bored him. Not even Zero was there. Richard's valet had taken the dog out for exercise; this had been done in obedience to Richard's own orders, but it now seemed to him in the light of a grievance. The grievance became more acute when his servant returned without the dog.

"Very sorry, sir; I wouldn't have had it happen for anything. I was walking in Regent's Park, with the dog at my heels, and all of a sudden, he made a bolt for it. I whistled and called, but he went straight on. And when I started running after him, he made a dash into a big shrubbery. That was how he foxed me, sir. While I was hunting him on one side, he must have bolted out on the other. Never known the dog act like that before. It was just as if something had come over him. Speaking in a general way—"

"Well, what did you do?" asked Richard sharply.

"I spoke to the park-keepers, and to a couple of policemen outside, and then I went on to Scotland Yard. The address is on the collar, sir. I should think there's no doubt you'll—"

"That'll do!" snapped Richard. "I thought you could be trusted to take a dog out, at any rate. Well, my mistake."

With a further expression of contrition, the man withdrew, and almost instantly the telephone-bell on Richard's desk rang sharply.

He went slowly to the telephone, and managed to put the concentration of weariness and disgust into the word "Hallo!"

The voice that answered him was the voice of Mr Murray.

"That you, Staines? . . . Right—yes, quite well, thanks. . . . I wanted to say when Jane got back this evening she found Zero waiting for her outside our front door. . . . He's here now, and seems quite cheerful about it . . . . Thought you might like to know."

Richard rapidly changed his tone of dejection for that of social enthusiasm. He thanked profusely. He would send for the dog at once.

"Well, look here," said Mr Murray, "Jane and I have got a night off—dining alone. If by any chance you're free, I wish you'd join us. Then you can take the intelligent hound back with you."

Richard said that he was free, which was a lie; and that he would be delighted to come, which was perfectly true.

He subsequently rang up a man at his club, cancelled an engagement on the score of ill-health, and went to dress. Such was his elation that he even condescended to tell his servant that the dog had been found and was all right.

Zero had done wrong. He must have known that he had done wrong; but he welcomed his master with gambols in the manner of an ecstatic bullock, and showed no sign of penitence at all. It was the habit of Richard to punish a dog that had done wrong, but he did not punish Zero. He called him a silly old idiot, and asked him what he thought he had been doing, but Zero recognised that this was badinage and exercised his tail furiously.

At dinner, Mr Murray said that Zero was an interesting problem. The dog was apparently a fine judge at sight of the stability of structures, but could not find his way home.

"That's not proved," said Richard, laughing. "He knew his way home all right, but he was trying to better himself. He's not fed at tea-time in St James's Place."

"He's had nothing here," said Jane.

"Really, Jane," said her father.

"Practically nothing. A few biscuits and the least little bit of wedding-cake for luck."

"Pity I didn't take him to the reception; then he could have had a vanilla ice as well."

"Wrong," said Jane. "They hadn't got vanilla—only the esoteric sorts. I know, because I tried. Never you mind, Zero. When the election comes on, you shall wear papa's colours round your strengthy neck and kill all the collies of the opposition."

"By the way," said Richard, "how's old Benham?"

"Poor old chap, he's still dying," said Mr Murray. "It makes me feel a bit like a vulture, waiting for his death like this. Still, I suppose it can't be helped."

Benham was the sitting member for Sidlington, and Mr Murray had been predestined to succeed him. Murray had fought two forlorn hopes for his party, and had pulled down majorities. He had fairly earned Sidlington—an absolutely safe seat. He had moderate means and no occupation. He had taken up with politics ten years before—shortly after the death of his wife—and had found politics a game that precisely suited him.

The discussion for the remainder of dinner was mostly political, and Jane—as was generally the case when she chose to be serious—showed herself to be a remarkably well-informed and intelligent young woman.

"I've no chance; she's too good for me," said Richard to himself—by no means for the first time—as he looked at her and listened to her with admiration.

Jane had just left the two men to their cigars when a servant entered with a card for Mr Murray.

"Where have you put him?" he asked the man.

"The gentleman is in the library, sir."

"Good! Say I'll be with him directly. Awfully sorry, Staines; this is a chap from Sidlington, and rather an important old cock down there."

"Go to him, of course. That's all right."

"I'm afraid I must. But here's the port and here's the cigars. When you get tired of solitude, you'll find Jane in the drawing-room. Smoking's allowed there, you know."

Staines got tired of solitude very soon. In the drawing-room, the conversation between Jane and himself took a new note of earnestness and intimacy. Zero slept placidly through it all.

An hour later Mr Murray came back to the drawing-room with the news of Benham's death. He in return received, with goodwill and no surprise, the news that a marriage had been arranged, and would shortly take place, between his daughter and Richard Staines.

4

During the engagement, which was brief, Zero found that two people—of whom his master was one—had very little time to talk to him; but he was not absolutely forgotten.

"What are we to do with Zero while we're away?" asked Richard.

"Could we take him with us?" asked Miss Murray.

"I don't think so," said Richard. "There would be bother at these foreign hotels; and there's the quarantine to think about."

"Suppose I said that if Zero didn't go, I wouldn't go either?"

"Quite simple. In that case, I should go alone."

And then they both laughed, being somewhat easily pleased at that time. Zero was offered to Mr Murray temporarily as an election mascot, but Mr Murray was not taking any risks—one of his principal supporters had a favourite collie. Finally, it was decided that Zero should pay a visit to his former master, Smith, until his master returned. He made one brief appearance at the wedding reception, where his supreme but honest ugliness conquered the heart of every nice woman present. He refused champagne, *foie-gras* sandwiches, and vanilla ices offered to him by the enthusiastic and indiscreet. However, he managed to find Jane, and Jane found bread-and-butter until word was brought that a person of the name of Smith had called for the dog.

"Bit fat, you are," said Smith, as he ripped the white rosette off the dog's collar. "Been doing yourself too well. Ah, now you're going to live healthy!"

Smith was as good as his word. Zero was sufficiently and properly fed, and given plenty of exercise. He mixed with some very aristocratic canine society, where the sweetness of his temper was much commended and imposed upon. After two months his master called for him, and Zero once more behaved like an ecstatic bullock.

"Yes," said Smith, "he's in good condition, as you say. Otherwise, he's not much changed. He's as big a fool as ever he was. If a toy Pom growls at him, he runs away; and if a collie tries to get past him alive— well, it can't. He'd tear the throat out of any man as struck you, and if the cat next door spits at him he goes and hides in the rhubarb."

"Seen any more of that wonderful instinct of his?"

"No, sir, I have not. But I should have done if there had been any occasion for it. It's a fact that I never feel so safe as I do when I've got that dog here. Don't you believe in it yourself, sir?"

"Sometimes I do—Mrs Staines does absolutely. If there's nothing in it, then there has been the most extraordinary lot of coincidences I ever came across."

Richard Staines and his wife had agreed that they would live principally in the country, and one day during their engagement Jane took Richard down to Selsdon Bois to show him the house of her dreams, known to the Post Office as Midway. Then, when he came to select, he would know the kind of thing to look for. Jane had known Midway in her childhood, and had loved its wide and gentle staircases, its fine Jacobean panelling, its stone roof, and its old garden with the paved walks between yew hedges.

"Well," said Richard, "if you are so keen on the place, why shouldn't we wait for a chance to get it, instead of looking for something more or less like it?"

"Because you can't," said Jane. "We're general public, and general public is never allowed to buy a place like Midway. People live in it till they die, and then leave it to the person they love best, and that person lives in it till he dies. And so on again. It never comes into the market. Things that are really valuable hardly ever do."

The conversation took place in the train which was conveying them to Selsdon Bois.

"Ah, well," said Richard, "what is there? It needn't be very big to be too big for us."

"Not a big house at all. I never counted, but I should think about twenty rooms." She made guesses as to acreage of garden, orchard, and grass-land. She admitted that they were merely guesses.

"The only thing that I really remember is that it was thirty-six acres in all. Could we do it?"

"Yes," said Richard; "we ought to be able to do that."

"Still, it doesn't matter," said Jane despondently, "because, of course, places like that are never to be got."

Then they stepped out on to the platform of Selsdon Bois Station, where a man was busily pasting up a bill. It announced the sale by auction, unless previously disposed of, of Midway.

"Miracle!" said Jane, subsiding gracefully on to a milk-can. "It's ours!"

And a fortnight later it was really theirs. The house was as delightful as Jane had said, but it was an old house, and during the last ten years had not been well kept up. There was a good deal to be done to make it quite comfortable and satisfactory. The work was to have been finished by the time Richard and his wife returned from the honeymoon.

"It's been simply funny the way we've been kept back," said the builder cheerfully. "But you might be able to get in, say, in another week or so."

They remained for a month in town, and this gave Jane time to discover that it was not possible to teach Zero to do trust-and-paid-for, and to look up a really admirable train by which Richard might travel from Selsdon Bois to the city every weekday morning.

"Yes," said Richard, a little doubtfully, "it's quite a good train, but—"

"But what?"

"Oh, nothing. I shall probably take it whenever I go up, though it's a bit earlier than is absolutely necessary. You see, I don't regard my presence at the office as so essential as I once did. My partners are most able and trustworthy men, and they like the work. Of course, I shall keep an eye on things."

"Then how many days a week will you go up?"

"Well, just at first I shall go up—er—from time to time."

"Come here, Zero," said Jane. "See that man? He's idle. Kill him!"

"Idle? Why, I shall have any amount of things to do down at Midway! Gardeners and grooms want a deal of looking after at first, until they pick up the way you want things done. Then there's that car your father gave us. I've got to learn how to drive it; I've got to know all about its blessed works right up to the very last word. The man who don't is open to be robbed and fooled by his chauffeur. That won't be done in a week. Then I've had an idea that we might lay out a golf-course—quite a small affair, just for practice."

"Richard, you're a genius! (You needn't bite him after all, Zero.) That will be the very thing for guests on Sunday afternoons—not to mention us ourselves."

"I was thinking principally of us ourselves."

"Where is that big-scale plan of the land? We'll pin it down flat on the table, and start arranging it now. We shall probably have to alter it all afterwards, but that don't matter."

5

Six years had passed; and Zero had got a new master, a somewhat dictatorial gentleman, but with genuine goodness of heart, aged five, bearing the same name as his father, Richard Staines, but never by any chance addressed by it. His father called him Dick. His mother called him by various fond and foolish appellations. He was known to the servants of the household as the Emperor. He had two sisters, whom he always spoke of collectively as "the children." He always spoke of Zero as "my dog."

Zero was rather an old dog now, but hale and hearty. In his own circle he was highly valued, but his formidable appearance still struck terror among strangers, willing though he was to make friends with them. The tradespeople, who had at first approached very delicately, had now grown used to him; but the tramp or hawker who entered the garden at Midway, and found Zero looking at him pensively, as a rule retired quickly to see if the road was still there. No further instance had occurred of Zero's mysterious powers, and in consequence they tended to become legendary. Richard Staines had now definitely adopted the theory of coincidence.

"Zero's a good old friend of mine, and I love him," he said; "but we must give up pretending he's a miracle." Jane's faith, however, remained unshaken.

And then, one summer evening, Dick came into the drawing-room with determination in his face.

"Mother," he said, "I want a stick or whip, please."

"Well, now," said Jane, "what for?"

"To beat my dog with. He's got to be punished."

"That's a pity, Dickywick. What's he been doing?"

"He won't let me go out into the road. Every time he caught hold of my coat and pulled me back. He's most frightfully strong, and he pulled me over once. He wants a lamming."

"I wonder if he would let me go out," said Jane. "Let's go and see, shall we?"

"Right-oh," said Dick, perfectly satisfied.

In the garden they found Zero cheerful and quite unrepentant. As a rule, he rushed to the gate in the hopes of being taken out for a run. But this evening, as Jane neared the gate, he became disquieted. He caught hold of her dress and tried to drag her back. He ran round and round her, whimpering. He flung himself in front of her feet.

"Now, you see," said Dick triumphantly.

"Yes, I see."

"Well, I shall go and fetch a stick."

"Oh, no. Zero does not want us to go out because he believes there's some danger on the road."

"O-o-oh! Do you really mean it?"

"Honest Injun."

"Then he's not a bad dog at all, and I told him he was. Come here, Zero." He patted the dog's head. "You're a good dog really. My mistake. Sorry. What are you laughing at, mother? That's what Tom always says. Now let's go and see the danger on the road."

"Well, it wouldn't be quite fair to Zero, after all the trouble he's taken. Besides, I want to see the rabbits at their games. They ought to be out just now."

"All right," said Dick. "You follow me, and I'll show you them. But you mustn't make the least sound. You must be very Red-Indian."

Dick's mother followed him obediently, and was very Red-Indian. The rabbits lived in a high bank just beyond the far end of the garden, and what the gardener had said about them before the wire-netting came could not be printed. Jane watched the rabbits, and conversed about them in the hoarse whisper enjoined by her son, but she was thinking principally about Zero.

Then Dick went to bed, and his father came back from the city. He went up at least one day a week, and came back full of aggressive virtue and likely to refer to himself as a man who earned his own living, thank Heaven.

At dinner Richard said: "By the way, I'd been meaning to speak of it—what's the matter with Zero?"

"Why?"

"He won't leave the gate. He was there when I drove in. I called him in, but he went back almost directly. I saw him through the window as I was dressing, and he was still there—lying quite still, with his eyes glued on the road."

And then Jane recounted the experience of Dick and herself.

"You may laugh, Richard, but something is going to happen, and Zero knows what it will be."

"Well," said Richard, "if anybody is proposing to burglarise us tonight, I don't envy him the preliminaries with Zero. But, of course, it may be nothing. All the same I've always said there ought to be a lodge at that gate."

But to this Jane was most firmly opposed. A new semi-artistic redbrick lodge would be out of keeping with Midway altogether. "And what are you going to do about Zero?"

"Oh, anything you like. What do you propose?"

"I don't know what to say. Whatever is going to happen, apparently Zero thinks he can tackle it by himself. Still, you might have your revolver somewhere handy tonight."

"I will," said Richard.

Zero remained at his post until the dawn, and then came a black speck on the white road. Zero stood up and growled. The skin on his back moved.

Down the road came the lean, black retriever, snapping aimlessly, foam dropping from his jaws. Zero sprang at him and was thrown down and bitten. At his second spring he got hold and kept it. The two dogs rolled off the road, and into the ditch.

At breakfast, next morning, Richard was innocuously humorous on the subject of revolvers, burglars, and clairvoyant bulldogs. He was interrupted by a servant, who announced that Mr Hammond wished to speak to him for a moment.

"Right," said Richard. "Where is he?"

"He is just outside, sir," said the man. "Mr Hammond would not come in."

Hammond was a neighbour of Richard's, a robust and heavily built man. As a rule, he was a cheerful sportsman, but this morning his countenance was troubled. His clothes were covered with dust, and he looked generally dishevelled.

"Hallo, Jim," said Richard cheerily. "How goes it? You look as if you'd been out all night."

"I have," said Hammond grimly. "So have several other men."

"Why? What's up?"

"Outbreak of rabies at Barker's farm. He shot one of the dogs, but the other got away. There must have been some damned mismanagement. A lot of us have been out trying to find the brute all night."

"But, by Jove, this is most awfully serious. Can't I help? I'm ready to start now if you like."

"Thanks, but I found the dog five minutes ago—dead in a ditch not twenty yards from your gate. He's there still."

"Who shot him?"

"Nobody. That's the trouble. He had been killed by another dog, as you'll see when you look at his windpipe. The chances are the other dog got bitten or scratched, and he'll carry on the infection. It's the other dog we've got to hunt."

"Could it be—" Richard paused.

"I'm afraid so," said Hammond. "Not many dogs would tackle a mad retriever, but your bulldog would. And it was close to your gate that the retriever was killed."

"If you'll wait half a minute, I'll see where Zero is."

But the dog was not to be found. Nobody had seen him that morning. In truth, Richard had not expected to find him. He left word that if the dog came back, he was to be shut up in an empty stable. And then he and Hammond went out together.

"You've got a revolver, I suppose," said Richard.

"I don't hunt mad dogs without one. This is most awfully hard lines on you, Richard. He was a ripping good dog, Zero was."

"He was. It's Dick I'm thinking about. The dog was a great pal of his."

They found young Barker watching by the dead retriever. He explained gloomily that he had sent a boy for a cart. The body would be taken back and buried in lime. "And even then, sir, we've not got the dog that killed him."

"We're just going to get him," said Richard quietly.

They walked on in silence for a mile and then at a turn of the road they saw Zero, apparently asleep in the sunlight in the white dust.

"I ought to do this," said Richard, "but I wish you would."

"Right, old chap. It'll be over in a moment, and he'll be dead before he knows he's hurt. Look the other way."

"Richard turned round and waited, as it seemed to him, for a long time, waiting for the shot. Suddenly he heard Hammond's voice behind him.

"No need to shoot. The poor beggar's dead—been run over by a motorcar, I should say. It's a lucky accident."

"I wonder," said Richard.

"Wonder what?"

"Wonder if it was really an accident."

The One Before

Mr. Ernest Saunders Barley, aged forty-two, a gentleman of independent means, lived with his wife at The Chestnuts, Shalton, Surrey. It was a newish house, with a couple of acres of garden, about a quarter of a mile outside the town.

At ten in the morning, Mr. Barley was generally to be found in his workroom on the first floor. He was a man of many occupations, principally futile. He had no great knowledge of botany, but he had recently taken to pressing flowers and mounting them on sheets of, cartridge paper. He spoke of this as his *Hortus Siccus*, reserved a table for it in the workroom, and thought a good deal of it. Another table was set aside for fretwork, spoken of by Mr. Barley as carving; a dust-cloth was spread under this to save the excessively florid carpet. A third table bore his typewriter; his diary, as well as any letters of length and formality, were always typed by him.

A big cupboard opening into the room had been converted into a photographic dark room. A present from Mr. Barley was extremely likely to take the form of one of his own photographs of part of his own garden, mounted by himself and placed in a fretwork frame of his own construction. He was interested also, more than most men, in household economy; he could, and did, mark glass-cloths and dusters with extreme neatness.

One morning in August he stood in his workroom, surveying through the window the scene in the garden below. He was a thin and narrow-chested man of medium height. He had rather scanty fair hair, a distrustful eye, a prolonged and pointed nose, a thin-lipped and peevish mouth, and somewhat prominent ears. He was clean shaven, and his light flannel suit seemed out of tune with the wearer.

Below on a seat in the garden he could see his young guest, James Havern. James was smoking cigarettes and reading the morning papers, as if there were nothing else to do in the world. Barley turned back to his room and prepared for a strenuous morning. As he was taking his coat off, one of the things that he had meant to remember flashed across his mind. At the same time, he recognised a step in the passage outside. He opened the door, and said, in a special low vibrant voice which he reserved for servants—

"Jane."

Jane did not hear him.

He did not raise the note, but he increased its length and volume—

"Ja-a-a-ane!"

She heard, and turned back at once—a tall girl, good-looking, with the impress of immaculate respectability and respectfulness all over her.

"Yes, sir," she said. Her air of pleased deference was alone worth more than her wages.

"Every morning, Jane, a certain amount of—er—chips and small pieces of wood are removed from the dust-cloth under the table where I do my carving. I wish to know what becomes of them. What is done with them?"

"I cannot say at all, sir. It is Ellen who does this room. Shall I inquire, sir?" Ready delight in meeting the slightest wish of E. S. Barley seemed to radiate from her face.

"Do so," said Mr. Barley, tersely, as he robed himself in a white apron, preparatory to work.

When Jane got downstairs the air of pleased deference wore thin, and the natural girl shone through. Servants do not always call one another by their official names, and Jane addressed Ellen as Maudie.

"Maudie dear, that silly old devil wants to know what you do with the little bits of wood from his room when you do it in the morning?"

"Sew 'em up in a bag and wear 'em next my 'eart. Tell him so, with my love."

"Oh, Maudie, you *are*! Do cheese it. He's waiting to know. Truth he is."

"What's he think I do with 'em? Is he afraid I eat 'em? I throw 'em away with the other rubbish, and I wish I could throw him on the top. Tell him that instead."

"Right. Now I will. You see if I don't. Now you've done for yourself, my girl." Ellen received this assurance with incredulous laughter.

When Jane reached the workroom, the message as actually delivered, with an air of some concern, ran as follows:—

"So far, sir, it seems that the chips have been thrown away. Ellen is very sorry if that was wrong, but she had no special orders about them."

"I thought as much," said Mr. Barley, with marked restraint. "For the wood I use for my carving I pay from fourpence to a shilling a foot. You understand? From fourpence to a shilling per foot. For bundles of firewood in the winter I pay—I forget the exact sum, but it mounts up. This must not go on. It is wasteful. In future Ellen must get a large cardboard box and save these—er—chips. They will be useful for lighting the fire with in the winter."

"Very useful indeed, sir," said Jane, with conviction. "I am sorry we didn't think of it before. I will tell Ellen at once, sir."

And this was the way she told Ellen: "I say, Maudie, here's the latest. You're to keep his 'oly blessed chips and use 'em for the fires."

"Why, certainly," said Ellen-Maudie, ironically. "I suppose he didn't 'appen to mention what we're to do with the orange-peel and the nutshells?"

"Slipped his memory," said Jane.

"Pity too. They'd do to trim a 'at." And there was another burst of ironical laughter.

But it was not given to Ernest Saunders Barley to see himself as others saw him. He imagined in times of great self-abasement that there might be a difference between the way people spoke of him and the way they spoke to him, but he never had the slightest idea how great the difference was. Contented with a good work well done, he now began to paste down the pattern on the wood. He was engaged upon this when his wife entered.

She was a kindly woman, whose ordinary common sense was always doing battle with her excessive belief in her husband, and almost always being vanquished. Her fear of him, and her affection for him, and the necessity for humouring and managing him, had made an occasional liar of her. She was some years younger than her husband and still passably pretty.

"I've seen cook, Ernest, and she says the lamb won't do minced for luncheon. Not enough."

"Strange," said Ernest, caressing his chin. "I was thinking as I carved it last night at dinner that it could be made to do very well."

"Yes, Ernest; I saw you were." She was guiltless of irony, and merely wished to agree with him. "You see, when you get it off the bone—"

"Quite so. I'm sure I don't wish to stint anybody. I needn't say that. But all that is wanted is a little management. Tell cook to put the mince on toast, thick toast. And—well, some poached eggs on the top would make it look more of a dish perhaps. Eggs—I don't know what eggs are this week. They've been very dear lately. Never mind; pay, pay, pay! There's no end to it."

"Are you quite sure, Ernest, that you like to have people staying at the house? Sometimes I think it seems to put you out a little. Of course, it does add to expenditure."

Without intending it she had touched him on the raw. She had assailed his character as a host.

"Now, why you should say that, Mary, except to annoy me, I can't think. There is nothing I enjoy more than the exercise of hospitality within reasonable limits. I dislike recklessness; but what has that to do with it? I suppose you wish to imply that I am not a good host?"

"Of course, that would be absurd, dear."

"I should be extremely sorry for James, or any other guest of mine, to leave my house with the impression that he had not had enough to eat. The position of a host carries with it its duties. I feel that as a point of honour. It is like the old *noblesse oblige.* Now, with regard to the luncheon, let me think. Yes, we will have the pressed beef on the sideboard. There is no occasion for you to make any allusion to it; but have it there. If he wishes for it, he will mention it. James is like that. However, he is your brother-in-law's brother, and, after all, he leaves this afternoon; we must be rather more careful after he has gone. I suppose you wish to play tennis with him this morning."

"Well, yes—I think so. There is nothing more for me to do in the house."

"I should not say that. Only this morning I detected a piece of careless waste that a little supervision might have prevented. But I make no objection. It is our duty to entertain our guest—I realise that. Hospitality demands sacrifice. I shall be down myself at half-past twelve—half an hour before luncheon, and half an hour taken from my morning, simply on his account. Now, if you stop chattering there I shall never get to work."

But she had hardly reached the bottom of the stairs before she heard him calling her from the top. He leaned over the banisters.

"I only wished to say it, while I remembered it, that I have left a cutting from a paper on the clock in the dining-room. You might look at it when you have time. It refers to the use of newspapers as blankets and bedcovers. Said to be very warm; but I don't know if there's anything in it."

Returning to his room he fitted a new saw, and began to cut out the pattern on one side of an ornamental wheelbarrow. In so far as that wheelbarrow could have been of no earthly use to anybody for anything, it may be considered to have been an instance of art for art's sake. The vine-leaf pattern on the side was pretty, and he was pleased with it. It was his habit to sing as he worked. In a subdued husky voice, he went through a repertoire composed of such scraps as he could remember of hymns and sentimental ballads. Plying the fret-saw furiously, he sang—

If the night would only last,
And never the daylight come,
In a love-dream we would live, while our hearts beat fast,
And only our lips were dumb.
All alone, my dusky queen,
We would live and love unseen
'Mid the singing of the woodbirds and the—

Here the saw snapped. Possibly the suggested association of Mr. E. S. Barley and a dusky queen was too much for it. Mr. Barley stood up. He did not swear, but his brows contracted and his eyes closed. He was suffering. When he opened his eyes again, they happened to sight the wastepaper basket. He kicked it to the other end of the room, sighed, and sat down to fit another saw. Soon the work was progressing smoothly again, while Mr. Barley huskily intimated that he haply might remember, and haply might forget. The morning had begun badly, and he saw the world very dark. It was a world of reckless waste and pleasure-seeking; he would buy his fret-saws elsewhere in future. His temper was working up for a storm.

CHAPTER 2

Punctually at half-past twelve, Mr. Barley approached the tennis-court. His misfit smile showed that he was now in the part of the genial host. Over his shoulder he carried a skipping-rope. The players should, Mr. Barley considered, have flung down their racquets and come to welcome him. But they neither saw nor heard him. The interest of a close finish had transformed them. James Havern, a good-humoured and pleasant-looking young man as a general rule, wore an expression of mad and murderous hate.

The tame and submissive Mary was changed into a bloodthirsty leaping tigress. Vantage out. Jimmy, with his white teeth set and breathing hard, delivered a swift and vicious service. The tigress leaped, and the ball came back hard and low to the far corner. Jimmy just reached it, and the rally went on. Two people playing for their lives could not have been more concentrated. At last, a well-placed one beat Jimmy, and he returned it into the net. Game to the tigress. At once they resumed the normal expressions of decent and civilized people. "Good game," said Jimmy.

"Excellent!" cried the genial host, with intent to attract attention to himself.

"You there?" Jimmy called to him. "Shan't be long finishing this sett."

"You don't mind?" added the submissive wife.

He minded very much. It was selfish; and on the part of a young man like James it was disrespectful. Why could they not have abandoned the game and resumed it after luncheon? What did they think he had come out for? However, in the role of the genial host, it was necessary to make sacrifices. So Mr. Barley, with a fine imitation of a careless and cordial manner, said—

"By all means. Finish the game, of course. I can wait."

He took a garden-chair, and unconsciously assumed the expression of a Christian martyr. The game went on, and a further triumph for the tigress finished the sett. Then, somewhat perfunctorily, they asked Mr. Barley if he wouldn't play. Mr. Barley's tennis was of a childish pat-a-cake order, and they accepted his refusal with equanimity.

"No, thanks," he said. "I've got rather tired of it. I like to strike out a new line now and again. Now, did you ever try this?" He swung his skipping-rope carelessly.

"Don't know," said Jimmy. "Expect I did when I was in the nursery."

"Very much the answer I expected, James. Now, when people laugh at skipping, I generally say, 'Yes, but can you skip?' There's a good deal in it. Apart from plain skipping, there are the variations. It is a grand exercise. I generally take a few minutes of it in my dressing-room before my bath in the morning."

James very properly suppressed a desire to ask if he couldn't have a photograph.

"And," Mr. Barley continued, "it takes some little skill, especially when you come to the variations. I don't profess to be anything much at it myself. What do you say? Shall we try a little competition?"

214

"I don't mind, just for the fun of it. Will you start, Mary?"

"I've tried it. I'm no good. You begin."

At his tenth skip James broke down; Mr. Barley, who had been counting, was delighted:

"Ah! you see there is a little art required for it, after all. Of course, what is essential is a perfect coordination of the eye and hand. I will show you where you are wrong, afterwards. In the meantime, I have to beat ten."

He began to skip with great solemnity and precision. At his eighth skip James suddenly screamed out—

"Look behind you!" Mr. Barley was startled, caught his foot in the rope, and nearly came over. James was much amused.

"My win! What price perfect co-ordination?"

Mr. Barley glared at him in silence for a moment, and then hurled the skipping-rope from him and strode rapidly in the direction of the house. The storm had burst.

Jimmy gave the low whistle which indicates surprise.

"Sorry I annoyed him," he said. "It hadn't occurred to me that a grown man could lose his temper over a skipping-rope."

"I don't think he's lost his temper," said Mary, mendaciously. "I think he just happened to think of something suddenly."

"Yes," said Jim, drily; "he thought of something all right. I'm glad he had the delicacy not to say it. I hope for your sake it won't last long."

"You've got quite a wrong idea of Ernest. He's one of the best and kindest of men, really. You listen to everything that that wicked old man, Uncle Nathaniel, says. He's always been prejudiced against Ernest."

"Oh, I shouldn't say that—one may like a man all right even when one recognises his little weaknesses. And uncle's distinctly fond of you."

"He needn't talk about weaknesses, with a memory that absolutely cannot be depended upon for a single thing. I think you go there far too much. You came from him to us, and now you are going back to him again. Ernest doesn't think that he's at all a good influence for you. Oh, I must go and see about luncheon."

She ran into the house; Jimmy followed leisurely. She went straight upstairs to the work-room, and found the door locked. Within the room Ernest Saunders Barley, that best and kindest of men, was lying on his back on the sofa, with his handkerchief over his face. He repeated in a bitter and determined whisper—

"Swindler and blackguard! Swindler and blackguard! Dirty swindler! Swindler and blackguard!" He chastised the sofa cushions without mercy.

A gentle tap at the door caused him to stop suddenly. "Who's there?" he asked, in the sepulchral voice of imperfect resignation.

"It's me, dear," said Mary. "Aren't you coming down to lunch?"

"No; I have a headache."

"I'm so sorry. What shall I have sent up to you?"

"Nothing. I couldn't eat anything."

"Ernest, James says he's sorry if he annoyed you by his silliness."

"I was not in the least annoyed or surprised either. That has nothing to do with it. I went away because it seemed impossible to get him to play fairly. It was of no consequence to me in the least."

"You'll see him before he goes?"

"If I am well enough. In the meantime, I wish to be left alone, please."

The storm had given place to a deep depression. He took a half-sheet of notepaper from the fret-worked tray in which he kept such treasures, and wrote on it as follows:—

No noise of any kind in this passage please.—E.S.B.

He opened the door to affix this notice outside, and a slight smell of luncheon greeted him. It was not unpleasant. It was even appetising. Should he? Headaches might, and frequently did, pass away very suddenly. No, it would be absurd. He fixed his notice, locked his door again, and returned to the sofa. His absence would mean one unclaimed poached egg; probably James would have it. Eggs were dear. What was that riddle about them? If an egg and a half cost three half-pence, how many herrings— And here Mr. Barley fell asleep.

He awoke at two with an undeniable hunger. Beyond the need for posing as an interesting invalid was the need for luncheon. Why not? Voices in the garden showed him that Mary and James had finished luncheon and were safely out of the way. The servants would be occupied with their own dinner, and had probably not cleared the luncheon-table yet. It was reasonably likely that he would be undiscovered. He opened his door and listened. There was not a sound in the house. No one was about.

He removed the notice from the door, crumpled it up, and threw it into the wastepaper basket. Then, on tiptoe, he went along the passage and down the stairs. He felt adventurous and rather good. There was no one in the dining-room and—Oh, joy!—the pressed beef was still on the sideboard. Its proportions told Mr. Barley's practised eye that James had been at it—in spite of that extra poached egg; but even this could not entirely damp his satisfaction. His place was laid for him at the table. This was very much all right.

CHAPTER 3

Mr. Barley carved for himself with an unusual liberality. He also poured out for himself a glass of claret. He sat down to the table and was contented. Reaction had set in, and he was for the moment convinced that all was for the best in the best of worlds. But almost with his first mouthful the trouble began. He heard a step coming down the path which he could not mistake; it was Mary's step. And he was not anxious that Mary, or anybody else, should have a doubt of that headache and total loss of appetite. When she came past the window, she would certainly see him.

There was only one thing to be done—to get below the level of the table, so that the friendly cloth screened him from sight. With wonderful rapidity he changed his seat from the chair to the floor beside it, taking his plate and glass with him. He was now invisible from the window. The table, like a protecting rampart, rose between him and it. He rested his plate on the seat of the chair, and went on with his luncheon.

Mary—he felt this as a legitimate personal grievance against her—lingered some time at the window. Why should she? It was tactless. It was keeping him in a position that could not be considered dignified. He was just deciding that this was really too bad when worse befell him. He heard a well-known whistle coming down the passage. That was James, and considering all that James had had for luncheon he might have had the decency to keep out of the dining-room. The interesting invalid was even more anxious that James should not catch him in the act of a hearty luncheon.

But what was he to do? If he arose, he then became visible to Mary at the window. If he remained as he was James would see him as soon as he entered the room. There was again only one thing to be done—to crawl under the table and hope that James would not stay long. To that twilit seclusion he at once retired, still taking his plate and glass with him. They constituted evidence. If they were found, he might just as well be found himself. James wandered about the room in an undecided sort of way. Presently he said, in a low distinct voice—

"Oh, where's that cigarette-case!"

"Found it?" called Mary through the window.

"Not yet," said Jimmy; "but I'm quite certain I left it here. I shall have it in a moment. I wonder if you'd mind tightening that net a little? I shall be there by the time that you've finished."

Mary moved on. Ernest Saunders Barley, in his position under the table, felt distinctly uneasy. Suppose that James took it into his head to think that his cigarette-case had fallen on the floor and looked under the table. Soon, however, immunity gave him confidence. He began to experiment on a method for the noiseless consumption of pressed beef. It was entirely successful, so far as the beef was concerned; the fact that he knocked his wine-glass over on to his plate was extraneous to the experiment. But it made enough noise to arouse the curiosity of James.

Now, when you find your host sitting under the dining-room table, in a cramped position, nursing a plate which contains an injudicious mixture of pressed beef, claret, broken glass, and mustard, you may be pardoned for coming to the conclusion that the strain has been a little too much for him.

"What on earth's up!" Jimmy exclaimed.

"It's all right," said Mr. Barley: with limp hilarity. "I was just going to have a little joke with you. If you wouldn't mind taking this plate, I'll get out."

Jimmy put the plate down on the table. "I see. And is this—er-mixture part of the joke?"

"No, I had an accident with my glass. Unfortunate. It's spoilt the whole thing. Would you mind ringing? The fact is that my headache passed off suddenly, the way these things will, and I thought the best thing I could do would be to get a little luncheon. Then I heard you coming, and I thought it would be good fun to get under the table and then jump out at you. These jests don't always come out right, you see."

"Yes," said James, reflectively. "Talking of things coming out, there's a good deal of claret on the carpet under the table. Ah! here's my case that I was looking for. Well, I'll see you later. I'm just going to play one final sett with Mary."

On his way to the tennis-court he thought it over. The notion that Mr. Barley had ever intended to perpetrate a joke was too monstrous for consideration. Besides, if he had intended to jump out, why on earth had he not done it?

"I almost think," said Mary, "that I ought to go and see how poor Ernest is before we begin. He may be suffering still. Perhaps I could persuade him to take something."

"His headache is better. I found him under the table in the dining-room. He was sitting up and taking nourishment. He said that he had gone there in order to jump out at me for the joke of the thing."

"Really? You're sure he's all right? It's so unlike him."

"Oh yes. It's not like him, and he's broken a wineglass in his little frolic; but he's quite all right. I expect he'll be out here directly."

Mary's eye fell on the skipping-rope that Ernest had hurled from him in his rage.

"Then," she said, "I think I'll just put this out of the way." She interpreted Jimmy's inquiring look. "You see," she added, "he doesn't like things to be left about."

Only his sense of his position, and—still more, perhaps—his regard for Mary, stayed Jimmy from intempestive laughter.

By the time that the sett was finished, with another victory for the tigress, Mr. Barley had appeared on the lawn. Apart from a further increase in his disapproval of Jimmy, he was now normal

"I don't want to interfere in any way with your plans for the afternoon," he said to his wife, "but there are several matters connected with the house that require your attention." He turned to Jimmy, who was now wearing a grin that Mr. Barley disliked extremely: "I don't interrupt your game at all, I hope?"

"Not at all, thanks. We'd finished. The fact is that I thought I'd just run up and say goodbye to the Derrifords."

"You went to say goodbye to them yesterday," said Mary.

"No; I went to see if I could get a round at golf yesterday, only the old man was out."

"But you were there for hours."

"Yes; Mrs. Derriford was at home."

"And Hilda, by any chance?"

"Let me see. Yes; she happened to come in."

The assumption of carelessness in giving this answer was not convincing, and Mary smiled knowingly as she gave him her messages for Mrs. Derriford.

"And now," said Mr. Barley, when his guest had gone, "I will thank you to come and see the way in which the so-called polishing of my brown boots is being conducted at present."

"All right, Ernest," said Mary, meekly. "I'm sorry if they aren't right."

"Nothing is likely to be right where the servants have no proper supervision. Another thing: for the second time this week I've found your storeroom unlocked. I will not have it. It seems to me that you think about nothing but this stupid tennis. That's not all. On going into the storeroom, I found no labels on two of the tins. If there's one thing, I hate it's disorder. There's no excuse for it. I am always ready and willing to type neatly for you any label that you may require. You have only to affix them. Apparently, even that is too much trouble. I don't wish to speak sharply, but—well, there are some things that must not be."

"Of course. I'm sorry."

They had reached the house. "Now, please go to the storeroom at once, and ascertain what the contents of those two tins are. Then come up to my workroom and I will type the labels for you."

He went upstairs, took the cover off his typewriter, put in a sheet of paper, drew up his chair and sat down. Mary entered.

"I'm ready. What is in the first tin?" he asked.

"It's empty. They're both empty."

Mr. Barley replaced the cover on his typewriter with some violence.

"And now," he said, "with reference to those boots."

James returned from his call on the Derrifords in excellent spirits, and just in time to catch the up train. He thanked Mary heartily, and hoped that she would let him come again one of these days. Mary said, "Of course." Mr. Barley, with an unnatural smile, shook him by the hand and wished him a pleasant journey.

When the cab had driven off, Mr. Barley turned to his wife.

"I think that I have played my part sufficiently well."

"I don't quite see what you mean, Ernest."

"I mean that I have done my duty as a host, however distasteful it might be. And I may tell you now that that young man will never darken these doors again. My appearance of geniality may have deceived him and you. It was intended to do so. I dislike him and I disapprove of him, and I've done with him, altogether."

"Oh, Ernest! Why?"

"I am sorry to have to say it of a man who is a connection of yours by marriage, but he is a man of no character—prying, dishonourable, and unprincipled. Formerly I was deceived in him. Now I have found him out."

"You aren't thinking about that skipping-match still, are you?"

"That and other things. Trifles are often important as indications of character."

"He only did it for fun, you know."

"I'm glad you can accept that explanation. I cannot. Then there are these visits to Mr. Nathaniel Brookes."

"But Mr. Brookes is his uncle."

"That may be. But I know something of Mr. Brookes. He is not a good influence for any man. It is to him that I trace James's downfall. It's over. Never again—never again." And, with these fateful words on his lips, Mr. Barley strode off to play the fool with his *Hortus Siccus*.

Jimmy calmly slept in the express to London, without any idea that he had had a downfall, and that sentence of banishment had been pronounced upon him. He would have been sorry to hear that he was not to visit Shalton again. And yet he did not go there for the beautiful eyes of Mr. Barley, nor for tennis with Mary, though he was very fond of her, nor for golf with old Mr. Derriford. At any rate, these did not constitute his principal reason.

CHAPTER 4

Punctually at ten o'clock, by the rule of the house, the nice-looking parlour-maid Jane, and her intimate friend Ellen, surnamed Maudie, went up to their room. It was supposed that they went to bed at once, and that the gas in their room was put out at half-past ten. But their practice did not always correspond with this hypothesis.

Having made a fair division of one pennyworth of pineapple drops, Jane kicked off her shoes and stretched herself on her bed. Ellen took up a similar position on the other bed.

"I must, and will have the gas put out by half-past ten," said Jane, giving a passable imitation of E. S. Barley.

"That's all right," said Maudie. "I'll undress when I like. No sooner nor no later. And if he don't like it he can leave it."

"It ain't a bad plice," said Jane. "He's near, of course. But he knows where to stop if he wants them that understand good service."

"That's where he's so rum," said Maudie. "He's a perfect fool, and yet he ain't, you know. You see what I mean."

"He's like no gentleman as ever I come across. Yet there's the money. What are you to say? He wants a good taking up and setting down. But—bless yer!—she'll never do it."

"You don't need to tell me that."

"There was something up today, if you arst my opinion. If he went off his head sudden, it wouldn't never surprise me."

"Well, I never noticed nothing."

"Didn't you? But I did. He never come in to lunch, and I could see as she were upset. Mr. 'Avern seemed as usual. Now, that's a young gentleman that is a gentleman. And it ain't only that he's free with his money; it's his way as I like. Nice-looking, too reminds me of George, in some things."

"Oh, you and your George! But what 'appened?"

"Nothing much, except to them as can put one thing and another together. I happened to go down the passage, past what he calls his workroom. There was a notice on the door as there were to be no noise in the passage. Now, there never is no noise in that passage no-how; who's to make it? I went on down, and next moment he was down, too, and in the dining-room. He was there some time; I won't say how long, for I didn't happen to cast my eye on the clock, but it was a good time. Then, he rung just as we were finishing our dinners. You were off, it being your afternoon, but me and Mrs. Dawes was still at it. I found him with a plate of the beef, and a glass smashed over it, and the wine all in the plate. 'Take this away, and bring a clean plate,' he says.

"So, I did. So far it might just have been a mischance, and I shouldn't have thought no more about it. But, then, he says to me: 'Some claret has been spilled on the floor, too, under the table. See about it.' So, I did again. That had been just done, and it were right in the middle. It couldn't have been done, except by somebody sitting under the table. Now, I'm one to put things together. I thinks of that, and of his not coming to lunch, though there's company, and the way as she wasn't herself, and the notice on that door, and all. It looks to me as if he were touched."

"Don't you," said the sensitive Ellen-Maudie. "You fair give me the shivers. We might be all murdered in our beds!"

"But, then, you have the opposite. He were just the same as he always is at dinner, though speaking of Mr. 'Avern in a way as I shouldn't care to be spoken of. All I say about it is that there's something up. It may be as you think, or it may not. Maudie, there's his step coming down the passage. Put the gas as low as it will go."

Mr. Barley frequently came down the passage to see if he could detect a light under the door of either of the servants' rooms, and

Maudie was not perturbed. On the contrary, it seemed an indication that Mr. Barley had not yet lost his characteristics. The steps lingered for a moment or two outside the door, and then moved off again. Maudie put up the gas.

"He's his old sweet self still," said Jane.

"Ah!" said Maudie. "When he's mad enough not to be particular about half a farthing's worth of gas, he'll be pretty mad, and no error. That always makes me just as angry as if it was the first time. If we were late in the morning, then I wouldn't say. But rules, just for the sake of rules, is what I never could stand. Oh, he's a beauty!"

"Anyhow, I ain't got much more of it. It'll be Christmas, George thinks."

"How you can—and with the examples as you've got in this house, too! Look at Mrs. Dawes."

"Well, her husband don't trouble her much."

"No; but just look at it. And all because there was no watercress. 'Goodbye,' says he, 'I'm off.' 'Where to?' says she, 'Egyp,' says he. And from that day to this she's never set eyes on him. She's told me the story many a time. Where'd she have been if it hadn't happened that she were a good cook? Then there's Mrs. Barley. She has all the comforts; but look at the life he leads her. He's for ever interfering and poking his nose into what don't concern him. She daren't call her soul her own. She spends all her time trying to keep his temper smooth. I remember once, when he was away, I was doing her room, and I come on a letter from him.

"Not knowing what it was, I just glanced through the first two pages. It were nothing but blowing her up because she hadn't had the chimney of his blessed workroom swept, saying she had no initiative, and a lot of beastly things like that. Then, seeing it were a private letter, of course I put it down. I dare say the rest was no better. No; with warnings all around me, I choose to keep my independence."

"You do talk such socialism. What are women meant for if it ain't to marry? I call it wicked the way you go on about marriage. What's the Bible say?"

"It don't say you've got to marry whether you like it or not. Anyhow, you're warned."

"Why, you talk as if my George were like that old idiot. George is a very different sort."

"He is now. I dare say as Mr. Barley were civil enough when he was courting. It's afterwards the misery begins. None for me, thank you."

"Anyhow, I'm not like her. I have got a little spirit of my own. You wouldn't catch me almost arsting to be trampled on, like she do. But you know, Maudie, I don't take much notice of what you say. One of these days love will awike in your heart."

"Then it'll get put to sleep again."

"That ain't so easy done," said Jane, sentimentally. "It's like—well, I can't tell you. It's like nothing else. It comes over you in a wave, and there you are. One of these days, as I tell you, you'll know it, and then you'll think very different."

"When I do, I'll write and tell you," said Maudie, with a yawn, rising from her recumbent position. "Talking about courting, I had a word with Mr. 'Icks, the Derrifords' gardener, on Sunday; and from what he tells me, I think I know what brings Mr. 'Avern to Shalton."

"I'd guessed that myself. I wonder what Miss Hilda thinks about it. She's one of the disdainful ones. She don't need anybody to tell her she's a beauty, She's found that out for herself. So, you saw Mr. 'Icks again on Sunday? Poor Mr. 'Icks!"

"What's the matter with him?"

"As if you didn't know."

"Well, I ain't going to marry Mr. 'Icks. That's flat. And he's been told so once for all. Let him find some other girl, like yourself, as don't mind giving up her independence. Now, 'old your row, my dear, for half a moment; I'm going to say my prayers."

Ellen-Maudie dropped on her knees. Jane, with a pensive and abstracted expression, began to wind the cheap American alarum.

CHAPTER 5

Mr. Nathaniel Brookes was a gentleman of commanding presence. He had thick white hair and an ivory skin. His face was remarkably mobile, and his eyes remarkably bright. Though he had the sweetest of tempers, he inspired instant respect in strangers who met him, and it was not only because he was on the committee that the club waiters were so specially attentive to him. In his younger days, abandoning the bar as soon as his profession threatened to become lucrative and tiresome, he travelled much and curiously, and had seen many strange things. He had several times been in imminent danger of being murdered, but never, he was wont to say, in the slightest danger of being married.

At any rate, he had always remained a bachelor. His memory was immense; all his life the bright eyes had been noting, and the capacious head had been storing; he asserted that, to the best of his belief, he had never forgotten anything. But the memory had a drawback in that it was by no means always available; he could not always recall things when he wanted them. There were the facts in the store-house, but the door was temporarily locked. He was capable of forgetting—or, at least, of being for a while unable to recall—his own name. On such occasions his secretary or his valet would act as a handy book of reference. But everything that he temporarily forgot ultimately came back to him.

Sometimes the interval was long. For instance, once in telling a story he forgot the name of the man who had interested him so much in Port Said, and finished his story without it; six years afterwards he recalled the name. It was Smith! Mary, as has been seen, regarded this curious memory as an affliction; so, did many others; it is probable that Mr. Brookes himself was secretly rather proud of it. For the rest, he was a somewhat complicated mixture of the dreamer and the man of the world.

"It's no good your saying anything, Jimmy," said Uncle Nathaniel, as he finished soup on the evening of Jimmy's arrival. "Mary doesn't approve of me. Our beliefs are not identical, and we've got differently coloured hair. Besides, she loves Ernest Saunders Barley, and I don't even like him. That explains itself. Even if she wanted to approve of me, that ridiculous little squirt wouldn't let her. Never mind; she's a very good sort. I can't speak as to her tennis, about which you're so enthusiastic; but she's a kindly person, and looks nice, and is generally sensible—always, in fact, except where Ernest Saunders is concerned. By the way, let's abuse Ernest Saunders."

"But I've just come from accepting his hospitality."

"Anybody could see that; you've lost weight. What's the abuse matter? It's all in the family. I'm your uncle, and your brother Percy's wife's younger sister married Barley. It's not as if you were speaking to a stranger. Tell me, has he got a fretwork paperknife in his bathroom yet?"

"No," said Jimmy, laughing.

"You surprise me. When I was stopping at Lynthwaite years ago, when you were in Paris, Ernest and his wife were there. He made seven fretwork paperknives there and then—each one more filthy and useless than the last. He used to take them round for everybody to admire. I asked him what he was going to do with them; I thought they must be for a bazaar; they were the kind of thing you never see anywhere else. He said he should find them very handy about his house. Why, there must be a fretwork paper-knife in the bathroom by now; it's very nice of you to pretend there's not, but there is, of course. He's a baby, you know—a mean baby—always has been."

"You knew him before his marriage, didn't you?"

"I'd met him once or twice. I know all about him. He had three thousand a year on his father's death; Papa Barley made it in soap. He's never spent it. I doubt if he's ever spent a third of it. But his house is a kind of fetish with him; when he does spend a few pennies it's mostly on the house. What a curse that man's dinner must be to him-naturally rather greedy, and naturally very economical! Dinner? Why, it's a civil war. Even in those days his favourite reading was the store catalogues, and he knew more about the details of household management than I consider decent in any man. I once saw him tell a story; it appeared to be a dramatic and impressive kind of story. He raised his voice when he came to the triumphant point, and I caught the words: 'The same bacon-absolutely the same bacon and a halfpenny a pound cheaper!' That's Ernest Saunders Barley. I believe his notion of heaven is that it's a place where you get the same bacon a halfpenny a pound cheaper. He's always been like that."

"It was Percy's idea, and it's mine too," said Jimmy, "that he's got worse these last few years."

"What? Has he taken to drink? I'm glad to hear it. It was always my complaint against him that he had no vices."

"No, he's not taken to drink, but—well, I can't think how Mary manages to live with him. It's pretty serious. It's a good deal her own fault too. She spoils him. When he behaves like a sulky child, and ought to be rotted most unmercifully, she apologises, and tries to smooth him down, and *kow-tows* generally. The house-fetish is worse than ever, too. He considers that every moment is wasted when she's not actively engaged in housekeeping. He brings her in from tennis because there are a 'few matters in the house' that he wants her to see about.

"He is always giving her orders and directions. I'll do him the justice to say that he tries not to be rude to her; but when he's lost his wool he doesn't always succeed. But I haven't begun to tell you half about him. He's taken to pressing wildflowers and to playing with the skipping-rope. I happened to humbug him yesterday when he was skipping, and he hurled the rope away, stalked into the house, and refused to come down to lunch. He's a double-dyed ass, and a little tin domestic tyrant."

"You're quite right not to abuse him, Jimmy."

"I didn't mean to. I only meant to tell you the facts. But it's not so easy to stop when you once begin talking about the beggar. What I wanted was to ask you whether, for Mary's sake, something couldn't be done. She doesn't complain, of course; but she must be having a pretty bad time. Percy and Jennie think so. Couldn't someone tell him what an ass he is?"

"Undoubtedly; but he wouldn't believe it. No; of course, he ought to have been sent to a public school and a university, and then sent round the world. By that time a lot of the nonsense would have been knocked out of him. Now, I don't suppose anybody could alter him, except Mary—and she won't."

"It couldn't be suggested to her? Suppose Jennie, for instance, were to—"

"I shouldn't advise it. It's been said that it's dangerous to monkey with a buzz-saw. Well, monkeying with a buzz-saw is a pleasant and harmless occupation for children compared with interfering between a wife and her husband. I've been told that I can't know anything about women because I never married; but I'm sure of that, at any rate. No. Extract the comedy from the situation, and then leave it. You can't mend it."

The conversation passed to other subjects. The two men were dining in Uncle Nathaniel's flat in Kensington. As a rule, Mr. Brookes took his nephew to dine at the club, but the club was closed for cleaning, and Mr. Brookes disliked the hospitality offered to its members elsewhere. It was a comfortable flat; Mr. Brookes considered that he had done enough roughing it, and that his years required comfort. It was not artistic in the Regent Street sense, and perhaps it was a little too full of mementos of Mr. Brookes's foreign travels.

The small dining-room opened into a larger library, where Mr. Brookes, with the assistance of Mr. Johnson, his secretary, was wont to devote a part of his day to the composition of a work to be entitled *Travels in Strange Places*. The work progressed slowly, and Mr. Brookes was wont to complain that Johnson, a pimply and anaemic young man, with ambitions towards a university degree, cut out everything that was really interesting. Over their coffee in the library Jimmy suddenly observed—

"By the way, uncle, I came on an old friend of yours at Shalton. Do

227

you remember a fine old chap called Derriford?"

"Johnnie Derriford? Why, of course I do. Met him at Cairo, I'm afraid to say how many years ago. He wasn't so very old then. He'd no qualifications for travelling except a pot of money, the English language, a good temper, and the gall of a canal horse. Yes, he was never afraid of asking for what he wanted; and he got along very well too. Remember Derriford? I should think I do. Why, it was only this morning that Johnson cut out my account of a little—er—exploit that Johnnie and I had together. Ah, the place was very different then from what it is now. He'd got his wife with him, a jolly little woman, and two kids—the prettiest little girls I ever saw in my life. I didn't come back to England for years after that, and so lost sight of them. How are they all?"

"They're all well. The old man's as hard as nails—practically lives in the open air. I used to play golf with him, and on the days when he's in form he takes a deal of beating. His wife is rather a pal of Mary's."

"And the girls? It's a queer thing that these pretty children nearly always make ugly women."

"That rule's broken down in their case."

"Oh? And which is the prettiest? Johnson would be down on me for saying that, by the way."

"The younger, Miss Hilda Derriford. But the other, Agnes Derriford, is very pretty too. She's to be married shortly, to Sir Charles Hyrley's eldest son."

"Good. And is Hilda engaged?"

"No," said Jimmy, moodily, as he lit his cigarette. "Nor likely to be."

"Why not?" asked Uncle Nathaniel. "What's the matter with her?"

Jimmy surveyed his uncle with a look of pity. "Well, of course you don't know her. She won't be engaged, solely because I don't see how any man is to have the cheek to ask her. She's too good for men, and she knows it. Nobody could be kinder and gentler up to a point—beyond that an icicle."

"Now, where," said Mr. Brookes, thoughtfully, "have I heard something of that kind before? No matter. So, you don't think of trying anything in the nature of a thaw."

"Me!" exclaimed Jimmy. "There are fifty better men than I am that want to marry her, and she won't look at any of them."

"This," said Mr. Brookes, still meditative, "throws a certain sidelight on your sudden rush off into Surrey, when you might just as well have stopped here until we go North together next week. In the meantime, I'll take you to see a ballet, I think. It's too late for any of the theatres. And don't forget to tell Ernest Saunders Barley, because it will horrify him. If I can get the reputation of a *debauchee* by a visit to a County-Council-inspected music-hall, with both its eyes on its licence, then let me have it. I never could resist these cheap bargains."

Suddenly, while Tarver, Mr. Brookes's man, was helping them on with their coats, Mr. Brookes exclaimed—

"Jimmy, I've got it!"

"Got what?"

"Got the very thing to redeem Ernest Saunders Barley. What he wants is, The One Before."

"And what on earth's The One Before," asked Jimmy.

"Why, it's—" Mr. Brookes stopped short, and put one hand to his forehead. "Dear me!" he exclaimed. He turned to Tarver. "Did I ever happen to mention to you, Tarver, something that I called The One Before?"

"I believe not, sir," said Tarver, gravely. "I have no recollection of it."

"Then it's no good, Jimmy, until I remember it. It will come back; but for the present it's not available. Hansom's there, Tarver? That's right."

CHAPTER 6

As they sat in the library on their return from the music-hall, which had soon bored them, Mr. Brookes became rather interesting on the subject of dancing. Dancing was the primary expression of emotion and the rudiment of the drama; it was also one of the foundations of religion. He spoke of the processional dances of the natives of New Britain, of the "Powder Play" of the Moors, of the "*Potlach*" of the Alaskan Indians, and wildest and weirdest of all—the Fire Dance, the *Hosh-Kon* of the Navahoes. He was speaking of the religious dance as still extant in civilized countries and citing the cathedral of Seville, when he stopped suddenly. He had been pacing to and fro. He now sat down, and began to fill his capacious *meerschaum*. He wore a gratified expression.

"Seville," he continued. "That gives me it. Now I recall all about The One Before. It is the name of a ring, of gold and bronze, now in my possession, which was given me on his deathbed in Seville by my friend Marcel Desormeaux."

"Who was he?" asked Jimmy, as he removed the wire from a bottle of seltzer water.

229

"That was not his real name—he told me so. Nor was he a French-man. But what his name and nationality were I never knew. I supposed him to be a Russian; but it was only guess-work. He did not speak about his private affairs, and of course I did not question him. He could master a language or dialect more quickly, and could get into sympathy with the natives' point of view more quickly, than any other traveller that I have ever met. He was rather a taciturn beggar. But he was a good sportsman, absolutely without fear, and never forgot a service that had been done to him—or an injury either."

"But this ring—you said it was to work a reformation in our friend Ernest. I don't think I quite tumble to it."

"You will in a moment. I will read you the description of the ring as it appears in my book of travels. Johnson, with his usual beastly discretion, has cut a lot out, but it will give you an idea. It is a ring which possesses magical properties—undoubtedly, for I happen to have tested it myself."

He went to a writing-table, and produced a stack of typewritten paper.

"I must say," he observed, as he turned over the pages, "that Johnson is the tidiest little creature that's ever been reared in captivity. I always know where all my papers are since I've had him. Let me see—here we are."

He began to read, with parenthetical comments.

"I may as well begin here. 'In handing me the ring my friend was careful to repeat to me again the strange properties that it possessed, and to exhort me to use it, if at all, with extreme discretion. The circumstances under which it had come into his keeping were sufficiently curious, but need not be detailed here.' (That last part is Johnson's, of course; he said that Desormeaux might have some relations living who wouldn't like it. Careful chap, Johnson. But however). "The ring, which is of antique workmanship, is fashioned in gold and bronze. It bears on a tablet in Persian characters the inscription *Sahib-i-dírína*, which may be roughly rendered The One Before. It possesses, as I have established by experiment, the power of transferring personality.'"

"Power of which?" said Jimmy.

"That's just Johnson's stately way of putting it. You'll catch on directly. I'll go on. 'The wearer acquires the character and temperament of the person who last wore it.' (See? If you wore it, and then I wore it, I should become like you). 'The rapidity and completeness of the acquisition may vary in different cases. The new character may be acquired instantly, or it may be a slow process extending over years; it may be acquired fully or only partially. The removal of the ring at night or for similar short periods does not affect the transfer, except perhaps to retard it slightly.' (I wrote, 'to slightly retard it,' but Johnson's death on split infinitives). But when the use of the ring is discontinued altogether the acquired character disappears—here again with varying rapidity in different cases. It is always the original character and never the acquired which is transferred.'"

"Let's see," said Jimmy. "How does that last work out."

"Why, this way. If I wear the ring after you, and so become like you, and then hand the ring on to Johnson and he wears it, he doesn't become like you in his turn; but he becomes like what I was before I put on the ring. He gets my original character, and not what I've become through wearing the ring."

"Here's another point. You wear the ring after me, and, in consequence, become like me. You take it off at night, and put it on again next morning. Then the last wearer is not me, but you. Therefore, you ought to become yourself again."

"No. The ring never returns a man to his original character. Johnson points that out when he says that the removal of the ring for short periods does not affect the transfer. I'll read on a bit. 'I am well aware that these statements will be received with incredulity. But I have already established the truth of them to my own satisfaction by a series of experiments. I have seen the nature of one man transferred to another in a way which seemed miraculous.' (Do remind me to tell you about the bishop afterwards. Johnson thought it was better not to put it in the book).

"'And it is possible that at a later date I may take steps which will put the marvellous qualities of the ring beyond the possibility of dispute, though, for some years past, my experiments have been, for personal reasons, abandoned. In the meantime, I attempt no explanation. Every traveller in the strange places of the East comes on problems with which the science of our boasted civilization is simply unable to cope. The treasure-house is broken down, and much of the old wisdom of the East is lost; but now and again some token comes to light to show—' Oh, this last part is all pure Johnson. I needn't read that. What do you make of it?"

"Seems rum—about the rummiest thing I ever heard. And you seriously believe in it, uncle?"

"How can I help myself? I've tried it often, and I must believe the evidence of my senses if I am to believe anything. It was not I alone who noted the marked change in the natures of those who tried The One Before. Friends and relations noticed it, and thought it inexplicable—for at that time I never spoke of the mysterious power of the ring to anybody."

"What was that about the bishop?"

"That was most unfortunate. He was a colonial bishop, stopping in London. You won't mind if I don't give you, his name. He was not a bad sort, but he was bumptious. He was bragging to me that he had not got one single superstition. He had already annoyed me by doubting perfectly true stories of mine. I suggested to him that in that case he perhaps would not mind wearing for a few days a ring that I had which was supposed to have extraordinary powers. He laughed at me, and put the ring on, as he said, to give me a lesson. For the moment it had slipped my memory, but the last person to wear that ring had been a hardened and irreclaimable gambler.

"He was a good fellow in many ways, and I had had hopes that, by means of the ring, I might break the spell, and give him a chance of reclaiming himself. In this I was fairly successful; but I should, of course, have remembered that the next person to wear the ring would inevitably inherit the temperament of an habitual gambler. I never thought about it. Two days afterwards I was going to the Derby; I was going by rail to meet friends there. On Victoria platform I met my friend the bishop. He was in his usual clothes; but he had got a bundle of sporting papers under his arm, and his field-glasses, in a yellow leather case, were slung over his shoulder; he was attracting a good deal of attention. He saw me, and came up to me at once.

"He said that we could travel down together; he had got a good thing, and was ready to bet his last gaiter on it. It was a long while since he had done anything of the kind; but he would soon pick it up, and he was going to have a jolly good time. Really, it was most embarrassing. I said it would be delightful, and, by the way, would he mind giving me back that quaint Persian ring that I had lent him? Not a bit of it. The ring was a mascot, and he was not going to spoil his luck. The only thing to do was to appeal to his gambling instinct. I said the ring was no mascot, and I could very soon prove that by tossing him for it. 'Done with you,' he said. 'Best out of three. Come along to the refreshment room.' The place was full, and everybody was staring at him; but he didn't care.

"He ordered a brandy and soda, chaffed me because I wouldn't have any, and pulled a half-crown out of his pocket, and wanted to pitch it up there and then. I explained to him that it would have to be done surreptitiously, or he would stand a chance of being thrown out. You may smile, Jimmy, but it was the most painful and awful moment of my life. I won the toss of course; I had no trouble in that, for he was a mere baby in such matters. He handed over the ring, and I slipped it into my pocket; but for some time, it did not make any difference. I was horribly frightened, for Desormeaux had warned me that, though the acquired personality might disappear the moment that the ring was removed, it was also possible that it might linger for years, and that often when the ring took effect most quickly, its effect remained longest.

"However, by getting him on to wrong platforms, I managed to make him miss two of the Epsom specials. Then he got angry, and said that I knew nothing about it, and he should go and ask a porter. But even as he was speaking, I saw a change come over his face. The next moment he was tearing off those field-glasses and concealing them and the sporting papers under his coat. The change back had come at last. 'Well,' I said, 'do you admit that the ring that I lent you has a curious and supernatural power?'"

"And what did he say?"

"Denied it. Said that he had been hypnotised, and that I had done it. He was furious, and accused me of trying to ruin him. It appeared that he was due to lunch at Fulham—at the palace—that day. Ungrateful beggar, after all the trouble that I had taken to stop him from compromising himself any worse!"

"And that was why you gave up the experiments?"

"No, I gave them up because I was unable to remember for the time who was the last wearer. I am still unable to remember that. It will come back one of these days, because I never really forget anything, but at present my mind is an absolute blank on the subject. I have a vague idea that it was a man or woman engaged in an unusual profession or avocation, but beyond that I can't go. However, our friend Ernest. Saunders Barley could not very well be changed for the worse, and I don't think you need have any fear in giving him the ring and asking him to wear it for your sake? That's what you must do. I'll take my chance of getting the ring back when I want it."

"I don't quite like it. If the ring has the powers that you say, then it's far too risky a thing. For all you know, the last wearer may have been a drunkard or even a homicidal lunatic."

"Personally, I would sooner be both than be Ernest Saunders Barley. However, in that case, which is improbable, I should have no objection to your taking any steps—even forcible steps—to make him give up the ring again."

"That might be too late. And if the ring had no effect whatever it would be a disappointment for you, and useless trouble to me."

Uncle Nathaniel's eyes became a shade brighter. He smiled.

"So, after all that I have said, you are not quite sure that the ring has any powers at all. Very natural; but you only leave me one course, Jimmy, and that is to convince you."

A deep-toned clock struck a solemn note.

"One o'clock!" exclaimed Uncle Nathaniel. "What on earth would the esteemed Ernest Saunders think of us? More debauchery! Come to bed at once, Jimmy."

"And when I'm asleep," said Jimmy, "you come and slip that infernal ring on my finger?"

"Not at all. You're safe. You have eaten my salt, and a deuce of a lot of it there was in that soup too. But you're going to be convinced. On that I am prepared to bet one hundred guineas to a halfpenny stamp."

"That's simply irresistible. I take you."

After Jimmy had gone to his room, Mr. Brookes unlocked with care a small safe, and took out the ring in question. He surveyed it for some moments and seemed on the point of putting it on his own finger. Then he changed his mind and locked it up in the safe again. He wrote one or two directions for his servant on a memorandum tablet on the table, and then switched off the lights and went to bed. He had quite decided what to do.

CHAPTER 7

Jimmy sat down to breakfast looking very fresh and young and gloomy. He had been communing with himself in the night watches, and the results had not been satisfactory. He had risen with an extremely low opinion of himself and a very good appetite.

"Mr. Brookes has already breakfasted, sir," said Tarver.

"Oh? What time was that?"

"About two hours ago. He desired me to tell him as soon as you came in."

"Very well, Tarver. Devilled chicken? Well, yes, I think so."

A moment or two later Mr. Brookes came in from the library

where he had left Johnson wrestling with his correspondence.

"Morning, Jimmy," he said cheerfully. "You're a pretty lazy beggar, don't you think?"

"I'm a hopeless slacker all round," said Jimmy, with an air of settled melancholy.

"Well, at present you are taking your much-needed repose. Of course, when you start painting again things will be different."

"It would be if I went back to Paris. I did really get some work done the years I was there. And it would be all right if I took a studio in London. But stopping at home at Linthwaite I shall never do anything."

"Percy always tells me that you're free to do as much toil as you like there."

"So I am, in theory. He's a very good sort. He's run me up no end of a fine studio there, and five days out of the seven I never go near the place. There are too many other things to do. There are Percy's horses to ride, and now there will be his birds to shoot. He and Jennie are hospitable people, and there are always visitors stopping in the house. No one could work there; I don't believe anybody can work at home. You'll see, the place will be simply full up when we get there. And Percy's a lazy beggar, except where sport is concerned, though he'd lose his wool if he were told so. Laziness is infectious, and I go off with him and lose my morning.

"Besides, I can't get any models there. The atmosphere is all wrong. When we go up there on Thursday, I'm going to tell Percy that I've got to clear out. He won't like it, but that can't be helped. If you are going to do any painting you can't play about with it. It's do it or leave it. I shall find a studio for myself somewhere Chelsea way, and get to work again properly. I can't stand this kind of thing any longer."

"Bit sudden, all this?" said Uncle Nathaniel.

"Not very. I was talking about it to somebody a few days ago."

"And what did he say?"

Jimmy began with great discretion. "What was said was with regard to slacking generally, but I couldn't help applying it to my own case. She's a girl that—" And now the secret was out. "I suppose," said Uncle Nathaniel, grimly, "that I am right in supposing that the girl in this instance is Miss Hilda Derriford."

"Well, as a matter of fact—er—yes. But don't misunderstand it, uncle. One may have a great respect for a woman's opinion, and be anxious that she shouldn't think one any worse ass than can be helped,

235

and yet at the same time—"

He paused abruptly, and then added, "Besides, what would be the use if I did?"

"Speaking plainly," said Uncle Nathaniel—and his manner was not altogether unsympathetic, "do you mean to marry Miss Derriford?"

"Children may want the moon."

"Now, look here. I don't come the antique and advisory uncle over you much, as a general rule. You're too old for it, and, besides, I'm thankful to say you don't need it. But I'll make a suggestion. As far as the painting goes, I think you're right, and I'll tell your brother so. You began well. Last Academy—"

"Oh, that means nothing."

"It may mean very little. But my point is not so much that you have done well as that the men who ought to know tell me that you might do much better. The accident that you have sufficient independent means should improve your chance; you can afford to do your best. But you can also afford to do nothing."

"Which is precisely what I have done for the last year."

"Very well, then; go ahead and come to London. It will be pleasant to have you handy, and I won't interrupt your work anymore than is good for you. But, as far as Miss Derriford is concerned, I think you are in danger of being a little too abject. Modesty is all right, but there are limits. If we only married the women that are no better than ourselves, the few marriages that did take place would be better undone. It may seem queer advice from an old bachelor, but"—and there was a touch of bitterness in his voice—"one may learn from failures."

"Ah!" said Jimmy; "but you don't know her."

"I knew her when she was a child, and she gave every promise then that when she grew up, she would be human. It is quite possible that she will never care or you in the least; but if I were you, I should not decide that without consulting her. And now I've got a bit of news to give you about that ring."

"What ring? Oh yes, The One Before. I hadn't been thinking about it. It would be interesting to have a look at it."

"I'm afraid I can't show it to you. It's gone."

"Not stolen?"

"Oh no; but I sent it off by post an hour ago, in a registered parcel addressed to our friend Barley. I sent him a nicely worded telegram at the same time, to tell him that a ring was sent to him, and asking him to wear it. I'm afraid that I took the liberty of signing the telegram with your name. I hardly knew him well enough to send him the ring myself. But it will be all right. If anything goes wrong, I will take all responsibility, and clear you."

"I say! But really, uncle, you shouldn't."

"Yes, technically I shouldn't. But I doubted whether you would send it at all if you were left to yourself. I know of no one in the world that I value less than Ernest Saunders Barley, and he was therefore a suitable person on whom to recommence my experiments. I do not know, of course, with what character and temperament the ring will invest him, for I am still unable to remember who was the last wearer; but the chances are that he will be greatly improved. Should the ring turn out disastrously, I will of course stop it as soon as I can."

"I don't half like it. I'm not particularly sweet on Ernest, but I don't want to do Mary a bad turn."

"Nor do I. I seem to have been precipitate; but there is really much less risk than you suppose. For one thing, I feel sure that if the last wearer had been a criminal, I should have been too much interested in the experiment to forget about it. And there is another point: the ring in most cases takes effect very gradually. It was not so in the case of my friend the bishop; but it is generally so. If I found that the thing was developing badly, I should get the ring away again."

"But how are you to know? And how are you to get the ring back?"

"I've written to old Derriford, and I shall hear from him, though of course he knows nothing about the ring. Probably I shall go down there later. Possibly you might be able to run down again yourself. And one can get any ring if one only knows where it is. One can ask for it, or buy it, or steal it. I've taken a certain amount of liberty with your name, and for that I'm very sorry, of course; but I expect it will turn out all right. What are you going to do with yourself this morning?"

"I'm going to one or two house-agents for orders, and then I'm going to look at the studios right away. The new *régime* has begun."

"Good," said Uncle Nathaniel, meditatively. "Let me see. It's a pretty situation. You are improving yourself. Perhaps it would be more accurate to say that Hilda Derriford is improving you. In the next room is the anaemic but grammatical Johnson, who is improving me; at least, he's trying it on. And finally, I, by means of The One Before, am improving Ernest Saunders Barley. I wonder which of us will make the biggest mess of it!"

CHAPTER 8

Mr. Barley sat at breakfast looking like a vindictive ferret. Beside his plate lay a newspaper cutting that showed some slight traces of wear. Mary watched him rather anxiously. She had already been told what was the matter. He stabbed his poached egg to the heart, glanced at the grim carnage on his plate with ferocity, helped himself to pepper, and resumed—

"I remember it perfectly. It was on the day that James Havern at last relieved us of his presence. I called to you from the top of the stairs that the cutting was on the top of the clock in the dining-room, and I asked you to read it. I find it now, not on the clock but behind it—crumpled, dusty, and unread. This kind of thing is enough to make a man despair."

"I didn't know that it was of any immediate importance. You said yourself that there might be nothing in it, or something of that kind."

"(Toast, please. Thank you.) Pray do not make silly excuses of that sort. You would do much better to say simply that you thought my wishes need not be regarded in the least, and therefore you forgot it."

"Really, Ernest, I don't want to disregard any of your wishes. I was just going out, and I didn't think you wanted me to look at it at once. Then, afterwards, I forgot it. There isn't one man in a million that has your marvellous memory for little things. Do let me read it now."

He had known that she would ask to be allowed to read it, and it had been his intention to say that no power on earth would induce him to let her read it after what had occurred. But Mary's servile flattery had somewhat soothed this twopence-halfpenny tyrant.

"If my memory is at all remarkable," he said, "that is due—partly, at any rate—to the fact that I have taken trouble with it—trained and schooled it. Here is the cutting, if you wish to see it. You will notice that it is stated that these paper bed-coverlets have already been tried in a cottage hospital and have been found satisfactory."

Mary read the extract through piously, and did her best to flog up some semblance of an interest in the question.

"Were you thinking of using these paper blankets?"

"Not in my own house. It would hardly be in keeping. I was thinking rather of the thriftless and improvident poor. Suppose I give away a lot of blankets at Christmas—the usual blankets?" (This picture of a beneficent Barley succouring the poor of Shalton was a piece of the most undisciplined imagination). "How am I to know that those blankets will be used as I intend? In all probability in a few days they are pawned, and the money spent in drink. Now, the paper blanket would put no temptation in their way; a pawnbroker wouldn't look at it. Besides, they could afford to provide these paper blankets themselves, and thus a risk of pauperization would be removed. I often ask myself what right I have by an act of ill-considered generosity to destroy a man's self-respect and to—"

But at this moment Jane entered with a telegram on a salver. Mr. Barley tore open the envelope and found that the message covered more than one sheet. He read it through, frowned, and said that there was no answer. As soon as Jane had gone, he turned to his wife again. "Mary this is a telegram from that man James Havern. I will read it to you. And I may premise that there was no necessity to telegraph at all. It is from first to last an act of mad extravagance. The address is: 'Ernest Saunders Barley Esquire. The Chestnuts, Shalton, Surrey.' (Barley, Shalton, would have been ample). It goes on:

'I am sending to you in a registered packet a small memento of my delightful visit. It is of no great value, but you may be interested in it as a curio. The ring is of old Persian workmanship, and if you consent to wear it, I shall be greatly complimented. With renewed expressions of gratitude and my best love to yourself and Mary, Jimmy.'"

"But it's not the least bit like Jimmy," exclaimed Mary. "He never talked like that."

"I am afraid it is only too much like him. All that is important in that telegram, which cost upwards of six shillings, could have been sent for sixpence. And, as I have already pointed out, there was no occasion to telegraph at all. That telegram is an act of foolish and criminal extravagance, and for that reason it is just what I expected from James Havern. His present will be returned to him of course. I do not keep an hotel, and I have no wish to be paid for recognising and amply fulfilling the duties of a host."

"But I don't think that's Jimmy's idea at all. You see, he points out that the ring he is sending you is of no money value. It's only interesting."

"I think," said the irritated ferret, as he rose from his chair, "I am fairly capable of understanding exactly what James Havern means. At present he is under an obligation to me: I prefer to leave it so. There is no more to be said."

Mary did not contest the point at the moment, but later in the day when the registered parcel arrived, she took it up to Ernest's workroom. Ernest happened to be in the Christian-martyr phase.

239

"I suppose," said Mary, "I may just have a peep at the ring?"

"By all means, if you wish it," said Mr. Barley. He was rather curious to see the contents of the packet himself.

"But it's charming," cried Mary. "I wonder what the inscription means. Look, it fits this finger exactly."

"It will be sent back tomorrow. Until then you can wear it of course, if it gives you any pleasure. He was probably correct in saying that it was of no value. I hate meanness. But it does not matter. As I have already told you, I have done with that young man finally. I hope that he will now understand that, and give me no more trouble."

Mary did not attempt a word in poor Jimmy's defence. But the ring gave her a quite peculiar pleasure, and she did not mean to relinquish it, if she could help it. Possibly Ernest would be less severe after dinner—that sometimes happened. In the meantime, she still wore the ring.

But after dinner she found that a change had come over her point of view. For the first time in her life her affection for her husband took the form of an effort to prevent him from being silly.

"About that ring of Jimmy's," she said. "You can't return it. It would be absurd."

Mr. Barley stared absolutely aghast. Had Mary gone mad?

"You see," she continued, playing with the ring on her finger, "if you take offence with Jimmy about what was, after all, a mere trifle, and make a family quarrel of it, you will be laughed at; and it will be very unpleasant for me."

"Are you venturing to question my conduct?" exclaimed Mr. Barley, vehemently. "Do you presume to dictate to me what I am to do, and what I am not?"

"Please don't shout. It is rude, and I don't like it. I'm only saying that if you do as you propose it will be very inconvenient and unpleasant for me. Of course, if that makes no difference to you, there is no more to be said."

"Well," said Mr, Barley, feebly, "if you put it like that. Mind, I am not going to wear that ring, or to have anything to do with it."

"You needn't. I mean to wear it myself. I've taken a fancy to it. All you have got to do is to write a civil letter of thanks to Jimmy."

"I have a little pride. It may be wrong, but I have it; and I have the greatest objection to taking a present from that class of person."

"Please don't speak of him as if he were a criminal, or an inferior. It is quite enough to say that you don't like him. If you are so anxious to even matters up, you can send him a present afterwards—a piece of your woodcarving, for instance."

This last suggestion was not altogether unwelcome to Mr. Barley. The output of his futile fretwork was, as a rule, largely in excess of the demand for it. Here was a *bonâ fide* opportunity for planting a piece on somebody.

"Well," he said, "I have a little thing in hand just now that might be suitable. It is intended for the mantelpiece, to—er—to hold small objects. Shaped like a wheelbarrow, with a decorative design on the sides, and an ornamental wheel. I thought it rather an ingenious idea when I saw the pattern."

"I'm sure Jimmy would appreciate it. And you will write a letter that won't let him see—".

"In these little matters of social diplomacy, I think you can trust me." He grasped his small chin, and unconsciously assumed a Machiavellian expression. "If occasion arises, I can wear the mask, and, perhaps, it would take a man more astute than James Havern to penetrate it."

"You do these things so well. I should love to see that letter."

"You shall do so, if you will wait a minute," said Mr. Barley, as he took the cover from the typewriter The letter ran as follows:—

"My Dear James,

"I am very glad to hear that you enjoyed your visit to my humble abode. Pray believe that I welcome your charming present as it deserves. I hope that my thanks may shortly take the more solid form of a small example of my woodcarving, if you will be kind enough to accept it. Thanks also for your reckless, and very expensive telegram. Mary has taken a great fancy to the ring, and I know that you will join with me in giving her permission to wear it.

"Yours, etc."

"Splendid!" said Mary. "You do put these things so well. And you hardly stopped a moment to think about it. Thanks so much, dear. I will tell Ellen to post it at once."

It never occurred to Mary that for the first time in her life she had made her husband do what she wanted, in opposition to his own determination. It did not even strike her that she had accused him of being ridiculous, had told him not to shout, and had said that she meant to wear the ring, without even going through the form of asking his permission. If she had been told that her subsequent flattery was given as one might give a biscuit to a dog that had done its trick correctly, she would have been surprised. Nor had her husband recognised that here was the beginning of the end of his despotic government. But, all the same—faintly and very gradually at present—The One Before was getting to work.

CHAPTER 9

A few days later the hireling cab that had been bidden to take the Barleys to dinner at the Derrifords' waited in the drive at The Chestnuts. It was twenty minutes to eight, and in Mr. Barley's opinion quite time they started. He paced the hall impatiently. His white silk muffler was carefully packed round his stringy throat; his latchkey was in one pocket, and a shilling reposed in another for the purposes of *largesse* if that should not be decently avoidable. He was ready, ready almost to over-ripeness, and Mary was keeping him waiting.

It seemed to him that during these last few days something had come over Mary; it was time to make a pretty determined stand, and here was the opportunity. She came down the stairs at last, with an irritating appearance of not being in any particular hurry, and James assisted them to their straw-perfumed equipage. So far Mr. Barley had checked himself; but the fire burned within him, and as they passed down the drive, at last he spake with his tongue.

"Once and for all, Mary" he said, "this kind of thing cannot go on."

"It is rather bad. But the provincial four-wheeler always is abominable. I don't think it would do much good to make a row about it. It always seems to me to be a pity, as we've got stabling—"

"Kindly allow me to explain what I mean, and don't rush to your own conclusions. You kept this cab waiting in the drive for eight minutes, for which I presume a charge will be made. And you also kept me waiting in the hall for a similar time. There I walked to and fro, in a strong draught, perfectly ready—and that kind of thing cannot continue."

"Well, it hasn't continued. It stopped when I came down." (And could this be the timorous Mary that scarcely a week before had hidden the offending skipping-rope from the eyes of her husband lest it should awake his wrath again?) "How can you be so childish, Ernest? If you didn't like the draught in the hall, you could have gone into the library—if you hadn't been hunting for a grievance. And if you think that I'm going to sit on the doorstep to welcome this broken-down flea-box at the moment of its arrival, you're very much mistaken. That cab will have to wait just as long as I choose." It was said smilingly and good-temperedly; but it was actually said, and apparently it was meant.

"Am I to understand, then, that you propose to disregard my authority and my wishes entirely?"

"Now, don't you worry about your authority, dear. That's all right. You needn't be always measuring it and taking its temperature. As for your wishes, I'll do anything you want that's reasonable. Only you are not to get cross and make a fuss about nothing, or you won't get any fun."

Mr. Barley observed gloomily that if he wanted any fun, he would mention it. It was not a satisfactory observation; the more he thought about it the more he felt that. And before he could qualify himself further for the International Gold Medal for Pure Fatuousness, Mary had begun to talk about something quite different.

In the meantime, Mrs. Dawes having asked and been accorded the evening, The Chestnuts was left in the sole charge of Jane and Ellen (surnamed Maudie).

"Look here, my girl," said Jane, shortly after Mr. Barley's cab had left, "I'm not going to set in the nasty old kitchen. Let's go into the library. There's comfortable chairs there. Besides, I want to write a line to George, and I like their notepaper better than what I've got myself."

"Well, I'm agreeable," said Ellen, rather despondently. "In about a month's time I shan't be setting along of you, my dear."

"Still harping on it?" said Jane.

"Yes, that worries, me, that does. And it's not only the chance that I'll get the sack, for I don't suppose as I should be long without a place. It's that I do hate to have forgotten anything. I rather prides myself on my memory."

"I tell you again that you're all right, and no one will be any the wiser. That registered parcel what came for Mr. Barley was from Mr. James Havern, though the writing on it wasn't his. I know all about it, because I heard them talking about it at dinner next day. It was a present of a ring to him, though it's she as wears it. So that letter as was given you to post was just a letter thanking Mr. 'Avern. That won't be none the worse for having laid in your work-basket a few days. It ain't like a letter as wants answering. Mr. 'Avern will get it tonight or tomorrow morning, and all he'll think will be as Mr. E. S. B. has took his time."

"I hope it may be so. Of course, there may have been other things in the letter as you don't know about. How I come to do it I can't think. I just put it down for a moment, my basket happening to be there, and then it went right out of my mind. Never give another thought to it till I found it there this morning. Mrs. Dawes said to me, 'Could you spare me a needle of black thread?' I said that of course I could—my motto being to oblige them that obliges me.

"I went to my basket and there was that letter. It turned me quite faint. Mrs. Dawes noticed it. She says: 'Whatever is the matter?' 'Matter?' I says. 'This should have been in the letterbox three days ago.' I was as white as a sheet, and I could feel my heart going. Without no more words, she poured me out a little drop of the cooking sherry, and made me take it off. That do make you cough too. Then she give the letter to Simmonds's boy to take at once, and told me to hope for the best, same as you do. She's a kind woman, that Mrs. Dawes, you know. Her 'usband was a fool to leave her; but then, most men are fools."

Ellen picked up her workbasket.

"I'll leave this door ajar," said Jane, "so that if by any chance the bell should ring, we shan't miss it."

They went on into the library, lit the lamps, and made themselves comfortable—Ellen in an easy-chair, and Jane recumbent on the sofa.

"That don't look much like writing letters to your everlasting George," said Ellen.

"Time enough for that. It'll be eleven or after before they're back. It's a comfort to put your feet up. That's a funny thing—some shoes do draw the feet and some don't, and you never know."

"I don't think shoes has much to do with it. It's more the being on your legs so long. I know some days the muscles of mine—well, it's more like the toothache than anything else. Talking of toothache I say, why don't he wear that ring himself?"

"What? Mr. Ernest Saunders? Well, I've not arst him yet. Some men don't care about jewellery. George don't."

"What? Don't George wear the fam'ly diamonds?"

"Don't you be too funny, my girl. A small pin in the tie and his watch—that's as far as George ever goes, even on a Sunday."

"Still, it ain't like darling Ernest to go giving her a ring."

"I dare say as he's making it do for her next birthday. Besides, it ain't much of a ring, and that's a fact. It don't look to me as if it were gold. And there's no stones or anything. I were quite surprised, for Mr. 'Avern is a generous man, as a rule."

"And is that still going on between Ernest and her—you know—that what you told me?"

"Rather! I should think so. More and more. You mark my words, he must have just gone a bit too far one of these days, and that's roused her spirit at last. If things go on as they is going on, in a very few weeks she'll be the master. Oh, there was one bit I meant to tell you. It was last night at dinner. Seemed that the ongtry wasn't what he wanted. He worked himself up about that, and spoke to her—well, very sharp and cross it was.

"She give him a laughing answer, but there was a look in her eye, and when I went out I hung round the door for a minute. My word! She just did give it him straight. Quite quiet—no shouting and no weeping—but she just took the skin off him. I can't remember the half of it, but it was all good goods. He didn't hold out long; he was soon begging her pardon. And he was a bit scared, too; all the rest of dinner he was just as civil to her as he knew how."

"I never! Well, it will do him good. I can see how it's come about. I think, Mr. 'Avern must have noticed that Mr. E. S. B. wanted taking down a peg. Either he gave her the tip direct, or—what's more likely—he managed to get a hint dropped through her sister, what married Mr. 'Avern's brother."

"No, that's not it. She's different all round. She's got a look now, when she's telling you anything, that she never had before. It's my belief that it's some kind of a conversion—like what they has in the Salvation Army."

"Anyhow, it's one more warning against the married state, at any rate, for them that know how to read it. Here you get two people side by side, quarrelling which of them is to be first. Where's your peace and quietness? Love's nothing but a snare. I wonder a smart girl like you can be taken in by it. Begins too hot and ends too cold, as I've heard Mrs. Dawes say often."

"She's prejudiced. It's a nice lookout for you. Work hard all your life till you gets too old for it. Then you may die and get buried by the parish. Nice sort of treat that. No, I'd sooner have a man to work for me, thank you."

"And I'd sooner work for myself. A girl of spirit and sense and ambition, won't never come to the workhouse. I've got my independence, and I've got my ambitions too."

"It ain't every cook as would learn you things, the way Mrs. Dawes do."

"I know that. And don't I go outside my own work to help her? After this, I'll get a regular cook's place, and then work up. And in five years' time or less, I'll be doing the superior jobbing. Well-paid work,

245

and holidays to suit yourself. You can take a three months' job, and then you can afford to have your fortnight at the seaside, and put by money in the bargain."

"But you don't look at the loneliness of it."

"I'd sooner have that than be as you will, with half a dozen squalling—"

Jane sprang to her feet with indignation. "If you get talking like that, Maudie, you and me will quarrel. I won't have it." She went over to the writing-table and sat down. "Why, here's that funny thing of his—stylographic thingamy. 'Ow'd it be to try writing with it? The silly thing won't make no mark. What ought you to do? Jerk it? Like that? 'Arder? Oh, I say, Maudie, blest if I ain't fetched the point up against the table! I do hope it's not hurt it. These things are too cranky for my taste. I'll try one of the other pens. Here's a beauty. How do you spell Tuesday? That's a thing I never could remember."

CHAPTER 10

Among the guests at the Derrifords' was Mr. Carvell Smythe, a young Oxford don, of some repute as an Oriental scholar. He was a distant connection of Mrs. Derriford's, and wished to make the connection somewhat closer by marrying her daughter Hilda. Unfortunately for this scheme, Hilda had no intention of marrying Mr. Carvell Smythe. For the rest, he was a particularly neat, well-groomed little man, with commonplace good looks, and a manner that was a shade too confident.

He took Mary in to dinner, and during dinner she noticed once or twice that he was looking attentively at the rings on her left hand. When the men came into the drawing-room afterwards, Mary was playing with Hilda's bull-dog, talking to him as if he had been her son, and teaching him to sit up. He had not the sweet temper possessed by most of his kind, and in theory he was never allowed in the house at all. In practice he sometimes came to look for Hilda, and, if the family were quite alone, succeeded in remaining for the evening; but he was always kept out of the way when guests were present or expected.

On this occasion, however, through somebody's negligence or his own intelligence, he had found his way to the drawing-room. A few days before, Mary would have welcomed the instant order for his removal. Now she caught him by the collar, and pleaded that he might stop for a little. It was immediately evident that she was perfectly safe with him. Of the other ladies, with the exception of Hilda, he took no notice whatever. Ernest Saunders Barley was fond of money, but not for one thousand pounds would he have attempted to take the liberties with that dog that his wife was doing? and if he had, Peter would in all probability have made the thousand pounds of more interest to his heirs and assigns than to Ernest Saunders personally.

When the men came in, Peter rushed forward, with his coat up, and with every other indication that he wished to eat Mr. Carvell Smythe. Mary caught him, and pulled him back, spoke to him, and spanked him gently. Peter calmed down. Possibly he had observed that the last person to enter was Mr. Derriford, who, with all his good humour and easy-going ways, did not spoil his dogs, and was deeply respected by them.

"That's rather a dangerous plaything for you, Mary," said Mr. Derriford. "Get out, you scoundrel!"

"Speaking to me?" asked Mary, maliciously.

"Not the last remark. That's for Peter. And, you see, he knows it." The dog trotted out of the room, with an expression that suggested a misunderstood but resigned gorilla. "And he knows that he's got no business to be in here at all."

"It's my fault," said Mary: "I wanted him."

"You shall be forgiven, on the condition that you give us a little music presently." (Ah! that "little music!" and how much it is!)

Mr. Carvell Smythe made his way to the vacant place next Hilda Derriford. Possibly Hilda did not observe it; possibly she did; at any rate, she crossed the room and sat by Mr. Barley. Now, there was nothing clandestine and devilish about Ernest Saunders Barley, but all the same, he was rather flattered, that the prettiest woman in the room seemed to desire to converse with him. They spoke of her sister, who was away, stopping with the Hyrleys. Mr. Barley permitted himself a little badinage. It was heavy, but delicate and very little used; it only came out on these social occasions, and it suited him about as well as the costume of the ballerina would suit a bishop. He could not have told you exactly how it was that subsequently their conversation concerned itself with Jimmy Havern.

Hilda made sundry disparaging remarks with regard to that poor young man, and Mr. Barley was lured on. He concurred heartily, and permitted himself to be satirical on the subject of Jimmy's pictures. Then Hilda suddenly turned round, and defended Jimmy hotly. A moment later, she was telling her father that it was wrong of him to monopolise Mary, when everybody was dying to hear her play. Mary went to the piano, and Mr. Carvell Smythe followed her there, watching her hands as she played. She had been well trained, and, though her natural gifts were not remarkable, her rendering of the familiar waltz of Chopin's would not have made a musician ill; it was accurate, at least. When the murmurs of thanks had died away, and the audience found itself free to talk again, Mr. Smythe said—

"I wonder if I might look at that very curious and interesting ring of yours."

Mary took it off and handed it to him. "It was given to me only the other day."

"It is very interesting." He examined it closely. "I suppose no consideration would induce you to part with it?"

"Well, I didn't bring it out with a view to selling it. No; it was a present, and I never sell presents. I sometime break them, or lose them, or give them away; but I don't sell them. In fact, I can't remember that I ever sold anything."

"You must forgive me for the suggestion. The ring has, unless I am mistaken, rather a curious history, I know of people who would be very glad so get it on almost any terms."

"Yes?" said Mary, without much interest. "I knew it was rather a curiosity. It's funny how the craze of collecting gets hold of one."

Mr. Carvell Smythe was about to say that this was not exactly what he meant, but at the moment he saw another opportunity, and this time he was more successful in securing the attention of Hilda. She led him gently and tenderly on, to make an idiot of himself. He struggled and got deeper. The ghastly sense that he was not doing himself justice seemed to paralyze him. He was a clever man, and he found himself talking like a fool—not a particularly well-bred fool either.

It was almost a mercy when the vicar's daughter, a portly young lady, sang to a cheerful and presumably Old English strain, that she would "trip it, trip it, trip it, trip it, and tree-hip it up and down." Then, as the congregation repeated the usual responses, a euphemistic servant announced Mrs. Barley's carriage.

On the following day Mr. Carvell Smythe returned to London, where he was engaged in British Museum research. For the present he allowed the British Museum to wait, and, after luncheon, he walked towards Leicester Square. In a back street in that musical neighbourhood there is a small and dirty shop, its noticeboard indicating that the proprietor is "E. Carcow, dealer in pictures and works of art." Its grimy windows are filled with objects of this description, mostly rubbish.

But that notice is an understatement. Mr. Carcow does indeed deal in pictures and works of art, when they come in his way; but he is also prepared to deal in almost anything else, from a second-hand frying-pan upwards. The shop's appearance of poverty is also misleading; if you have ten thousand pounds' worth of diamonds that you are prepared to part with for half that sum, Mr. Carcow will not keep you waiting an hour for your money.

As Mr. Carvell Smythe entered the shop, Carcow emerged from behind his desk. He was a man of sixty, completely bald, and emaciated with the fever of a thousand bargains. His eyes peered short-sightedly from under the thick brows. His air was patient and humble. One long yellow hand played nervously with his ragged grey beard. His shoulders were stooping and his back bent. He was a mixture of nationalities, but he had been in England forty years, and spoke the language well enough.

"Ah! Good morning, Mr. Smythe. A long time, sir, since I have had the pleasure." "Morning," said Mr. Smythe, as he sat down on the stool by the counter. "If your prices were a little better you would see me a little oftener."

"But I have some things now that are cheap enough for any man. You buy old carved ivories, I remember. Well, you come on the right day. A chance that will not be again in London. And I tell you why—"

"Hold on a minute, Carcow. Do you remember telling me a cock-and-bull story about a ring of gold and bronze?"

"It was a true story. That ring—the 'Sahib-i-dírína'—is worth, perhaps, one sovereign, if you take it to other shops. I give one hundred pounds for it. It is no cock-and-bull. Hand me over the ring: I pay at once."

"Don't get so excited about it. You say you heard about it from a friend of yours at Bussorah."

"Yes, a friend in the trade. He instructed me, and I told one or two other friends in the trade in London—not many, for there are few who could read the inscription, and many whom I could not trust. I also told you, because you know the Oriental languages. Now, sir, a hundred sovereigns for it!"

Mr. Smythe lit a cigarette leisurely.

"Look here," he said. "Who is the real buyer? Who is going to pay your friend in Bussorah for it?"

"That I do not know. He was instructed by an agent, and that agent in turn by another. My friend at Bussorah says that he thinks it is a religious thing—what you call hanky-panky. It must be a powerful man, a man with much money. For years he has been scratching up all the world to find it."

"Penny plain, and twopence coloured. Any more?"

"I do not know who the great man is, nor where he is. My friend at Bussorah does not know, nor does the agent who instructed him. We are like links in a chain, and what the other end of the chain is we cannot say. I have told you all that I know. Now, sir, have you got it?"

"You've not told me all you know, and I have not got the ring. But I saw it last night. I was away in the country, and only returned this morning. It was worn by a lady, and she will not sell it—she said so; and she very much gave me the impression of a woman who means what she says. She was a stranger to me; I had never met her before. She let me examine the ring, though. It consists of a band of plain greenish bronze, with a tablet of gold about twice the breadth of the band. Two serpents in gold, entwined, run round the band, the head of one biting the tail of the other. One head and tail come at the top of the tablet, and the other pair at the bottom. The inscription on the tablet is cut deep, and is quite unmistakable. It is, as you say, '*Sahib-i-dírína.*'"

Carcow seemed to be agitated. "Ah! That is it," he exclaimed. "Found at last! Now—well, what shall I say? I am ready to do anything you wish. You will tell me the name of this lady, and where she lives. I cannot offer a gentleman a commission, of course. But expenses—shall I say twenty or twenty-five for expenses? Or you might prefer it in another form—a little souvenir. Those ivories I spoke of are very fine. You might wish to select a nice important piece, sir. I will meet you any way you like."

"I don't take commissions from dealers, not even when they're disguised as expenses or souvenirs. And I'm not going to give you the information you want. I suggested to the lady that I knew of someone who would give a very high price for that ring; that was as far as I could go for you; and I got snubbed for my pains. I'm not going to be the means of her being bothered any further about it. You know now that the ring is still in existence, that it is in England, and that it is not in London. That's all you'll know from me. Incidentally, if I happened to have the ring myself, I should want a thousand pounds for it—and you would pay it. You are rather keen on getting that ring, you know, Carcow. Now let me hear no more about it; my mind's made up. You can show me those ivories if you like."

Carcow grasped the lapels of his coat with both hands; he seemed on the verge of an outburst of fury. Then, possibly, an idea occurred to him. His manner changed at once.

"Well, sir, this is a great disappointment to me. I had no idea you would take it like that. It does seem hard to come so near a thing, and then miss it. But I know, of course, how you gentlemen are hampered by your rules and regulations. I cannot complain. I show you the ivories."

Mr. Smythe bought a couple of pieces at a very moderate price, and Carcow seemed well content.

"And where shall I send them?" he asked, with his fingers on the pen.

Mr. Smythe, totally unsuspecting, gave the address of his hotel.

"The boy shall bring them round tonight," said Carcow.

But it was not the boy who took the ivories round that evening. It was Mr. Carcow himself. And he managed to have a conversation, of great interest to himself, with the second boots.

Later on, that obliging boots met Mr. Carcow in the private bar of a neighbouring hotel.

"I've got it for you," said the boots, exultingly. "There was one foreign, which I wrote down to make no mistake."

"Never mind that."

"There was an Oxford label, and a fresher one which was Shalton. The others were all London stations."

"Thank you," said Carcow. "That will do. Here is your money."

He still lingered after his informant had gone. He sipped his *absinthe* and reflected. So far, he was satisfied. Thanks to the evidence of the labels on Mr. Smythe's luggage, the field of search was now narrowed down to Shalton for the time being. If the ring was not there, then the lady who wore it was a visitor, as Smythe had been, and it would be necessary to start again.

But Smythe had said nothing to imply that the lady was a visitor, and the clue was quite good enough to follow up. And by the time that Carcow had finished his *absinthe*, he had quite made up his mind how to follow it up.

CHAPTER 11

It was in the billiard-room at Linthwaite that Mr. Barley's letter of thanks for the ring, forgotten by Maudie and subsequently forwarded by that spotted secretary Mr. Johnson, was handed to James Havern. He was not more than pleasantly tired after the day's shoot, and had

251

still enough energy to watch a game. He glanced carelessly through the letter until he was pulled up short by the passage which informed him that it was Mary, and not Ernest, who was wearing the ring. Then he began to be rather nervous.

It seemed almost impossible to believe that a ring could really alter a personality. Yet Uncle Nathaniel absolutely believed in it; and Mr. Nathaniel Brookes was not a man who believed with any profusion. James felt that he would be happier if he could have a word with his uncle, just to be assured that the talk about The One Before had 'merely been a joke on his uncle's part. He found Mr. Brookes, who had not been shooting that day, hard at work in the library.

"Hullo!" said his uncle. "Where's everybody?"

"Don't know. Playing bridge, some of them. Henderson and McAnvers are in the billiard-room. And I expect some of them are asleep. Look here. I've just got this letter, and I want to ask you about it. It's a letter to thank me for the ring (and our friend Ernest Saunders has taken his time about it); but the point is that he's given the ring to Mary, and she's wearing it. I suppose you were merely pulling my leg as to the ring's magic powers; else I must say that I should be feeling rather uncomfortable."

Mr. Brookes looked thoughtful. "No," he said. "If I had been getting at you, I should have hit on something much more probable. If Mary is wearing the ring, she is inheriting the nature and temperament of the person who last wore it. I ought to have foreseen this possibility. I had a charming letter from old Derriford yesterday, and I think if anything much had been wrong with Mary, he would have been bound to have mentioned it. The ring may not take effect at once, and it is not always the entire personality that is inherited. But all the same, I think it had better be got away. It's no end of a journey to Shalton, but that can't be helped; I'll see Percy, and leave by the early train tomorrow."

"Then you really do believe in it? I don't feel that I shall ever be able to do that until I've actually seen its effects. At the same time, I can't altogether disbelieve; if I could, I should be a good deal more comfortable. Can't I go instead? You could tell me how to get the ring away."

"That is precisely what I couldn't do without knowing how the land lies. In the course of my experiments with the ring I have frequently had to get it from people who did not want to give it up; as a rule, I have stolen it, and I'm afraid you have not had enough experience to make a good clean theft of it. I have even, on one difficult occasion, had to have recourse to drugs, and I'm afraid you don't understand drugs. No; it would be much better for me to go—thanks all the same. Besides, I am the responsible person. It was I who sent the ring in your name."

"It's a pity," said Jimmy, "that you can't remember who it was that wore the ring last."

"My dear boy, you're talking nonsense. There is no man in the world who has a better memory than I have. I remember everything, to the last and minutest detail. The only trouble is that the memory is not always available. The facts that I wish to recall come back, but they take their own time about it. At any moment I may be able to recall who was the last wearer of The One Before. I never forget anything; my memory is miraculous. But one must give it its own time to operate."

Of course," said Jimmy, without conviction. "This kind of thing bothers me, uncle. It's all very well for you, who have travelled all over the place, and are used to the Orientals and miracles generally. But I'm a twentieth-century, commonplace Britisher; and this kind of thing puts me off and makes me nervous. I don't understand what to do with it. It's not in the books. Speaking frankly, I wish I'd never had anything to do with it."

"But you haven't. It was I who suggested the ring, feeling sure that any change in Ernest must be an improvement. It was I who sent the ring. It is I who am going to leave tomorrow in order to get the ring back again. Yet I don't distress myself. Oh, wait!"

Mr. Nathaniel Brookes flung himself back in his chair with both hands pressed to his forehead.

"What is it?" asked Jimmy. "You remember something?"

"Yes. At least, I have always remembered it, but only now become conscious of it. It is a warning that Desormeaux gave me on his deathbed—a warning that, I am sorry to say, I have neglected. I recall the scene vividly now. He was lying in a whitewashed hut outside Seville. He was a thin yellow beggar, wrapped up in a gaudy silk counterpane. It was just after he had told me to use the utmost discretion in my experiments. And he said, 'Do not let the subjects of your experiments, or anybody else, know that the ring possesses any magic powers. If you do, they will speak of it, and such talk spreads rapidly and far. That would enable the searchers for the *Sahib-i-dírina* to locate it; the search will go on always and everywhere. Once they know where it is, nothing on earth can stop them from getting it.' Those were his exact words, and after all these years I can recall them accurately. That's not a bad memory, I think."

"It's a pity you did not recall it before. And have you spoken to many people about the magic powers of the ring?"

"Fortunately, I have not. In one or two of my experiments I may have admitted that the ring possessed powers of some kind, but as a rule I said nothing about it. The only people to whom I have told the whole story are Johnson and yourself. I shall warn Johnson, and of course I shall cut the whole passage out of the book. In the meantime, do you happen to have mentioned it to anybody?"

"No; and I won't. It's lucky, for I have been on the verge of talking about it to Percy once or twice. By the way, you never told me how Desormeaux got it."

"No; Johnson cut that out. Well, as a matter of fact, he stole it. In justice to him I must tell you that he would have been quite willing to buy it, only the thing was not for sale; incidentally, he had to shoot a man, who had himself stolen it previously."

"And who are the rightful owners—the people who are searching for it?"

"Desormeaux never told me. He gave me a hint, and I think I know, but I'd rather not talk about that."

"Still more mysterious. If ever I get hold of that infernal ring, I'll drop it in the Thames. A thing of that kind ought not to be about; it's an anachronism, and a dangerous anachronism. Even if it does not possess the powers with which you credit it, there are apparently a number of fanatical people on the hunt for it. Suppose they find out that it is in Mary's possession, it might be uncommonly unpleasant for her."

"Undoubtedly it might. But is it probable? There will be no public talk about a magic ring, because neither Mary nor anybody else in Shalton knows that it is any more than a toy bought at a curiosity shop. The change in her character may be noticeable, and probably is; but no one will connect that with the ring. I have not the least doubt that she might wear it there all her life without it ever coming to the knowledge of the searchers.

"Even if I had recalled the fact that this organisation was hunting for the ring, I should still have sent it. If they did find that she was wearing it, nothing worse would happen to her in all probability than that she would sell it at what she would think an absurdly high price.

It would be awkward for me, for it would mean that I had lost the ring for ever, which I should be sorry to do. But it would be rather pleasant than otherwise for her."

"And if she refused to sell it?"

"Then I admit that there might be trouble. But the chances are millions to one against it, and it is really not worth thinking about. Besides, I start for Shalton tomorrow myself, and if I find that the ring is deteriorating Mary in any way, I shall bring it back with me."

"I wish you would bring it back in any case."

"No. It may be doing a good work. Then it will be interesting to watch the experiment. Leave it to me. If anything goes wrong, I take the whole responsibility."

Jimmy slept badly that night, and dreamed of many murders. Consequently, he was very late in coming down the next morning. The only person that he found still at breakfast was Mr. Nathaniel Brookes who should have started for Shalton about two hours before.

"Hullo!" said Jimmy; "missed your train?"

"No; I am not going, after all—at any rate not at present. I have explained to Percy that I had a letter by the first post which made it unnecessary. As a matter of fact, my memory has been getting to work again. I have recalled who was the last wearer of the ring—a very decent man indeed, not unlike Mary in many respects, but with some fine qualities added."

"Well," said Jimmy, impatiently, "who was he?"

"He was by profession, and also by sheer love of it, a lion-tamer. He had a *troupe* of performing hyenas as well."

"Yes, but as Mary doesn't happen to have any lions or hyenas—"

"But she has a husband—a snappy little suburban-souled wife-bullying husband; and she'll tame him

She may even succeed in making some kind of a cheap imitation of a second-hand man out of him. That ring is doing a good work. It is our plain duty to leave it alone. In a week or two you'll be going to town to commence this serious work that there's been so much talk about. At the same time, I'll accept John Derriford's invitation, and run down to Shalton to see him. Then I shall see how the land lies. Leave it all to me, my boy. It's going splendidly."

And Jimmy, utterly bewildered, and hoping against hope that he might merely be the victim of some elaborate practical joke, was forced to assent.

CHAPTER 12

(Extracts from the Diary of Ernest Saunders Barley.)

Personally, I should say that it was some long-arrested development of character. I have heard of such things. In some ways it is a gain. The condition of the table silver lately has been most satisfactory; the cleaning and polishing have been thoroughly done. And, speaking generally, the servants seem particularly anxious to please her. I should almost have said that they were slightly afraid of her, but for the absurdity of the idea of anybody being afraid of dear Mary. With her attitude towards me I am less satisfied. There is a something wanting.

It is almost as if she had lost the power to appreciate me in the way that she used to do. I had invented two or three little variations with the skipping-rope, and called her in to see them; she did not seem in the least enthusiastic. There was a word or two as to my ingenuity and agility, but she said that they would be better employed in some real game. She does not disobey my commands, but she is forming a habit of getting me to withdraw them. Of course, I use my judgment in such matters; one must allow for these late developments of character, and for the present I frequently give way.

I have the feeling that I do not know exactly what will happen if I do not. Naturally, I shall return to my old position as soon as I become more used to the situation. I am convinced that the old methods of expressing authority are of no use; they invariably put me wrong, and appear to represent me in an odious light. She is also much more exigent than she used to be. She wishes me to do things or not to do them; and she never seems to mind saying so. There never used to be anything of the kind. She shows a tendency to inquire into the relation of expenditure to income, and is far less easily satisfied on this point than was formerly the case.

She makes no secret that she would like to have a horse to ride, and that she thinks I should provide it for her. The question of expenditure is a grave one, but I am unable to tell her that it would be quite impossible. It might, perhaps, be wiser—temporarily, while this crisis lasts—to give way. Indeed, her passion for animals has grown very much of late, and causes me some nervousness. She frequently takes Hilda Derriford's bull-dog out with her—a very dangerous animal, that should certainly have been shot long ago.

The *Hortus Siccus*, a collection to which for the past year I have given a considerable amount of my time, has now been destroyed.

For some days past I have had hints that Mary did not really think very much of it, and yesterday afternoon, when we were alone at tea, she spoke quite plainly about it. She said that if it had been part of a genuine study of botany, she would have said nothing about it, but that the love of doing neat things with gummed labels was merely childish, and people would laugh at me, and she did not care to have her husband ridiculed.

It is, as I said above—the faculty for appreciation seems to have disappeared completely. I was naturally a little put out. I went upstairs, fetched the *Hortus Siccus*, and took it out to the greenhouse stove. I then called Mary out, saying that I had something that I wished to show her. "There," I said, "is a collection which represents practically a year's work. Apparently, you disapprove of it. Tell me to destroy it, and I will do it at once. I have matches here for the purpose. But if you do not care to go as far as that, pray refrain from criticisms of this kind in the future." I did not say it crossly at all, though perhaps with a certain dignity. It was certainly my idea that she would shrink from this rash and necessarily final step.

On the contrary, she said, "That's very good of you. I think you'd certainly better burn it and get quit of it altogether. I'd much sooner you gave the time to some outdoor game or sport, and Mr. Derriford is longing to teach you golf."

"Say no more, Mary," I said. "If you ask for this act of wanton and stupid destruction, you shall have it. But do not attempt to justify it." I then set fire to the *Hortus Siccus*, turned away, and went straight up to my workroom. I must say that I expected that she would come up shortly afterwards to give me an apology, or at least a detailed explanation of her action. She did nothing of the kind. At dinner she thanked me profusely for yielding to her wishes, and said that I had made up my mind and behaved like a man. Of anything like regret for the *Hortus Siccus*, there was not one word. Really, it is very difficult to know what to think.

★★★★★★★★★★★★★★★★★★

I have just come back from my first lesson in golf. Mary seemed to wish it, and Derriford, who is an enthusiast, was very pressing. I can see many objections to the game. There is an element of chance in it which I deprecate extremely. For instance, my first drive was very good. Mr. Derriford said so himself. Later, when I had really gained in experience, I seemed to be able to do nothing right. However, Derriford wishes me to go on, and so does Mary. It might possibly prove a useful exercise, if limited to one hour a day. I should be sorry to spend longer than that on what is, after all, merely a game.

★★★★★★★★★★★★★★★★★

I have made no entry in my diary for the last few days, I see. When one is first learning a game, it is probably better to give a good deal of time to it, and to get over the initial stages as soon as possible. I find that with continual practice one's improvement is very rapid. Certainly, at first, I was inclined to exaggerate the element of chance in the game. There is more skill in it than I had supposed. Had I known how very much there was in it, I should certainly have started it years ago. I fancy I have been prejudiced against it by the talk of some duffer who had tried it and found himself no good. Derriford, by the way, is extremely pleased with my progress.

It is astonishing to see that Mary, who can play, does not care in the least about it. She is really most good-tempered about being left so much alone. I have given her permission to hire a horse occasionally, so that she can ride with Hilda Derriford. But hiring is very expensive, and not satisfactory. I have gone very carefully into the question of figures with Derriford, and he is coming here to look at the stables, and see what would need to be done. But I have given no actual promise at present. Certainly, men who to my knowledge have a much less income do manage to keep horses.

★★★★★★★★★★★★★★★★★

I am really becoming very remiss in the matter of this diary. I allow days and days to elapse without making an entry. I have had to see after the few alterations that Derriford thought would be wanted in the stables. There has also been golf, of course. Unfortunately, Derriford has Mr. Brookes staying with him at present, and Mr. Brookes does not play golf, and is therefore of no use: what is worse, he prevents Derriford from playing. It is unfortunate, as he was about the only man that I could depend on for the mornings; as it is, I have to go round by myself.

In the afternoons one can always get a game; but so many men let their business interfere with it in the mornings. I find the game of the utmost benefit to my health and appetite; otherwise, I should not give so much time to it. I am not quite sure that Derriford has not got rather an exaggerated idea of his own form; he is certainly very good on his day, but it is by no means always his day. He is not what I should call a very consistent player.

Mr. Brookes and the Derrifords are to dine with us tonight. I do not altogether approve of Mr. Brookes. There are some queer stories told about him, and on one occasion he was distinctly rude to me personally. It was Mary who suggested the dinner, and I felt sure she would not like me to object. It may be, as she says, that it is worthwhile to make almost any sacrifice to avoid that most odious form of quarrel—the family quarrel.

It may be also, as she says, that I somewhat misunderstood young James Havern. Mr. Brookes is certainly more civil than I have known him to be before. I keep up my authority most strictly in a general way, but in these details, it seems from experience that things work out more pleasantly if Mary is allowed to manage them herself. After all, I have other things to do. This is so much the case that in future I intend to abbreviate this diary considerably, and only record really important matters. Mary thinks it quite right that many minor points with which I used to concern myself should be relegated to her entirely. A man has business, or his golf, or some other matter that requires his attention, without fussing about the house. There is some truth in this, perhaps; in any case, Mary has made it quite clear that she prefers that it should be so.

★★★★★★★★★★★★★★★★

At dinner last night Derriford confessed that he could no longer give me a stroke a hole. I have seen this myself for some days past.

★★★★★★★★★★★★★★★★

On the new arrangement we halved the first five. Then Derriford's luck went wrong. He was in every bunker, broke his favourite club, and lost his ball. I won by two holes. He seemed annoyed, and wished to play it again tomorrow before breakfast. To this I have agreed.

CHAPTER 13

Rebecca (wife of E. Carcow, dealer in objects of art—and most other things) sat in a small, stuffy, overcrowded room, finishing her supper. The table-cloth was spread at her end of the table; at the other end sat her husband, who was taking no part in the supper. He ate little, and never at regular and stated times. He was letting the water drip slowly into his *absinthe*, and smoking a fifteen-centime Belgian cigar, on which duty had not been paid. Mrs. Carcow did not object to the smell of tobacco, even at meal-times; and it would have been all the same if Mrs. Carcow had objected with all the vehemence of which she was at times capable.

She was an untidy, rather greasy, woman, and she was engaged upon an untidy and very greasy supper. She had been at the age of eighteen, when Carcow married her, distinctly good-looking. After marriage she had rapidly attained a state of permanent over-ripeness. Her figure was unrestrained, and her chins numerous. Her hair was still black; her eyes had been beautiful once, at the time when her face had been thinner; her mouth was widely and generously apologetic. She was a sentimentalist with a strong business instinct—a very common combination. She was supping in the loose gown that she had breakfasted in. Money to Carcow meant extension of business; the idea of making his private life more comfortable and luxurious had never entered his head.

"I say again, advertise," she said. "Put it in the local Shalton paper. Something like this: 'Lost! A ring, of gold and bronze, design of snakes, curious inscription, believed to be Chinese. A reward of five pounds will be paid to any person bringing it—' and so on."

"You are talking like a fool, Rebecca," said Carcow, without passion, as he slowly sipped his *absinthe*. "I tell you things plainly, and even then, you do not see them."

"And perhaps—well, you tell me why I am a fool. Then I shall become wiser, no doubt. I want the *Sahib-i-dírína* as much as you do, and the five thousand also; but for all that, I do not see the sense of throwing away money and time. We are busy in the shop. There are always Americans every day, sometimes you cannot be there; if I am away too, then we lose money. Now, an advertisement—that risks little."

"Still more folly. If I advertise, the lady will not give up the ring. Smythe would have had it if she would have given it up. We are not the only people in England who are looking for the *Sahib-i-dírína*. I was made to instruct four people myself. True, if they find it, and send it to Bussorah, I have my commission. But I am not going for a little commission; I am going for the five thousand pounds. And it is likely that there are many more of whom we know nothing who are also looking for the ring. That advertisement would tell them that some one believes that the ring is in Shalton or near it. They may squeeze in in front of me. And then my pains are wasted; I do not even get my small commission. No; I know something, and I am not giving it away to strangers. I go for the five thousand."

"And the shop?"

"Bah! When do I go out? Almost never. If it is necessary, I can have your brother. He will be safe; for I know so much about him that he is a little frightened."

"That is an innocent lamb, and has done no wrong, though many lies are told about him. He will treat us fairly if you keep an eye on him, and he is, besides, the best salesman in London. If I go, what is it you want me to do?"

"What you were doing when I married you. You take a nice big room in a good place for the business, and also a small bedroom anywhere. You are Madame Fortunata, the renowned palmist. You advertise in the papers. You have bills out likewise. Your fees are pretty high, since you do not wish to waste your time on servants. You tell character only, for the police might make a bother, and you do not want your name to appear. (Besides, it is not as if you were depending on this for a living.) The ladies will flock to you. They take off their gloves, and put their hands on the cushion under the lamp. If on one hand you find the ring, you follow the lady. You tell me where she lives, and all that you can find out about her. I do not ask you to try to get the ring away from her—that is my work; you leave that to me. Once you find it, I give you a velvet dress. I give you anything you like. Now, then—you can do it?"

"Oh yes, I can do it. I can read the hands all right. But if I never see the ring?"

"That may very well be. I am not mad. I do not expect that every lady in Shalton will come to you. But see—this is a woman who is very fond of a ring with quaint snakes on it and an inscription—which she cannot understand. That is the kind of woman that comes to have her hand read. I know that type of fool just like my pocket. Still, if she does not come, I have other cards to play. You will stay at Shalton for a fortnight, and then, if you have seen nothing, you come home again."

"Very well, Ezra my dear, I go. And I waste my time."

"Five thousand pounds!" exclaimed Carcow. "If we both of us waste ten fortnights—twenty fortnights—and get five thousand in the end, does that matter?"

He finished his *absinthe*, put the bottle back in the cupboard, and locked it up. "I am tired," he said. "I worry too much. I go to bed."

A few nights later, in their room under Mr. Barley's roof, Jane and Ellen (also known as Maudie) finished a light repast of mixed biscuits and paregoric lozenges, while Ellen narrated her extraordinary story, and Jane commented thereon.

"For a girl like you, Maudie, making but twenty-two pounds a year, to go and throw away ten shillings on a thing like that,—I call it

261

downright wicked. However, did you come to do it?"

"Along of a bill that was shoved into the letterbox. I just kept it to look at, not taking it in with the letters, because, of course, they don't want no advertisements. That said as Madame Fortunata were a world-renowned palmist and mystic, and were in Shalton for a few days, at a room over Mr. Borkin's in the Igh Street. Then there were a lot about some people having wonderful powers as might make their fortunes, if they only knew they had 'em, and that was how Madame Fortunata had always done.

"And testimonials to prove it too, though the names left blank out of secrecy. I turned it over in my head, and I thought to myself that I should just like to hear what she had to say about me. The price was stiff, ten shillings being the lowest. But then I'd just got my month's money, and of course any one with them out-of-the-way gifts like Madame Fortunata, isn't going to work for nothing. I didn't say a word about it to you, nor to Mrs Dawes neither, for I knew you would put me off. But next day, being my afternoon, I went there, bold as brass." "Well," said Jane, virtuously, "you know what the Book says about witchcraft."

"Witchcraft, my aunt!" said Maudie, elegantly. "That Madame Fortunata's no witch. Why, she's a great fat woman. Dressed a good deal for show, I thought. And if the stones was real in them rings she was wearing, they was a king's ransom, I says. "Can I have my hands done? I've got the money with me.' She says that certainly I could. I had to set down against a table, and put my hands on a pink cushion, just under the lamp which she lit, though it was broad daylight. There was nothing stand-offish about her, and she talked to me, and I to her, while she was getting things ready. Then she started, going over the lines with a ivory penholder; and it was an absolute miracle.

"She'd got me just as if she'd known me all her life. My own mother couldn't have done it better. 'You are in domestic service,' she said; but you are too good for it, and I see here qualities which should place you in a very different position. You have some special reason for coming to see me, and it is connected with some wish or ambition that you have very much at heart.'—How they know these things is what gets me—'You are exceedingly ambitious, and you have good reasons to be. You have pride and great discretion; you could be trusted to keep a secret. You are fond of your freedom and independence, and, though you are attractive to the opposite sex, you remain cold to them.' You know what a blooming icicle I am with men yourself,

262

don't you?

"And so, she went on, and every bit of it as true as truth. She said I had been in danger from fire, and I was just going to tell her that it was wrong there, when it flashed across my mind about that lamp going over in the kitchen a fortnight ago. After that I felt she knew all about me; it was as if she could see through and through me. There was lots more, and I don't remember all of it. When she had finished, I paid her the money, and said it was all very good, but I should have liked to hear something about the future. She said as she were not allowed by law to tell that for money, but she said as she wouldn't mind telling me *gratis* that I had nothing to fear, for I had long life before me, and only one serious illness. And it would be lucky for me to wear a ring of mixed metals—gold and silver or silver and copper. 'Perhaps your lady wears one,' she said. 'Not she,' I says; for you know as I'm one to keep up the credit of a place where I am. 'Real gold and real diamonds is what she wears, and nothing else—leastwise not in the way of rings.' Never come into my mind till afterwards that she does wear a ring of mixed metals, after all—you know—that little thing that Mr. 'Avern gave her. Then I came away."

"And you've wasted your money."

"It's ten shillings gone, of course. But I never knew before what a world of wonders this is. Oh, you did ought to go and see what she says about you! It is encouraging, you know."

"Not if I was the Bank of England twice over, I wouldn't do such a thing, for I don't hold with it. And, even if I did, any money as I can put by will come in nicely when me and George—"

"There's your blooming George again. It's just as if you couldn't keep him out of your head a minute."

"P'r'aps I can't; p'r'aps I don't want to."

"Well, sooner you than me. I knows a bit too much about men."

"You don't know anything against George. Nor you don't know anything against Mr. 'Ick's, either, if only you'd listen to the voice of your 'eart, instead of taking up with socialism and witches."

"It's no good for Mr. 'Icks to get you to speak for him, nor Mrs. Dawes neither. I've give him my answer once for all, and he knows it."

"That was a cruel thing. You didn't see him as he was that next Sunday afternoon, when he came up with a letter from Mrs. Derriford. You was out. His face was a ghastly, deathly white, and his spirits was all gone to nothing. He didn't speak much. He pulled a small cucumber out of his breast-pocket, and handed it to Mrs. Dawes. 'She's partial to 'em,' 'e says, in a melancholy way, not mentioning your name, though of course Mrs. Dawes knew. 'Shall I say as it's a present from you, Mr. 'Icks?' she says. He just shook his head. 'Say a gift from a friend,' 'e said. 'No good to mention my name.' There's heaps of other girls would marry him, for he's not too old, though old enough to be steady; besides, he's a clever gardener, and makes good money. But he won't look at any of 'em. I've seen him of a Sunday, setting all alone up at the cemingtery, smoking his pipe and reading the paper. Oh, that sort of thing makes my heart bleed. And as for asking me to speak for him, he wouldn't dream of it."

"And it wouldn't be any good if he did."

"I only hope as you may live to change your mind. Strange things does happen in that way. Look at His Royal Highness Mr. Ernest Saunders Barley, Esquire."

"Yes, she's boss now. But then, look at the years as she's been put upon. And it may change round again yet. No, there's too much uncertainty about marriage."

"She's a bit different too," said Jane.

"Yes, there is a something; you can't hardly say what it is. There's a look in her eye, and there's a way of speaking."

"She's as pleasant-spoken as ever she was," said Jane.

"I don't say she ain't, but there's a way with her. You has a feeling that she could speak very different if there were reason, and pretty nigh take the skin off you. If there is anything wrong—and that don't happen often in my work-I don't make no excuses. She used to look at you; now she looks right through you. Now, ain't it so?"

"It's something or other anyhow. She don't make no threats, and yet I knows that if the silver weren't up to the mark she'd think nothing of giving me the sack. Never worked so hard since I've been here, and that's a fact. It wouldn't suit my book to have to go. I'm comfortable enough, and I don't want another change for the short time afore me and George are married."

"And I don't want to leave neither, not until Mrs. Dawes has taught me all that she knows. I'd sooner have it as it is than like it was when he was always hanging round, and wanting to know what you did with small bits of string from parcels, and saying as he wouldn't have them wasted. He was a corker. What I say is that I can make allowances for anything except worrying and wangling."

"Well, there's something in that." Jane paused before the looking-glass and tried an effect. "I say, Maudie, how'd you like me with my 'air like that?"

"Oh, a treat!" said Maudie. "You looks like the Queen of nothing."

CHAPTER 14

Extracts from a letter from Nathaniel Brookes to his nephew James Havern.

You are by this time very savage that I have not written to you before to report progress. It is a case where no news is good news, but undoubtedly, I should have written sooner but for the fact that I find writing such disgusting and laborious work. If I'd only got my secretary down here, it would be different. He would take me down in shorthand, transcribe me, punctuate me, make the requisite repairs in my grammar, address me and stamp me, and save me a mint of trouble. I'm afraid I should not have thought of writing now even, but that it seemed a more desirable occupation than watching a contest at the royal and idiotic game of golf between my cheerful host and—

Can you guess the name? Ernest Saunders Barley. And that's a fact, Jimmy. Ernest Saunders is converted into a golf maniac and quite un-recognisable. And it's the blessed work, indirectly, of The One Before.

The lion-tamer was a man of strong, almost mesmeric, personal influence, and Mary has inherited it. She has made an improved version of Ernest Saunders. He is still ridiculous in many ways, and always will be, but the domestic pettifogger and tyrant has vanished. "Mary seems to wish it," is a final argument with him now. The Hortus Sic-cus has been destroyed. The fret-saw is laid aside; to my knowledge he has not made one filthy and ineffective paper-knife or one putrid and untrustworthy bracket since I've been here. I've grave doubts if he could tell you offhand the exact price of his breakfast bacon.

He let Johnnie Derriford give him one lesson in golf, and since then golf has marked him for its own. The original lesson was because "Mary seemed to wish it," but golf itself has gone on with the good work. Derriford tells me that he's by no means a bad player, consid-ering how short a time he has been at it. He plays every day, and is inclined to talk it in the intervals; but I've known better men than him to be thus afflicted. The out-of-door exercise has done his health good, and by mixing more with other men and different sorts of men, he has gained more sense of proportion. He is even beginning to spend some of his money—I fancy that "Mary seemed to wish it." He is going to embark on a carriage-Johnson would never pass that sentence—and is at present modernizing his stables under Derriford's directions.

The changes in Mary—the direct result of The One Before—are

less remarked, but not less remarkable. That quality of domination, which she has acquired from my old friend the lion-tamer, shows itself in subtle ways, in a look of the eyes, in an inflection of the voice, in a quickness of decision and an absence of timidity; and naturally in ordinary social converse it has no occasion to show itself at all. But they chaff her about her sudden craze for animals—he even made friends with a performing bear that two abominable French scoundrels were dragging round the place. So far as her complete ascendency over Ernest Saunders goes, they have probably got some vague idea that she has asserted herself. But it certainly has not occurred to them that she has become to a great extent somebody else altogether.

Well, Mary did her duty to a member of the family and asked me to dinner. I fancy her distrust of me has diminished rather; more probably because I am a friend of the Derrifords' than for any merits of my own. Ernest Saunders follows her lead. Also, he regards me with pity because I don't play golf. And I regard him with contempt; and we're both very civil to each other. After dinner we had one of those weird card games that they have in the provinces; you've never heard of it before, but they tell you that you'll soon pick it up. The chief point of this game seemed to be that every three minutes everybody had to pay Ernest Saunders six fish-counters, which seemed to give him a good deal of pleasure. I lost my head (through excitement) and gambled like a madman—thereby, I am sure, incurring Mary's gravest suspicions.

And the more heavily I plunged the more luck went against me. By the end of the game, I felt as if I had lost my entire fortune twice over, and the only thing to do was to go home and blow my brains out. I had run through no less than two hundred and ninety-eight fish-counters. This, by the way, represents in cash six shillings and twopence-halfpenny. Ernest Saunders said he had never seen anything like it before. One talks all the time, and it's a nice bright game. I must teach it them up at the Club. It's a pity I've forgotten the name of it.

Well, you see, The One Before is doing an excellent work. In fact, the work is done. The spell has been broken, and Ernest Saunders would never get back to his old position as penny domestic tyrant and general nuisance. I return to London next week. I was extremely glad to see the Derrifords again, and they've done everything to make my stay pleasant, but the provinces are the provinces, and I'm too old to learn the way of them. It's all right for a while, but I'm not equal to much effort, and Paris, London, and Central Africa are the only places where you can really rest. I will bore you further on this point when

I see you. But I have already written at an unconscionable length, and there is still another point to touch on, one of more personal interest to you.

Hilda Derriford is well. I would add that she is beautiful, but I remember that you have already remarked that. So also has her father. "I want Hilda's portrait painted," he said to me. "She will be in London this winter, stopping with her aunt, and it would be a good opportunity." I agreed with him, and asked him if he had any particular artist in his mind. "Well," he said, "that was where I wanted your advice. I don't want one of the highest-price ones. I've lived a long time, and I've looked at the public sales. It's a dangerous thing for a man who isn't right in the know to give a very long price for a portrait by a modern artist. I want a man who is going to get the big prices one day. If he does, then people say that Johnnie Derriford ain't such a fool as he looks. If he doesn't, then there's no great harm done."

It was not, perhaps, the highest point of view to take in a matter of the kind. But then Derriford is the kind of man who would cheerfully spend a hundred pounds to save himself from being done out of a penny; few men who are so open-handed are also so shrewd. Well, I gave him a few names of coming men who would be suited with such a subject; of course, your own name was on the tip of my tongue, and equally of course I had the decency not to mention it. But old Derriford did. "The man I was thinking about," he said, "was Jimmy Havern. He gets things like. I remember his Lady Harston in the Academy, and he'd got the old witch to the life. Then the papers talked about him as if he were going to be somebody. But of course, he hasn't a studio in London, and since his Academy success I suppose he wouldn't look at a commission for a full length under seven hundred."

I told him that you had a studio in Tite Street now, and he took down the address, remarking that it could do no harm to write and ask. If he does, your natural inclination will be to fake up some ingenious arrangement by which you paint the portrait for nothing, and make him a present of it. Don't do that. Derriford wouldn't have it.

Didn't you rather give me the impression that Hilda was very proud? I should like to point out that the appearance of extreme pride is often the result of extreme shyness. I could tell you a great deal more about that young lady; but I shan't. I had thought of stealing The One Before before leaving. But I have promised to come back later for a day or two with the partridges, and I can do it then. And I think this about enough letter-writing for the present.

CHAPTER 15

Rebecca stood in the big room over Borkin's shop in the High Street, and looked pensively out of the window. It was her last afternoon in Shalton as Madame Fortunata, and so far, she had not found the ring. Otherwise, the palmistry had been very fairly successful, far more so than in the days of her early struggles, when her fees had been much lower. and her need for money had been more immediate and pressing. She even felt a mild satisfaction that she had not found the ring. Ezra should have taken her advice and advertised. If she had found it, the satisfaction would have been more full and material, but she had proved herself right; she had also made between four and five pounds when all her expenses were cleared, and she did not propose to hand that over to Ezra, not, at least, if she could help it.

As a matter of fact, Rebecca knew little or nothing about palmistry, but she was shrewd at forming a rapid estimate of anyone at first sight, and she had also found unexpected assistance from the fact that Borkin was a photographer. She had read Borkin's hand for nothing on the first day that she started business, and had told him that he ought to have been an artist. Mr. Borkin said he was well aware of it, and seemed pleased. He showed her some of his recent work, photographs of local people, and chattered about them.

Rebecca had an excellent memory, and, thanks to that chatter, was later enabled to do what appeared to be miracles, so that her fame became great in Shalton. She had a stock of useful phrases to suit most cases; and she was well aware that her clients did not want to be told that their character was what it was, but that it was what they would like it to be. The accusation of remarkable ambition or a strong will was always welcomed.

As she stood looking out of the window a carriage drove up, and presently two ladies—Hilda and Mrs. Barley, to be precise—were shown in.

"This lady wishes to have her hand read," said Mrs. Barley; "and I should like to stop and hear how it's done. Is that all right, or shall I be in the way?"

"Not in the least in the way, *madame*. Pray be seated. Perhaps you will be tempted to have your own hand read afterwards."

"I don't think that's very likely; but thanks. Take off your gloves, Hilda. Which hand do you want, Madame Fortunata?"

"Both hands, if you please."

Hilda spread out her two pretty hands on the cushion under the lamp, and Madame Fortunata went over them carefully.

Borkin had shown Rebecca a charming portrait of Hilda, of which he was very proud, and had mentioned as that it was a queer thing that she was not engaged. That was all that Rebecca had to go on; but it was more that she generally had.

"A most interesting hand," she said. "I see that you had some special reason for coming to see me, and it is connected with some ambition or some wish that you have very much at heart." From the corner of her cunning eye Rebecca noticed that the young girl blushed slightly. "It is a wish," she repeated, "that you have very much at heart. You are not married. Why, this is very strange, you are not even engaged. You are extremely attractive to the other sex, far more so than you suppose, but you are not vain, and care far less for general admiration than for more important things. You have pride and great discretion; you could be trusted to keep a secret. In some matters you carry your reserve to excess; you should be warned of this, for it may be against your interests. I am not allowed to tell you the future, or else—"

"Oh, please do!" exclaimed Hilda.

"Yes, let us hear it," said Mary. "We won't tell anybody."

"Your hand indicates that you will be engaged before the end of the year."

"Is that all?" said Hilda.

"No," said Madame Fortunata; "that is not all. After you are engaged, you will try to break off the engagement."

"I am quite sure I shouldn't," exclaimed Hilda. Then she realised that she had implied more than she intended. Mary smiled sweetly and provokingly.

"You see what I mean," said Hilda.

"Oh, quite, quite!" said Mary.

"Don't be horrible. I only mean that I never change my mind after I have once decided anything. Isn't that so, Madame Fortunata? Isn't that written in my hand?"

"Certainly. I see here that you are a lady with a great independence of thought. You take your own line and you keep it. But in an affair of the heart, you would be guided solely by the heart." This last was a pleasing sentence of which she had professionally made frequent use. She proceeded to give Hilda a little more for her money, endowing her with a keenly logical mind and remarkable powers of organisation. She was just observing that if Hilda had been a man, she would have had great success as an electrical engineer, when Mary rose and came to the table.

"Look at my hand beside yours, Hilda," she said, drawing off her right glove. "Mine looks absolutely brown."

"A very interesting hand," said Madame Fortunata. "It would be a pleasure if *madame* would change her mind, and take off the other glove too. I feel sure I could give you satisfaction."

"No; thanks," said Mary, putting on her glove again.

If Mary had happened to remove her other glove, Rebecca Carcow would have found The One Before, for it was on her left hand that Mary wore the ring.

Rebecca waddled to the window, and watched the carriage drive off with her two clients inside; she watched it pensively and complacently. Had she known, in a state of the wildest excitement, with all the blood to her head, she would have been avalanching down the staircase, prepared to follow that carriage to its destination, even if she had to die—or take a two-shilling cab—in the attempt. As it was, she went to the mirror and patted her fat limp hair, and powdered her fat limp cheeks, for she had been bidden by Mr. Borkin to a farewell banquet-a tea in what he invariably called the "stoodio."

In the carriage, Hilda said that it was certainly very curious.

"Many of the things she said were absolutely right. I'm glad I saw her circular."

"Of course, my dear," said Mary. "But it's rubbish all the same."

"Well, how could she have known that I was not engaged? Really, I'm not so ugly as all that."

"No, you're so pretty that I was surprised she said that. But put another question. Can you believe that when a girl accepts a proposal that makes a change in the lines of her hand?"

"I suppose not. Do you know that you have changed a good deal of late?"

"Really! How?"

"I don't know exactly. You're more authoritative—much more. You used to be rather timid and concessional with strangers. A month ago, you would have been more apologetic to that fat woman, and you would have given way when she bothered you to have your hand read."

"Should I?" said Mary. "Well, I suppose I've seen the error of my ways."

But that explanation did not satisfy Hilda. Nor did it satisfy Mary, who became somewhat thoughtful as the carriage rolled on to fetch

Ernest Saunders Barley, muddy and triumphant, from the golf-links.

CHAPTER 16

Mr. Nathaniel Brookes was not in a good temper. His morning letters had not pleased him. Tarver had annoyed him. When he went into the library he found his secretary, Mr. Johnson, irritatingly grammatical and exasperatingly polite.

After a brief salutation, Mr. Brookes began to dictate his replies to those letters.

"This is to those incompetent swindlers, Jordan and Sage, who've made a mess of the maps for my book. Take down, please."

The tone was peremptory, and the spotty but conscientious Mr. Johnson raised his eyebrows, and looked like a wounded leopard.

Mr. Brookes began: "Dear Sirs, I return the rubbish received from you this morning. I require maps which are clear, accurate, and in accordance with my instructions; and I have no use for this nonsense. Should you happen to have any one in your employ who is not a drunkard, or a cretin, or both, pray let him try to carry out the work, and with as little delay as possible. If not, I have only to say that I will not accept the so-called maps enclosed, nor will I pay for them. And I am surprised—Good Heavens!" He stopped abruptly, with one hand to his forehead.

"I beg your pardon, sir," said Mr. Johnson.

"It's nothing. Put that letter aside for a moment. I've just recalled something that I wished to say to you. You remember a passage in the book which deals with the *Sahib-i-dírína?*"

"Perfectly, Mr. Brookes. Certain parts of it had to be deleted."

"Well, it has all got to be deleted. Every reference and allusion to the *Sahib-i-dírína* is to be cut out. Understand?"

"I understand, of course. I should not have thought that necessary, and I should not have supposed that I had allowed anything to remain that was improper or indiscreet."

"Nobody's asking you what you thought, or supposed, or allowed." Mr. Brookes was certainly not in a good temper this morning. "I'm telling you what you're to do. Every line that refers to the *Sahib-i-dírína* is to be omitted. Secondly, have you said anything at all about that subject to anybody?"

"Have you ever known me, Mr. Brookes, to fail in the slightest degree to justify the confidence with which you have hitherto honoured me?"

271

The stateliness of that speech was absurdly out of proportion to the speaker, and if Mr. Brookes had not already been angry he might have been amused. He now became more angry.

"Don't talk to me like some fool on the stage. Give me a plain answer to my question."

Mr. Johnson was also rather angry, and rather frightened besides. But the stateliness of his diction still held out.

"I have never communicated any of your business to anybody, Mr. Brookes, and I never shall. I hope that this plain statement may save me from any offensive remarks and questions of this kind in the future."

He sat aghast at his own temerity.

Mr. Brookes changed his manner suddenly. He no longer looked angry or raised his voice when he spoke. He was quiet, and he smiled gently and sweetly. But he was somewhat grim all the same.

"Am I offensive to you, Mr. Jackson? Then I must apologise indeed. I mentioned to you a certain matter some time ago—it seemed then to be of no earthly importance;—if you had passed it on to every Tom, Dick, and Harry of your acquaintance, it would not—so I thought then—have mattered. I should not have cared two straws. If, as I suppose, you are fond of boring your friends, it would even have been natural. But when I found that this was a matter where thousands of pounds—and some graver interests still—were involved, I ventured to plead for your discretion. So that offends you, Mr. Jimson! Well, well—"

"My name is not Jackson or Jimson," said the lacerated secretary. "It is Johnson, as you know perfectly well. And I do not think your account of your case is entirely accurate."

"Really, Mr. Jobson? (You did say 'Jobson,' didn't you?) Let's see how we stand, then. I say that there are certain people who would pay thousands to get this ring, the *Sahib-i-dirina*—who would go further even than that. For that reason, I directed you not to talk about it. You tell me the statement is a lie, and the direction is offensive. Now, taking your word for this—"

"I never said it. You choose to misconstrue me, Mr. Brookes. However, it is of no use to argue the point. I'm quite resigned."

"Really?" said Mr. Brookes. "Then I accept your resignation. Fill up a cheque now for any sum that may be due to you, including what is customary in lieu of notice, and bring it to me to sign in the next room. There's not room in this flat for two people with tempers, and I happen to have a temper myself. You are an admirable secretary, and

I shall be glad to say so in a testimonial; and I quite realise that I have brought your resignation on myself, and have only myself to blame. People who have bad tempers, like myself, always have to suffer for it. Be as quick as you can with the cheque, by the way." And Mr. Brookes moved towards the door into the other room.

"I had no intention of resigning, sir," said Johnson, staring helplessly. "It is a misunderstanding, and I could easily explain it; I never meant to resign."

"No?" said Mr. Brookes, in the open doorway. "I look at it from your point of view entirely. It would be better for you to say that you resigned the post in consequence of my temper than for me to say— something different."

"Very well, sir. I will make out the cheque. I am paid monthly, but I think a quarter's notice would be customary—the monthly payment being merely a special arrangement in my case that you kindly consented to—"

"All right, all right," said Mr. Brookes, impatiently.

"There are also a few little things of my own that I should wish to get together before I leave."

"Do so as quickly as possible, Mr.—er—Marlowe. When one has to bear a loss like this, it is the time of waiting which tries one. The actual bereavement—but, however—" And Mr. Brookes passed abruptly into the next room, closing the door behind him.

It is perfectly true that Mr. Johnson was ridiculous, and stately, and nicely educated. It cannot be denied that his ideals were not of the highest, and that he had a keen eye for the main chance, or at least for the monetary side of it. But his ideals were not entirely his own fault, and regard for money is very much a matter of income. The people who have little think much of little; the people who have more think less of little. It may be added that the people who have most think most of little—in many cases, at any rate—but the fact remains that Mr. Brookes could afford to dismiss with impatient contempt a sum which seemed almost a question of life or death to his secretary.

Mr. Brookes, on the other hand, was a gentle and just man, but in this matter, he had neither behaved like a gentleman nor like an ordinarily fair man. One should not take that advantage of life's handicap, and bad temper makes fools of the best of us. Also, time flies, and there are several other copy-book headings, if space permitted quotation; but it may be doubted nowadays, if the most devoted lover of Dickens can read the scene in which Eugene Wrayburn triumphs over the

273

schoolmaster with entire satisfaction.

One may admire the conflict of wits, equally placed; but the triumph of the bounder over the fool is a sorry business. And it may have been that some such thought occurred to Mr. Brookes, for he sat down and wrote a letter to his friend, Sir Thomas Folmersham, F.R.S., recommending in the highest possible terms his late secretary. Mr. Brookes added that the fault which had led to their separation was entirely his own fault, and that he felt compelled to say that Johnson was quite justified in resigning his post.

Undoubtedly, Mr. Brookes was suffering from a twinge of conscience, and in less than a week that eminent authority on primitive people, Sir Thomas Folmersham, F.R.S., had engaged Mr. Johnson at a higher salary than he had hitherto received.

Every wrong (to refer back to the copy-book again) brings with it its own punishment; it may be added that it frequently leaves it at the wrong house. The wrong that Mr. Brookes had done might have resulted in his grave moral deterioration, but it did not; it resulted in the grave moral deterioration of Mr. Johnson.

To fill up the cheque and get his things together took Johnson precisely two minutes. But nearly a quarter of an hour had elapsed before he presented the cheque to Mr. Brookes for his signature.

"I was unable to put my hand on a note-book of mine," said Johnson, meekly and mendaciously, as he apologised for the delay.

As a matter of fact, he had been occupying his time in making a rapid shorthand note of those passages in the book which referred to the *Sahib-i-dírína*. He might, or might not be able to make use of them by way of vengeance on Mr. Brookes and remuneration for himself. He was by no means sure that Mr. Brookes had spoken the truth when he said that thousands of pounds were involved. But he took his treacherous chance, together with a cheque for a quarter's salary, and an introductory letter to Sir Thomas Folmersham.

CHAPTER 17

On the night of her return to London Rebecca sat in the stuffy little room and discussed matters with her husband. He took his disappointment philosophically, raking his unkempt beard with his yellow fingers, deeply meditative.

"After all," he cried, "there is no money lost. It is one card played— but I have more. Now I play the next."

"If you had only taken my advice from the first, and put in the advertisement—"

"Ah! Hold your tongue!" he interrupted. "Am I a fool that I should tell the others where to look for the *Sahib-i-dírína?*" He took the *absinthe* bottle from the cupboard, and prepared his opalescent poison with loving care. "Remember, I do not know how many are looking for the ring. At times I see thousands of them; when I dream at night, I see someone get before me."

"It is because you drink too much of that," said Rebecca, placidly.

"You will mind your own business. That is a weakness of your family, Rebecca. Your brother also—"

"You were glad to have Nathan to help you while I was away."

"Your brother is a dirty thief, if you wish to know."

"Why should you say that? Nathan is a poor boy that is not understood."

"Well, I show you that I understand him very well. And to begin, he is not a boy. He is nearly thirty, and he knows rather more than a little boy, your brother Nathan. Perhaps he has not taken much from me—maybe some cigarettes, maybe a few stamps, perhaps a little pin for the necktie that is not of value. He knows that I know something, and he is careful. I say he is a dirty thief, all the same. Look for yourself." Carcow gesticulated from the wrist, with the palms upwards. "He wears a better coat in the shop than I could at Buckingham Palace. He has patent boots and a silk hat and embroidered satin braces—all very good. His watch and chain—I will lend ten pounds on them and take no risk.

"He has a club; he plays billiards; he goes to theatres; he backs nonstarters; he has all such luxuries. He never thinks twice of a week-end at Brighton; he takes cabs when he could walk; he sucks musk lozenges, and puts scented stuff on his hair. All of that is money, money, money! And where does it come from? Is he a solid man like me, with a good business, with some capital in it? No. Nor does he work if he can help it."

"He would work if he could find anything that really suited him. In all London there is not a better salesman."

"He can sell anything; I know that well. I am not telling you he is a fool—I am telling you he is a thief; and I wish I knew how he did it. He was sharp enough when you were away. Neither of us, I know, has breathed a word to him about the *Sahib-i-dírína*. But he knows we have some big business on. I could see he knew, and that he would like to have a finger in it."

"I told him it was my health—the shortness of breath again—and that the doctor had made you send me away a little."

"Yes, and I told him the same story; and do you know what he said? He said, 'Rats!' When I asked him why he mentioned those vermin, and what he was thinking, he said it was a funny thing he was not told where you had gone; so, I told him at once you had gone to Hastings. Then he asked for the address. No, he is not honest, your brother Nathan; he is a dirty thief; but he is sharp enough, and he suspects we have something on. The day after tomorrow I go down to Shalton, and I play my second card, which will perhaps take the trick. I leave you with him. You want to have your eyes open, and to tell him nothing at all."

"I shall be careful," said Rebecca. "I have a great love and affection for Nathan, and I do not like to hear people speak ill of him. It would be wrong for me to put temptation in his way. The *Sahib-i-dírína* is ours—we have heard of its value, and he has not—we know where to look for it, and he does not. If by any chance he got it away from us, though he is my own brother and I love him, I would spit in his face and never speak to him again. Ezra, you will not have another *absinthe* tonight, will you?"

"You will mind your own business," said Ezra, as he placed the spoon carefully in position. "That will give you enough to do. You will tell Nathan that I have gone to attend some sales in the country. If he wishes to know more, you can say that is all I have told you—which will be true. And you watch him as a cat watches a mouse."

"Nathan is a very good boy in many ways, and he is a clever boy too. But he is not clever enough to get over me. Five thousand pounds—no; that is not for Nathan."

A few days later Rebecca had some occasion to doubt her perfect security. Nathan was in charge of the shop, and he had had a fairly good morning. He had sold three people things which they did not want, at prices which they could not afford to pay, prices largely in excess of the value of their purchases. And he had sent them all away with the conviction that they had done well for themselves, and got the better of the resplendent young man behind the counter. He now stood in the doorway of the shop, smoking one of Carcow's cigarettes, and surveying the street. But for the fact that he had bulbous eyes, a pronounced nose, and a greedy mouth, he would have been distinctly a good-looking young man. To him approached, hesitatingly, a small telegraph-boy.

"Carcow?" said Nathan, sharply.

"Mrs. Carcow," said the boy.

"Right. Give it here." He spoke dictatorially. As it was his profession to be servile, so it was to his recreation to be dictatorial when safe occasions offered.

The envelope was addressed to Mrs. Carcow; but Nathan tore it open. The telegram had been handed in at the Shalton Post-office, contained the single word, "Found," and was signed, "Ezra."

"There's no answer. Be off with you," said Nathan, and took the telegram through to the little room at the back of the shop, where Mrs. Carcow was concocting one of this year's out of two of last year's. In matters of her wardrobe, she loved show and economy.

"Rebecca, my dear," said Nathan, "I opened this by mistake. I was expecting a telegram from a customer who was thinking of buying some enamels, and I only noticed the name Carcow. But I am very sorry; I hope there is no harm done."

"Well, I wish you would not open things that are not meant for you." She glanced through it and flung it aside. "It is nothing."

"Eh? Well, that is not like Ezra. He does not telegraph for nothing—not usually."

"I suppose you want to know all about it?" said Rebecca, bitterly.

"Not at all," said Nathan, meekly. "If he has some business that he does not wish me to know about, that is all right."

"It's nothing to do with business. He wrote to me to send on his pocket-book. I wrote back that I knew he had taken it with him, and that he must have mislaid it. Well, I was right. Now he telegraphs that he has found the book. That is quite simple—eh?"

It was not bad as an impromptu, perhaps, but it was far from being a perfect lie. Rebecca had, in her time, told many better. Had it been the truth, Ezra, in all probability, would not have telegraphed; if he had, he would have addressed it "Carcow," and not added the "Mrs.;" and, even if he had added the "Mrs.," Rebecca would not have been annoyed at an accidental opening of the telegram. These points occurred to Nathan.

"Then, it is nothing. I am not curious, and I am not a man that wants a commission out of everything, as Ezra thinks. It is only that I do not like to be mistrusted. I tell you, Rebecca, no one yet has ever lost money by placing confidence in me."

Rebecca said that she knew all about that; and something in her manner seemed to suggest that nobody had lost money on that risk, because nobody had taken the risk. But Nathan did not appear to be offended by her manner. She was lying; he was lying; and each knew the other was lying. But neither thought it worthwhile to say so. He went on, still in the part of the injured lamb—

"Well, however, I have to go out for an hour. I am to meet a man. He has a gas-stove—something quite new—twenty *per cent.* less gas and fifty *per cent.* more heat. If that is right, that will be great business. Then all other gas-stoves will be scrap-iron. There will be this one and no other."

"You were always a great one for gas," said Rebecca, sardonically. "And where do you come in?"

"Well, it is to be a company. I can introduce some friends, if it is worth my while. Oh yes, I put you and Ezra in too! I am not one that wants to keep a good thing all to myself."

If this was said with any idea of arousing the feelings of remorse and generosity in Rebecca, it failed in its purpose. Rebecca had a quite sincere affection for Nathan. But with her affection was affection, and business was business. Business was Number One A, and affection came rather lower down in the catalogue. So, she said—

"That is right. And you know very well either of us would do as much for you, and be glad of the opportunity."

Nathan put on his silk hat—a hat of unnatural and suspicious glossiness, and made his way to the Sceptre Club. The Sceptre Club is a new proprietary club. The subscription is low, and there is at present no entrance fee, and it is as near Pall Mall as you have any right to expect for the money. It is entirely free from any of that carping and critical spirit that we regret so much in other clubs; the management sends out its touting circulars from time to time; it goes out into the by-ways and hedges, and compels them to come in.

At its birth it sent invitations to sundry celebrities to become life members without money and without price. Celebrities are not always men of the world, and though the majority put the invitation in the waste-paper basket, well knowing that what is offered for nothing is worth just that, a few lent their names. There are nice patient scientific celebrities in the country who hardly know that they are celebrities at all; they took the invitation as a compliment, and wrote four-page letters to accept—well-worded letters in the best taste, letters which would look well in a biography. There are also celebrities in London whose arrival is so recent that they are not yet quite convinced, and welcome any confirmation. Their names formed the bait that the proprietor threw out to the smaller fry.

It is a wonderful club; it has refused nobody; and yet it has been accepted by quite good people. Its objects are set forth as being social, literary, artistic, scientific, and imperial—that's all. And it has a real committee, though the committee is nothing like as real as the proprietor. If it should ever be your lot to enter the Sceptre Club, you can leave your hat and umbrella in the hall, but I do not recommend that course. There have been one or two little accidents there through carelessness.

Nathan left his sheeny hat and his silver-mounted Malacca—by arrangement—in the hall-porter's cupboard. He went on to the reading-room, whose only occupant was a pimply-faced young man who was reading the *Times* with an air of great seriousness. And he was not the inventor of a new gas-stove. Nathan rang the bell; after a few seconds he appeared to grow irritated, and rang it again and more considerably. A waiter in a noisy livery appeared.

"Bring me the atlas," said Nathan.

"Ver' sorry," said the intelligent Swiss, "dere vos no atlas."

"Well, a map of England would do."

"I'm afraid dere vos no maps, neither."

"Go away, then. You're no use!"

They are really a little too harsh with the waiters at the Sceptre Club. Those waiters should not be made to suffer for the sins of others; they have some of their own.

"Scandalous! Disgraceful! Abominable! No atlas!" Nathan might have been soliloquising, but he appeared rather to be seeking the sympathy of the pimply stranger.

The stranger was our ambitious young friend Mr. Johnson. The circular had fallen upon him at the critical time when he had plenty of money in his pocket. The circular of the Sceptre Club is most alluring. Johnson felt that he should embrace the opportunity. It was true that he had no friends at the club, but he had friends elsewhere who would be impressed by its note-paper. He was elected by return of post, and had felt rather a dog ever since. Here was an opportunity to make a club acquaintance—an excellent opportunity.

"I beg your pardon," he said; "I don't know if I could be of any assistance, sir. I happen to have rather gone into geography."

"That is very good of you," said Nathan. "I was wanting to know where is a place called Shalton."

"It is a small town in Surrey, not very far from Guildford. You go

279

to it from Waterloo."

"Thanks very much indeed," said Nathan, as he sat down. "Of course, every club ought to have an atlas. The fact is, our committee is rather slack."

"It certainly seems an omission," said Johnson. "You could have got it in Bradshaw, of course."

"So, I might; of course. Tell me, if I am not taking a liberty, do you know the position of every town in England like that? It seems to me an extraordinary feat of memory."

"I think I know most of them. In this case, I must admit that I had come across Shalton quite recently—well, in connection with rather an interesting affair."

"My business at Shalton is a little out of the way, also," said Nathan.

"This was an affair where thousands of pounds, and, even graver interests were involved. I act as a confidential secretary, and, of course, I cannot speak more fully of matters that come to my knowledge professionally."

"Of course not. Quite right. Very proper. I was just going to take a sherry and bitters before lunch. I wonder if you would do me the honour to join me."

Johnson signified his assent in the usual manner. The prismatic waiter brought the fire-water. Nathan, who appeared to have taken quite a liking to Johnson, chatted freely. He confessed that, as a confidential financial agent, he had frequently to conduct negotiations where many thousands were involved, but he did not allude further to the subject of Johnson's little mystery.

Warmed with sherry and gratification, Johnson talked a good deal about himself. The names of his former and present employers came glibly off his tongue. His intentions in the direction of a university degree were touched on. No, he had not been to the Earl's Court Exhibition yet; he had been sticking hard at work. He assented to Nathan's observation that one must not overdo it; and to the suggestion that they should dine together at Earl's Court on the following night.

"This is just a little bit of sheer luck," said Nathan to himself as he returned to the shop.

The inexplicable absence of the man with the absolutely new gas-stove did not seem to weigh on his mind at all.

"Here you are," said Rebecca. "Well, what about that gas-thing?"

"Nothing settled. I am not satisfied about the patents yet. But it may all come right. Perhaps I have to be away again. When does Ezra come back?"

"It will be tonight or tomorrow morning, I expect."

But Ezra did not return that day or the next. It is one thing to find the *Sahib-i-dirina*, and another to get possession of it.

CHAPTER 18

Mr. Carcow's method had been simplicity itself. He took down to Shalton with him a small stock of Persian rugs, Benares ware, and more or less Oriental jewellery. He procured the requisite licence, and a boy with a handcart to take his goods. He wore his oldest suit of clothes—and they were very old—with one or two added touches, which were intended to suggest the far East. With these he went round to likely houses, and on the second day he arrived at The Chestnuts. The circumstances were narrated by Jane the same evening in the kitchen after supper.

"Just missed getting myself a silver bangle today," she said.

"Ho!" said the sardonic Ellen-Maudie. "I just missed getting myself a couple of di'mond necklaces as well."

"Now, don't you two girls get sparring," said the peaceable Mrs. Dawes.

"She won't do no harm, unless she cuts 'erself with being too sharp," said Jane. "But it's s'truth I did get the offer of that bangle, and a funny thing it was. I was upstairs this morning when I heard the front. So, of course, I ran down and opened the door, and there were such a queer old man. He'd got a yellow and red thing round his neck, and he wore one of them red cap things like what natives has."

"*Fez* is what you mean," said Mrs. Dawes.

"That's it. I had the word on the tip of my tongue. He'd got a boy with a handcart full of things just behind him. 'Good morning, young lady,' he says. 'Well, yes,' I says; 'but the back door's the place for you; so just you get round there if you want anything.' With that he just whips some silver bangles out of his pocket, and they looked real good too. 'I want to do a little business with the lady of the house,' he says. 'I come from Persia, and I have brought most beautiful rugs and embroideries with me—all very cheap. Now, if you help me to see the lady of the house, and I sell something, I come round to the back and give you one of these bangles afterwards; any one that you like to choose. I am a man of my word,' he says. Well, that looked all right, didn't it?

"So, I said I couldn't do no more than tell Mrs. Barley, and then it would be for her to say. So, I went and told her, putting in one or two things to make her curious like. She said she'd see him in the hall, but I was to stop there too. So, I brought him in, and he began to spread his rugs and things out. When he saw her, he give a kind of little jump, as if he'd been startled. The missus liked his things, and they did look good too, but the prices, they were something awful.

"Little bits of rugs, five and seven pounds apiece! And one long rug, what she took to rather, that he said was twenty pounds. 'Your prices are ridiculous,' she said. 'Pack up your things, and go away.' He said they were beautiful rugs, all silk, and took years to make, but he could not sell them, and he could not go on carrying them round. Look here, my lady,' he said. "If I give you the twenty-pound rug, will you give me that little ring on your finger for an exchange? I say it because I am superstitious. If I can get rid of one of these things, then the rest will follow, and all sell as a hot cake.'"

"What ring was it he meant?" asked Mrs. Dawes.

"Why, that one as were give her. It don't look like gold, and it's got no stones in it. I'd be sorry to give ten shillings for it myself. I can't say what the rug was worth, not being familiar with these 'ighpriced antique things, but it was worth a good many times more than the ring-anybody could see that."

"Why, he must have gone clean off his burner," said Maudie, pensively.

"So I thought. And I expected as she'd jump at it. But not she! 'No,' she said. 'I offered you a fair price for the rug, and you wouldn't take it. Now go, and be quick, please. I've nothing more to say to you.' And what come next will surprise you; leastwise, it did me. Very well,' he said. 'If I can't sell, and can't exchange, perhaps I can buy.' With that he dived his hand in his pocket, and brought it out full of gold sovereigns. 'If these will not be enough, I have some more,' he said. 'How much for the ring?'

"Think she'd listen to him? Not a bit of it. She had him out of the house inside of five seconds. And there was he crying pretty near, and the perspiration starting out on his face, and offering her anything she liked for the ring. And as soon as I'd shut the door, she turned on me, and said I ought to have seen that the man was drunk. I didn't answer her back, but I don't believe as he was drunk. A bit cracked, perhaps."

"These sunstrokes ain't uncommon in foreign parts," said Mrs. Dawes. "And I have heard as that's liable to come on again afterwards. So, he wouldn't give you the bangle?"

"I went round to the back, but he never come. That was all right, because he only promised it if he did business."

"Pity he didn't come," said Ellen-Maudie. "He might have took a fancy to my 'air-pins. I'd have sold him the lot for a pound apiece."

"Poor man!" said Jane. "I felt sorry for him. I expect it was one of them sunstrokes. I only hope as he's feeling better now."

"That might be," said Mrs. Dawes, who was the kitchen authority on medical matters. "I've known a case where they passed off quite sudden-like. Other times they leaves a weakness. Well, it should be a lesson to you gels not to go running out with nothing on your heads."

Carcow took his rugs and embroideries back to the little inn where he was staying, and packed them up. He would not require them again. He dismissed the boy with the handcart, and sent off the telegram to his wife, which Nathan intercepted. Then he sat down to think. He had found the *Sahib-i-dírína*; his satisfaction at that success overcame his disappointment at his failure to get it. That was only a temporary failure. He could not admit the possibility that, having found the *Sahib-i-dírína*, he would be unable to get it. That was merely a question of time, and of thinking out a suitable way.

He had taken the precaution to bring down with him a couple of fat glass bottles, filled with the *absinthe* of Pernod. He fished one of these out of his bundle, mixed himself a draught in a cracked mug, and stretched himself on the untidy bed in his grimy attic. How to get a ring from a lady who does not wish to part with it? That was the problem. So far—to himself he admitted it—he had been tactless. It was no wonder that Mrs. Barley thought he was drunk, and declined to have anything to do with him. And he had made a great mistake in not going round to the back door afterwards. He might have gained some valuable information.

It was not any excessive regard for the shilling silver bangle that had stopped him. It was simply that in his excitement at having found the *Sahibi-dírina* he had forgotten all about it. It was pardonable, perhaps; he had been taken by surprise, and had not done himself justice. His next move must be far more tactful. And how was tact to get a ring away from a lady who apparently did not care about money, and did not want to part with the ring? The longer that Ezra Carcow stared at the dirty ceiling, the less he seemed able to arrive at a solution. It was so unexpected; he was quite unused to having anything to do with people who did not wish to swindle him. They represented a type that he did not know. And it seemed a little bitter that the woman should have got the better of him, not because she was sharper than he, but because she would not take advantage of what she undoubt-edly considered his deplorable condition

Supposing he put tact aside and tried something else. Something else suggested itself at once, but it was an illegal something. It would be vain to pretend that Carcow had any moral objection to a breach of the law, but he had the gravest possible objection to suffering for it. To be caught would be unpleasant for him personally; it would also be injurious to his business. But much sooner—very much sooner— would he run the risk of being caught than of relinquishing the *Sahib-i-dírína* now that he had once seen it. The fervour of the chase was upon him. If he had been told that there was anything that he cared about more than money, he would have resented the insult to his character and understanding. But all the same, he was about to do, in order to get possession of a ring, something that he would certainly not have done to secure five thousand pounds in cold cash.

He consoled himself with the thought that if he wished to avoid being caught, he had only to be patient; it was necessary to wait for a favourable opportunity; he had already been too precipitate, and the mistake must not be made again.

He had waited three days, and the *absinthe* was finished, before he got the opportunity for which he was looking.

CHAPTER 19

Mr. Johnson, in his bedroom in a cheap Bloomsbury lodging-house, made elaborate preparations for the dinner to which Nathan had bidden him at Earl's Court. When he had finished, he looked at himself in the glass and was dissatisfied; he was a small man and his silk hat and frock coat did not suit him; also, though he felt rather a dog and wished, for the evening, to be rather a dog, he looked more like a cat that has been left out in the rain overnight. He put his hat a little on one side, and was immediately transformed into an inebriate and fallen Sunday-school teacher. He restored it hurriedly to its original position, and pinned the flowers in his button-hole.

Even then—he felt it acutely—he did not look smart; he looked as if he had put the flowers into his coat in order to look smart, which happened to be the fact. His spotty complexion, his nervous mouth, his mild and beneficent eye, behind his spectacles—all annoyed him. Well, he had done his best; anyhow his hat had been ironed and his boots hurt; very likely he looked better than he thought. So he took courage and the 'bus to Earl's Court.

His appointment with his new acquaintance, Mr. Nathan Rosenstein, was for half-past six, but Mr. Johnson arrived at four. When you pay a shilling to go in it is just as well to have your full shilling's worth. He had not been to the exhibition before, and he thought it a dream of loveliness, and a perfect palace of Sybaritic luxury. He began by having a whiskey and soda, not because he wanted a whiskey and soda but because it seemed to him to be in the part.

Then he sampled various side-shows, until his head reeled with wonders. He attempted a mild flirtation with a middle-aged lady who presided over a cigarette stall; she seemed to him to be one of those remote and irresponsive women.

In time he realised that he might just as well try to flirt with a stone wall. So, he went away saddened with fifty cigarettes, his original intention having been not to go beyond the threepenny packet. Then he listened to music, and smoked some of his fifty. He watched the ladies who passed him; in the faces of some he seemed to see a friendly interest. It was either that or amusement. Punctually at half-past six he was at the place of meeting that Nathan had appointed, at the bandstand opposite the Welcome Club, and found his new friend already awaiting him there.

"I say," said Johnson, with some dismay, after the first greetings, "you're in evening things. Ought I to have been?"

"Not at all," said Nathan. "Some do and more don't. It's simply that I've got the habit of it," which by the way was untrue.

"You see," said Johnson apologetically, "I was here early this afternoon."

"Quite so. You hadn't seen the place before. Dull hole, ain't it? The English, you know, can't do these things."

"That's what I've always said," replied Johnson, with conviction. "What I should like to see would be a little more of the French spirit." It may be added that he did not in the least know what the French spirit was, did not want it, and if he had got it would not have liked it; the wretched little impostor was merely talking for effect and saying what he thought was required. O spectacled martyr to a misapprehension of the *comme il faut!*

Nathan did not pursue the subject. "Anyhow," he said, "let us come and get a drink. I've booked our table. It's at the back of the room, but it was the only one I could get."

So, Johnson drank the first cocktail of his innocent life, and was taken for a short stroll round the gardens before dinner. Nathan's con versation was genial and flattering. He showed considerable deference to Johnson's opinions. Johnson's self-respect came back to him in a flood. Life was very rich and rosy.

At dinner Johnson could not but feel that he was in the midst of a scene of unexampled splendour. The lights were pretty. The band without discoursed sweet music. There were any amount of beautiful dresses, and some of them were worn by beautiful women. The long menu promised in the French tongue strange mysteries. The champagne reposed on the ice. It was a gay world. And Mr. Rosenstein was paying for Mr. Johnson, and Mr. Johnson's heart was light within him. He felt like a monarch.

If Mr. Johnson felt like a monarch at the soup, one asks a little nervously what he would feel like at the end of dinner. But it was no part of Nathan's plan to reduce his new friend to a bestial condition. His own sensitive regard for appearances rebelled at the idea. All he required was a warmed, expanded, genial Johnson, with his judgment just off the right balance, a Johnson who could be aroused to do a little bragging, and in return for the confidences that he had received make some confidences of his own.

"Look here," said Nathan, "I know you are a man of the world, and I wish you would give me your advice about a private matter. As a rule, I can make up my mind for myself, or for other people. The other day I had one of the Rothschilds in. He'd got a new thing, and wanted to know what I thought about it. I only looked at the first page of the prospectus. 'Don't touch it, Alfred, my boy,' I said. 'Leave it alone.' And he did. I'll bet he's thankful he did too. Yes, I'm not often at a loss. But in this matter, I should like a second opinion."

"I haven't had very much to do with business," said Johnson, modestly.

"Perhaps not, but I think you know human nature, and that's what the point turns on. (Waiter, do open that bottle of champagne. What are you thinking about?) I am not supposed to mention what I am going to tell you. But in your case, I know it will be all right. The other day a man came into my office and said 'I want fifty thousand pounds. I am told you can find it for me.' That sort of thing happens every day in the course of business. 'Well,' I said to him; 'I perhaps know a few people who would put that sum into a good thing, but I do not know of anybody who wants to give fifty thousand away. What have you got for it?'"

"A very good answer," said Johnson, solemnly.

"Oh yes, you have to talk to these chaps pretty straight. Well, it turned out that he was an inventor, and if half what he said was true, the thing was worth a good deal more than he was asking. I'd only to put my head out of the window and whistle and I could have got the money for him. The thing was a gas-stove, and it worked out seventy-five *per cent.* cheaper than any gas-stove on the market."

Johnson pronounced that so far it was so good. He emptied his glass, and Nathan refilled it.

Nathan continued—but we have already met that mythical gas-stove. Nathan mixed up the inventor with a rival inventor; he raised questions of patent law; he told how the original inventor had borrowed a sovereign from him and not repaid it. It was rather a long and complicated story, and Johnson drank and ripened as he listened. The final question, which Nathan had been unable to settle for himself was whether he ought to trust the original inventor entirely. "Now what do you think of it, Johnson?"

"Norrentirely farrisactory." He pulled himself together. "I mean it is not en-tire-ly sat-is-fac-to-ry." That was better, though the enunciation was perhaps even too clear. He did not see things double, and the dimness of the lights was doubtlessly due to the atmosphere of the room. He felt particularly well and splendid. "I shouldn't trust that man," he continued; "not, at any rate, without further enquiries." Yes, he could speak all right if he gave a little attention to it, and not too much attention. But as a precautionary measure he drank no more champagne.

"I'm much obliged to you for your opinion, and I shall follow it," said Nathan. "That's a weight off my mind. Funny, that the chap should live at Shalton, and that you should have important business there too."

"It wasn't strilly speaking, my business. Strict-ly spea-king, it was business of Mr. Brookes's. And it wasn't exactly business either."

"I shouldn't think that Mr. Brookes can have had much eye for business, or he would never have got rid of you."

"Gorrid of me? He did not get rid of me. There isn't a man living who has ever got rid of me."

Nathan thought that that man would come into existence, however, later in the evening, when Johnson had told his little story. Johnson continued:—

"I gave Mr. Brookes the sack myself. I found that he told lies—and it was about this same business that he told them. No good to ask me to stop after that. Wild horses couldn't have done it."

"You are quite right. A man must have some spirit."

"I don't know if you know the kind of man I am."

"I know you are a man that I have trusted at sight with some very important secrets."

"Thash the kind—I mean, that is the kind of man I am. And I trust you just the same. Though I've only known you a shorrime, a very short time, I'm going to tell you something. Thousands involved. I can't tell you here because there's too many people."

He observed a red face, with fishy eyes, that stared hard at him through spectacles, and recognised slowly that it was his own reflection in the glass, and that the flowers in his button-hole had—very properly—died of disgust.

"Just as you like," said Nathan. "Anyhow it would be pleasanter to take our coffee outside. I'll find a place where you won't be overheard."

As Johnson rose from his chair, all the lights in the room appeared to take a sharp swerve upwards. He steadied himself, took his hat from the waiter, assumed an expression of extreme severity and walked in an absolutely straight line out into the gardens. To the hypercritical the exit might have seemed to wear rather too much the air of a performance; also, he had left his umbrella and gloves behind, but Nathan brought them out to him. Johnson's gratitude at their restoration was a little excessive.

Nathan found a table sufficiently remote from the crowd to satisfy Johnson, and the coffee was brought to them. "Well," said Johnson, as he lit his cigarette, "I'm glad to sit down again. I don't want it gellarary known—I mean gellenary known—but my boots are rather tight."

Nathan suppressed the *tu quoque* which arose to his lips. "Well, now," he said, "what was that about the way you scored off Brookes?"

Johnson had three tries at the words "solemn secrecy," and having cleared this obstacle and been reassured by Nathan, plunged into his story.

Progress was slow at first, but his head cleared as he went on; his sentences became less spasmodic, and he no longer spoke loudly; his words gave him no trouble, and finally he became sorry that he had ever embarked on the story at all.

Nathan sat with his hands under the table, and occasionally made unseen a pencil note on his shirt-cuff. He was greatly interested. He did not believe in the account of the magical powers of the ring in the least. But he had little doubt that it was the ring that Ezra had gone to Shalton about. The telegram that he had opened had probably referred to it. But Ezra had not returned; Nathan was inclined to think that this was because Ezra had not got the ring, though he had found it. He had no doubt that the ring was of great value—either as a curio or perhaps for some sentimental reason. His brother-in-law, Ezra, did not take trouble for nothing.

As Johnson began his story, an old gentleman of distinguished appearance sat down at the next table. It is an expression which Johnson would never have pardoned, but his back and the old gentleman's back faced each other. The old gentleman ordered a cup of coffee which he did not drink, read a letter that he drew from his pocket—or at least seemed to read it—and did not remain more than a few minutes.

After the story Nathan proposed another turn through the gardens. In the crowd Johnson had the misfortune to lose Nathan; at least, that was Johnson's idea of what happened; Nathan's was somewhat different. He had really no more use for Johnson, and he had a good deal to think about.

Johnson was tired, and the 'buses were full. He permitted himself the luxury of a hansom. But even that could not revive his departed feelings of splendour. The fires were out and the ashes were cold. His boots were a perfect torture, and he was aware that he had made a fool of himself. On the hall-table of the shabby boarding-house lay a letter addressed to him in a handwriting that he recognised. It had been delivered by messenger. Johnson did not wait to remove those boots; he tore the envelope open, and standing under the gas-jet read as follows:—

Dear Mr. Johnson,
I do not know whether you will be sufficiently sober on arriving home to understand this letter. When I saw you it did not seem probable. But I require you to be at my house at nine tomorrow morning punctually, as I may have to call on Sir Thomas Folmersham at nine thirty.
Faithfully yours,
Nathaniel Brookes.

"I'm done for," said Johnson aloud. "Utterly done for."

Then he sat down on the stairs, took off his boots, and wished very sincerely that he was dead.

CHAPTER 20

"Good morning, Mr. Johnson," said Mr. Brookes, politely. "Here you are, back in the old familiar rooms, where for so long we worked together."

"I have come," said Johnson, doggedly, "in answer to the letter I received from you last night."

"Here it was that you delivered that parting oration which you reproduced in public, with my name attached, for the benefit of your foreign friend last night. I cannot repeat your pronunciation, because at the moment I don't happen to be drunk enough, nor do I wish to shout, as you did. But I recall the words: 'Mr. Brookes, you are a liar. I will have nothing more to do with you, sit down and write a cheque for what is due to me—I leave you at once—this minute. Refuse—and take the consequences. That is what you told your friend you said to me, and you told him that I answered that I had brought it on myself and must submit. Now, Mr. Johnson, did you ever say anything of the kind, and did I ever speak to you in that spirit?"

"No," said Johnson, gloomily. "Then it would seem that Mr. Johnson is the liar."

"I had taken too much wine."

"*In vino veritas*—except in the matter of bragging." "He had taunted me in saying that you had dismissed me. I hardly knew what I was doing. I am ready to write any letter you please to my friend, withdrawing what I said and telling him the truth."

"Thanks, Mr. Johnson, I won't trouble you. Apparently, the opinion of that greasy young man to whom you were talking is of some value to you—at any rate, when you're drunk. But I'm afraid I could never get drunk enough to think it of any importance to me. You may take my repute into the fried-fish shop, but don't expect me to follow it. No, Johnson, if that had been all you said, I should not have fetched you here this morning. The trouble is that your imagination broke down and you went on with the truth. You told the story of 'The One Before,' and your friend with the dirty hands wrote names and addresses on his shirt-cuff under the table."

Johnson's mouth opened with amazement. "I never saw that," he said.

"Of course, you didn't. You didn't see me sitting within a yard of you. You didn't see that you were being pumped dry by an overdressed uncleanly scamp. You didn't see anything. So, you broke the agreement which you made with me when I first employed you—made on your word of honour. And you have probably done a great deal of harm—not to me, on whom you thought you were revenging yourself, but to another whom you don't know."

"I'm very sorry. You saw I was excited with drink—to which I'm not used—but that's no excuse. I see what it all leads up to."

"It leads up to your dismissal by Sir Thomas and your ruin, if I do my duty. But I'm not anxious to ruin you. Take that sheet of paper and write down your friend's name and address."

"His name is Rosenstein. I do not know his address. I met him at his club."

"Put down the name and address of his club then. What's the fellow's trade?"

"He told me that he was a financial agent-I think he said he had done business for the Rothschilds."

"Ah! Well, you needn't trouble to write that down," said Mr. Brookes, sardonically. "Now give me that paper, and listen. I wish you never to mention to any one any of my private business. That applies also to Sir Thomas's private business, since I was fool enough to recommend you to him. And as a natural corollary, I wish you to become a total abstainer. Secondly, I wish all that has passed at this interview to be kept from—er—Rosenstein, who must not know that I have his name and club address."

"All that I am prepared to swear on oath to—"

"Stop! You're not a man of honour, and your oath's worth nothing. I won't take it. I won't even listen to the farce. But as to Rosenstein—I tell you plainly that if you breathe a word to him, or give him the slightest hint, I shall know it. His conduct will tell me it. In that case I shall show you no mercy. As for the rest, you've already had a lesson, and perhaps will not want another. But I'm going to have an eye on you—and there again the slightest indiscretion will meet with no mercy. That's all I've got to say. No, I don't want any assurances—I tell you I don't value them from you. Leave me. Get out. That's all."

As the depressed and repentant Johnson withdrew, Tarver brought in a card. "Yes," said Mr. Brookes, as he glanced at it. "In here, please."

Tarver ushered in a commonplace-looking young man, who seemed to have clerk stamped all over him—and was not a clerk.

"Good morning," said Mr. Brookes, speaking rapidly, as he handed to the new-comer the sheet on which Johnson had written. "That's the man's name and club address. I want to know where he works, if he does work anywhere, where he lives, what his character is, and

291

anything else that you can find out by one o'clock today. Of course, you must have longer if it is necessary."

"The time's short," said the private detective," but it seems all simple enough. I know a little of the Sceptre Club; it can be worked easily. I'll start at once, sir, and be back as soon as I can. Good morning."

When the man had gone, Mr. Brookes went to his writing-table and wrote three telegrams. The first was to Mrs. Derriford, and ran as follows:

"May I take you at your word, and come down for a few days. I should arrive tomorrow morning, if that is really quite convenient to you. Kindest regards to you all."

The second telegram, to Jimmy Havern at Chelsea, bade him come to lunch at one and hear some important news. These telegrams were signed with his name. The third bore no signature whatever, was addressed to Mrs. Barley, and ran:

"A sincere friend recommends you not to leave the house today or tomorrow. You would be in some danger."

"Have those telegrams sent at once, Tarver. Pay replies to the two signed telegrams—not, of course, to the other. If they ask for a name and address on the back of the unsigned telegram, you're not bound to put mine."

"Quite so, sir. I understand," said Tarver.

Then Mr. Nathaniel Brookes dismissed the subject from his mind, and set himself to work upon his book of travels. In the course of the morning, he had a reply from Jimmy, saying that he would come with pleasure, and another from Mrs. Derriford welcoming her guest heartily. At twenty minutes to one the detective returned with a brief but sufficient report. At a few minutes past one Jimmy and his uncle sat down to luncheon together.

"Well," said Jimmy, "and what's the important news? Good or bad?"

"Last night it was bad; this morning it's better. In fact, it's going to be all right. But we'll speak of it after lunch."

When they had taken their cigars into the library, Mr. Brookes told his story.

"Last night I went to the club to play piquet with a man, and found a note from him to say he'd got pleurisy, Beastly selfish of him, I thought. I picked up a paper and saw the advertisement of the Earl's Court Exhibition. It struck me that it would be pleasanter out-of-doors than in, and that I night stroll through the gardens and hear the music for half an hour. So off I went. As I was passing a group of tables outside one of the refreshment places, I heard a voice from one of the tables say loudly: 'Mr. Brookes, you are a liar!' Jimmy, don't smile, it's irreverent.

"I looked round. There sat my ex-secretary Johnson, and with him a greasy young swell in evening things, with dirty paws and an obvious nationality. Johnson (who by the way was considerably drunk) was giving his friend a dramatic account of the way in which he, Johnson, dismissed me, Brookes, from his service, so I sat down at the next table with my back to Johnson. In a minute I saw that our greasy swell was pumping Johnson as to The One Before; and the poor idiot was blurting out all he knew about it. When I left, our greasy swell was privately taking a note of Ernest Saunders Barley's address under the table on his shirt-cuff."

"What? Do you think Johnson's pal is one of the people who are after the ring?"

"Not one of the regular lot. But he has found out that it means a good deal of money, and he will try to get it. If I know anything of faces, he's on the make and he's quite unscrupulous. Well, I sent Johnson a note last night that brought him early this morning—a bloodshot and repentant Johnson. I found from him that his friend's name was Rosenstein, that Johnson had met him at some pig-stye of a club, and knew nothing about him. I also had here a private enquiry agent, whom I've employed before, and sent him off to find out what he could. He brought me his report just before you came."

"Well, what does he say?"

"He got at the club's hall-porter. Rosenstein is a clever fellow, always smartly dressed, gambles, and does little work of any kind. Of late he has been helping in a curio shop kept by his brother-in-law, a man called Carcow, who's away now. The police were after Rosenstein three years ago, in connection with some long-firm frauds, but had not enough evidence to go on."

"That doesn't seem much."

"No? Well, my agent found a little boy taking a letter to the post to oblige Mrs. Carcow. Carcow's present address is a public-house in Dowse Lane, Shalton."

"Then Carcow's after the ring too?"

"Possibly. Possibly it's only a coincidence, and his business in Shalton is something quite different. One thing's rather queer, if Carcow and Rosenstein are both after the ring, they are not working together—otherwise, Rosenstein would have had no need to pump Johnson.

Yet a curio dealer would be just the man that would be employed to hunt for The One Before; possibly Rosenstein got some suspicions from Carcow, and pumped Johnson to get fuller information. Anyhow, I don't like the idea of either of those blackguards trying to get the ring from Mary; their methods would possibly be unpleasant. So, I've arranged by telegram to go down to the Derrifords tomorrow, when I'll save trouble by stealing the ring myself. I shouldn't like Mary to get hurt, and I should be extremely sorry to lose the ring."

"But you ought to be in Shalton now, uncle. Why wait till to-morrow? anything may be happening today. Then, again, unless these brutes know that Mary no longer has the ring, they may still go on annoying her. It seems to me the very deuce of a business, anyhow. Couldn't the police be put on to it?"

"Jimmy, in these times of stress you lose your head; you hurry; it has been well observed that haste is of the devil. Take it that danger threatens Mary from Rosenstein and Carcow. Rosenstein may possibly have gone down to Shalton this morning. If he has, he will, from his regard for his own safety, try fair means first; there is nothing to fear from him before tomorrow, Carcow has been away some time; he may have now got the ring, in which case we need not trouble. He may just be on the point of trying objectionable methods—perhaps violent methods—of getting it.

"But if he had been intending to resort to them, I think he would have done it before, and we should have heard of it. It does not seem to me probable, but I have guarded against the remote possibility by sending Mary an anonymous and melodramatic telegram, warning her not to leave the house today or tomorrow. So long as she stays at home, she will have the strong right arm of the esteemed Ernest Saunders—and other right arms—to protect her, if needs be.

"Yes, I decided I could quite keep my dinner engagement to-night, give Mrs. Derriford twenty-four hours' notice of my visit, and run down to Shalton tomorrow. It will be time enough if I steal the ring then. And, when I've got it, I have an absolutely certain way of convincing Carcow and Rosenstein that the ring is not in Shalton, and that they may abandon the search for it. You shall hear about that later."

"I'm not so confident about it as you seem to be, and I wish to goodness we'd never had anything to do with the ring. But it's your responsibility."

"I accept it cheerfully. Nobody's going to get hurt; make your mind easy about it. Let's talk of something else. How's your work going? Fixed up everything with Derriford?"

"The work's not as bad as it might be," said Jimmy. "By the way, I must get back to it at once, for I told my model she could come again at three. I begin Miss Derriford's portrait as soon as she comes to London, and that's to be in a few days, I think. I wrote to old Derriford last night."

He had; he had also written to Miss Hilda Derriford, but he was not going to mention that just yet.

"That's all right," said Mr. Brookes. "If Romney could have painted her!"

"Then you'd have got a good picture but a poor portrait. Look at his Lady Hamiltons—all different. Still," he added modestly, "If he could have painted her, I'd have let him. It's just possible that I shan't do much better."

CHAPTER 21

On the same morning, Mary was on the point of starting out for a walk when Mr. Brookes's anonymous telegram was handed to her. She thought it over for a minute or two. What on earth could it mean? Probably it was some imbecile joke of Jimmy's, and the explanation would arrive later. She never dreamed for a moment of taking the warning seriously. It was a glorious morning; she had a new hat, and liked herself in it; she felt younger, prettier, and in better spirits than usual. The anonymous telegram did not frighten her in the least; it merely puzzled her to imagine what the joke could possible be.

In the road at the bottom of the drive she hesitated for a moment, and then took a path across the fields. A shabby-looking old man who was loitering down the road, noted the direction she took and followed her. In the first three fields he kept a long way behind her, and then he quickened his pace. In the fifth field she heard his quick steps close behind her and turned round. She recognised immediately the horrible drunken old man who had come to the house to sell his Oriental rugs, and had said that he wanted to buy her ring. She showed less fear than she felt.

"Go on, please," she said, "I don't like to have people walking just behind me."

"It is all right," said Carcow, a little breathless. "I do not want to hurt you, if it can be helped. I want your ring—the ring that I offered to buy the other day. I must have it. I will still buy it if you will sell, and

295

pay the money now. If you will not sell, then I must take it—even if I spoil your pretty dress—even if I break your finger—even if I murder you for it. It is no good to scream. There is no one near, and if you scream, I strike at once with this stick."

Mary looked round; it was true that there was no one near.

"You don't frighten me in the least, and if you don't go away you will get yourself into trouble. The other day I thought you were drunk; either you are still drunk or you are mad. In any case the police will be after you, if I know anything about it. How dare you—"

"Stop that. Be quick, now. I must have the ring. Do you sell or do I take it?"

"What is the use of talking of selling? I want thirty pounds for that ring, and you have not thirty pence."

"Ah! I am not so poor as I look." He pulled a greasy bag from a pocket inside his waistcoat. "I count out thirty golden sovereigns for you. Off with your glove, and let me have the ring."

Carcow was greatly relieved; he did not want to use violence, and was terribly afraid of the consequences. Mary's plan was of the simplest; she intended to drop some of the money; when he stooped to pick it up, she meant to push him over and then run for it. With the start she would get in this way, she had no doubt she would be able to escape; she was an active woman and he was an old man, he would not be able to go far. But another form of deliverance was close at hand. Through the gate at the further end of the field came a young lady and her dog. The lady was Hilda Derriford, and the dog was the brindled bull-dog, Peter. Mary whistled, and the dog came rushing towards them.

"Put up that bag and run for your life," she said to Carcow. "If that dog catches you, you're a dead man."

Carcow took in the situation rapidly. He did not like dogs—especially bull-dogs—and it seemed to him that this bull-dog was coming in a hurry and on business. He did not even stop to swear; he ran—ran faster than he had run for years. Mary called after him that she was going straight to the police-station, and then she devoted herself to stopping Peter. As Carcow tumbled and rolled over the stile at the end of the field, a hurried glance backward showed him that Mary was having some difficulty in keeping the dog back. Peter was torn betwixt his native common sense and his acquired education.

His common sense told him that the whistle had been urgent and his assistance required; the fact that the man ran was evidence of his guilt, richly supported by his personal appearance; and obviously his first duty was to kill the man that ran. In all of this his common sense was quite correct. On the other hand, his education had shown him that he must always obey Mr. Derriford, Hilda, Mary, and the coachman's youngest little girl, aged six. And at present Mary was hanging on to his collar, spanking him, and telling him to lie down and not make a fool of himself. Finally, he yielded under protest to education—a sweet old idiot of a dog that feared nothing, would fight anything, and let a child of six make him ridiculous with her own sun-bonnet, tied rather too tightly under his chin.

It was true that the dog had elected this ruling syndicate himself; but, once elected, he did not question their right to rule. He quite understood that Mr. Derriford was a just man, and would shoot him if necessary; that Hilda was his mistress; that Mary was his best and most sympathetic friend; and that one must be careful and gentle with a little golden-haired girl of six. But he could never understand that the vicar had called with no intention of stealing the aprons, nor could he even approve of Mr. Ernest Saunders Barley—though afterwards, in deference to Mary, he learned to tolerate him.

Hilda came running up, and put the dog on the lead. "Who was that man? What was he doing? Why didn't you let Peter go after him? (Good beast, Peter.) We came just in time. I was coming to see you." Hilda was much more excited than Mary.

Mary laughed, and told Peter that he was an angel of light, though he might not look it—a statement which Peter found gratifying but inconsistent with the fact that he had been spanked. With many inter-rupting questions and exclamations, she told Hilda the whole story, as they walked back to The Chestnuts.

"But who sent the telegram?" asked Hilda. "It must have been from somebody who knew that this brute might attack you."

"But he wouldn't have told anybody he was going to do it. No, the telegram was a coincidence, and part of some idiotic practical joke of Jimmy's, I expect."

"He wouldn't have done such a thing. I'm quite sure of it."

The tone was very positive. Mary raised her eyebrows. Hilda blushed; her new habit of blushing was infinitely becoming. "I mean, I don't think he would. O Mary, I had a letter from him this morning, and they're so glad at home, and you were the very first person I was going to tell!"

Mary's immediate reply was to kiss Hilda with enthusiastic affection "Dear Hilda! Really and truly? I can't begin to tell you how delighted I am. I knew it all along, and, now it's happened, I can hardly believe it. Tell me everything at once, dear. Have you answered? When will he know? I want to telegraph my congratulations to him."

"He will know this afternoon. He asked me to send a messenger with the reply—if it was—well, if it was what it is. So, William's going up by the one-thirty, and will get to the studio by three. *And perhaps he'll bring me another letter back with him.*"

(And was it for that model, or was it for this messenger, that Jimmy had insisted on being back at the studio by three?)

There followed many and almost indiscriminate eulogia on that pleasant young man and quite decent artist, James Havern. Peter heard them all, as he trotted docilely at his mistress's heel—and being a well-bred dog—heard them without a smile. Conscious that subjects for congratulation were in the air, he wagged his tail, with as much enthusiasm as could be expected from a led dog.

Hilda accompanied Mary to the police-station. There Mary told a polite and perplexed inspector a somewhat confused story of an elderly tramp with a beard and a bag of money who had threatened to murder her in the fields. Possibly, she would have made a better story of it, if the fresh excitement of Hilda's engagement had left her mind clearer. No, she didn't want to charge the man with anything, only she did think the police ought to do something; they might find the man, and frighten him a little, and tell him to go away. The inspector made a note or two and sighed patiently. He was a married man himself, and not unused to the workings of the feminine mind.

Mary bore Hilda off to lunch with her. Ernest Saunders Barley was away, having gone in great glory, a new suit, and a first-class smoking-compartment, to establish the repute of Shalton golf on some far-distant links. At lunch the conversation returned to the subject of the ring again.

"And what would you have done if Peter and I had not turned up at the critical moment?"

"Dropped his money—pushed him over as he stooped to pick it up—and then run for it. I couldn't have given him the ring in any case, because I hadn't got it with me."

"Really! I thought you always wore it."

"I always have done. But today it wasn't comfortable when I put on my gloves to go out; so I left it on the table in my room. O Hilda, I've got such a splendid idea. It was Jimmy who gave Ernest that ring—so you shall wear it until Jimmy gives you a ring for yourself—it will be a sort of deputy-understudy to your engagement ring."

"But I shall be so afraid of losing it. You say Mr. Smythe told you it was valuable, and this mad tramp offered you bags of gold for it."

"But Jimmy said distinctly that it was of no money-value."

"Did he? Then it isn't. Whenever he does give an opinion it's always right. I've noticed that, and he knows any amount about curios and out-of-the-way things. Those two lunatics must have mistaken it for something else. I should love to have it, if you really don't mind, and I'll give it back as soon as I get the real ring."

"Then you shall have it now. Jane, run upstairs—no, don't, because we shall want you in a moment—tell Ellen to run upstairs and find a ring with two gold snakes on it. I think it's on the dressing-table-or possibly the mantelpiece—but she must find it and bring it down."

"Certainly, ma'am," said Jane, respectfully. She gave the message in the kitchen as follows:—

"Maudie, my dear, you 'urry; you're to fetch the duchess's ring—you know, the tin-pot one. And if it ain't in one place it's in another, and that's all she knows about it. And if you've not got it inside of a minute, you'll have your head chopped off."

Ellen placed her thumb to her nose, extended her fingers, and with a slow and stately grace passed up the back-stairs. She found the ring at once, and—being in a humorous mood—put it on her finger. She was still wearing it when Jane came into the kitchen for the *soufflé*.

"There you are," said Ellen, as she took the ring off. "If she wants my ring, she can have it. And if she'd like my diamond ear-rings as well, she's only got to ask. You say so."

"I'll mention it," said Jane.

Ellen had scarcely worn the ring for a minute, but it was enough to give her for an hour or two that afternoon some touch of Mary's nature. Had Mr. Hicks called that afternoon, he might have found his hopes revive considerably. Mrs. Dawes and Jane noticed that Ellen was quiet and pensive, and had things to say to her on the subject. But, on the whole, it is just as well that the faithful gardener did not call, for by the evening Ellen had returned to her normal state, and the hope revived would assuredly have been quenched again.

In the meantime, Hilda wore the ring, and therewith began gradually to assume some of the more prominent characteristics of Ellen-Maudie—Ellen-Maudie's eye for the main chance, Ellen-Maudie's contempt for men, and Ellen-Maudie's scorn for the married state.

It was a good thing that Mr. Brookes was to arrive on the following morning; his intervention was beginning to be most urgently required. Whatever the good work The One Before had done in the past, by enabling Mary to reform and improve her husband, it obviously was on the way to dealing disaster now.

CHAPTER 22

But on the evening before Mr. Brookes's arrival, another gentleman, also much interested in the *Sahib-i-dírína*, stepped out on to the down platform at Shalton station; and when it is said that this was an overdressed young gentleman, that he had bulbous and apologetic eyes, and that he stepped with a third-class ticket out of a first-class carriage, his identity is perhaps sufficiently indicated. Mr. Nathan Rosenstein carried with him a small brown bag, refused the offer of a cab outside the station, and made his way to the Railway Hotel, not more than a hundred yards distant. He thought that hotel would supply his simple needs.

With commendable caution—or, if you prefer it, with his native suspiciousness—he thought he would investigate further before definitely engaging his room. And therefore, he selected, not the hotel entrance, but that which bore on its portal, in a mosaic of stained glass, the words "Saloon Bar." In that august and crimson-plush retreat was seated one man only, an old man with a ragged beard and restless eyes, and with a heterogeneous bundle on the floor beside him.

He no longer wore the ragged garb in which he had affrighted Mary in the fields that morning. He wore the decent silk hat and thin black overcoat in which he had arrived at Shalton. He was aware that the police might be looking for a tramp, and would take no notice of the decent bagman that he now appeared to be. He sat in an attitude of the deepest dejection, his head in his hands, with an unfinished glass of brandy-and-water on the marble-topped table by his side.

He turned, as the glass door swang, and Nathan entered. But Nathan had had just one glance before the turn, and had no difficulty in spelling out the absolute. failure depicted in Carcow's face.

"Well, Ezra, my boy," said Nathan, easily, "you look surprised to see me. I am surprised to see you, too; but we are always well met, good friend, brothers-in-law, eh? Packed up to go home, I see. That is funny also. Your business at Shalton is finished just when mine begins."

"Ah? Very pleased to see you, Nathan. You are a damned thief—I have always known that. Perhaps you come a little too late for your

300

business; perhaps that business is done already. But never mind—I do not want your secrets. I only ask you one question, though I know you will not tell me the truth. What has Rebecca told you?"

"Why, I have no secrets, I put all my cards down on the table. I am here to get the *Sahib-i-dírína,* which is a curious ring for the finger, and is worth little, but fetches big money. I have known of it a long time, but only last night did I get the finishing touch. Rebecca has told me nothing. What should Rebecca know about the *Sahib-i-dírína?* Besides, I never talk business to Rebecca-except just the matters in your shop, you know. Perhaps I am too late; I can only go up to The Chestnuts and try. But then-this may all be Greek to you. You came down here to attend a few sales, I was told; very likely you know nothing of the *Sahib-i-dírína.* But then, I do not want your secrets either. There, Ezra, my boy, we won't talk business now. After shop hours, eh? Come, you will finish that and take a glass of brandy at my expense. What?"

Ezra was not a fool. He collated the principal facts in one rapid mental flash. He himself had failed to get the ring, and it was no longer safe for him to remain in Shalton; Nathan (no matter how) was aware of the value of the ring and where it was to be found. Therefore, he would do better to cling on to Nathan and save something out of the wreck. He also guessed that Nathan had some use for him, and in fact could not get the business completed without him; for undoubtedly otherwise Nathan would never have said a word about the ring, would never have put a card on the table, and would have spun off a string of lies as to abnormal gas-stoves or other fantastic business.

And Ezra was entirely right. The important fact that Nathan did not know, and wished to find out from Ezra, was where his market was. Nothing is of more value than you can get for it, and a ton of diamonds is worthless to the lost traveller in the desert. And Nathan had not the least idea where he ought to sell the *Sahibi-dirina,* if he ever secured it. If the worst came to the worst, he believed he could get a few pounds for it from Mr. Brookes, but he felt pretty certain that he would get nothing like the top-price there. He doubted very much if Mr. Brookes knew himself what the top-price was; Nathan's opinion on the subject was formed much more from the fact that Ezra had thought it worthwhile to spend days and days in Shalton in order to get the ring than from anything that the intoxicated Johnson had told him.

It was a pretty duel, but the result of it was almost a foregone conclusion. Nathan, as things stood, had by far the better chance of getting the ring; Ezra had by far the better chance of selling it to ad vantage. The voice of cold reason said distinctly "Halves!" And now, as on many previous and many subsequent occasions, Ezra realised the beauty and profit of the position of the middleman.

"Always the same, my dear," said Ezra, with his best imitation of the indulgent smile. "Light-hearted, dressed in fine clothes, ready to stand a drink to anybody, ah, yes—and giving away all the little things that you should not speak of to anybody! O you are a damned old thief, Nathan." But the words had changed their character altogether now, and the tone of Ezra's voice made them to blossom forth as a term of affectionate endearment. "Well, I do not reproach you for it. When you speak to me alone, you speak to me alone. You know it and I know it. I drink some brandy-and-water with you with pleasure, for in these country-places one cannot get *absinthe*, and I have yet an hour or so to wait for the up-train. Well now, you have put your cards on the table. I do the same—and perhaps even more frankly. I have been after the ring, and I have not got it.

"I am the only man in England who knows where to get the money for it. Perhaps, I wished to make you a little surprise—to set you up in a business as Rebecca has so often asked me—but I need not speak of that. All I say is that I have failed to get the ring, and that it is better for me to leave this hole of a town immediately. I tried a big coup, a very daring *coup*, and the bottom has dropped out of it. It may be that in time I should have come back again, should have tried something else and should have secured the ring. That would have been good for you, for I do not forget those of my family, but this is better.

"You also have found out about the ring. I thought I was the only man in England that knew where to get five thousand pounds for it, but I see I am mistaken. You have found that out, too. Very well, my boy, go in and win. Do not mind me; I have the little shop, and do not need to take anything from you. I wish you luck. I drink to it. No, the five thousand for Nathan! Come, drink!"

And the most cunning thing in this speech was that Ezra, overcoming his natural instincts, actually named the real sum that he would receive for the ring—if he ever had it to sell.

"Come now!" said Nathan, as he made himself perfectly comfortable on the crimson-plush. "I know you have a regard for your family. Believe me, Ezra, I have always known you were my friend; but I am not a man without heart—not I either. There is no reason why we should not share this. Perhaps I can get money for the ring. Mr. Brookes would pay it. (Ah, I see, you do not know about Mr. Brookes;

well, never mind that.) But he would not go so far as five thousand. 'Two thousand'—that is what he always says to me—'Two thousand, Nathan, my dear boy, if you get back my ring for me If I share with you, that is five hundred pounds better money for me.' If I do not, that is two thousand for me and nothing for you. Only, if we are to share, you must tell me the whole story."

From long experience, Ezra was enabled to sort out the principal lies from Nathan's friendly statement. He knew nothing about Mr. Brookes, but he did not believe that Mr. Brookes had ever offered two thousand—if he had, then Nathan, knowing no better, would have snapped at the offer, and would not have taken his brother-in-law into his confidence. None the less, Ezra judged it better, with certain reservations, to tell the whole story.

"Very well, Nathan. Perhaps my failure may help you to succeed. That is all I ask. On the terms you have mentioned, I tell you everything that I know and everything that I have done. I do not want anything in writing, we are of one family. I take your word as I would take the word of my own mother if that blessed woman were still alive on earth; well then, I happened to hear that five thousand pounds was to be got in a certain quarter—which I need not mention yet—for this ring, which was accurately described to me. If I had a pencil I could make you the inscription on the tablet of the ring, myself with my own hand. Then I received information which led me to think that the ring might be in Shalton. I did not come with the address all ready as you do; I was not so fortunate; I had to hunt about and find; and I found. Then I tried to buy the ring; the lady would not listen."

"You mean Mrs. Barley or the daughter?"

"I mean Mrs. Barley. There is no daughter." Nathan's attempt to show an intimate knowledge had somewhat overreached itself, but he did the best he could with his blunder.

"Anyhow, you think there is no daughter. Very well; we need not go in to that, and what next?"

"Today I tried some violence—well, a threat—I had found her alone in some fields, and what else was there to do? Everything seemed to be going well, and then there came a bull-dog. It came after me, and I was much embarrassed. I had a stick in my hands, but my head was lost, and then these bull-dogs are not quite like the other dogs that one keeps off with a stick. I had to go away immediately."

Nathan lay back on the crimson-plush lounge and chuckled heartily.

"You laugh!" Ezra continued. "I tell you, it might have been my life. And after that the lady went to the police, and so it is better for me to leave Shalton for a little while. I said to myself that there was you, Nathan, and that I could send you to try for the ring and give you a thousand pounds if you found it. I pay for the little bedroom that I have had, and go straight to the station. There is no train for a long time, and I come to this place to wait. Suddenly in you walk! Now, is not that a special providence—except that you ask for more. And that I must put up with. Well, how do you go to work?"

Nathan had stopped laughing. He sipped his liquor reflectively. "And what are the servants like at The Chestnuts? You worked them, I suppose."

"Well, no. I was not trying that. Perhaps that would have been better."

"Couldn't have been much worse, could it? What made you try to get the ring by violence?"

"I saw no other way."

"And what made you cut and run, just at the moment when you were getting the ring? You had that big stick in your hand. I do not care whether it was a bull-dog or not; one good whack on the skull with that, and you might have finished your business without trouble."

"Perhaps. It was not expected, and, as I have said, my head was lost. Then my nerves are not those of a young man."

Nathan made a contemptuous exclamation. "Nerves? You have none; they are gone into the *absinthe* bottle. And your brains seem to be going the same way. See what a nasty mess you have made of this business; and that makes it all the more difficult for me. Does it seem to you a right and just thing that you should distrust me, have secrets from me, blunder and spoil everything, and then ask me for a present of two thousand and five hundred pounds? That is what it comes to. Now, if you had said to me, 'Give me the ring, and I find a five-thousand buyer for twenty *per cent.* com.,' then that would have been talking."

And at this Ezra Carcow arose in his fury and spake with his tongue

"You damned thief! You dog! You reptile! You ape! My brains was good enough for Nathan Rosenstein still. Look at this!" He tapped his left forefinger with his right. "If you could have got on without you would. You cannot. So, when you bluster, I smile. Bring the ring to me, and I will give you two thousand five hundred pounds for it. If you can get that anywhere else, then get it. But—and I tell you this seriously—if you say any more that you are not treated fairly, my price for that ring is one five-pound note."

"But then there is Mr. Brookes."

"Everything you have said about Brookes is a lie, and I know it. If you pretend that it is not a lie, then my price for the ring once more is one five-pound note. Father Abraham! Have I nurtured this young man; have I saved him from the police; have I paid him commissions—always liberal; and then is he to turn on me and treat me as a swindler, and eat his own words? For yes, Nathan, it was you that said halves."

"All right," said Nathan. "This *absinthe* makes you get excited. I was only just talking, and I do not want to go back on my word at all, especially with an old friend. Cards on the table again. I shall see the ring—perhaps in church. I shall have a copy made. I shall work the servants, get the real ring in my hand, exchange it for the copy, and scoot before the exchange is found out. Get your money ready; I shall call for it in a fortnight."

"Now that is sense," said Ezra, appeased. "And how was the health of Rebecca when you left?"

CHAPTER 23

Mr. Nathan Rosenstein slightly changed his plans; they involved too much delay, and he was not a gentleman who allowed grass to grow under his feet. Next morning, he might have been found at the back door of "The Chestnuts" in conversation with Jane. He had for sale some elegant little gun-metal watches with gunmetal bows attached, on easy terms. The system (which he ascribed to the *Times* newspaper) was sixpence down, and the rest when you felt like it.

"Not me," said Jane. "Never was in debt in my life, and not going to begin now. Still, if they're as good as they look, and you didn't want much for them—ready money—then I don't say."

"Good as they look, miss? Why, they're better. What some put into extra finish in the cases, we put into the works. It wouldn't pay me to sell a watch that wouldn't go, and I'll tell you why—I trade to make trade. In a few months I shall be round again with another cheap line, and what chance should I have if I had sold rubbish before?"

"Well, you wouldn't find me here anyhow."

"What?" Nathan winked. "I see. The young men about here have some judgment; but there, I always come too late for everything. Well now, what prettier ornament can a young lady have on a wedding-dress than a watch like this? Being a special case, I shall say eight shillings."

Jane smiled; it would not even be incorrect to say that she giggled. "If you like to sell it for seven, I'll have it."

"Why, miss, each of these watches costs us seven and sixpence to make. I cannot afford to give money away, like that cracked old man who was selling the carpets down in the High Street just now."

"We had him here the other day. Missus thought he was drunk, though it was not what I should call drunk. He wanted to give her twenty pounds for a ring, the old fool."

"Perhaps not such a fool. If there were some fine stones—"

"Why, it was a little old ring you wouldn't have given a pound for. No stones in it at all."

Nathan was vastly amused. "Well," he said, "I should like to have a look at that ring—just to be able to say I've seen it when I tell the joke to my friends."

"Now, I might have shown it you if you'd come yesterday, for she left it out on her dressing-table. But now it's gone."

"I see. So, she's sold it to that cranky old chap after all?"

"Oh no! She gave it away to Miss Derriford—a lady friend of hers. Now, am I going to have that watch for seven shillings?"

"Well, I never could stand out against a pretty girl; that is why I am such a poor man. You shall have it for seven. And so that ring has gone to Miss Danford, in the little house by the bridge—I know it."

"Not Danford. It's Derriford—big place at the corner where you turns off to Frelingham. Now, you might sell some of those watches there."

"I dare say. I will take it in my round. Well, good morning, miss. And my best congratulations to that happy young man."

His own superior watch, as well as his healthy appetite, told Nathan that it was time for luncheon. He went to the nearest hotel to feed and meditate. He was also unable to resist the temptation to torture his brother-in-law by the following telegram:

"The article wanted has changed hands and disappeared."

Besides, it was just possible that Ezra might in his frenzy be driven to increase his offer of two thousand five hundred pounds.

After luncheon he lit his cigar, inquired the way to Frelingham, and walked thither at a leisurely pace. He arrived at the back door precisely as Hilda Derriford passed out at the front door, joining Mr. Nathaniel Brookes, who was about to take her for a walk. Mr. Brookes assured himself of the presence in his ticket-pocket of a small brass wedding-ring, of the cracker variety, value one halfpenny. Peter was safely chained otherwise, since he disliked extremely the appearance of Mr. Nathan Rosenstein, he might have come out once more as the saviour of the *Sahib-i-dirina*. But he would have wasted his trouble, for Rosenstein sold no watches, got no information, and left in a wickedly bad temper, while Mr. Brookes (with that brass ring in his ticket-pocket) was pursuing his designs on the ring at some distance from the house.

Hilda had spent a wretched night, had been gloomy and depressed at breakfast, and had received Mr. Brookes's congratulations with a faint smile and no enthusiasm. And at this Mr. Brookes would have been greatly surprised—for he had long guessed correctly the real state of affairs—if he had not noticed a certain ring on her finger. Hilda had taken no one into her confidence; she felt that she had made a mistake, and she was heartily ashamed of it. She ought to have known her own mind, and it had seemed to her yesterday that she knew it definitely and beyond the possibility of a doubt. She felt equally sure now that she had been wrong then.

She could not marry Jimmy; she could not marry anybody. Marriage was a surrender of one's independence—it was a generally-accepted slavery with which she could not possibly have anything to do. And yet she was very fond of Jimmy. The break must be made gradually—during the time that she was in London, and sitting for her portrait, that could be arranged. But how much she wished that she could speak of it—that she could take counsel with somebody! To confess her own imbecility of mind to her own nearest relations was impossible—an imbecility that involved cruelty, as it were.

Mr. Nathaniel Brookes had known her as a child. He was sympathetic to her. Also, he was a man of the world, and she had never known him to be in the least surprised. In her interests—as well as in the interests of his favourite nephew—he would counsel her well. Could she bring herself to speak of it?

They lingered on the bridge over the river, a mile away. Mr. Brookes leaned over the parapet, and discussed cheerfully the advantages of drowning over other methods of suicide. Suddenly he broke off.

"What was that ring that you were wearing this morning? Surely it was the same that Jimmy sent to our esteemed friend, Ernest Saunders."

"It was. Mary was wearing it, and she lent it to me because it came from Jimmy—until—well—I suppose—"

"Really, how very unlucky to wear a ring that Jimmy sent to somebody else! What made me speak of it was that Jimmy thought the inscription on it was oriental—wanted me to have a look at it; but I happened to be away at the time, and somehow I didn't."

(Oh, Mr. Brookes! And what of the sacred character of truth?)

He gazed pensively at the floating weeds and running water as if he had finished with the subject.

"Oh, but you can look at it now if you like," said Hilda, drawing off her glove. "See—there it is."

She handed it to Mr. Brookes, who turned it over critically in his fingers. "Dear me!" he said, "this is very curious."

"Mind you don't—" Hilda began. But before she could finish her warning to him not to drop it, the time for the warning had gone past. A sudden catch with the hand-a flash in the air—a little splash in the water—and under her very eyes the ring had gone.

But what her eyes did not detect was that the ring which Mr. Brookes had dropped into the water was not the ring which she had handed to him. It was, in fact, as the intelligent reader has already surmised, not "The One Before," but the brass ring from his ticket-pocket.

"Oh, what have you done?" exclaimed Hilda; "and what shall I say to Mary? Can't we get it back?" She leaned over the parapet, looking in vain into the weedy bed of the river.

"I'm afraid there's not a chance of it. It's all my fault—my appalling clumsiness. I will explain and apologise to Mary as best I can this afternoon; but there's no hope of recovering her ring, I fear."

Hilda's back being turned to him as he spoke, he examined leisurely "The One Before," as it lay in the palm of his hand. He smiled a sweet smile of satisfaction, and slipped his prize into his pocket.

Hilda turned away from the parapet. "It's no good," she said. "I can't see the slightest trace of it." She sighed deeply.

It may have been a sigh of regret for the loss of the ring, or it may have been a sigh of relief. For quite suddenly the cloud that had come over her the evening before, and had rested on her ever since, passed away; her great happiness came back to her; she was deep in love again, and her will was her lover's will, and she did not want any beautiful independence in the least bit. Mr. Nathaniel Brookes watched her as she still spoke of the ring, threatening him with a variety of nursery punishments, and radiant with smiles. At the back of her mind, she was wondering if it could be true, as he had said, that it was unlucky to wear a ring that your lover had given to some other person.

Mr. Nathaniel Brookes was quite reassured, even before Hilda said suddenly, rather as if it were a grievance—

"You knew Jimmy long before I did."

"Well, yes; it's not my fault entirely."

"Then, tell me everything about him, please. What was he like?"

"Like? Oh, the ordinary sort of boy."

"What a wicked thing to say!" said Hilda, with conviction. "No, I want to know the real truth. And—I wanted to ask you—do you believe in palmists?"

CHAPTER 24

Some weeks later, Mr. Ezra Carcow and Mr. Nathan Rosenstein held conversation together. The last part of it may be reported.

"Then it comes to this," said Nathan, his face flushed and his manner excited. "I give weeks of my time and my work. The ring has gone—because you played the fool and frightened the woman—and I find out where it has gone. You could not have done it; but I did it. I have to spend money like water, and give away valuable watches to servants to make them talk. I get bitten by a beast of a dog. I go on still, and find the ring has been dropped in the river, and I find the exact place where it was dropped. I pay two men—all this out of my own pocket—to search the bed of the river for me. It was not my fault that it failed; there was not one more thing that any man could have done. If I had got the ring, you would have had half the profit. Therefore, if I fail, you should pay half the loss. Let us be reasonable, Ezra."

Ezra sipped his *absinthe* complacently. "You know what I think of you, my dear Nathan, for I have told you sometimes. You tried to rob me of two thousand five hundred pounds, and because you were too much a fool to be able to do it, you want me to pay you some of my hard-earned money for a consolation. That is like you. You are a swine, and the son of a swine. You are a dirty thief. And I pay you nothing."

That, undoubtedly, is not the way in which one speaks to one's brother-in-law. And with impartial justice it must be admitted that when Nathan flung the tumbler of *absinthe* into his brother's face, broke a chair to bits, and flung the bits into the grate, cursing at the top of his voice in three different languages simultaneously, he went beyond the limits of the retort courteous. His sister Rebecca, entering upon this scene of violence, was probably correct in going instantly into hysterics, and in subsequently charging her brother for the breakages. Also, a casual customer, who had sauntered into the shop below and heard the row, only acted naturally in leaving at once without waiting to complete his purchase.

It is also necessary to record a few observations made about the same time in the servants' hall at The Chestnuts, Shalton, Surrey.

"It may be only my fancy," said Ellen, surnamed Maudie, "but to my mind she's gone back to just what she used to be. She humours him the same as she used. And if I makes an excuse for anything she listens to it just as she used."

"But he ain't gone back to what he used to be," said Jane, pensively. "For which my humble and hearty thanks. Remember, how he was always messing about, with his gummed labels, and his gas-out-please, and all the rest of the half-farthing business? I'd no patience. Nowadays, we never see him—for when it's not golf it's the garden."

"Quite right too. If I had my way, I'd never allow any man in my house at all. They're not wanted there."

"Now, that," said Mrs. Dawes, judicially, "is what I call going too far."

"And Mr. 'Icks wearing himself to a shadow," added Jane, by way of further reproach.

"Wearing himself to your grandmother! Engaging himself to the coachman's daughter; that's what he's doing. And if she wants such rubbish, I'm sure she's welcome. Oh, I say, have you seen Mrs. Barley's new ring?"

"Yes. That with them blue stones—what do they call them?—it's in the Bible, I know, along of Ananias. Well, it don't matter. That came from Mr. Brookes, I heard. Wonder what he give it her for?"

"Don't know, I'm sure," said Maudie, sardonically. "If you'll kindly touch the bell, I'll inquire of Mrs. Barley."

The two Miss Derrifords were married on the same day. Jane was unusually sentimental, and Ellen was unduly caustic on the subject; but it was a great day at Shalton. During the latter part of their honeymoon, Hilda and Jimmy wandered by the lake one beautiful evening, and said how different their love was to any that had ever existed in the world—finer, deeper, grander. There was a pause, and Jimmy saw with awe and terror that tears came into Hilda's eyes, and he asked his princess-angel-dove to tell him what was the matter, adding that he would much rather have his heart cut out than that she should have one sad thought.

"It's nothing, heavenliest one. Only—there was a time when I almost very nearly didn't love you as much as I ought. It was when I was wearing that ring you sent to Mary—and Mr. Brookes said it was unlucky—and he dropped it in the river—and oh, how horrible it was of me, my own star-gem!"

To which Mr. James Havern replied that she was a dear white soul, without one fleck upon her; also, that the best man on earth had never done enough to deserve one millionth part of the ecstasy of being loved by her. She was never in all her life to have one moment's unhappiness. He added that possibly the ring really was unlucky.

At his last remark she looked at him somewhat inquisitively.

"Dearest fairy-giant, I believe you know something about that ring."

In reply Mr. James Havern said that it was not his own secret, and suggested that his dearest and loveliest moon-nymph had better ask Mr. Brookes herself.

And there came a day when Mrs. Havern did ask. Mr. Brookes rubbed his forehead.

"Yes, my dear Hilda, there was a certain something about that ring, most extraordinary. I have the best memory in the world, and ultimately nothing escapes it. But for the moment my memory is not acting, and I can recall nothing whatever about that ring.

It was on this same day that Mr. Rosenstein and Mr. Johnson met in the reading-room of their club, and each came away with the firm and satisfying conviction that he had cut the other.

Mr. Brookes has decided to have his book of travels printed for private circulation only; this gives him more latitude—of which neither you, nor I, nor Mr. Johnson could possibly approve.

"The One Before" still lies forgotten in Mr. Brookes's safe. Jimmy's portrait of his wife was universally admired. Mr. Ernest Saunders Barley is the proud winner of a silver cup. Peter, that excellent bull-dog, is dead. And the story is ended.

LEONAUR

ALSO FROM LEONAUR

AVAILABLE IN SOFTCOVER OR HARDCOVER WITH DUST JACKET

MR MUKERJI'S GHOSTS by S. Mukerji—Supernatural tales from the British Raj period by India's Ghost story collector.

KIPLINGS GHOSTS by Rudyard Kipling—Twelve stories of Ghosts, Hauntings, Curses, Werewolves & Magic.

THE COLLECTED SUPERNATURAL AND WEIRD FICTION OF WASHINGTON IRVING: VOLUME 1 by Washington Irving—Including one novel 'A History of New York', and nine short stories of the Strange and Unusual.

THE COLLECTED SUPERNATURAL AND WEIRD FICTION OF WASHINGTON IRVING: VOLUME 2 by Washington Irving—Including three novelettes 'The Legend of the Sleepy Hollow', 'Dolph Heyliger', 'The Adventure of the Black Fisherman' and thirty-two short stories of the Strange and Unusual.

THE COLLECTED SUPERNATURAL AND WEIRD FICTION OF JOHN KENDRICK BANGS: VOLUME 1 by John Kendrick Bangs—Including one novel 'Toppleton's Client or A Spirit in Exile', and ten short stories of the Strange and Unusual.

THE COLLECTED SUPERNATURAL AND WEIRD FICTION OF JOHN KENDRICK BANGS: VOLUME 2 by John Kendrick Bangs—Including four novellas 'A House-Boat on the Styx', 'The Pursuit of the House-Boat', 'The Enchanted Typewriter' and 'Mr. Munchausen' of the Strange and Unusual.

THE COLLECTED SUPERNATURAL AND WEIRD FICTION OF JOHN KENDRICK BANGS: VOLUME 3 by John Kendrick Bangs—Including twor novellas 'Olympian Nights', 'Roger Camerden: A Strange Story', and ten short stories of the Strange and Unusual.

THE COLLECTED SUPERNATURAL AND WEIRD FICTION OF MARY SHELLEY: VOLUME 1 by Mary Shelley—Including one novel 'Frankenstein or the Modern Prometheus', and fourteen short stories of the Strange and Unusual.

THE COLLECTED SUPERNATURAL AND WEIRD FICTION OF MARY SHELLEY: VOLUME 2 by Mary Shelley—Including one novel 'The Last Man', and three short stories of the Strange and Unusual.

THE COLLECTED SUPERNATURAL AND WEIRD FICTION OF AMELIA B. EDWARDS by Amelia B. Edwards—Contains two novelettes 'Monsieur Maurice', and 'The Discovery of the Treasure Isles', one ballad 'A Legend of Boisguilbert' and seventeen short stories to cill the blood.